The Gifts of Pendrall

By

R. L. Scott

A Passionately Fair Publisher
Manuscript formatting, cover designing
By
Pat Simpson
www.apfpublisher.com

© 2010 R. L. Scott
All rights reserved. No part of this book may be reproduced, stored in a retrieval system or transmitted in any form by any means without the prior permission of the publishers, except by a reviewer who may quote brief passages in any review to be printed in a newspaper, magazine or journal
ISBN #: 978-0-557-32086-8

Author Foreword

I have always been a lover of fantasy. Perhaps that is because as a small boy it was an escape from the all-too-real world around me. Having been born into a poor and, for the most part, illiterate family, I had very little intellectual stimuli. I found myself reading more and more about worlds beyond the harsh reality around me, worlds that took me deep into my imagination and beyond. Books became a refuge where I could blast off into space or ride the tail of a comet and fly to unknown universes. I became well acquainted with Flash Gordon, King Arthur, Superman and scores of other fictional characters that helped to inspire within me a love for the world of the imagination.

As I grew older, I became familiar with some of the greatest fantasy writers of all time. Writers like William Morris, Edith Nesbitt, T. H. White, and J. R. R. Tolkien were familiar names to me. I discovered Edgar Rice Burroughs, who created not only the Tarzan legends but also memorable characters on other worlds. Robert E. Howard, the great pulp fiction writer and the creator of Conan, was another writer who helped establish the swords and sorcery genre which influenced me so much. With all these noted writers for inspiration, my love of fantasy grew. What is contained within these pages is my feeble attempt to emulate the writers who inspired me in my youth. May they forgive me.

Roger L Scott

Contents

The Dark Wood	Chapter 1	Page 1
Grinold	Chapter 2	Page 10
The Crystal of light	Chapter 3	Page 20
He Who Wears the Crown	Chapter 4	Page 30
Preparing for War	Chapter 5	Page 40
The Meeting	Chapter 6	Page 50
Revelations	Chapter 7	Page 61
With an Iron Hand	Chapter 8	Page 74
The Alliance	Chapter 9	Page 85
The Caravan	Chapter 10	Page 97
A Fruitless Encounter	Chapter 11	Page 109
A Power Revealed	Chapter 12	Page 116
A Like Trust	Chapter 13	Page 129
The Council of Twelve	Chapter 14	Page 139
Beauty in an Unusual Place	Chapter 15	Page 152
To Meet a King	Chapter 16	Page 163

Contents

To Capture a Queen	Chapter 17	Page 173
A House Divided	Chapter 18	Page 183
To Plan a Rescue	Chapter 19	Page 194
The Confrontation	Chapter 20	Page 202
A Force of Thousands	Chapter 21	Page 215
Prelude to War	Chapter 22	Page 225
The Return of the Queen	Chapter 23	Page 234
The Conflict Begins	Chapter 24	Page 245
The Past Revisited	Chapter 25	Page 253
The Past Revealed	Chapter 26	Page 259
The Caves	Chapter 27	Page 270
The Circle Completed	Chapter 28	Page 276
The Battle of the Caves	Chapter 29	Page 290
The Assault	Chapter 30	Page 297
How Great a Sacrifice	Chapter 31	Page 304
A Kingdom Reborn	Chapter 32	Page 314

Dedication

To all the people who made this book possible,
I would like to express my appreciation.
To all my teachers at Celina Elementary School,
Especially Mrs. Roberts, thank you for
the great stories that turned me onto reading.
To my mother and father,
Thank you for allowing me to be a dreamer.
To my siblings I am grateful for your support
in the growing-up process,
which can be harrowing at best.
To my late wife Elizabeth, thank you for all
your love and encouragement through those times
when I doubted my ability to write.
And to Amelia, thank you for keeping me
on a sane and steady course in the real world
and for always being there for me.

~~*~~

Chapter One
The Dark Wood

The solitary figure moved quickly in a shuffling gait over the ridge of the hill, pausing only long enough to cast furtive glances back into the direction from which it came. Assured at last that no one was near to witness, he took an object from the long cloak that covered his hunched form and held it in his hand for a moment, silently debating what he should do. He opened the leather pouch and shook something into his hand. Even in the dark, the object gave off an eerie light, as if catching the beams from the moon and amplifying them until the area around the stranger seemed bathed in its glow. The crystal appeared to pulsate as if it had a life of its own, and the creature holding the object stared at it until he seemed to lose all motion and stood statue like, looking into its depths. Suddenly, he shook himself as if waking from a trance and placed the crystal back into the bag. He looked around him, memorizing the landscape, and then moved to a cluster of rocks at the base of the hill he had been walking. Within these rocks he placed the leather bag and covered the cavity with larger stones. He carefully brushed the area with leaves until only the most discerning eye could have discovered that any activity had ever taken place there.

He stood for a moment, searching the landscape for something he seemed to sense but could not see. Surveying his surroundings to assure himself he could find the spot again, he resumed his path along the hillside. The sound of barking dogs in the direction from which he had come seemed to put new energy into his movement, and he hurriedly struck a course toward the river where he hoped he could lose his pursuers. This was the Dark Wood, and the fleeing figure seemed to know as if by instinct that only those who had no other choice would ever come here. He would be safe from his

The Dark Wood

pursuers, but he did not know at what cost his safety would be bought. As this tableau played out in the darkness, another pair of eyes had been witness to the night's activities as they unfolded. He noted with growing interest the stealthy movements of the man who had crossed the hillside and was now wending his way toward the river that flowed into the Dark Wood. Only the most brave or the most foolish would go into these woods at night. He, too, had heard the baying of the dogs, and he knew that the fleeing figure was taking the only recourse open to him. Still, he knew that many men would stand and face certain death rather than confront the unknown dangers that lay in the dark embraces of the forest. Surely, this hunted being had a strong will to survive, and the reason might be in the small leather bag he had hastily deposited in the rocks.

The watchful figure moved quickly from the place where he had been concealing himself and ran across the short expanse that lay between the woods and the rock structure wherein lay the bag. Moving the few large rocks that concealed the cavity where the bag rested, he reached into the crevice and extracted the pouch. Placing it into his jerkin, he moved to a large tree and quickly climbed its branches toward the top. Reaching a convenient place, he moved from one limb to another and then into a neighboring tree and continued in this manner until he was safely away from any danger of the hounds, who would not be able to find his scent in the high trees. Having reached what he considered a safe distance, he paused and rested against a large branch midway in one of the trees.

He had barely completed his concealment when a large group of dogs burst into the area where the pouch had been hidden. Sniffing the area around the rocks, they took to baying afresh and lunged with their handlers in the direction of the river. While the men wrestled to restrain the frenzied animals, one man examined the area carefully. He observed the markings around the rocks and moved each one in turn.

"Master Tobias, there is sign of activity here. It looks as though these rocks have been moved more than once tonight. The object is not here, so he must have it still. Perhaps he plans to hide it somewhere in the Dark Wood."

The man referred to as Tobias looked at his chief tracker doubtfully. Their quarry would not use the Dark Wood for shelter. Knowing the people of the area to be superstitious and fearful of that which they did not understand, it was unlikely that the man they pursued would enter there.

"I think not, Grinold," said Tobias, addressing the tracker. "Our quarry is not of sufficient courage to seek succor in such hostile environs. He will go into the river to elude our hounds, but he will not go deeper into the woods. Think you he still has the object we seek?" The tracker again looked about and mused for a moment before replying.

"The signs seem to indicate he tried to conceal the crystal here, but I see it not. Perhaps we were upon him before he could do so. He will not be taken with the object we seek. I fear he has managed to conceal it somewhere along his route tonight. We will find him without the crystal, but as you are aware, Master, I have means to make the most reluctant speak those things we need to know." Indeed Tobias did know of Grinold's dark gift. This is one of the reasons the tracker was so invaluable to him. It was as if the tracker had the innate ability to know when another was lying. Just by looking into a man's eyes, he could transfix him and extract the darkest secrets against the creature's most iron will.

"We will need your talents, Grinold, hopefully before this night is over. Our hounds are close upon him, and if he has not the crystal, your services will be sorely needed. We must not fail to recover this object. Without it, I have no hope in fulfilling what destiny has waiting for me. With it, my power will be limitless, and those who have aided me in my quest will be richly rewarded as well."

Grinold listened as his master told of the glory and riches awaiting them when the orb was recovered. He had no desire for glory, nor was he an ambitious man. The riches were another matter. With the wealth the orb could provide, he could buy power. He was satisfied to wait and share in the riches that his talents might bring him. And if he were patient enough, maybe he would eventually have the object for himself. He was a loyal servant to Tobias, but there was a limit to his loyalty, especially in regard to such a valuable treasure.

"There is little that we can do here in the dark," spoke Grinold, again casting his eyes over the spilled rocks as if therein lay a clue to the object they sought. Something troubled his senses, and his senses were never wrong. Whatever had occurred in this spot involved more than just one man. If someone else had entered the game, then the finding of the crystal would be decidedly more difficult than they had thought. Did their quarry have an accomplice or was this just a chance encounter? Whatever events had occurred here this night, Grinold knew he would uncover their purpose once their prey was caught.

Knowing the answers they sought lay elsewhere, the two men mounted their horses and took the direction the hounds had taken toward the river. The going was difficult and progress was hindered by the small shrubs and prickly bushes that seemed to block their way at every turn. But these obstacles only encouraged their efforts as they realized, as difficult as it was for them to maneuver through the cover around them, it must be twice as difficult for a man on foot.

The baying of the hounds, now only a short distance in front of them, indicated that the prey must be near at hand.

Hroldolf gasped for breath as he labored toward the edge of the Dark Wood. He knew he would never make the river at the rate the hounds were closing on him. If he could make the edge of the forest, perhaps his pursuers would abandon the chase rather than face the unknown. He struggled through the morass of scrub bushes, nettles, and marsh that barred his way and made fast travel impossible. If he died here, no one would know where the crystal was hidden, and all his efforts would have been in vain. The king needed the crystal to preserve his kingdom now more than ever since he had taken ill. With the object in the hands of Tobias, no village would be safe from his rapacious nature. The thought spurred his efforts and he broke into a clearing, and before him lay the Dark Wood.

Hroldolf knew the nature of his pursuer. Having been a servant in the house of Tobias for a number of years, he had seen the capricious and vengeful nature of the man at its heights. He knew there would be no reprieve if he were caught. The beatings he had experienced for failure to please Tobias during the years he had served him would be minor in comparison to the punishment that would be administered now. It was this cruel nature that had convinced Hroldolf that he must act when it became known that Tobias had acquired the crystal after years of searching. How he had found the crystal was a mystery that would never be known to Hroldolf, but he knew it could not remain in the hands of a man whose cruel nature would turn it to use that would doom the kingdom forever. So when Tobias had gone to bed that night after acquiring the crystal, he had placed it on a cushion near his bed to gaze upon until he fell asleep. He had no fear that it would not be safe. Guards were always posted outside his bedroom, and no one was permitted entrance.

Hroldolf knew the bedchamber of Tobias as well as any part of the castle. He had been in it numerous times during his

The Dark Wood

servitude. He was the only one who knew of the small entrance that lay directly behind the bed. Probably at some time in the past, the previous owner had built it to serve as an exit if the need arose to leave the chamber in a hurry. It was this avenue that Hroldolf had used to gain entrance to the bedroom without the knowledge of the guards. He had taken the crystal and fled the castle, hoping to get the treasure to the king and foil the plans of Tobias forever. The baying that Hroldolf heard gave him little hope that he would ever get the crystal to the king. The Dark Wood seemed far away and his strength was fading. He could not outrun hounds or men on horses. Frantically, he summoned his last ounce of strength and found himself at the edge of the forest.

He plunged into the darkness and had run only a few feet when he found himself trapped in a murky bog that pulled at him more tightly with each effort to extricate himself. The hounds raced into the edge of the forest and would have plunged into the same pit had not the handlers instantly seen the nature of the danger.

"He's in quicksand, Master!" yelled the nearest handler. "What are your orders?"

"Don't let him go under. If he has the crystal, we will lose it forever. Keep him above the surface of the bog."

The handlers quickly tied the hounds to the nearest tree and immediately secured a limb which they placed across the bog for Hroldolf to grasp.

"Get me out!" Hroldolf screamed as the murky water pulled at him with each new effort.

"Quit struggling, you fool, or you will go under," Tobias said nervously as he envisioned Hroldolf and the crystal sinking into the quicksand to be lost forever.

Tobias made his way forward, taking care to avoid the trap into which Hroldolf had fallen.

"Quickly, give me the crystal," he urged. "It would not do anyone a service at the bottom of this bog."

"I do not have it," cried Hroldolf. "Please, Master, do not let me die in the Dark Wood."

"Give me the crystal, and I will have my men pull you from this pit. The crystal is mine and you stole it. It is only right that it should be returned to me. Give it to me and you will be rescued, and I will make you head of the servants in my castle. That will be my forgiveness to you and my reward."

"I do not have it, Master. I would gladly give it up to be rid of this bog and this wood forever."

"Grinold, come forward," said Tobias, beckoning to the tracker, who, to this point, had remained a safe distance from the entrance to the forest. He, too, had grown up with the superstition surrounding the Dark Wood. He was in no hurry to test those superstitions. Grinold carefully made his way forward and arrived at the edge of the pit where Tobias was now kneeling, imploring Hroldolf to tell him the whereabouts of the crystal. When it became clear that the imprisoned man was not going to produce the object or reveal its location, Tobias turned to Grinold.

"The gift that you have I now need," said Tobias. "Look into the eyes of this man. Listen to his pleas. Tell me if he has the crystal."

Grinold stared into the eyes of the frightened man before him. Hroldolf's fear clouded the efforts that the tracker was making to extract the desired information. Gazing even more intently, he began to question.

"Do you have the crystal, Hroldolf? Confess and let us pull you from this swamp. Do you have the crystal on your person?"

"No, the accursed object is not on me," screamed Hroldolf, feeling himself sinking more into the slime around him as he gripped the limb even more tightly.

"He is telling the truth, my lord. He does not have the crystal on him."

"Then he must have hidden it somewhere along the way. Ask him where he has hidden it."

"Where did you put the crystal? Tell us so that we may rescue you before it is too late," urged Grinold.

"It is among a pile of rocks to the side of the roadway along which we came. Now, please release me, and I will go with you to reveal its location."

"Liar!" screamed Tobias. "The crystal is not there. We saw the stones. The crystal is not among them."

Hroldolf's eyes widened in surprise and horror. "No! That cannot be true. I placed it there tonight with my own hands. No one saw me. It must be there."

Grinold had continued to stare intently into the eyes and the soul of the doomed man before him.

"He is telling the truth, my lord. It must be there. Perhaps we overlooked it in the darkness. We must pull him out and take him with us. It is only then that we can be sure of its location."

Grinold looked beseechingly at Tobias as he spoke. He, like Hroldolf, knew the cruel and unforgiving nature of the man before him. Hopefully, if the crystal were found, Tobias would forgive Hroldolf, or at least forget him in his joy upon recovering the object. Grinold had the greedy nature of Tobias but none of the cruelty that so often accompanies the trait. He did not want to see Hroldolf die for his actions. He had been brave enough to steal the crystal for his king. Such bravery should not be punished.

"Ask him again to be sure the rocks on the hillside are the location," commanded Tobias.

"Did you put the crystal among the rocks?" Grinold asked

again.

"As surely as I stole the crystal, the location of its hiding is also true," responded Hroldolf, now convinced that Tobias would release him.

"Remove the limb and let him sink," ordered Tobias. "He can tell us no more."

"My lord, you gave your word to release him if he told the truth," Grinold implored. "Release him and let him return to his family. By all that is holy, leave him not to perish in such a place as this."

"I gave no such promise. Though if I did, I can just as easily rescind it. The man is of no importance to me. He stole from me and this shall be his reward. Let this serve as a warning for those who choose to defy me in the future that the punishment will be harsh."

Grinold could say no more, for he realized he could just as easily be at the bottom of such a bog himself should he dare to thwart Tobias. He stood by helplessly as the handlers pulled the limb from Hroldolf's grasping hands. As the bog closed around the sinking Hroldolf, Grinold knew that it would only be a matter of time until he well might meet a similar fate. He must plan for that time.

In the trees not far removed from this small group of men, two hard and dark eyes stared at the proceedings. The figure descended the tree and moved in the direction of the Dark Wood until he disappeared into the murky void of their embrace. In his hand he was holding a small leather pouch. Behind him, the group of men were hurriedly moving toward the hillside where lay the pile of rocks in which Tobias hoped he would find the crystal. In the Dark Wood, the pit made a gurgling sound as it closed forever over the sinking form of Hroldolf, again insuring the superstitions would remain as long as there were victims to perpetuate them.

Chapter Two
Grinold

Grinold was an odd creature. Nature had given him an even odder gift. As a small child, he had come to sense that he was unusual. As he grew and became a young man, he realized that he had an intuitive way of knowing when people were deceiving him or others around him. It was almost as if he could look into the eyes and straight to the soul of anyone he met. Eventually, he came to the knowledge that most people were out to help themselves, often at the expense of others. His gift was at once a blessing and a curse. He could avoid those who would try to take what was his or who would try to win him with false praise. Thus, he knew who his true friends were and also those who only pretended to be friends to curry favor. But it was the dark side of this gift that shaped what he eventually became. Coming into daily contact with people like Tobias was to jade his perception of mankind in general. It seemed that the people who were honest and generous were outnumbered by those who preyed on others for their gain. It was to be a perception, regardless how misconstrued, that would lead him into the company of men like Tobias and forge a mindset that would be resistant to change.

Grinold had no family nor close ties to anyone. His most vivid memories of his childhood were of the family who nurtured him as a boy. He had come to them as a small child, not even a year old, and they had brought him up as their own. Who his birth parents were he never knew. His foster parents were quite old when he came to them one dark night, delivered by a tall man cloaked in black. He had knocked on the door and left the child with the admonition that he be watched over carefully. They had cared for the boy as if he were their own. Misfortune, however, spares no one. Grinold was only thirteen when a raid on the village left his foster parents dead and their home burned to the ground. This was to be Grinold's first encounter with Tobias though he did not know him at the time. Since that fateful day, Grinold had been on his own with nothing to guide him other than his gift, which he had to use often to survive.

Not having any skills in a trade nor training in combat, Grinold had to resort to other methods to survive. Using his intuitive gift, he became skilled in games of chance where the understanding of how the opponent thinks is important. If shells were used, it did not matter how quickly the three shells were moved around, Grinold always knew under which one the pebble lay. In a game of Tok he could always find the card with the skull. Whether it was sleight of hand or a game of chance, Grinold would always win merely by looking into his opponent's eyes and reading the secrets there. Such a gift has to be used wisely, for those who play at these games do so for survival. To always win might prove fatal, so Grinold learned early to lose enough and win enough to survive. Life was a series of adjustments, and a quick mind and a quick wit were both necessary in the life that he had chosen.

As were most events in Grinold's life, his meeting Tobias was by chance. Grinold had taken to frequenting the small tavern in Vorkna, a small village which lay in the territory that Tobias hoped to rule some day when the crystal came into his possession. Grinold would lure hapless wayfarers into games that he would invariably win, and his victims would be none the wiser, for he preyed primarily on visitors to the village for his gain. After they had lost, they simply moved on, none the wiser to the gifts of the man who had taken their purses. It was on such a day that Tobias came into the small tavern in Vorkna and saw the man who would eventually take his quest to rule closer to reality.

Tobias often visited Vorkna, which could provide an outlet

for his many passions, whether it be gambling, women, or whiskey. Vorkna was comprised of small farms, small hamlets, and people with small ambitions. They only desired to be left alone and be allowed to tend their farms and raise their children. A man like Tobias was a dark cloud on their village when he visited there to drink at the nearest tavern or to partake of the pleasures that the wenches of the village could provide. He was a man of many passions, and his greatest passion was not only one day to control Vorkna but all of the other villages that lay in the realm that belonged to King Malvore. The king was old in years and in ill health. Should the fire of misfortune be the king's destiny, it would be Tobias who would provide the spark.

To turn that spark into a flame, Tobias knew he would need men who would be loyal to him for the revolt that was to come. If loyal followers could not be found, he would entice them with the dream of riches that would be theirs under their new ruler. In Grinold, fate was to provide him with a man who could make that first step a large one.

As Tobias drank from the mug that the innkeeper had been diligently refilling every few minutes, he watched carefully the activities of the young man sitting at a table across the nearly empty room. Grinold had not been able to entice the few strangers he had seen that day into the games he played. Therefore, he had added little to his purse. The two players now sitting with Grinold had been steadily losing for an hour. Due to the lack of players, Grinold had been less careful to let the two men win occasionally. The two players had been drinking steadily, and the drink combined with continual losses to the young man across from them had shortened their tempers. As the game continued, and Grinold proceeded to win turn after turn, the conversation among the three men grew heated.

Tobias had watched the game with increasing interest. As the bets were placed, the young man stared intently into the faces of his opponents, which, as the game wore on, only tended to make the men more uncomfortable and edgy. It was a look of intense concentration as if he could peer through them. Nothing else about the young man was remarkable. He looked to be eighteen years or about. His features were fine and his face was smooth, devoid of a beard or the scraggly hair that adorned his playing companions. His long hair fell down over his face, covering it as he bent forward save for the piercing blue eyes that seemed always to be in intense concentration each time a new hand was played.

Unable to bear the stare or losses any longer, one of the men rose quickly, turning the table and chairs over in his fury.

"You're cheating!" he screamed at Grinold. "No man can be that lucky. I know you have played foully in the winning. Do you deny it?"

"I do deny it," answered Grinold more calmly that the situation dictated.

"You have won every hand," spoke the second stranger. "My companion is not amiss in his claim that you won unfairly. Return our money or defend it with your life."

"As you can see I am unarmed. Would you take sword to an unarmed man?"

"A rascal and armed or a rascal and unarmed, it matters not to me," spoke the first man. "We will have the money or your life."

As the hostility had intensified, Tobias had moved across the room unnoticed and now stood directly behind the man who was speaking.

"Perhaps the young man is telling the truth," he said as all three men turned toward him as one.

"And who are you? What is your part in this?" asked the

man who had made the accusation.

"Just someone who would not like to see an innocent man injured. His play was fair. I have been watching the game, and nothing was amiss. Perhaps the drink has made you rash in the gaming. Thereto should be placed the blame. A sober man thinks before he takes the risk. A drunk man thinks not at all. My young friend will leave with his winnings and in the doing no lives will be at risk."

"Say you now?" blustered the first stranger, slowly removing his sword from its sheath. "Do you intend to make this your fight? If so, I and my companion are willing to defend what is ours."

"There need not be any bloodshed among gentlemen such as we," spoke Grinold in an attempt to assuage the tempers of the three men. He had made a mistake in winning too frequently and inciting the two gamblers. He was not a man who wanted to see any life taken. If he could end the confrontation peacefully, all would live to gamble another day.

Grinold looked at Tobias and read in his countenance the fire that burned there. It mattered not if the cause was just. Tobias lived for the encounter, not the cause. To a soldier a battle is a battle, and Tobias had been inactive too long.

"Gentlemen, put away your swords. My lord, shed no blood in my cause. Let them pass."

"Nay, these knaves would call you a rogue and insult me. I have killed men for less."

"But they are drunk and unworthy opponents for one of your obvious skill, my lord. It is I who am at fault for taking advantage of them. I stand for them."

Tobias looked at the young man and weighed his words. This obviously was a man of breeding though his clothes and general appearance would belie that fact. He doubtless had a talent that Tobias could use. Perhaps tolerance would be best practiced for the moment.

"Then away with you two cowardly dogs and return not, or I will show you the punishment for insulting those of rank."

The alcohol induced fog now lifting from the brains of the two men, they suddenly began to realize how close they had come to death and backed toward the door. As the door closed behind them, Tobias slapped Grinold on the shoulder.

"I see that you are a peacemaker," he laughed. "The game you play determines that you need the skills that I possess. I think you will be called upon again to defend yourself. Mayhap on that occasion I will not be around. It would be best if we can help each other in this regard."

"How can I help you?" asked Grinold. "I am a mere gambler by trade. No soldier am I as you can attest by my actions here."

"Your skill lies not in the sword. I have men who can fight. Your value will outweigh many swords in the days to come. If you wish, I can teach you skill with the sword, but you must give me the service I need in return. This is no life for a man. Here you will simply be a gambler, risking his life with each new game. With me you will have rank and a purpose. Eventually, you will have your own land which you may rule as you wish. Is this not better than what awaits you if you follow the path you've chosen?"

Something in the bearing of the man before him told Grinold that he should refuse this offer and go it alone. The eyes of Tobias were cold and, looking into them, Grinold saw only ruthless ambition and cruelty. What could he learn from this man that would improve his lot? He did not know the answer, but something within him told him that his future was somehow connected to Tobias. What that connection was he did not know. But his life was ruled by his instincts, and he could not turn against them now.

"I will accept your offer. I have little here to hold me. I am a gambler by nature, and this is simply another risk that I will take. Whether it lead to fortune or failure, I will play the die as it is cast. I am not a soldier and do not kill others for gain. If that be your wish for me, speak now and we will go our different ways. Yet, I am not averse to material wealth, and if I profit in your venture, am I not doing that which all men seek to do?"

Tobias smiled as he listened to Grinold debate with himself the merits of casting his lot with such a mercenary being. Here was a man who could be trusted and who would be intensely loyal if the cause was just. Tobias would not be able to conceal his plan to such a man as Grinold. His instincts were too refined for secrets to be kept very long from him. But his failing was that of many men. The desire for wealth and the benefits that are derived from such can lead a man to go against those principals he holds most dear. He would use Grinold's gifts until he was not needed, and then he could dismiss him as easily as he did the drunken men in the tavern. For now, Grinold was a valuable asset, and he must be allowed more leniency than he would accord most others.

That chance meeting at Vorkna had occurred almost two years ago. During that two years, working for Tobias had only deepened Grinold's conviction that mankind was inherently selfish and self serving. Why should he not be the same? If no lives were lost because of his actions, he could justify his course of action. Thus he reassured himself, even as Tobias continued his ruthless quest for power, that he was merely an instrument in that quest.

The crystal they sought was not found. Time and again Tobias sent search parties along the road Hroldolf had taken that fateful night. The searches yielded nothing and with each new failure, Tobias grew more and more obsessed in his quest.

Though the king was gravely ill, Tobias was not yet powerful enough to proceed with the rebellion on his own. There were too many men still loyal to the old king who would rally to his side if a battle for the kingdom should happen. Thus he had to be content with the small raids on the surrounding villages, hoping that in his failure to quell these, the king would lose favor with the people and they would seek a new ruler. With power second only to the king, he would be the logical choice to govern. The king had no heirs, having lost both his small sons in a daring raid on a caravan carrying them and the queen. The queen had been unharmed, but the infant sons had not been returned. The awaited ransom notes never came, and nothing was heard from them again. The tragedy was to continue to haunt the king for the rest of his life. His sorrow, no doubt, hastened his sickness which now was threatening to take his life.

Tobias had been more shocked than anyone at the events that had taken place in the kidnapping of the king's sons. This very deed he had planned for months and had set events into action that would have achieved his desired ends. He realized the two sons would grow to become formidable opponents in his desire for the crown. With heirs at hand, he would never be king. The kidnapping had been planned with this in mind. Indeed, no one other than he could have planned and executed a raid so well. Yet, the raid had taken place only a short distance from where Tobias had stationed his men in preparation for the attack on the royal caravan. All his efforts to discover the whereabouts of the king's sons were in vain. They seemed to have vanished into thin air, and after a time Tobias, like the king, assumed they were dead. Whatever had happened to them had simply made his job easier. Now, only the king stood in his way to obtaining the crown.

Tobias had been patient since those events so many years

Grinold

ago, but a man obsessed with power has his limits. The king had lived longer than he expected, and who knew when a man would turn up professing to be the king's son? There were many as ruthless and cunning as he. He had worked too long to let another assume the position he had coveted for years. The crystal was of vital importance if he was to be assured of victory. Its discovery and subsequent loss so quickly had devastated Tobias. He had found the crystal, and the power he desired had lain in the palm of his hand only to be taken away by a mere servant. The time and opportunity were at hand. All that was missing was the crystal and someone knew its whereabouts.

Grinold watched with interest the continuing efforts of Tobias to find the crystal. What strange powers did it possess that would drive a man to murder countless people in order to obtain it? He had heard of such an object as a small boy but had accounted it as superstition, much like the fears of the Dark Wood. He knew the crystal would never be found on the road that Hroldolf had taken that night. Someone else had seen the crystal being hidden and had removed the pouch assuming that it contained gold. Who could it have been and what might he have done with the crystal upon realizing that it was just a piece of glass for which he had risked his life? It could very well be at the bottom of some lake or river by now. Seeing the effect the deprivation of the object had upon Tobias's nature, Grinold thought that would be just as well. He knew that regardless of the situation concerning the crystal, Tobias was impatient, and it would not be long before he would make his move. When that time came, he would have to make a choice because numerous lives would be at stake. He had to be sure the wealth he sought for himself would be worth the price his soul would have to pay. Once the gauntlet was cast, there would be no turning back. Where he stood at that moment would have to be where he stood forever. This choice would not be long in coming.

Chapter Three
The Crystal of Light

In a small hut deep in the Dark Wood, Cyrean sat on a stool, staring at the leather pouch he had deposited on the wooden table in front of him. The hut was roomier than most and comfortably outfitted with crude but functional trappings. The walls were built with sturdy timbers fashioned from trees cut from the forest. Cyrean's father had been a woodcutter, and the hut and all the furnishings in the house he had built with his own hands. What they lacked in fineness they made up for in comfort and sturdiness. The hut itself was situated deep in the Dark Wood. No visitors ever came this far into the forest, so Cyrean lived a life of solitude, encountering other beings only when he traveled outside the dark confines of the forest. His father had built the hut over twenty years ago before Cyrean had been born, and with the death of his parents, he had stayed there, preferring the solitude to the capricious nature of the few people with whom he had come into contact. Why his father had chosen such a life in such a secluded location Cyrean never knew, but as he grew and played in the forest, he discovered many wonders that few mortals who feared to come into the forest would ever see. He did not understand their fears, but he came to appreciate the life he lived more and more as he witnessed the behavior of the people outside his domain. So he had chosen to stay in the Dark Wood and to let the world outside his realm do as it wished. He knew the forest and its inhabitants, and even the deadliest of these he preferred to the world of the men he had seen at the edge of the woods.

Close to the fireside lay a large mastiff, Cyrean's most loyal companion. The dog was now in its middle age, being almost six years old. Cyrean had found the animal trapped in one of the many pits that could be found all through the forest. Just a small pup at the time, it had been set out by travelers who had come through the area, and it had wandered into the forest, unaware of the dangers there. After falling into the bog, it had lain there for two days without food or water until Cyrean had heard its plaintive cries and rescued the half-starved animal. Luckily, it had been small and light in weight and had managed to stay atop the quagmire that otherwise would have swallowed it as it had Hroldolf. Since that time, Cyrean and the mastiff he had named Wolfen had become inseparable companions. They hunted together and ate together. The dog held the esteem in its master's eyes that normally is accorded only to a most true and loyal friend, for indeed he was. When food was needed, the two companions often had to venture outside the forest, for few animals roamed within its hostile environment. Cyrean had quickly discovered his companion to be fleet of foot and strong of jaw. Indeed, the power that the animal possessed in its jaws was formidable. Once an animal or object was in its powerful grip, it could only be released when he chose to do so. Many deer or like animal had felt that grip and succumbed to its power.

Wolfen now lay staring at his master with a puzzled expression as if he also was deliberating upon the contents of the bag. He whined softly and rose and shook himself, trying to throw off the effects of sleep. He moved to the table and sniffed at the bag and then looked at Cyrean as if to say there are more interesting things in the woods. Cyrean smiled and stroked the head of the large animal as he, too, stood and stretched. Being that his nature was an inquisitive one, it was unusual that he still had not looked into the bag. Though he was inquisitive, he was also cautious when it came to anything that involved the outside world. He had seen a man killed for the contents of what lay inside the bag. He was in no hurry to examine the object within, preferring to deliberate at length

The Crystal of Light

and perhaps learn more before he chanced to examine it closely. He still remembered the traveler bathed in light from the glow of the crystal and reasoned that such an object merited obtaining more information than he now possessed.

The two companions walked outside into the cool evening air. Darkness came quickly to the forest. Little light ever found its way into the denseness of the tall trees that covered all but the small clearing where stood the small hut of Cyrean. For a few hours each day, the sun filtered into this clearing and allowed brightly colored plants and flowers to bloom in what otherwise was a gloomy and hostile setting. It was only this that Cyrean missed in the world of his fellow mortals. The Outworlders could roam hill and forest, valleys and fields unencumbered by the dangers posed by the Dark Wood. Though he knew its entrapments and knew how to avoid them, it was only his greater fear of the dangers of the outside world that kept him here.

But as great as his yearning was for the beauty of what lay outside his realm, greater yet was his desire for a human companion. Since his parents died, he had not felt a closeness to any other person. He missed the daily presence of his mother, who had been a calming influence on his life during those times that he had rebelled against the restrictive nature of his existence and would have left its gloomy confines save for her pleadings. In his limited excursions outside the Dark Wood, he had often spied caravans passing through the area. Occasionally, he would see young girls, dressed in bright attire who talked and laughed and stirred longings within him that he had never felt before. He knew that the yearnings within him would never be quelled until he left the dark forest to walk among the men he despised.

As Cyrean stood musing outside the doorway of his hut, Wolfen emitted a low sound that started as a rumble in his throat and grew into a full growl. Suddenly, a stone flew from the branches of one of the trees providing the perimeter of the forest surrounding the hut and fell just feet away from Cyrean.

"Ah, Ah, Ah, Ah," came the sound of mocking laughter high in the tree several yards from where Cyrean stood. Wolfen ran to the base of the tree and growled menacingly.

"Here, Wolfen!" Cyrean commanded, and the large dog returned to his master's side, gutteral warnings letting the intruder know he was still there.

"Ah, Ah, Ah, Ah," came the laughter again.

"Bartold's aim is getting better," came a voice from the top of the tree. "Soon he will be able to topple the mighty Cyrean with one of his missiles. Then Cyrean will fear the presence of his mightiest enemy."

"Bartold's aim is as it ever was. If a braying fool such as Bartold be Cyrean's mightiest enemy, he will never have to fear for his safety. And should such fool ever improve and be lucky enough to hit Cyrean, Wolfen will make him pay for his impudence."

At the mention of the dog's name, the laughter stopped and a small figure descended the tree until Cyrean could see the dwarflike creature standing on a limb above him.

"Bartold would not hit master Cyrean," the dwarf said, eyeing apprehensively the large creature by Cyrean's side. "Bartold and Cyrean are friends. Do I not bring you news of the outside world? Am I not your greatest spy and informer?"

"What need have I for your news? I care not what happens to the Outworlders."

The dwarf descended to the last limb of the tree and dropped agilely to the ground.

"Bartold has news that master Cyrean will welcome. I travel among the Outworlders and see and hear many things. They look upon me with loathing and take me for a fool, but I hear and remember. Creatures such as I are fit only for the Dark Wood, but one day I and my brothers in the dwarf kingdom will rule, and Cyrean will be grateful that I, the great Bartold, spared him."

"What news could you have that I want, boastful one? The woods are my home. I need no communication of the Outworlders."

"I have seen strange things," said the dwarf, moving closer as if to convey his message so that others might not hear. Wolfen growled at his approach, and Bartold quickly stepped back.

"What things? Stop prattling and speak what you know or return to the trees and to your brothers in the wood."

"I have seen great numbers of men gathering from all over the provinces. They flock to Tobias at his command. Large armies are being formed, and I fear the king's days are numbered."

"Why do you care? What changes would such an event, should it come, have upon you and your kind?"

"I have seen the cruelty imposed upon his own people by Tobias. What chance would creatures such as I have if Tobias were to rule? We would be eliminated. A man such as he has no fear of the Dark Wood. He would lay it bare and destroy all its inhabitants. Such a man can never be allowed to assume the throne."

Cyrean listened to the small creature before him and knew his fears were sound. He, too, had just recently seen the dark nature of Tobias and his ruthless drive for power. He did not have any love for the dwarf clan, but they were a life form just as he was and had a right to live. If Tobias was putting an army together, a war would be a certainty and all would suffer, including the inhabitants of the Dark Wood.

"Tobias would never come here. It is the unknown that men fear, and Tobias is just a man," reassured Cyrean. "Still, it is best that we know his whereabouts and what he is planning. You must keep me informed, Bartold. We must be prepared if that day comes when Tobias attempts to overthrow the kingdom."

"Bartold the Bold sees and hears all. Perhaps when I unseat the powerful Tobias, I will allow you a position in my kingdom. It would be wise on your part to pay me the reverence I deserve now, looking toward those days when I shall rule."

"Get you hence and go about those duties I have given you," Cyrean said, picking up a large stick and tossing it at the dwarf. " Such an ugly creature is fit to rule only the Dark Wood. That will be your domain and lucky you will be to have it."

Bartold skipped nimbly about, easily avoiding the wooden missile and climbed swiftly back into the tree.

"Bartold will help Cyrean but he will remember the harsh words and perhaps Cyrean will be only a servant to Bartold when he becomes king."

Cyrean had picked up a stone to throw at the dwarf, but he had rapidly disappeared into the safety of the trees.

His encounter with Bartold and the news he had brought had stifled any desire Cyrean had to hunt that day. He turned back toward the hut and Wolfen reluctantly followed him, knowing that the hunt would have to wait until another time.

Cyrean knew that Tobias could never be allowed to come into possession of the orb. He did not understand what destruction so powerful a weapon in the hand of one such as Tobias could inflict, but it must be formidable and it must be denied him at any cost.

He moved to the table and lifted the bag. Slowly, he untied the string and let the object within drop into his hand.

The Crystal of Light

For a moment he stared at the object, but the small candle within the rapidly darkening room provided inadequate light for close examination. He moved closer to the candle and placed the crystal directly above the flame. Instantly, the room became bathed in light. It flooded the room and flowed through the two small windows of the hut, illuminating the outside of the hut as well.

Wolfen had reacted instantly, fleeing the room and seeking the comfort of the woods. Astonished and frightened by the intensity of the light which had filled the room so quickly, Cyrean dropped the crystal and fell to the floor, temporarily blinded by the brilliance of the colors emanating from the object. For moments he lay there as the light gradually dissipated within the room.

When he could see again, he found the crystal and placed it back into the pouch. Putting the bag in its former place on the table, Cyrean sat down and rubbed his eyes. It was not only the light that had weakened him. His very essence seemed to have been absorbed by the rays flowing from the glass, and he sat shaking while he tried to recover his strength.

Such power Cyrean had never felt before, and he knew that only a fraction of its power had been captured by the small candle in the room. A man with full knowledge of its secrets could rule the world. This was the power that Tobias was seeking. With the crystal he would be all powerful. Now Cyrean realized why the fleeing servant had fought so desperately to escape and get the crystal to the King. It could never fall into the hands of anyone such as Tobias. He had to finish the mission the servant had begun and get the crystal to the king. He paused in his thinking when he realized what this mission would entail. He would have to leave the Dark Wood and travel to Eustan. In so doing, he would be open to all the evil and malevolence of the outside world. Perhaps this was the impetus he needed to do that which he had so often thought about. If he were ever to venture into the realm of the Outworlders, this would be the time. He could sense that the fate of the Dark Wood and perhaps the entire kingdom depended on his delivering the crystal to the king.

Cyrean took the bag from the table and placed it into his jerkin. He would not feel safe until the bag and its contents were delivered to the king. He vowed to start the next day and began making preparations for his journey.

Wolfen had lain in the woods until the glow within the hut disappeared. His flight had taken him to the edge of the Dark Wood, and he had rested there until he felt it was safe to return to the security of the fire in his bed near the fireplace. The comfort of the light from the fireplace was warm and embracing. The light he had just experienced was different from anything he had known before. It was frightening in its intensity and even he instinctively knew that its purpose was not warmth or comfort.

Suddenly, his senses came alert. Something was moving in the forest. The smell that came to his nostrils was not of the game he chased with his master. This odor was much like that of his master and called for inspection. Silently, he made his way in the direction of the scent. Using the skill he had honed in many hunts with Cyrean, the animal crouched in the grass and waited and watched.

Soon a figure appeared within Wolfen's range of vision, but he remained motionless, and he watched the actions of the man. This was not some animal to hunt. It was a man creature and more dangerous than any animal. Patiently, he crouched and watched as the man came to the hillside where lay a small stack of stones. The man examined them carefully as if looking into each rock for a clue to a great mystery. After a thorough examination of the rocks, he stood and looked at the area around him. He sniffed as if somewhere in the air lay the answer to what he sought. A hint of something in the wind drew his attention to the forest in the direction from which Wolfen had come in his flight. Slowly, picking his way through the scrubby brush, the man began to move in that direction.

Seeing the figure slowly approaching, Wolfen silently made his way back into the woods and started in the direction of the hut. Surely the light would now be gone, and he could go back to the comfort of the fire. With any luck, his master would have a large bone to give him from the night's supper. The man now forgotten as the image of food took its place, the large dog moved more quickly toward home.

The tracker had sensed he was not alone. Somehow he knew eyes watched his movement. He knew not where they were or what form they took, but they had been there. Now there was nothing and he turned his attention to the scent of smoke that he had detected coming from the Dark Wood. Why would smoke be coming from such a place this late at night? Who would dare to go into the forest when the dangers lurking there would be at their height?

Grinold paused and sniffed again. The scent of smoke was undeniable, and its source was far into the forest. He continued his way toward the scent, pausing occasionally to look at the ground before him. Even in the darkness he could detect that something had been there. His senses told him it was not human. Was he being stalked by some creature, and, if so, why did he not detect its presence now? He looked at the forest before him and the fears returned. Something or someone was in the forest. Therein might lie the answers to the questions he sought, but he was not so foolish as to seek them tonight. He would not be in haste to put his own life into jeopardy for Tobias. Tobias had been absorbed in gathering his army for the battle to come and had turned the finding of the crystal exclusively over to Grinold with the admonition that it must be found quickly. The fact that Grinold alone had been accorded the responsibility of finding such a valuable object attested to the admiration that he had for the tracker's abilities. Grinold would not disappoint Tobias, but the hunt into the Dark Wood would have to wait until daylight.

Chapter Four
He Who Wears the Crown

Far to the West in the province of Eustan lay the castle of King Malvore. Built centuries earlier by his ancestors, the castle of the king was a monument to time. Constructed of stone taken from the mountain that loomed behind it, it was an imposing fortress. Many battles had been fought around it, and though the battles that had been waged there had inflicted damage upon the structure, each time it had been rebuilt stronger than before. It would take an imposing force indeed to conquer those who fought within the walls of this great edifice. To the left and right side of the castle, long walls fanned out from the structure hundreds of feet to jut against the mountain itself. Above each of these walls ran a fortified walk from which the inhabitants could throw hot oil, stones, and arrows upon any potential enemy below. The only entrance was through the gate, a magnificently constructed portal built of massive timbers which would repel almost any force thrown at them. The castle could withstand any siege as long as water and food were plentiful. The inhabitants of Eustan could find refuge inside the walls of the castle when the need arose. This had not been necessary now for almost two decades. The king had been a strong leader, and the province had grown in size and strength under his guidance. If the outlying provinces had been as adequately prepared, the king would have stood in even more favor with his subjects.

Vorkna was a good example of how the king had been lax in his rule of the outlying regions. Regardless of how strong the leader was that king Malvore placed in one of the lesser provinces, Tobias proved to be stronger. His raids had weakened the king's strength in all the eight provinces save that of Eustan itself. Tobias was not yet of sufficient force to challenge the king and his army in Eustan, but each day he grew more and more powerful as mercenaries flocked to him, seeing the opportunity for wealth in the new regime. Vorkna, like the other provinces, had suffered the tyranny of Tobias until any change would have been preferable to them if it meant getting rid of the plundering and looting they suffered regularly.

The king knew of the discontent of his people, but his failing health had kept him from taking a personal hand in the conflict. He had been confined to his bed for almost a year, and the heavy burden of leadership and the tragic loss of his two sons and heirs had left him despondent and uninterested in affairs outside the castle itself. Only the queen seemed to be able to provide the support and comfort necessary to keep the king's will to live strong. It was she more than the king who daily took stock of the situation with Tobias, and the news she received made her fear for the safety of the inhabitants of Eustan. She knew the former strength of the king would be needed in the battle that was certain to come. Yet, she had found no way to console her husband after the disappearance of the two princes, nor had she been capable of restoring his spirit sufficiently to rule. The sickness was more in his mind than that of a physical nature, and even his greatest physicians had not been able to cure such an illness.

Most of the matters of government that required overseeing on a regular basis had been placed into the hands of the king's chief advisor years earlier when it became evident the king could not do so in his present state. Lord Hadreon had been in the king's service since his coronation many years ago. They had fought in three campaigns together, defending their home against hostile invaders, and each man had proven his courage time and again. The king's trust in Hadreon was absolute, and for several years now, Hadreon had taken on more and more responsibility in the governing of the king's affairs. Lord Hadreon was more aware than anyone in the province of Eustan how powerful Tobias had become. He knew how absolute power could corrupt a good man. He had stood in the place of the king for more than three years, and during that time he had to fight daily against letting the position and the power lead him to believe he was more than the king's servant. If Tobias were to come into such a position, the intoxicating influence it would have upon him would endanger the world as they knew it. Now further news had come to Hadreon's ears that had troubled him mightily and made it imperative that the king be informed quickly.

"My good friend and counselor, you look unwell today," spoke the king as Lord Hadreon bowed to him upon entering the chamber. "Each day I have seen the gloom deepen upon thy face. Does the fate of the kingdom seem so desperate? Have we not fought many battles in the past and always defeated those who would enslave our people? When that day comes again, we will do as we have always done and defend the kingdom with our swords and shields, and with the grace of God we shall again prevail."

"Your grace, there is much to report since the last time we spoke. Our kingdom is not the same as during those long ago times when we fought side by side. The traitor Tobias has been gradually building an army with which he hopes to topple the very walls of Eustan itself. He grows bolder with each new soldier that joins his ranks. It will be soon now when he decides he is of such power to overthrow our forces, and I fear we may not have prepared well for that time. It is reported by our spies that he has come into possession of the Crystal of Light. If that be so, nothing will stop him in his quest."

"Think you the reports are true? Could he have found the crystal? I had thought it gone from our world forever. The stories of its disappearance put its last known sighting at the

Battle of the Two Mountains over one hundred years ago. At that time it created such destruction that King Raul ordered that it be thrown into the fiery mountain that stood where that last great battle had been fought."

"I heard the same stories, my lord. But I have also been told that the orb might not have been cast into the fire by the soldier to whom the duty was entrusted. Instead, he tossed a piece of glass into the fire and concealed the crystal in his cloak. This event was supposedly witnessed by a servant who had accompanied the soldier to the top of the mountain. The crystal had not been seen nor spoken about for over a century. Now it resurfaces, supposedly in the hands of Tobias. If that be true, no greater danger could the crystal ever impose than it does now."

"I have entrusted my kingdom to you, Lord Hadreon. The fate of my queen and my people rests in your hands. What do you need to carry on the fight against Tobias and his forces of darkness?"

"My king, if Tobias has the crystal and is prepared to use it in all-out battle against Eustan, we have nothing that will stop him. Our only hope is to acquire the power of the crystal for ourselves. With the object in our possession, Tobias would never dare to oppose us. Were the battle fought without the use of the crystal on either side, I fear we would lose to his superior forces. It is imperative if the crystal exists that it be the king who controls its power."

"Oh, if my sons were here, Lord Hadreon, the viper Tobias would never dare to challenge the throne. I do miss my sons most dreadfully in these times of crisis."

"I can not imagine your grief, your grace. It has been a great loss for the people of Eustan as well. I know how grievous it would be for me to lose my only child. She has been the light of my life for, lo, seventeen years now. With each passing day she grows more beautiful and reminds me of my dead wife in so many ways. The emptiness I felt with the passing of my Helena I can imagine you have experienced manifold with the loss of your sons."

"Yes, you still have Aurienna to comfort you, Lord Hadreon. She comes to my chamber often to read to me or talk of matters that she hopes will lighten my heart. She takes too much upon herself at so young an age. She should be toying with the affections of the young knights in the kingdom instead of spending her time talking to a tired old soldier."

"She finds it no imposition, your majesty. She has often said she finds the games that are required in courting do bore her, and the young knights that woo her are not of the mettle that you and I once were. The man who wins her heart will be fortunate indeed."

As Lord Hadreon finished speaking, a soft knock on the chamber door was followed by the entrance of Aurienna into the room. Approaching the king's bed as she had so often done before, the look upon her countenance was one that spoke her right to be there in the king's presence without the formalities that would have been only proper for others of lesser state. The quiet, yet assured, demeanor of her bearing was enhanced by her personal radiance, and the composite was beauty that would rarely ever be seen by men.

"Good day, Father. I hope I am not intruding upon matters that are not womanly in nature. I know that you and his majesty have many urgent matters to discuss of late. If so, I can attend his majesty later."

"Nonsense, Child," spoke King Malvore. "We have finished with our business and had we not, you would still be most welcome. There are no secrets among us. I know well that anything discussed here would never fall on traitorous ears. Lord Hadreon, we will discuss the crystal tomorrow. If there is a chance that Tobias has it in his castle, perhaps one of our spies can inform us. If it be there, we must take immediate action to acquire it."

"I have planted a spy there, your majesty, in the guise of a servant. I have not received communication from him of late, but he is brave enough and resourceful enough to steal the crystal if the situation should present itself. Should I receive good news from him, I will hasten to inform you of its nature."

"Be it so, Lord Hadreon. We have had great days, and greater days are yet before us. I can feel that fortune will smile on us in the battle if it does come."

Lord Hadreon bowed and moved quickly from the room, and Aurienna assumed her usual station in a small, comfortable chair at the king's bedside. She opened the volume from which she had been reading for several days but suddenly closed the book at looked at the king intently.

"Your majesty, is it true that the kingdom stands in peril and that war is imminent? If it be so, I must learn to do battle as a knight would do. After all, I am as capable as any of the muddled brained knights that I have rejected of late to defend my home. I am strong and I would fight as bravely as any soldier in the kingdom. If his grace so ordered, I would defend with my life the king and the realm."

King Malvore laughed at these words so earnestly spoken and then quickly replied.

"Forgive me, Child. I do not laugh at you. Your words are indeed noble and have touched my heart. Would I had a thousand knights like you, I would not fear for the kingdom. But there are other things that you can do that would better serve my cause. There will be many things for which to prepare. Food and water will need to be stored so that it will be ready when the siege does come. Medicines and bandages must be prepared for those who will be injured, and your spirit and the spirits of all the wives and daughters of the soldiers will be needed once the battle begins. Then if the need of a sword in your hand becomes apparent in a hopeless cause, I will bestow upon you one that I have used in battle. Let us hope that day does not come."

"Perhaps I could be the spy that is planted in the house of Tobias," spoke Aurienna, now caught up in the adventure and her imagined part in its coming.

"Child, we would never put you in such danger. Your father would not agree, and I have already lost too many close to me."

"But Tobias knows me not. You and my father have talked of how my beauty affects men. Would it not also affect Tobias?"

"That is a surety if he indeed be a man. But that day will not come to pass. Your safety can only be assured behind the walls of this castle. Should the day come when those walls seemed doomed to fall, only then would we send you out to seek safety and to face whatever destiny awaits you. But not until then."

Aurienna listened as the king finished speaking. She placed her hand on his brow and looked into his face. He had drifted off to sleep with his final words to Aurienna and now seemed to be in peaceful slumber.

It was in the nature of Aurienna to be like her father. She was proud and fearless, and had she been a male, she doubtless would have been a great soldier and leader. But fate had given her another calling. Regardless of what that calling might portend, she would meet it bravely and without hesitation. If only she had met her true knight, a man she could stand beside proudly in their fight to save the kingdom. That had not happened and some intuitive part of her being told her that man was not inside the boundaries of Eustan. The world she had known in her seventeen years had been very limited, and she yearned to see what lay beyond Eustan and the walls of the castle. If she knew her father, he would want to send her to a place of safety before the battle began. She knew she could not defy his wishes, but that is not the way she wanted to leave her home. She preferred it be at her own choosing and in her own time. Maybe the war they feared would not come at all. For the last twenty years peace had reigned within the kingdom. Perhaps peace also had made them soft. If so, the kingdom would be lost.

As Aurienna ruminated on the possibilities of war, beyond the gates and beyond the boundaries of Eustan, a huge army was gathering. Emboldened by the lure of fame and fortune, renegade soldiers from provinces far and wide had gathered onto Tobias, pledging their lives in return for his promises that everything would be shared with them. None of these mercenaries had ever had honorable treatment from tyrants they had served in the past. Was it the nature of these kind of men to live for the moment, hoping that at some time in their wretched lives, a man of honor would actually lead them and live up to the promises he made? Such delusion seemed to be the stuff on which they thrived, and their pledge of loyalty to Tobias would once again only lead to disappointment. To live and die as a soldier was their lot. Many would never live to see their dreams fulfilled, and those who would survive the coming battle would never realize anything more than what they carried onto the field. Such would ever be their destiny whether it be Tobias or another ambitious pretender that would lead them to destruction.

Tobias watched day after day as his army grew, and he knew the time was now close at hand when he would be able to carry out his rebellion. The men who gathered to him were a

He Who Wears the Crown

rag-tag lot, but they were bodies to throw at the fortifications of Eustan. Enough of them would eventually be weight enough to bring down the walls of the mighty castle. True, the crystal had not yet been found, but he felt that now his army was of sufficient strength to win the day without the power it could lend to the fray. Grinold might yet find the crystal, and if he were to do so, that would only ensure the victory. Regardless, the time was now, and within the coming weeks the soldiers would be sufficiently prepared to do battle.

A day's ride from the camps where the army gathered, Grinold was seeking to fulfill the mission given to him by Tobias. As he arose with the morning light, he saw before him the Dark Wood, and he sensed that within its ebony clutches lay the object he sought. He wondered what he would do if he actually found the crystal. He disliked war and the pain and suffering it brought. He was merely a pawn in a game that men play, and he wanted to have no part of what now seemed to be inevitable. He preferred the solitary life of the woods and fields to the company of Tobias and his army of cutthroats. He had still not decided where he would cast his lot once the actual battle began, and he had many times thought of leaving the provinces to seek his fortune in some unknown land. Whatever path he chose, he felt he could not give the crystal, should he find it, to a traitor.

As he stood pondering his options, Grinold once again felt eyes upon him. This time they seemed to be distant. He knew that danger lurked everywhere for a lone man on the roads. Highwaymen were common to the region, and it was his ever-present instincts that had kept him out of danger up to this point. If the peril lay in the Dark Wood itself, it would probably not be a creature like himself that would pose it. The hazards that would be confronted there Grinold would not have seen before. Again, he suppressed the urge to turn and travel in a direction away from the Dark Wood and from the army of Tobias. He did not have time to deliberate long, for suddenly a beam of sunlight reflected off an object in a tree at the entrance to the Dark Wood, and Grinold, his curious nature aroused, picked up his bag and moved quickly in that direction.

Chapter Five
Preparing for War

Queen Ofra sat quietly as her handmaidens prepared her dress for the activities of the day. Her mind was preoccupied with thoughts of her husband and the crisis that he and Lord Hadreon must somehow avert if the kingdom were to survive. The last few years had taken their toll on her once beautiful countenance. The burden of carrying on the daily activities of the castle coupled with the king's sickness had placed a dire responsibility upon her that she had been ill-equipped to handle. She had weathered adversity bravely, but the years of worry and constant attention to those duties that should have been the king's had left their mark. It was a rare occasion indeed when a smile could be evoked upon her face. The gay laugh that had lightened the hearts of those who knew her was now rarely heard. The face that had enchanted men in her youth with its beauty was now lined, and her eyes reflected the torment of the soul within. She had suffered no less than the king with the loss of her sons. With her sons gone and the king nearer death with each passing day, she had been denied almost everything that made her existence bearable. She knew the time was coming when a great change would take place. She feared for her husband's life and the lives of those who depended upon the king for protection. She sorrowed for those days when the king ruled with a firm but wise and gracious hand, and the only responsibility she had was to her husband and young sons.

"Your majesty, I had started to worry," Aurienna scolded mildly as she entered the queen's chambers. "You are stirring unusually late this morn. I have spoken to the king who is astir and asking for you. I think he has some news of much import to give you today. Will you speak to him?"

The queen smiled wanly at the young woman standing

before her and thought how beautiful she looked. That same beauty had been hers not so many years ago. She envied Aurienna, who teemed with boundless energy and youthful enthusiasm. She feared for her most of all in the upcoming battle. Since the death of her sons, Aurienna had become like a daughter to her, always there to comfort her and the king and never asking for anything in return. What a match she would have been for her oldest son if he had lived. She and the king had lived full and useful lives, but Aurienna was yet to experience the myriad wonders that the world provided. How were they to ensure her safety when the battle was at its height and all might be lost? She hoped the meeting with her husband would resolve some of the questions that had been plaguing her mind for weeks now.

"My child, you have more important things to do than worry about an old woman. You are young and energetic. The day is beautiful and you should be riding or playing games instead of filling your mind with concerns about the king and queen. We have many servants to see that our needs are met. Get thee hence and torture those young men who seek your favor."

"I care not for such silly activities," replied Aurienna haughtily. "I have many important duties to fulfill. There are preparations to be made that will require the strength of a man and the delicacy of a woman. Until the castle is fully fortified and at maximum strength, my place is here. The king knows my value and has entrusted many duties to me that will help in the defeat of the tyrant Tobias should he be so foolhardy as to come against us."

"So much like your father Lord Hadreon. He and the king fought many battles together. My husband often spoke of the bravery of your father in battle and indeed owes his life to him more than once."

Preparing for War

"The debt was repaid more than once since," replied Aurienna. "Two soldiers such as they can lead our forces again to victory if Tobias dares to carry out his threat."

"Ah, if I were as assured of that as you are, but they are old in years and not the warriors they once were. Who will carry our banner now? General Draco has trained our army well, but many of our young men are untested in battle."

At the mention of General Draco's name, Aurienna frowned and her voice rose in irritation.

"Draco! That fraud! I don't trust him. He is ambitious and arrogant. What he does he does simply for his own gain, not that of the kingdom. I feel the king's trust in him is misplaced. My father speaks of him often but never in flattering tones. The king places too much power in Draco's hands, and I fear that trust will be betrayed and at a time when it will be most damaging to our cause."

"Even if your fears are valid, it is too late to make changes in leadership at this late point in time. The king and Lord Hadreon are much more knowledgeable than we to judge who should be in command. We can only hope their faith in General Draco's ability to lead is well founded."

Before Aurienna could reply, a chambermaid approached to inform the queen that the king and Lord Hadreon were without and would like to speak to her on an important matter.

"Of course. Admit them at once. Aurienna, come and attend me while I speak with our visitors."

Aurienna dutifully moved to the queen's side and began preparing her hair as the visitors were granted entrance into the chamber. The somber look upon the faces of the two men filled the queen's heart with foreboding, but she knew she would have to be strong for Aurienna's sake.

"Lord Hadreon, we are fortunate indeed to gaze upon the beauty of the two women closest to our hearts. Is this not indeed worth fighting for?"

"Assuredly, this is so, your grace. Men are the weapons of battle, but women such as these are the fire which will temper that metal to a white heat until defeat of the stoutest enemy is inevitable. We are fortunate indeed."

The queen smiled indulgently at the vain attempt to flatter them and arose to address the king and Lord Hadreon.

"If a glib tongue could win the day, we would indeed be victorious, but undue flattery sometimes conceals dark fortune. Our beauty does not draw you forth. What then is the nature of your visit, my lords?"

"True," rejoined the king, "our skills in the art of flattery, much like our weapons, have dulled over the years, but like our weapons, constant use will hone them to a new sharpness. That blade will be applied to our enemy when once we meet. At that meeting no words will be necessary."

"I have feared that this time would come, my husband. What is it that you wish of me in this crucial hour?"

"The forces of Tobias have swelled until he sees the possibility of victory even without the crystal in his possession. News from my spies has lead me to believe that that time is near. Before his forces march on the castle, there is one matter to which I must give immediate attention."

"Speak, my lord, and if it is within my power, I will attend your wishes."

The king looked at his wife and sought the words he had to speak. Lord Hadreon, seeing that the king was faltering in the delivery of his message, stepped to his side.

"The king and I have agreed that it will not be safe for those women of nobility to remain in the castle. We have planned for a caravan to transport you and my daughter to a place of safety. After our forces are victorious, we will again return you to your rightful place in the kingdom."

Preparing for War

Aurienna, who had remained silent until now, suddenly found herself facing her father and fighting the tears that were rapidly filling her eyes.

"No, Father, I won't go. The king has said that I will be needed here to fill a vital role when the battle begins. I will not leave like some coward when the kingdom needs me most."

"Hush, Daughter, this is not a decision that was made lightly. If the battle be lost, all who are of rank will be executed. Should the battle go against us, you and the queen will be needed to pull our people together. Your youth and courage will rally many to your side when we are gone. This will be the only hope we have of ever retaking the kingdom."

"Then you do truly fear that we cannot win. If that be so, send the queen under heavy escort to safety. Let me remain to be of use here where I am most needed. The daughter of Lord Hadreon should not flee into the night like an abject coward. What army would follow me after I am branded a deserter to our cause? Your majesty, speak to my father and let me do those things that you promised me just this morn."

"The burden of rule lays heavy upon my heart, my child. Your father is your counsel and your guide. I cannot go against his wishes for his only daughter. Follow the path he has chosen for you. In time your worth will be in your survival. Tobias will never be at ease as long as he knows you and the queen live. It is therefore decided."

Aurienna knew the king's word was absolute, and she sank dejectedly upon the bed and cried. The queen held her and stroked her hair as the king gave instructions before parting.

"Get those things ready that you will need for an extended stay," he said. "You will be taken to a remote province far to the north. The trip will take days by caravan and the time of return, if ever, will be indefinite. An armed escort will assure your safe departure and will guide you to the appointed place well beyond the reach of Tobias."

A noise outside in the courtyard cut short any other communication among the people in the room, and Lord Hadreon crossed swiftly over to the window to witness the din occurring just inside the palace gates.

"Your majesty, it is General Draco and it seems that a spy has been captured and is being interrogated in the courtyard. A large crowd has gathered to witness the spectacle. It appears that the prisoner has been severely beaten in the effort to extract information from him."

"Draco goes too far. Take the prisoner to a cell and bring the general to me," ordered the king. "We do not make inquisitions public spectacles. That is the type of behavior we would expect from Tobias, not one of our own generals."

"It is exactly the behavior I would expect from him," said Aurienna harshly. "The difference in the two men cannot be distinguished by their actions. Both are cruel and heartless. Both crave power and would do anything to achieve position. I trust him not, your majesty."

"The position that General Draco holds sometimes calls for a cruelty that we are not capable of, my child. The nature of war in itself is cruel and unjust. I do not condone abusing prisoners, yet I know that torture sometimes is the only way to get information vital to our cause. Still, it does not have to be a public spectacle."

"I have summoned General Draco, my liege," interjected Lord Hadreon. "He has had the prisoner taken to a compound where he will be closely guarded. Apparently, the man was captured just inside the city gates. He had entered in the guise of a peddler and had been observed by one of our soldiers making diagrams of our fortifications. No doubt, these would have found their way into the hands of Tobias. His spies are everywhere and we cannot know what secrets he already has in his possession."

As Lord Hadreon finished speaking, a large, imposing figure had been escorted into the room by one of the king's guards. General Draco did not speak as he stood facing the inhabitants of the room. His eyes took in the room in a swift glance. He bowed to the king and queen and waited for the king to speak. King Malvore looked at the soldier in front of him and knew this would be a formidable opponent in battle. Easily as tall as Lord Hadreon and bigger in stature than either of the other two men in the room, he stood composed and outwardly calm. He held his helmet under his arm. It was battle tested with the imprint of sword and axe in its metal. It had protected its wearer well. Yet Draco's face still bore the marks of battle, the most telling a scar that ran vertically from the top of his left eye to his chin. The eye had been damaged and now was covered with a white film that unnerved the strongest of those who gazed upon it. Many were the battles in which he had fought, and the scars he wore proudly as one would wear badges of honor. He did not seem ill at ease although he already knew why the king had sent for him. It was his business to know what others thought and what their actions would be in circumstances such as these. He knew well how to read people, and in the interrogation of prisoners he almost always was successful. The few times he did not get the information he needed, the prisoners had died in the process. He felt no compassion in these situations. It was part of war and any soldier who was captured knew this might be the fate that awaited him. A soldier rarely surrendered in battle, preferring instead to die an honorable death at the hands of the enemy rather than be subjugated to the cruelty of one such as General Draco. When a spy was taken, like the one the general had been torturing in the courtyard, it was the sadistic nature of Draco to make it a public spectacle. If there were other spies who witnessed the brutality, they were sure to abandon their activities and leave rather than face the possibility of capture and like punishment.

"You sent for me, my liege?" Draco asked, looking at the king but well aware of the two women in the room, especially the young one whom he knew to be the daughter of Lord Hadreon. Her beauty and grace he had marked many times during his frequent visits to confer with her father. He could see in her bearing that she would be a formidable opponent if she were a man. Even now she looked as if she could hold her own with most soldiers under his command. There was fire in every aspect of her being. Yes, she would indeed be fitting match for the man who could control her.

"Yes, General. It has been brought to my attention that you are having a public interrogation of a prisoner. Such inhumane treatment is not for us. This business will be done in private."

"Is it the king's wish that I release the prisoner? For if I cannot use the tactics necessary to loose his tongue, then we need to sent him back to Tobias without one."

"Is it necessary to abuse and humiliate prisoners to get information, General?" asked Aurienna, unconcerned that in these matters she was overstepping her bounds in the questioning of a man who had led armies into battle.

"Is it a woman's place to question my tactics, your majesty? Are we now answering to women who doubt our methods? If so, indeed we have fallen mightily, and Tobias will make short work of us all."

"My daughter has always spoken her mind, General," interjected Lord Hadreon. "If that is a fault in her, then it is my error that it is there. Yet she often sees more clearly than I on the issues at hand. I value her opinion most highly, though at times I wish she were more prudent in the voicing of it."

"Yes, I, too, have received the benefit of the wisdom she

has acquired at so young an age," added King Malvore. "But the business we must now conduct will not require wisdom but simply the means to take the queen and our young advisor to safety. We will retire to the planning room for our deliberations on this matter. If the queen and your beautiful daughter will excuse us, Lord Hadreon, we will continue to converse on these matters. My heart will carry a heavy burden until I know they are safe."

The men took their leave and walked down a long passageway that would eventually take them to the war room where so many strategies had been planned over the decades. Aurienna watched them go with a heavy heart, for she knew those plans would take her far from the conflict that was imminent. How she longed to be there for that battle, but she could not defy the king's orders.

"Don't worry, Aurienna, for them or for our safety. The king will take all the precautions possible to ensure we reach our destination. As for them, they will do as they have always done when danger has threatened. A warrior cannot be anything else. It is all he knows. These times of peace are for us and the villagers. They are not for the likes of Lord Hadreon and General Draco or even the king. To die in battle would be the death they desire, not to grow old and feeble and useless. Your help is not needed here. The king is right in his belief that we will serve better later to reunite the kingdom should it fall into the clutches of Tobias. Do not be of heavy heart in the parting. We will return and when we do, the kingdom will be as powerful as ever."

Aurienna listened to the words of the queen. Secretly she knew that the king and her father were making the right decision, and the kingdom would be better served with them safely hidden away from Tobias. Yet that part of her that was so much her father in nature yearned for the battle that loomed ever closer with each new dawn. She would obey their orders for now, but that time would come when she would take a stand for their cause. She did not know when that time would be, but something that welled up from deep inside her told her that day would not be far away.

Chapter Six
The Meeting

The flash of light that Grinold had observed in the outer fringe of the forest had not reappeared. Had it been his imagination? The part of him that was the hunter and tracker said it was not a vision conjured in his mind. He had felt that he was being watched, and that feeling had not completely dissipated. Knowing the fear that the inhabitants of the region had for the Dark Wood, he doubted that someone like himself had created the movement. As he made his way toward the area from which the light had emanated, he checked the ground he traversed carefully, looking for markings that would indicate that someone else had passed this way. There were no signs that such an activity had occurred. Still he proceeded with the caution of a man who had been in similar situations before and who knew the importance of being prepared for any eventuality.

The sun that morning had risen brightly, quickly taking the cold and moisture from the fields, but there was a coldness within Grinold's body that the sun could not touch. Every fiber of his body tingled as he drew closer to the forest. The birds that sang in the field where he had walked the day before did not sing here. Indeed, as he drew closer and closer to the woods, the only birds that he saw or heard were large rooks that flew with regularity in and out of the dark confines of the forest before him. A part of him was sure that the woods could hold nothing that a man in his position had not seen before. In the years that he had worked for Tobias, every conceivable aberration of nature and of human nature he had seen. Nothing really surprised him anymore. In Tobias he had seen the cruelty of mankind in its purest essence. No creature of the forest could reach the heights of depravity that a man like Tobias was capable of reaching. So with this thought providing some modicum of comfort, Grinold made his first steps into the Dark Wood.

Working his way carefully through the tangle of vines and trees, Grinold lifted his head and paused. Again, the morning breeze brought the hint of smoke to his nostrils. He sniffed the air much like a hound on the trail of game, and inhaled the odor. It was unmistakably smoke. During the time he had taken to pause and determine from what direction the smoke had come, he noticed a large crow pecking at a bright metallic object lying on the ground only a short distance from where he stood. He moved quickly to the object and got within reaching distance before the crow gave up on lifting the shiny piece of metal and flew into the safety of the limbs high in the tree above. Grinold looked the metal over carefully, finally deciding that it was a large stud that a man might wear in a belt or on a piece of clothing. Could the crow have been sitting in the tree with the piece in its beak, and the sun simply caught it for a moment and caused the reflection he had seen? The crow had probably found the piece in some field and was attracted to its shiny quality. This seemed to be the most plausible explanation, and it gave Grinold some encouragement as he looked into the darkness before him.

There was no path anywhere in the area where Grinold stood. If someone or something had traveled through the forest, it had not left a path or even a track he could follow. He looked along the limbs of the trees that surrounded him and at the many serpentine vines that climbed high into their branches. It would be possible to travel through the trees, using the vines as a means of quickly moving through the forest without ever touching the ground. It would be natural for some animals to do this, but if the scent that kept coming to his nostrils were made by a human, why would he want to hide his presence here? Once more, his senses tingled, and the

The Meeting

feeling he was being watched came to him again.

Vines and exposed roots of the large trees made travel difficult, and Grinold had to pick his way carefully forward. Ever present and even more dangerous were the innumerable sand pits that would swallow any unlucky victim who did not choose carefully his way around their edges. As Grinold worked his way forward, a large sand pit spread out directly in front of him. He had seen a man swallowed by one this size, and he skirted its edge, moving carefully to a firm section of earth a few feet to the right of the boggy mass. Suddenly, the ground beneath him gave way, and he tumbled headlong into a large pit, bringing dirt and limbs that had concealed the hole down upon him in the process. He lay stunned for several moments before he finally composed himself enough to gaze about his prison.

As he tried to focus his eyes in the darkness around him, he could tell he was not in quicksand. This was a large hole that had been dug out at some time to trap large game. Someone had placed a natural covering over it, and in his concentrated effort to avoid the quicksand, he had inadvertently stepped into another danger. The small torch that he had been using for light had gone out in his tumble into the pit, and the waning light that seeped into the forest gave him little aid. Gradually, his eyes began to adjust to the darkness, and he began to investigate the walls of his earthen prison more closely. Certainly, the pit had been created by someone. The walls showed markings of having been carved by some instrument. The depth of the hole indicated it had been intended for some large animal and not the warthogs, small deer, or other game that frequented the area. He had just completed his cursory examination of the pit when he detected a movement in one of the trees that he could see by looking directly above him.

"Ah, Ah, Ah, Ah, Ah," came a coarse and derisive laugh from high in one of the trees.

"Who's there?" shouted Grinold. "Show yourself and help a visitor to these woods to safety."

"Ah, Ah, Ah, Ah," came the laughter once more and Grinold tried vainly to locate within the darkness of the limbs a figure to go with the laugh.

"I implore you for help!" shouted Grinold once again and louder than before. "I find myself trapped in a crude pit created for some animal. As befitting any soul in peril, I would expect succor from a passing traveler. Drop me a rope and rescue me from this dark hole."

"The Outworlder needs my help?" came a sarcastic voice from the darkness of the tree. "This is unusual indeed that a hunter like yourself should require the aid of a lowly creature such as I."

Again Grinold's eyes searched for the source of the voice above him, and still no shape appeared from the darkness.

"I am a visitor to these woods!" he shouted. "I mean no harm to anyone or anything. I saw a movement and entered the woods thinking that someone might need help that I could render."

"Outworlders are full of lies. I saw you yesterday looking into the forest. It is a mission upon which you have come. Even the most experienced woodsman will fall prey to the Dark Wood, a fact to which you can attest. I care not for your lies nor do I have a great desire to help those who torment me and treat me as the basest of creatures. What do you have of value that might buy your way to safety?"

The bitterness in the voice of the creature in the tree above him gave Grinold pause, and he determined it would be best to be patient and win the trust of his would-be rescuer before making any other supplications in regard to his release.

The Meeting

"I have two gold dragons and a knife that once belonged to a great warrior chieftain. I won it in a game of chance, and it is purported to be made of the hardest metal ever forged. Encrusted into its hilt are rare jewels that could be sold which would make the bearer rich."

"If that is true," replied the disembodied voice above Grinold, "I might just wait and take the gold and the knife from your rotting body once the worms have done their work."

"Come forth into view so that I may see, however dimly, the heartless being who would fail to help a hapless traveler in distress. You speak of mistreatment and persecution by others, yet you have judged me in much the same way. You know me not, and still you have deemed me an outsider and unworthy. Am I not being accorded the same treatment that you purport to have received? Such hypocrisy, yes, I have seen in my own people. Perhaps you are more like them than you will admit. Regardless of the cause you champion, the gods will indeed punish you for the inhospitality you have rendered me."

"Your gods mean nothing to me. I worship my own way and to my own gods. I have found only one of your kind worthy of my trust. He, too, cares little for your world, preferring the company of my people to that of his own."

"Then someone does live in these woods. I knew such a thing must be true when I smelled the smoke. If you will not help me, at least go to him and he will deliver me from this dank and dark prison."

Another movement occurred above him, and Grinold was looking at a dark face which suddenly appeared over the hole. The head of the being upon which he gazed seemed much too large for the body, which appeared short and squat from his vantage point. A large nose was the most prominent feature on the face and even in the dim light around them, Grinold could distinguish the numerous warts that covered most prominently the dwarf's forehead and chin.

"Give me the gold and the knife," wheedled Bartold, "and I will go for help to pull you from the hole."

"Nay, I trust you not in this matter. You will take the gold and knife, and I will remain here until I die of starvation. Bring me help and I promise the gold and knife are yours. I give you my word that I can be trusted."

"Bah, your word means nothing. When rescue is brought, you will flog me for not bringing help more quickly. I know the ways of the Outworlders, for I have spent much time among them."

"Not all Outworlders are alike just as all dwarfs are not alike. I sense that you are not without compassion. Could I look into your eyes, I would see there a kindness that you would hide from me. But I know it is there. It is my nature to understand the workings of the mortals that I encounter, whether they be what you call Outworlders, or dwarfs, or the proudest and most reknown of kings. I know you will not leave me here to die."

"Perhaps Bartold will leave you here. Bartold can sense things also. You are not here because you are lost. There was a purpose for your travels to my forest, and I feel it is not for good. What benefit would it serve me or the inhabitants of the Dark Wood if your release were granted? We might be served better with your death and not know how your survival could cause us later grief."

"I mean the inhabitants of this wood no harm. Nay, even the Outworlder that you take for a friend need fear anything from me. Bring him to me and I will make this vow that you shall never rue your generosity."

Grinold did not know if his last words were heard, for the dwarf had disappeared. As he sank down against the earthen

The Meeting

wall, he was not sure what effect his words had wrought upon the conscience of the dwarf, but at present his only hope hinged upon what compassion he had sensed in the creature to whom he had spoken. He had no other choice than to wait. The silence in the forest deepened as the sun began to set, and Grinold reluctantly steeled himself for a sleepless night.

The fire over which Cyrean stirred the stew that was to be his supper had slackened in heat, and he cast two large chunks of wood into the coals. The stew had simmered for most of the afternoon, and the aroma it gave forth made Cyrean realize how long it had been since he had eaten. Wolfen approached the fire and gazed longingly at the pot, hoping that his master would not forget that he, too, had not eaten for some time. The events of the previous day had quelled Cyrean's appetite up to this point, but he had made the decision to take the crystal to the king, and he knew he would need his strength for such a trip. He had just ladled a large portion of the pot's contents into a wooden bowl when he heard a thud on the roof of his hut.

Cyrean paused in his ladling and he and Wolfen moved as one toward the door.

"Thud," came another sound from the roof.

"Thud, thud, thud," came the sounds repeatedly.

By this time Cyrean had reached the door and opened it, carefully peering out into the gathering darkness.

"Who's there?" asked Cyrean, peering into the night.

"It is I, Bartold, the Brave. Only I dare travel the Dark Wood at night. The great Cyrean dares not venture into my realm when the sun has vanished from the sky. He sits and cowers by the fire with his beast. Truly am I Lord of the Realm."

"Truly is Bartold like the large monkeys that live in the innermost parts of the forest. He jabbers, but few understand him. What do you want? Is once not enough in one day for me to have to endure your mindless banter? Now you torment me at night also. Go away and throw your rocks at the moor hogs that root the ground and litter the forest with their droppings. It is there that you may be Lord of the Realm indeed."

"Bartold will go away. The Outworlder can die, but it will not be Bartold's fault."

Cyrean had turned back into the house when the dwarf's final words registered in his mind.

"Stay!" yelled Cyrean at Bartold who was not retreating into a large tree. "What did you say about an Outworlder?"

"Is Bartold's presence now required?" smirked the dwarf, climbing down the tree and returning to face Cyrean. "Did you not say that one like I should be jabbering to the forest monkeys? Since I have nothing of importance to say to the great Cyrean, I will return to those who wish to hear about my great adventure."

"Perhaps I was too harsh in my judgment of you," said Cyrean, hoping to placate the angry dwarf long enough to gather the information concerning what must be an intruder into the Dark Wood.

"Yes, when Bartold can be useful, then he is welcome around Cyrean and the Outworlders. Once I am not needed, I am cast aside again."

Irritated by the delay as the dwarf voiced his displeasure at the unfortunate lot he must bear in an uncaring world, Cyrean reached out and grabbed Barto and lifted him off the ground.

"This is no time to whine about how you are mistreated, you irritating bundle of dragon dung! Where is the Outworlder? If someone has entered the forest, it is because he was sent here on a mission. The forest is a shelter to us only as long as the outside world fears it. We must make sure that others are kept out. If someone is in the forest, he must be

The Meeting

sent back immediately. Now where is he?"

As he spoke, Cyrean shook Bartold until he had difficulty catching his breath to speak. When Cyrean finally released him, he sat on the forest floor and began to cry.

"It is always thus that I am abused and mistreated. I meant merely to bring news that an Outworlder has fallen into a pit in the forest, and this is how I am treated for my compassion."

"A pit in the forest? He is lucky that he did not venture into the sand bogs. Show me where he is, Bartold. If you are telling me the truth, I will share with you some of the warthog stew that is over the fireplace."

"My reward will be much greater than that if the Outworlder speaks true," replied the dwarf.

"Save your riddles for another time, Bartold. Wolfen, you must stay here. We will have to go by the trees at night to avoid the hazards of the woods. We must move quickly. If someone is in the pit, there are beings in the forest who would prey on such a hapless victim. Lead me to him. If you are lying, I will cast you into the pit and leave you there for the bogbears."

The dwarf ignored the threat and got to his feet. Moving quickly, he ascended into the trees. Cyrean nimbly fell in behind him and they made their way through the limbs toward the pit where Grinold lay, glumly pondering his misfortune.

As Grinold looked about him, he began to wonder what his chances of survival would be if the dwarf did not return with help. He had been in more dangerous situations than this, and his wits had always extricated him when the situation seemed bleakest. He did not know what dangers other than the sand bogs and pits lay beyond the confines of this hole in which he found himself, but to simply make no effort to help himself was not in Grinold's nature.

He felt along the sides of the hole for jutting rocks, clefts, or any indentations into which he could get a hold. When nothing presented itself, he took his knife from the sheath and began to dig into the dirt wall. After a few minutes, he had managed to cut a hole in the side of the pit sufficient to place a hand or foot. He continued in this manner with five more holes until he had reached as far as he could above his head. Above the mark of the last hole still remained at least five feet that he would have to climb to be able to grasp the lip of the pit. He felt around in the pit and in the debris that had tumbled into the hole with him was a large limb. The diameter of the pit was too large for him to be able to brace against the opposite wall as he placed a foot or hand into the holes he had dug. He cut the limb to the length that he would need to reach the other wall and placed the knife in his jerkin where it could be easily reached. Moving carefully, he eased up the wall as far as he could until he attained the last hole. Placing the limb against the opposite wall, he leaned back against the blunt end until he was braced sufficiently to release his hands for digging. In the creation of any hole, the walls slope out with the bottom of the hole being narrower than at the top. This allowed Grinold to slant forward just enough to maintain a sufficient hold on the wall as he dug the next hole for his ascent. For what seemed like hours to his aching hands and feet, he inched his way up the wall. As he worked, he reassured himself that if he could not make the entire climb, he would have at least completed enough steps in the wall that he could make it out after he had rested the following morning.

    He was only two feet from the top of the hole when his knife broke. In an attempt to pry a rock from the hole he was digging, the blade snapped. In the darkness no one could have seen the ironic smile that came briefly to Grinold's face as he remembered the lie that he had told the dwarf about the strength of the metal in the knife. He had no such weapon, and the inferior blade that he did possess now had let him

The Meeting

down when he needed it most. It did not matter that the knife was not a fine weapon nor was it important that his pockets did not hold two gold dragons. The dwarf would not return. He wondered if Tobias would search for him when he did not return. The likelihood of his absence being important enough to warrant the concern of Tobias was not comforting. Letting the limb fall back into the pit, he released his hold on the wall and dropped to the ground. Leaning back against the wall, he resigned himself to wait until morning when he would be better able to assess his situation. He had just settled in when he heard voices in the trees above him.

"The hole is over here, Master Cyrean. Now you will see that Bartold does not lie. Bartold will be the richest of dwarfs with two gold dragons and a weapon that will make him feared wherever he goes."

Grinold stood up and listened. The voices had stopped. He could not see in the darkness around him, but his hunter's senses told him he had been joined by at least two figures. The dwarf's voice he had recognized. He knew the dark eyes of the other person standing at the top of the hole could see him even in the blackness of the pit. He could only hope the darkness of those eyes did not mirror a dark soul also. Grinold was suddenly shocked back into awareness when he realized the two figures had left the pit and he was again alone.

Chapter Seven
Revelations

A small bit of light had just begun to filter into the darkness of the forest when again Grinold heard voices approaching. He stood and shook the stiffness out of his body and cupped his ear to be sure that it had not been his imagination. He listened carefully and the voices became more distinct. He recognized them as the same ones that had spoken to him before. It had been an hour since they had left the pit. During that time Grinold pondered his fate and wondered if he would ever be rescued from the hole that seemed even deeper now that the partial light which filtered through the dense trees allowed him to see his prison more clearly. He shouted but no voice replied. He yelled again and this time a large vine was tossed over the rim and down into the hole beside him.

"Grab onto the vine and pull yourself up," commanded a voice from above him. "Be aware, trespasser, that we are armed, and any aggression on your part will be met with stiff retribution."

Grinold grasped the vine and began a slow ascension to the top of the hole. His muscles ached from the exertion of trying to dig himself out hours earlier, and twice he had to let go of the rough vine as his sore hands prevented him from getting a grip sufficient to hold his weight. A third time he began the ascent, and this effort brought him to the edge of the hole where he felt strong arms grasp his upper body and lift him from the pit and lay him, exhausted from his efforts, on firm ground.

Grinold looked at his rescuers and recognized the dwarf he had spoken to hours earlier. The other figure he could see clearly since enough light now shone into the forest to make shapes easily distinguishable. The man standing before him was dressed in rough leather clothing and carried a knife, which he brandished in his hand, and a bow and sheath of arrows on his back. He was a tall man with dark eyes and a tan face which told Grinold he did not spend all his time in the Dark Wood. His hair was long and fell onto his shoulders, and a dark beard obscured the other features of his face. Grinold could tell from his bearing that he was used to using caution in dealing with intruders, and he knew that the best thing would be to feel out the stranger before making any moves that might be interpreted as hostile. He sat up gingerly and rubbed the back of his head which he suddenly realized was aching and sending a dull pain into his eyeballs. He felt the back of his head and discovered a large bump which by now was encrusted with dried blood.

"You have received many bruises from your tumble into the pit," said Cyrean. "Why come you into these woods when stories of the dangers here are known to all but the most distant traveler to these parts? Only the most foolhardy would venture into this forest whether the time be day or night. There are bogs and sand pits that will close quickly on travelers not familiar with this area. Bogbears, warthogs, and other meat eaters prowl the forest in search of food. You are lucky to be alive. Bartold and I will escort you past the dangers and back to safety beyond these woods."

"Nay, before I take you and your companion up on your generous offer, at least let me know to whom I owe gratitude. I have met the dwarf and I thank him for bringing you to rescue me, but I know you not and it would be ill-mannered of me indeed to accept your kindness without knowing to whom I should be grateful."

"You owe me more than gratitude," said Bartold before Cyrean could reply to Grinold's request. "You promised me gold and your knife if I would bring help to you. I have done my part. Now you must give me the treasure you promised."

"I am sorry, my small friend, to have deceived you. I do not possess the items I have promised to you. The knife I described does not exist and its poor companion lies in the pit broken into two pieces. If I had two gold dragons, I would gladly give them to you, for even my poor existence has at least that value. But, alas, I am but a poor wayfarer with little except what you see upon my back."

"Oh, most deceitful of wretches. Base liar and false-hearted villain. Vile and dishonorable Outworlder. Like your brothers, you have used Bartold for your purposes and then cast him aside. I will run my knife through your heart and extract my payment in blood."

"Hold thy tongue, Bartold. It is most likely that this hole was dug by you and your clan for just this purpose. I have told you not to set traps other than for food. You are getting no more than you deserve," Cyrean scolded.

"To answer your question, stranger, I am Cyrean, master of the Dark Wood, and I do not like trespassers into my forest. I have witnessed the abominations that you and others like you have inflicted upon each other. I and the other inhabitants of this forest want nothing to do with your conflicts. So whatever mission has brought you here, know that it will remain undone, for I will escort you to the forest boundaries. Should you enter again, I will not be responsible for the horrible fate that will surely befall you."

"Let me lead him out, Master Cyrean," pleaded Bartold. "I know where lurk the bogbears, and they would welcome the taste of an Outworlder. Truly would he then know not to deceive Bartold."

"Away, impish dwarf, before I tie you to a tree and let the foul swampsweepers eat upon your live carcass. These monsters crawl through the swamps searching for easy prey.

Revelations

With their long snouts and powerful jaws, they would make short work of you. Even now I can hear their hiss as they slide through the water looking for food."

The dwarf looked quickly around and then turned and bounded into the nearest tree.

"I am Bartold the Brave and fear no creature, whether it be swampsweeper or Outworlder. I will go and organize an army that will conquer all the Outworlders and then you will pay obeisance to King Bartold."

"Go and organize your army. The forest monkeys have need of your skills. Try your jabbering upon them and anon you will have a furry army that will rival that of the greatest generals."

"Cast derision upon Bartold if you wish but soon all the world will bow to Bartold when he finds the all-powerful Crystal of Light."

Grinold had been tenderly examining the back of his head and trying to adjust to the situation in which he found himself while his two companions had been bantering back and forth. When Bartold mentioned the crystal, his senses became acutely alert and he looked to see what reaction the mention of the crystal had upon Cyrean.

Cyrean too had been taken aback at the mention of the crystal. Did the dwarf somehow know that he had the object? Bartold and other members of his clan were aware of all that went on in the forest. If he had been seen carrying the crystal, it was necessary that he find a good hiding place until that time when he could journey to see the king. He was aware of Grinold's eyes upon him, and he willed himself to show no surprise at Bartold's threat.

"The crystal is just a myth," Cyrean said. "It is just a superstition that old men like to talk about in stories around the fires to frighten children. Search for the crystal if it will get you from my sight. I last heard that it was in Alcinor, two weeks' ride to the north. If you leave tonight, you could be there and back in a month. Perhaps many of your clan would like to go also. I am sure you will need their help on your mission."

"Again you taunt Bartold, but you will see. Yes, you will see and when that day comes, then Cyrean will be a slave to me, begging for scraps from my table."

With these last words of warning, Bartold took to the trees and, moving quickly from limb to limb, soon was out of sight.

"A strange creature," mused Grinold. "Are there others like him in the Dark Wood? He would be a worthy opponent if his skill were a match for his boasts."

"There is a small clan perhaps three hundred in number in the forest," answered Cyrean. "They stay to themselves and only Bartold and a few others ever dare to venture into the villages. They are often persecuted by the villagers who treat them as less than human and abuse them at any opportunity. It is sad that life here in the Dark Wood is more preferable to them than living where the sun shines and there are bright meadows and flowers and fresh streams where fish may be caught."

"But you share their fate," observed Grinold. "Do you not long for those things also? The abuse and persecutions of which you speak would not be your lot. In the outside world, you would be no different than any other man that one might meet on the highway or at some tavern in the village."

"True, I look like you and the others that Bartold hates. But I feel much as he does in the dislike of those that live beyond the boundaries of the forest. In my encounters with those outside my world, I have seen very little that would lure me from these woods. The wars that are fought are never for noble causes. Misuse of power and moral corruption abound

Revelations

at all levels of society. Can you not see why I prefer my existence to the one you propose?"

"I, too, have seen these things," answered Grinold. "But I have also seen the good that man is capable of achieving. I was taken in when I was an infant into a peasant family who cared for me as if I were their own child. They were honest and hardworking, wishing only to live their lives in peace and helping those who sought the same for themselves. There is good in the world, for without the power of good we would not recognize the face of evil and know how to combat its forces."

Cyrean looked at Grinold and thought about his words. Here was a man who spoke openly and honestly. Such a man might be worth knowing at another time. For now, he needed to get him out of the woods and return to his hut to check on the crystal. The mention of the crystal by Bartold had caused a feeling of dread in the heart of Cyrean, and he must make sure of its whereabouts.

"Stranger," said Cyrean, "you have asked my name, and I freely revealed it to you. What should I call you if we ever meet again outside the confines of these woods?"

"I am Grinold, tracker and hunter. I was simply hunting for meat when I wandered into the forest," he lied, thinking it best not to reveal too much about himself and his mission until he knew more about the man before him.

"In this forest you would be the hunted rather than the hunter," warned Cyrean. "It is best if I return you safely to the fields and let you continue your hunt there."

During all the conversation that had taken place since his rescue, Grinold had remained sitting on the ground. His head still buzzed and he was hesitant to stand. At Cyrean's words, he slowly arose and instantly his legs began to wobble and he fell to the ground.

"It seems that my head has not recovered from the knock it received," he said. "I must remain here for a while until I can walk steadily once more. I will be fine now that I am out of the pit."

"It is not safe here alone," said Cyrean. "I will have to take you to my hut until you can move again on your own."

Before Grinold could voice a protest, Cyrean took his arm and moved slowly in the direction of his hut. He knew the risk of letting an Outworlder see where he lived was great, but he could not leave Grinold there in the forest. If he were a great tracker such as he professed to be, he would no doubt find the hut anyway if he chose to do so.

An hour later the two men came into sight of the hut. Cyrean had taken great care in bringing Grinold to his home. If he had been alone, the return to the hut would have taken a quarter of the time, for he would have used the trees to avoid the dangers of the forest floor. Having to pick their way through those dangers at night added to the time required to make the journey.

As they approached the house, Wolfen crossed the clearing from the house to the woods where they had now emerged. A low growl issued from his throat as he smelled the odor of a stranger.

"Quiet, Wolfen," commanded Cyrean. "We have a visitor tonight. The warthog stew will have to be warmed, for he has not eaten for a while."

At the command of his master, Wolfen sniffed at the stranger and then turned and moved back to the house, assured that Cyrean had command of the situation, and his help would not be needed.

Cyrean entered the hut with Grinold still holding gamely to his arm, and he laid him on the rough cot in the corner near the fire. He went to the fireplace and rebuilt the fire which was now just glowing embers. When the fire was sufficiently hot, he placed the pot of stew on the hanger above the blaze to warm. Fatigue had finally taken the last reserves from Grinold's will, and he had fallen asleep instantly. Cyrean knew it would be hours before he would awake, and the stew would be welcome at that time. He pulled a chair closer to the fire and sat for a moment looking at the sleeping Grinold and wondered what his purpose was here in the Dark Wood. He instinctively knew that somehow it had something to do with the orb. He knew the voice to be that of the man who had been leading the party the night that the servant had died in the bog. He was sure this was the man now because he had seen the instant recognition in his eyes when Bartold had mentioned the crystal. If that is what he was searching for in the forest, then he was doing so at the command of someone more powerful, probably the leader who had ordered the death of the servant. He had heard of the ruthless barbarian Tobias. He was sure this was the man Grinold served. Yet what would one like Grinold have to gain in the servitude of a murdering tyrant like Tobias? There were questions here that would have to be answered before Grinold could be trusted.

The thought of Tobias had made Cyrean aware that he needed to check on the safety of the crystal, and he moved quietly to the small cupboard on the wall next to the chimney and took a large pot from the hook hanging there. He placed his hand into the pot and felt the leather bag with his fingers. He extracted the bag and felt the roundness of the object contained therein. Comforted in the knowledge that the crystal was secure, he placed the bag back into the pot and again hung it in its customary place on the hook. Returning to the fire, he sat and made himself comfortable. He would be watchful this night and, as if knowing this night was unusual, Wolfen raised his head alertly at Cyrean's movements to let him know that he was vigilant in his duties as guardian of the house.

Cyrean awoke just as the first rays of light entered the hut. He stood and stretched his large frame, trying to get his body, cramped from a poor night's sleep in the chair, to respond more quickly. He stirred the fire until the live coals beneath the ash were uncovered, and then he threw more wood upon the fire. The stew began to reheat, and he went outside to relieve the full bladder that had finally fully awakened him.

The morning was crisp and the sun made its way into the clearing around the hut, warming a myriad of plants that had once bloomed in the fields outside the Dark Wood. On numerous occasions, Cyrean had taken bright plants from the meadows and moved them here to his hut. This small area was the only bright spot in the forest. Here, the trees had been cut for wood to build the hut and for fire, and the sun could make an entrance to feed the plants and grass that grew under Cyrean's nurturing hands. Interwoven amidst the flowers grew many medicinal plants, and Cyrean looked among them and, finding the specific one he desired, he pulled it up by the roots and took it back into the hut.

Removing the stew from the fire, Cyrean took a small pot from the hooks on the wall and placed the plant into its cavity. He poured some water from a basin into the pot and put it where the stew had been. Within minutes, steam was coming from the pot, and Cyrean moved it to a spot over the fire where it could simmer for a few minutes. When he was satisfied that the potion was ready, he poured the mixture onto a cloth and approached the sleeping Grinold. Shaking him gently but firmly by the arm, he aroused Grinold sufficiently to place the cloth beneath his head over the bruise that seemed to have enlarged overnight.

He let the cloth remain on the wound for a while and then, concerned that too much sleep might not be good when such a blow had been to the head, he again shook Grinold and brought him to full consciousness.

Grinold gradually became aware of his surroundings and sat slowly up on the bed, leaning his body against the wall. The pain in his head had lessened somewhat, but he still could not make any quick movements, for the pain from such a movement made him instantly aware of the fragile nature of his injury.

He looked about the hut and saw Cyrean standing and staring intently at him as he made a feeble attempt to put his feet onto the floor. He put his hand to the back of his head and realized that a cloth had been placed over the injury. He carefully removed the bandage and felt the knot which protruded through the thick hair on the back of his head.

"I would not attempt to rise yet," cautioned Cyrean. "You are still weak. Until you have eaten, it would be advisable to remain where you are. I have some warthog stew that should make your stomach aright very soon. I had begun to worry that the blow to your head had caused such injury that my potions could not cure. It is good to see you awake."

"I have suffered far more grievous injury. It is the nature of my business that I should suffer many wounds over a lifetime. A hunter will not always make the kill instantly and when he does not, a wounded animal is a dangerous quarry. I have many scars to show that an injured animal will fight to the last. Even more dangerous is the human animal. In games of chance, often a man will quarrel over a loss, and drink and a quick temper make for a poor combination. Many is the bottle that has been broken across my crown in such instances. Yet, I am here to bear witness that I am not so easily dispatched."

"Well, what wild animals and broken bottles have failed to do, my warthog stew may still accomplish," said Cyrean smiling as he handed Grinold the bowl he had just filled.

Grinold sniffed the stew and placed it on the cot beside him as he slowly brought a bit of the repast to his lips.

"You may be right, my friend, but for now the broth is welcome. I have not eaten for three days running. I could eat the warthog were he here."

Cyrean smiled again, encouraged by the good humor of his guest. Bringing the chair in which he had slept closer to the bed, he began to question Grinold.

"I know little of what is going on in the outside world. Perhaps you could answer some questions that I have about rumors that have come to me concerning the king. Is it true that the kingdom stands in peril of overthrow and that a traitor named Tobias leads the faction against the king?"

"That is true, and as it stands the king is in ill health and poorly equipped for such a conflict."

"What of the king's generals? Can they not defend the realm in such dire circumstances?"

"These are trying times," answered Grinold. "Tobias draws many soldiers to him and is more powerful than any force heretofore brought against the king. It does, to all accounts, look as if the king will lose the battle."

"What would the king have to do to turn the tide of battle his way?" asked Cyrean, looking intently at Grinold.

"Nothing save a mighty force could assure a victory now," answered Grinold. "Nothing short of the Crystal of Light could help the king."

"Then such a thing exists? I had thought it was just more babbling from Bartold. Have you seen the crystal?"

"Nay, I have not seen such an object, but I know it exists."

"If a person had knowledge of its location, it should be taken to the king, would you not agree?" questioned Cyrean again looking closely to observe Grinold's reaction.

"That is true if the finder is loyal to the king."

"And would it not be true that to fail to take the crystal to the king would be a traitorous act?"

"True also if the king has been a just and righteous king," answered Grinold.

"I have heard none say to the contrary, but then my life is secluded and no news reaches me here. Yet I know the king loves his people, and I would defy any man to say otherwise."

Again Cyrean looked at the face of his visitor for any sign that would suggest his disloyalty to the king, but Grinold's impassive countenance gave not a hint that he held ill will toward King Malvore.

As Grinold received each question, he knew their purpose and nothing that he said was untrue. He had not been disloyal to the king up to the present moment. Yes, he had done jobs for Tobias but nothing that could have been interpreted as a traitorous act. If he found the crystal and took it to Tobias, that would be treason, but he had not fully decided what to do with the object. He felt that to return it to Tobias would be wrong on many counts, and he had resolved within himself to see that such a thing did not happen. He had to make Tobias think that he was searching for the crystal, but he did not have to tell him that it had been found if he should be successful. As Cyrean continued to probe into Grinold's motives, Grinold began to formulate a plan of his own.

"As my rescuer and my host," began Grinold, "you are entitled to ask anything of me that you deem important. I know not the purpose of my inquisition, but I will not balk in the answering of your questions. I ask only that I be allowed to inquire of some matters from you in return."

"Ask and I will answer if I can. Remember though that my world is a small one with the world at large undisclosed to me."

"I have but one question and, as you have already asked it

of me, I feel I should have the right to ask it also."

The eager look that had come into Grinold's eyes as he spoke gave Cyrean the uneasy feeling that he had granted overmuch too soon to his visitor, but he had given his word and he would keep it.

"Ask your question but know that I have limited knowledge on most matters," cautioned Cyrean.

"Give me your hand," said Grinold. "The truth is an energy unto itself that can permeate the very being of he who is speaking. Your hand, friend, and then I will ask my question."

Reluctantly, Cyrean proffered his hand and Grinold took it into his own. Looking intently into the dark eyes of Cyrean, he spoke.

"Do you know the location of the Crystal of Light?"

"Yes," answered Cyrean truthfully, realizing he had foolishly played into Grinold's hands.

"Where is the location?" asked Grinold, suddenly impatient to get the news he so badly desired.

"You asked me to answer one question only," replied Cyrean craftily. "I granted your request and I will answer no others."

Grinold released Cyrean's hand. The questions did not matter now. He knew who had the crystal. He could sense it as soon as he looked into the eyes of Cyrean and touched his hand. He was close to the crystal. He could sense it and before he took his leave of Cyrean, he would know its exact location.

Chapter Eight
With an Iron Hand

Often the most important characteristic of a good leader is his ability to outwait his enemy. Patience is not a trait common to a lot of men, but Tobias was the exception. He had planned and waited for twenty years for this opportunity, and, to him, a few more days was of no significance if it meant he would strengthen his advantage. In less than two weeks, he would be battling for King Malvore's kingdom and with the army now at his disposal, victory was assured. He sat in his tent and studied the maps his spies had brought him. As he looked at the fortifications of king Malvore's castle, he knew now where the vulnerable spots were and, by exploiting those weaknesses, soon the castle and the province of Eustan would be his. Spies were reporting to him daily, and with each new missive he grew more confident that soon the crown would have a new wearer.

Tobias had just rolled the maps and cleared the planning table when a rider came swiftly to a stop in front of his tent. Immediately, a guard stepped into the tent with news that a courier had come with good tidings. Tobias sent for the rider and within minutes he was standing before Tobias and reporting his message.

"My lord, I bring you great news from the castle of King Malvore," said the messenger.

"Then speak, man, and if it be good news, five gold dragons will be your reward."

"Spies recently arrived from Eustan have made it known to our generals that a caravan containing the queen and Lord Hadreon's daughter will be leaving the castle tomorrow at noon to go to a distant province, thereby hoping to find safety in hiding. The caravan will be under heavy guard with over fifty soldiers as escort."

"Excellent! This is the best of news. If the king has seen fit to seek safety for the queen outside the castle, then he fears that it is not fortified well enough to withstand our assault. The reports that we have been receiving must be accurate. The castle now is at its weakest and open to attack. The time I have planned for so long is here, and fortune will smile on he who strikes when it is most opportune. Here, messenger, are the five gold dragons I promised. Carouse and spend them foolishly because this is a time for celebration. Soon the riches of Eustan will be mine. Then will all the provinces hail me as the new king."

The messenger exited the tent, and Tobias excitedly reopened the maps he had been folding. Looking over the roads that led from the castle, he was certain he knew the route over which the caravan would travel. With the queen for ransom, the battle would be brief. Fifty soldiers would be a force with which to contend, but with the element of surprise on their side and scores of soldiers eager for battle after having been inactive so long, the capture of the queen was a certainty.

Tobias finished perusing the maps and folded them. He had just settled into a comfortable chair to enjoy the news he had received when a guard entered the tent and announced that General Aberon requested an audience with him. General Aberon was commander of the legion that would be primarily responsible for the storming of the gates of the castle. The soldiers had spent the last few weeks preparing catapults and battering rams for use against the wall's huge doors. Weeks of nonstop training had taken their toll on the soldiers who were ready for the battle to begin.

"Lord Tobias, I greet you at the beginning of what will be a great victory for our army. The men are ready. When will we be ready to move against the king and his soldiers?"

"Patience, General Aberon. The time is near. Leaders such as we must be a settling influence on our men. They must see that only the foolhardy strike too early and give the advantage to the enemy."

"I fear they do not see the advantage of waiting any longer, My lord. There have been many outbreaks among the soldiers. Two have been killed and a score have been wounded in skirmishes among themselves. Their tempers are short and as of yet there is not a common cause to bring together so many different groups into one unit. Some soldiers have deserted our ranks under the cloak of night and gone back to their homes. I fear that if we wait much longer, more will follow their lead. Many of the soldiers who comprise our forces are mercenaries. If they see no reward soon, many will leave for more lucrative positions elsewhere."

"The time is soon, General. Tell the men that we will wait four more days. If Grinold has not returned at that time with the crystal, we will start our advance without him or the crystal. Has any news of his whereabouts been forthcoming from any of our numerous spies who frequent the provinces and outlying areas?"

"No, my lord. He was last seen three days ago entering the Dark Wood. The two men who witnessed his entrance say that he has not come back out. They fear he is dead and neither wish to enter the forest to confirm their suspicions. They have been advised to return to camp."

"Perhaps he is dead," replied Tobias. "But I will not give up this soon on my tracker. He has been in many dire situations before and always managed to escape unscathed. We will start without him, but I would not be surprised to see him when the battle begins."

"You have more faith in him than I do, my lord. I trust him not. He has a conscience that often betrays him when a cold, calculating demeanor is needed. I have witnessed his compassion for the weak and servile. Such a man does not make a good soldier and may betray our cause when we seem most assured of victory."

"Perhaps you are right, General Aberon. He has served me well for the last few years, but his talents will no longer be needed after I have defeated King Malvore. He may still bring me the crystal. The very quality that you find as a fault in him will compel him to bring me the weapon I need. It is called loyalty, General. A rare trait indeed and not often to be found in the motley soldiers now under my command. It will be with a great deal of sadness when I order his execution. Though he is loyal, I have often seen the disfavor with which he looks at me. He would not condone the ways that men like us use to maintain our power once it is in our grasp. If the Dark Wood has not claimed him as victim, he may return with the treasure I most desire. Whether he succeed or fail, death will be his reward."

General Aberon bowed and left the tent. Tobias turned back to his maps, and after a time he opened the flap of the tent and ordered one of the sentries to bring him the captain of his elite guard. Within minutes Captain Malaban stood before Tobias awaiting orders.

"Captain, a caravan will be leaving the castle of Eustan tomorrow noon. Before that time I want to know its destination and the route it will follow to get there. Send as many spies as necessary to gather the information I seek. Failure is not an option. Succeed and you will stand with me when victory is ours."

"Yes, my lord. I will see to it personally. You will have news before the morning."

Captain Malaban left the tent and mounted his horse. Taking a dozen hand picked soldiers with him, he started swiftly toward Eustan. In the company were Malaban's top two spies. Both men were masters of disguise and had been in and out of Eustan undetected on numerous occasions. Any news about the caravan carrying the queen and Aurienna they would ferret out if it could be done.

Assured that Captain Malaban would complete his mission, Tobias turned to other matters that required his immediate attention. All the news coming from his spies seemed to indicate that Eustan was ripe for the taking, but Tobias had his own source and a meeting had been arranged for that night to meet and talk with his informant. If he received good news from this source, he would start moving his army immediately. Within the four days he had planned, he could be outside the walls of the castle.

Tobias took four of his most trusted soldiers and left camp that night and pointed his horse's head toward Eustan. Traveling slowly and carefully to avoid any renegade highwaymen that might be in the area, Tobias rode into the hills that would eventually bring him within the borders of Eustan. Darkness found him at his destination, and he dismounted, leaving his men to stand guard as he quickly ascended a small rock outcropping toward a level area several hundred feet from where he had left the men and horses. A full moon gave him the light he needed to navigate the rocks safely until he finally reached his destination. He stopped and looked around. Seeing nothing out of the ordinary, he made three short whistles and waited. Within minutes a tall figure emerged from the trees and stood waiting as Tobias approached.

"You are early, Tobias. You crave good news from Eustan I would judge from your eagerness."

"I am content to wait as long as is necessary," replied Tobias to the voice from the dark. "The spider who is patient feeds often and well. If your news be of like nature to the other reports I have received today, then my patience will be justly rewarded."

"The time is near to do that which we have long planned, Tobias. The king is growing weaker in health and his forces are outnumbered by your army. The castle's fortifications will be the key to our success. The walls and gate are firm and heavily manned. The wings of the walls are the least fortified, but there are no ladders long enough to gain entrance at those points. Archers are stationed there and large boulders and hot oil are positioned to rain upon those who attempt access to the castle at those points. Entrance must be at the gate, and to achieve success there, you must have someone ready to man the pulleys which operate the large wooden bars that lock the gates. If during the heat of the battle I can get men stationed at those points, they can open the gates from inside."

"See that it is done," said Tobias. "I will rely upon your assistance in this matter. My superior numbers afford me little advantage unless I can get inside the walls."

"I must go," said the voice. "I will be missed if I am away for too long."

"What of the caravan that is leaving the palace at noon tomorrow? Do you know its destination?"

"No, I am not privy to that information. The king has not trusted me to know the details of this mission. Only his closest advisors know where the caravan is going. A select group of soldiers will escort the wagons. It will not be an easy matter taking the women from such a heavily armed guard."

"That will be my concern," replied Tobias. "Attend to those things we have discussed on the day of battle, and I will take care of the rest. Until then, have your spies keep me informed about any changes that might affect the outcome of the conflict."

With an Iron Hand

"It will be done."

The speaker faded into the darkness of the woods, and Tobias carefully made his way back to where his soldiers waited impatiently to return to camp and a hot meal.

As Tobias began his return to camp, he could not know that the plans he wanted so desperately would be carefully formulated that night within the planning room of the castle. King Malvore had spent the day in bed conserving his strength for the events that would happen in the next few days.

"Be of good cheer, my lord," said the queen, as she entered the room and placed a cool hand on his brow. "All is proceeding as planned and soon neither Aurienna nor I will be a cause for worry, having been carried to a place where Tobias cannot reach us."

"That is what I hope for," replied the king. "Where is Lord Hadreon? He has not been to see me today. We needs must meet and finalize those plans we have begun. Send a guard to summon him."

"I am sure, my husband, that he has thought of nothing else and has been busily making arrangements for the morrow."

As if he had been conjured from the air at the mention of his name, Lord Hadreon appeared at the entrance to the king's chamber and came to his bedside.

"Let my absence not be a cause for undue worry, my liege. I have been busy with fortification of the city. Such business has taken me beyond the walls of Eustan temporarily, but now I am ready to finish that which has occupied our plans for what seems an eternity. Tomorrow, our minds will be at ease and we will be able to concentrate our efforts on the defense of the castle."

"Help me to the planning room, Lord Hadreon. I will lean on your strong right arm that has fought for the kingdom so many times in the past. Come, come. We must hurry, for the morning will come quickly and the caravan must be ready."

The two men left the room and Queen Ofra sat down in a small chair by the doorway. She, too, was impatient for the trip to begin. She knew that the king would worry until they were safe. Anything that would lift this burden from his frail body, she was willing to undertake. Aurienna's reluctance she would not be able to overcome, but she would see at some later time the wisdom in such a move.

Within minutes the two men were busily poring over maps spread across the table in the planning room.

"This seems to be the wisest plan, your highness," said Lord Hadreon, pointing at the small road that ran southward from the castle to Parvidian, the smallest of all the provinces in the king's realm at the southernmost point of the kingdom.

"But would the original plan to go north to one of the stronger provinces there not be the wiser course?" asked the king.

"Perhaps it would be the wisest in terms of military strength. But if Tobias should discover this plan, which he might well do since his spies are everywhere, he would not hesitate to attack the caravan with superior numbers and our cause would be lost. We must be like the fox and use our cunning to thwart Tobias. In sheer force and numbers, we are not a match, but what we lack in strength, we can make up in guile."

"In these times I must depend on you more than ever, Lord Hadreon. My trust in you has always been rewarded. I will not hesitate now to heed your advice when the lives of the ones we love are at stake. Show me again the plan you have devised."

"Tomorrow at noon," began Lord Hadreon, pointing at the map, "a force of soldiers fifty strong will escort a large caravan to the northern province of Alcinor. An escort this large will indicate to anyone watching that a valuable commodity is being transported. Those who have been spying within the castle will carry the news to Tobias. When that caravan is raided tomorrow evening, as I am sure it will be, soldiers dressed in women's clothing will greet the bandits of Tobias with hard steel. If the battle goes against them, they will return here to the castle and fortify our number. Meanwhile, a smaller caravan, unnoticed, will depart the castle one hour after the major caravan has turned north. This caravan will be composed of only the driver, a small armed escort, and the queen and Aurienna, dressed in simple garments. In this guise, it is unlikely that anyone would take the effort to stop them with little to be gained from such an unlikely troupe. The distance to Parvidian can be covered in a little over two days which is half the time it would take to get to Alcinor, and the roads will be much safer from highwaymen."

The king had listened carefully to Lord Hadreon's words and smiled. The plan was well thought out and would likely succeed because of its simplicity.

"As I have come to expect from you, Lord Hadreon, you have hit upon an excellent ruse. My heart is lighter already. When the battle comes, I will meet it with the knowledge that those I love are safe, and damned be Tobias if he and I should meet when the battle is at its height. Then he will discover what strength I still have in these old limbs."

"Your majesty, you and I are the only ones who know of the second caravan. I have not yet told my daughter or the queen. Talk to the queen tonight and I will do the same with my daughter. Under no circumstances is anyone to know of this plan other than the queen and Aurienna. We will hastily assemble three or four soldiers tomorrow to be the escort and quickly get them on their way."

"I will call the queen to my chambers tonight and say my goodbyes," answered King Malvore. "Neither you nor I will be able to see them off tomorrow. To do so might give away to prying eyes the value of that which is contained within the wagon. God grant us good fortune in our deception."

Later that night Lord Hadreon went to the chambers of his daughter. She was asleep and he gently pulled her hair away from her face and looked at her for what he knew could be the last time. Should he fall in battle, this would be the last opportunity he would have to speak to her and prepare her for the future. She stirred and her eyes opened. She smiled sleepily at her father and sat up and kissed him on the forehead.

"Father, why are you up so late? Plans have been made for our departure, and little else needs to be done before the caravan departs. Are you worried about my safety? There is little need of that. I will take care of the queen and myself if danger should befall us. Go back to your bed and sleep. Dream of the kingdom as it will be when Tobias is defeated."

"There is yet more to talk about, my child. The king and I this night have devised a plan which will assure you of safe passage to a place where Tobias cannot touch you or the queen."

"Then we are not going north as we had been told?"

"No, you will be taken to the south by a small escort outfitted to look as plain as any peasant band which would travel the road on an ordinary day. There will be no chance that anyone will know of this other than the king, the queen, and we two. I feel that this is the wisest course for us to follow."

"And I have always listened to your advice. Since my mother died, you have been both parent and friend to me. Your love for her you have redoubled in me since her death. I will be the soldier you would have had in a son. I will face the dangers that come and when the queen is hidden, I will return at the head of an army that will stand against Tobias, and we will win the day."

"I believe you will, Child, but until that time stay with the queen and keep her from harm. We will meet again when the battle is won. Tomorrow, one hour from the time of the departure of the first caravan, meet at the east wall. There the queen will be waiting and you will take a wagon to the south. Until that time prepare yourself for the journey."

Lord Hadreon left the room and slowly walked to his own chambers. He knew it would be a long night.

When dawn came, all was made ready for the large caravan that was to journey to the north. Little effort was made to disguise its purpose inside the walls. When noon came, two figures attired in royal dress were helped into the king's carriage, and the procession pulled out of the city gates and headed north flanked by the king's elite guard. The king and Lord Hadreon were in attendance at its departure and watched until it passed through the gate and then returned to their business of preparing for war.

One hour later a small, simple carriage pulled up to an isolated part of the castle and took on board two women dressed in simple peasant dress. Escorted by only three men, the wagon pulled out and drove through the gates and slowly headed to the south. Looking from an advantageous spot high within the castle, two old soldiers who had fought many battles without any outward sign of emotion watched the departure of the second wagon. No one was present to see the tears that fell unashamedly from their eyes.

Chapter Nine
The Alliance

Several times during the night Grinold awoke from the throbbing in his head. Sleep continued to elude him, and he adjusted the poultice that Cyrean had prepared for him before they went to bed. He sat up and looked about the darkened room, now lit only by the fire which had burned low and was in need of replenishing. The nights in the Dark Wood were always cold regardless of the time of year, and Cyrean kept a large quantity of wood stacked close by the fireplace. Grinold arose slowly and quietly so as not to wake Cyrean, but he was more conscious that any abrupt motion worsened the pain in his head. Wolfen, who always slept on a mat close to the fire, stirred as he sensed the movement of Grinold. Always alert, he raised his head and watched the activities of Grinold as he took wood and placed it over the coals. In the time that Grinold had been with them, Wolfen had taken a liking to the stranger. There was something in his demeanor that told Wolfen there was no danger from this man. Still, the dog watched warily as Grinold performed his duty as tender of the fire. Grinold sensed the dog watching him and wondered at the loyalty of the large animal to its master. Such devotion could be found only in an animal. Human nature could never generate such unbridled loyalty and love from one to another. Other than the parents who had reared him, Grinold had never felt that kind of love, and he silently admired the man who commanded such devotion from any living thing whether it be human or animal in form.

After the fire had been sufficiently fed to last the rest of the night, Grinold returned to his cot and sat staring at the flames. His conversation hours earlier had gotten him the information he desired. Cyrean had the crystal, but the knowledge and the acquisition of the crystal were not the same. Where would his host have hidden the object? To leave it in the hut would be simplistic and foolhardy. If it were hidden somewhere in the forest, it would take some time to discover its whereabouts with the dangers lurking there. Cyrean was no fool, and now that he had revealed to Grinold that the object was in his possession, he would be doubly on guard to protect its hiding place. If the object were in the hut, Wolfen would be alert to anyone prowling to discover its location. Somehow, he would have to gain Cyrean's confidence sufficiently before he plied him with any more questions. And if he did not find the crystal and Cyrean were to take it to the king, he had decided that would not be such a bad thing. The crystal could not be returned to Tobias. Of this Grinold felt sure. In the short space of time that he had known Cyrean, he had found himself admiring the qualities the older man possessed. He had an air of quiet humility which assured Grinold that he would never want the crystal for personal gain. Cyrean would take the crystal to the king and never expect anything in return. Grinold could sense the goodness of the man who had rescued him from the pit and wondered why men such as this could not be king. Men like Tobias cared only for themselves and the power the position of king would bring them. Was it the will of some capricious god that mankind always be governed by such men? The old king had served long and well. Still, the provinces had been plagued by Tobias who burned and pillaged at will because not enough men had the courage to oppose him. It would take a mighty effort now to defeat the superior forces that Tobias had amassed. Over the last year in service to the tyrant, Grinold had felt his revulsion toward the man grow stronger each day. Now was the time to break the bonds he had forged with Tobias if he were ever going to do so. As he pondered his future in the regime that seemed inevitable, he sensed eyes upon him.

Cyrean had lain awake since the time that Grinold had rekindled the fire. He had silently observed the stoic nature of Grinold as he had ruminated over his future. Not having the gift that Grinold possessed to determine a man's character quickly, he had watched the actions of his guest. He had listened to his words and looked into his face and had seen no darkness of character present in this man. If he worked for Tobias, it would have to be an uneasy alliance because this was not someone who would kill and destroy at a whim. The nature of Grinold's wound indicated to Cyrean that he would have to be tended for another three or four days before he could be trusted to travel on his own. During that time he would discover those things that would tell him whether the tracker could be trusted. If he had an ally who knew the outside world, as Grinold most certainly did, the crystal would have a better chance to be placed safely into the hands of the king.

"You seem to be feeling better today, my friend," said Cyrean as he threw back the bogbear skin that kept him warm even when the fire chanced to burn out at night.

"My head yet doth ache," replied Grinold. "But I now can stand and walk without the thousand buzzings that have plagued my senses these last two nights. It has made me feel womanish to have to be waited on like a newborn babe. It is good that I will be able to travel very soon and not be beholden to you for further care. It is difficult for one such as I to be in debt to anyone. Still, I know that without your help I would be as food for the worms. For your part in the saving of my life, I will always be grateful. And know that when that time comes when you will need assistance from me, I will repay in kind the hospitality you have shown."

"That time for departure has not come yet," answered Cyrean. "You will need to have all your strength when we take you out of the Dark Wood. Plan for two more days, and if the warthog stew has not dispatched you in the interim, then we can safely say you are strong enough to travel on your way."

"Then if I am to stay yet a while longer, there should be some chores that I can perform to help pay for my keep. I am not an idler though my professional skills as a gambler are often looked upon as unworthy. A man must always be responsible for himself and, though I have often taken advantage of others, it has been only because they have made it so easy to be duped. Mankind by nature is a willing victim. A man will lose all he has in a game of chance and yet come back the next day and gamble the clothes off his back, thinking he can recoup his losses. He does not learn from his failures, believing instead that opportunity awaits at every turn, and he must only be there to achieve greatness. He is never at fault when misfortune strikes; yet he feels any success he achieves is his due because of his cleverness. Perhaps I am only different from those of whom I speak in that I recognize my weaknesses and use them to my advantage."

"I have not seen that ill-natured quality in you," observed Cyrean. "Perhaps you look at your fellows with a jaded eye. I am sure that you have seen more of the fallibility of mankind due to the nature of your work, but is there not a nobility in man that perhaps you have also seen?"

"At times, perhaps. I lost my parents when I was very young. In me, they tried to instill the nobility of which you speak. Perchance had they lived, I would be a different man. But the evil of men such as those that destroyed my village and killed my family seem to be so much more prevalent than those who would do good in the world. In the past few years, I have been responsible for only myself and for my actions. Perhaps it is time for me to take a broader look at what higher purpose I could serve."

"An admirable ambition," remarked Cyrean. "Mayhap we will have a chance later to talk on how this sudden conversion can help those who are most in need of the skills you possess."

"We have spoken at length about me," said Grinold. "I now nothing about your history or your purpose in being here. How came you to this dark existence? Would it not be better living with those of similar natures than living here among the darkness of these woods and having only creatures of death as neighbors?"

"I have seen the evils of which you have spoken in the outside world," replied Cyrean. "Perhaps in my own way I am more skeptical of human nature than you, my friend. I have often longed to seek the brightness of the fields and forests outside these confines. I have lived here for as long as I have a memory of myself. My father built this hut, and he and my mother lived here until the beauty she longed for outside these woods she eventually found in death. With her passing, my father withdrew into himself and the darkness of this forest is a thousand times brighter than the sorrow that tortured his soul. He never told me how he came here, but he often spoke of the treachery of mankind and how our existence in the Dark Wood is many times more tolerable than life among the Outworlders."

"Your father must have had a good reason to withdraw from the life he knew outside these woods. What is your reason for staying here? Let those things that isolated your parents be part of their past, Cyrean, not part of your future. You do not belong here. It is evident in every part of your being that you are destined for greater things. Can you not feel your destiny pulling you? It awaits and whatever it may be, it would be better dying for something in which you believe than dying here for something you do not understand."

"This existence is not one I would have chosen for myself,"

The Alliance

replied Cyrean. "It was chosen for me, and I sense there was a purpose that has not been revealed . If fate has plans for me, I believe it will be unveiled when the time is right."

"Sometimes Destiny needs a push. Perhaps I am the instrument Destiny has chosen to get you from these woods. It may be that our fates are tied to each other. If that be the case, in the two days that I will remain here, I will need to know more about the crystal that you say you have in your possession."

"Ah, the crystal again. Grinold, you are my guest but that does not entitle you to know all that I know."

"But you said that you have the crystal in your possession. What harm could it do to let me see it? If our fates are indeed intertwined, would it not be good that I should know about the existence of such a force?"

"I did not say that I had the crystal in my possession. I said that I knew of its whereabouts. I could know where it is and not be able to possess it."

"You bandy words with me, but I know the crystal is close. I can sense it."

"Yes, I have come to realize even in a short time that you possess a talent that enables you to discern those things that would remain a mystery to other men. How did you come by such a gift?"

"I know not its origin," answered Grinold. "But the gift can also be a curse which isolates me from others. Its power opens my eyes to things that others cannot or will not see. I have been surprised that I still have its use. God gives such gifts to be used for the betterment of others, not for the bearer. All my life, I have only used the gift for my base desires."

"Then perhaps it is fate that has brought us together, and you are the means whereby I will deliver the crystal to the king. Now the talent you possess can be put to the use for which it was intended."

"Perhaps you are right," mused Grinold.

"Let us venture into the woods today, Grinold. There are many things I wish to show you. Should you ever have need for sanctuary once you leave here, you may need to return. If so, the secrets of these woods may save your life rather than take it."

The two men took their weapons from the pegs on the wall and walked outside into the sunlight which illuminated the area around the hut. For about four hours each day, the small cabin was bathed in light until the sun's movement took it behind the tall trees that surrounded the cleared area which had been settled so many years ago by Cyrean's father. With Wolfen in the lead, the two men walked into the forest and Cyrean began to point out the dangers as they walked.

"Always keep your eyes to the path in front of you," warned Cyrean. "The quicksand bogs are everywhere. They can be spotted quickly by someone like yourself and easily avoided, but be careful that in avoiding one trap you fall into another."

"The bump on my head will serve to remind me of that," said Grinold as he felt the still tender spot on the back of his head.

"Yes, the dwarf clan have built their own traps, and they are not all for the animals of the forest. The rope snares are easy to spot if you know what to look for. There will be raw meat within the coil of the rope to entice game such as warthog. The hole into which you fell was probably dug for bogbear since it was so deep. They are large, furry creatures with claws that can slash like knives. They have long snouts with jaws full of jagged teeth which can tear and rend a victim in minutes. The weakness they have is poor eyesight. Since they live in darkness so much, their eyes are small and useless for all

The Alliance

practical purposes. They rely mostly on sound and smell to detect their prey."

"Are the dwarfs dangerous? The one I met that led you to me did not seem uncivilized for all of his ravings. Is there anything to fear from them?"

"Bartold and all of the dwarf clan have come here over the last century. Their small stature and gross features have made them outcasts. They were servants, primarily, in years past or entertainers who juggled and did tricks to entertain kings or wealthy aristocrats. But they were always ridiculed and abused by those who felt superior because the dwarfs were small in stature and ugly in feature. No one looked into the hearts of the creatures they spurned. If they had, they would have seen no difference in the dwarf and themselves. Perhaps, this commonality was their fear. In my dealings with the dwarf clan, I have come to discover that all cannot be based on physical appearance. Bartold may be a braggart and a fool in certain matters, but he would come to aid me if I were in need. It may be a bond we have formed because of the need to survive in these woods, but I think it is more."

As Cyrean finished speaking, he took Grinold by the sleeve and stopped his forward progress.

Overhead, suddenly the woods had come alive. Dozens of screeching howlers were running back and forth through the trees above the two men throwing burrnuts at something below just out of their vision. Dozens of these missiles flew from their hands as they continued the bombardment for several minutes. Wolfen froze for a moment, for he had detected a scent of danger. Warily, for Cyrean knew of the many perils lurking in the forest, the two men and Wolfen approached the small clearing where the howlers now had abandoned the attack and fled back into the trees. There in front of them they saw the reason for the viciousness of the tree monkeys. One of the smaller and younger monkeys had made the mistake of leaving the sanctuary of the trees for a burrnut it had dropped. Unwittingly, it had fallen victim to a large swampsweeper that was just now engulfing the last remains of the unfortunate monkey into its monstrous jaws. Seeing larger game before him, the reptilian creature turned and emitted a hiss that froze the blood within Grinold's veins. He had tracked and killed many animals, but he had never beheld in any other animal the dangers posed by this creature. Large scales covered the body of the lizard running from its head to almost the entire length of the tail, which whipped back and forth as the swampsweeper slowly moved forward. The tail was massive and one lick from this scaly appendage could disable most large animals. Its mouth was large and cavernous with rows of teeth meant for killing and devouring its victim.

"Separate and go to the other side," ordered Cyrean. "Make him concentrate on me and you can get into the trees. There's no need in both of us risking death."

"You can climb trees better than I ," responded Grinold. "I am a tracker and hunter and better able to confront this beast than are you. Seek shelter in one of the nearby trees, and I will quickly dispatch the intruder."

"Do not be foolish, Grinold. The creature has few vulnerable areas. He is covered with scales that are impervious to the most powerful of weapons. Your only choice is flight. Get to the safety of the trees while I distract him here."

"I will not abandon one who has saved my life. If we are to die, let it be together fighting this spawn from hell."

"If you will not listen to reason, then listen to what I say about this creature. It must be attacked through one of its vulnerable areas: the eyes, the mouth, or its underbelly. Its jaws have the force of a catapult in forward motion, but once its

The Alliance

jaws close, it is seconds before he can get them open again. During that time when the jaws shut, we must press our advantage. I will get the animal to close its jaws. When he does, you must jump astride his body and try to plunge your knife into one of the eyes."

"I am beginning to reconsider your offer to find safety in the trees," said Grinold weakly as he surveyed the length and girth of the creature before him.

"Once the jaws are closed, there is no power in them," said Cyrean. "Wolfen will attack on my motion and go for the jaws. Once he has a hold on them, nothing can pry them open. Hang on once you have a grip, for he will try to flip you off. When his underbelly is exposed, I will send an arrow into his heart."

Wolfen had circled the monster until he now stood facing the enormous jaws.

"Be prepared to move once I loose my first arrow," cautioned Cyrean as he fitted a shaft to the string of his bow.

The swampsweeper hissed loudly as he prepared to attack, and at this advantage, Cyrean let fly the arrow into the mouth of the animal. The action only served to infuriate the beast as he closed his jaws to snap the arrow into splinters. At this distraction, Grinold hurled himself upon the back of the reptile and stabbed at the eyes. In the same instant, Wolfen had rushed forward and taken the jaws into his mouth. Now finding himself victim to attack from three directions, the swampsweeper twisted his body and swung his tail in an arc that almost caught Cyrean before he could position himself for his second shot. With Grinold still holding on, the beast rolled to try and throw its attacker, whipping his head in the same motion in an attempt to dislodge Wolfen. At the precise moment when its underbelly was exposed, Cyrean let fly his second shot which flew true to its mark. In the same moment,

Grinold had succeeded in driving his knife into the eye of the creature and into the brain. With one final convulsion, the creature threw Grinold into the air and rolled once more and for the last time.

Moving quickly to Grinold's aid, Cyrean lifted his head and checked for signs of life. Stunned, Grinold moaned and opened his eyes, becoming suddenly alert when he remembered what he had been doing. Seeing the creature at his feet, he started and backed quickly away as Cyrean laughed.

"It is good to see you so agile after the beating you took, Grinold. I had thought that maybe you had escaped one danger of the forest to be consumed by another."

"It is good that you can see the humor in my pain. The next swampsweeper we encounter, you can climb on his back and I will shoot the arrows."

During the excitement following the kill and the attention directed toward Grinold, Cyrean had momentarily forgotten that Wolfen had been part of the battle. Looking back at the monster, Cyrean realized that Wolfen was still locked onto the monster's jaws. Stunned and in obvious pain, he had never relinquished his hold upon the deadly jaws.

"We must get him back to the hut," said Cyrean. "I fear that he has broken ribs which will need immediate tending."

"How are we to get him loose from this foul lizard?" asked Grinold. "His hold is firm and unbreakable. He is not conscious to listen to your command to release the jaws."

"My skill with the bow will do us no good here, but your prowess with the sword would be welcome . If we can cut through the head of the creature, we can take Wolfen with his teeth still firmly locked onto the creature's severed jaws."

"An unseemly trophy but our only choice as I see," agreed Grinold.

Taking the sword high above his head, Grinold brought it

The Alliance

down with all the force he could manage. The finely honed blade made little impact upon the scaly head.

"We must turn him over until the underside is exposed. My sword has no effect upon his scales," observed Grinold

The two men grasped the trunk of the animal and with some effort finally managed to get it in position to swing the blade at the soft area under the neck. With two strokes, Grinold had severed the head of the large lizard. Taking the burden of lizard head and dog into their hands, the two men made their way back to the hut.

After carefully placing Wolfen on his own cot, Cyrean began to prepare herbs which he could apply to the bruises that Wolfen had absorbed while being tossed during the fray. Taking small limbs, he placed them on the ribcage of the wounded animal and laced them tightly with strips of cloth to hinder movement when the dog awakened. The ribs would take time to heal, and other poultices he needed could not be found in the Dark Wood.

"I must go immediately to an old hermit who lives in the valley outside these woods," said Cyrean. He has remedies that are unknown to me. He will be able to give me the medicines to cure Wolfen of his injuries."

" I will go also," said Grinold. "He fought bravely and deserves all the efforts we can put forward."

"Then let us go quickly. He will sleep for a while. We must be back before he awakens and tries to remove the restraints I have put upon his ribs."

The men picked up their weapons and left the hut, moving rapidly in the direction of the road that ran just outside the Dark Wood. If it is true that fate plays a part in the lives of mankind, the alliance of these two men would begin the web into which would be woven the destinies of many people, including the inhabitants of the Dark Wood.

Chapter Ten
The Caravan

As the carriage carrying the queen and Aurienna moved over the well traveled road from Eustan to Parvidian, Aurienna tried not to think about what she was leaving behind. She had been promised a prominent part to play in the war that was to come, and now she was fleeing like a cowardly thief that had just been caught lifting a purse. Every fiber of her being ached to turn back and do the duty that the kingdom required of her. She looked at the queen who sat in the opposite seat with her eyes closed and a sad look upon her face. She knew the queen could not disobey her husband's wishes any more than she could disobey those of her father. How cruel was fate to deny her the chance to serve her king in such a glorious encounter! She looked out the window at the countryside, but even the beauty of the pastoral scene that flashed by her could not lift her spirits. The dress she wore was not of the fine material she wore at court, and she constantly itched as the rough fabric rubbed against her tender skin. How she longed to have just common breeches and jerkin at a time like this. She would have preferred to dress like a man and ride a horse. No one would have known her in such manly garb. However, the queen would not have agreed to such accouterment and the suggestion was never proffered.

A sudden jolt rocked the carriage as it hit one of the numerous ruts that made the roads so uncomfortable to travel. The queen sat up and opened her eyes and glanced at her traveling companion.

"I would not have objected," said the queen, "if my husband had furnished us with a better vehicle for our travel. The journey will be a long one, and my old bones are not what they used to be. How quickly we get used to the finer things and forget what the masses have to endure daily. I should

The Caravan

count myself fortunate to have known the luxury of the palace for so many years. It may be some time before we know the like again. You look sad, Aurienna. Am I complaining like some old woman?"

"No, my queen. I have been distracted since we left the castle. I feel as if I am neglecting my duty in going to safety. I should be with my father and the king. They will need all able bodies in the next few days. What good do I serve in hiding when I can handle a sword? My father was wrong to send me away."

"No, Child, it is best that we continue as it has been planned. If either of us fell into the hands of Tobias, we would be the tools whereby he could take the palace without a blow struck. Our leaders need to be able to concentrate on the battle without having to worry about us. It is best that we not be there."

Aurienna did not answer. To talk of the thrill of battle to the queen was useless. She would never understand how that single moment in time when a person meets his enemy hand to hand can define who he is. She looked out at the soldier riding beside the carriage. Three men and a driver for protection. Should they happen upon bandits, they would have little chance of escape with such a small guard. She should at least have stowed a sword within the carriage. A shout from the driver brought her mind back to the present moment.

"Your majesty, we will stop for a few minutes when we reach the river. The horses need water, and we can refresh ourselves there."

"Such an ignorant man," Aurienna said caustically. "He shouts out your title so that all will know this carriage carries the queen. Any bandit within a mile will be upon us if he does that again."

"Calm yourself, Aurienna. The man does not think as you

do. I see why your father cultivates your advice so much. You think like a soldier and plan for any eventuality. It is that part of you more so than your beauty that endears you to soldiers like the king and Lord Hadreon."

"If they thought so strongly of my soldierly qualities, they should have let me stay to do battle. I can be of little help hidden away in some hut in a village that I have never seen."

The queen smiled sadly. She knew how much it meant to Aurienna to stay and be part of the battle. She, too, would have preferred to stay and be at her husband's side even if it meant her death. Life without her husband she could not imagine. In all the battles that had been fought securing the kingdom all those years ago, she had been with him. They had been young and fearless and where he fought she was near to comfort and give aid when needed. Now times were different. The king feared for the safety of the queen and Aurienna in a battle that he felt they could not win. The king's command was law, and even the queen could not change his mind.

The carriage began to quicken in pace as the thirsty horses smelled water. Within minutes they had arrived at a small clearing near the river where travelers were accustomed to stopping and camping or just to refresh themselves before they continued their journeys.

The driver opened the door and Aurienna stepped out unassisted. She gave her hand to the queen who stepped down and walked slowly toward the river, trying to restore the circulation that a cramped space in a carriage tends to restrict. She sat down on a small stool provided by the driver and fanned herself as the driver and the guards watered the horses and filled their flasks. The road that morning had been relatively untraveled. They had met some pilgrims traveling, some on horseback and others walking, and two small peddler's wagons but nothing that would warrant extra caution on their part.

After the horses had been watered and rested, they resumed their journey. The stop had been about thirty minutes in length and due to the lack of travelers on the road, they were making good time. If good fortune remained with them, they would be beyond the section of the road that ran by the Dark Wood before nightfall. Travelers were always aware that the Dark Wood loomed before them on long trips and planned their travels accordingly so as not to be too close when night fell. No one spoke of the dangers there, but it was understood that this area was to be avoided at all costs.

"Your majesty, what makes the Dark Wood such a fearful place?" asked Aurienna as she heard the driver comment on its proximity to their chosen route.

"Stories of the Dark Wood are as common as the birds in the air, my dear," answered the queen. "The village folk all have their stories and no two of them seem to be the same. There have been tales that have grown into legends about great battles that were fought in that area. It is said that the forest had once been a paradise bright with sunshine and filled with flowers and beautiful birds and animals of all types. Nothing evil existed in that Eden, and everything lived in harmony. In the middle of this paradise grew a tree that produced gold apples which the gods used to decorate their great city and for their weapons and jewelry. Mortals could enjoy all the benefits of this paradise, but they could not kill any animal or pluck any plant. Most importantly, they could not take any of the gold apples from the tree. For hundreds of years the wood was beautiful and peaceful. Then one day a traveler came to the wood from a distant land. He had heard of the legends of the forest, and he wanted to see them and to see especially the tree that produced golden apples. As he gazed upon the tree, the temptation became too great and he plucked one of the fruits, assuring himself that the gods would never miss one apple from a tree that produced a never-ending supply. When he picked the apple, immediately the skies darkened and the wood began to change. The flowers withered and died, the sun disappeared from the sky, and all became dark. Huge pits of quicksand formed from the once clear lakes, and the trees dropped their leaves and turned dark. They grew in size until they blocked the sun, and the beautiful animals became hideous monsters that preyed upon any unsuspecting victim that should wander into the forest. The unfortunate mortal who plucked the apple fell into one of the many sand pits and died taking with him the golden apple that had destroyed a paradise."

"Surely, your majesty surely does not believe in such fantasy!" interjected Aurienna.

"No, Aurienna, I am too rooted in the rational world that says there is no paradise other than the one we can create for ourselves. When mankind ceases to hunger for power and wealth and the great battles have all ended, then that will be paradise. The gods will not build it for us, but they give us the ability and the choice to make one for ourselves."

"As long as men like Tobias rule, that will never be," said Aurienna sadly as she turned back to the window to look at the rapidly approaching section of the province known as the Dark Wood.

"Yes, Tobias would pluck the golden apple from the tree and doom us all. It would be best if he were taken to the forest and left there as was done in the past with criminals and traitors," said the queen.

"Men have been sent to the Dark Wood for crimes?" asked Aurienna.

"Yes, and none have been heard from since. The king, my husband, once banished one of his most trusted advisors to

The Caravan

the Wood many years ago. I know not the reason and he would never speak of it, but it was a very sad time in his life."

"It would have to be a grievous offense for the king to commit such an act. He is a proud and honorable man. I have never seen him do an unjust thing in all the time I have known him," Aurienna replied.

"Though he is a king, he is still but a man and prone to mistakes as we all are," answered the queen.

The darkness of the forest was now a presence as the wagon traveled rapidly toward its destination. The river that flowed on its course less than a mile from the road on which they traveled seemed to be a dividing line between light and dark with the bright meadows and fields on one side of the carriage and the Dark Wood on the other. Aurienna felt an involuntary shudder run through her as she looked at the forest in the distance.

Through that forest Cyrean and Grinold were now making their way toward the hermit's hut. The two men moved quickly on the ground with Cyrean as guide to carry them past the sand pits and other dangers that Grinold was now all to aware existed, having fought through two of them himself. They had just left the forest and were crossing the distance between the river and the road when the sound of men on horses came to Grinold's ear. He motioned for Cyrean to stop, and both men moved quietly toward the grove of trees from where the sounds came. Travelers on the road were not uncommon, but this group of riders had taken great effort to conceal themselves within the little grove of trees and bushes about a hundred yards from the main path. When they had gotten close enough to see the band clearly, Grinold scanned the riders to determine if they were Tobias' men. He did not recognize them, but that would not be unusual considering the size of Tobias' army. This was a rag-tag lot and they had all the earmarks of common bandits who frequented the roads and robbed travelers of their goods. They were not soldiers but even these unskilled ruffians were dangerous in enough number.

Grinold counted eight riders who were apparently waiting for the next unlucky caravan that came by. Rarely was anyone seriously hurt in these raids, but they were so common that they had become a real nuisance to the kingdom. King Malvore had often sent soldiers out to hunt down these bands of outcasts, but as soon as one was group was eliminated, another sprang up to take its place. Most of the members of these bandit groups were men from the villages that Tobias had destroyed, leaving them homeless and without families.

As Grinold scanned the group, another sound came to his ears. A small caravan of riders was approaching and soon would be nearing the spot where the men were concealed. Realizing what was about to happen, he motioned Cyrean forward and they moved quietly toward the group of men. Grinold knew he would not have time to warn the caravan before it came under attack. He moved quickly to where Cyrean had now stopped awaiting another signal.

"We do not have time to warn the caravan," Grinold whispered. "How far and how accurately can you send one of those arrows?"

"Accurately enough to dispatch any of the riders hidden in that grove of trees," Cyrean assured his companion.

"Can you send one far enough to hit that approaching wagon without harming its occupants?" he asked.

"That would be a distant target indeed," replied Cyrean. "The range of my bow will be tested with such a shot. I will need to get closer."

"Move quickly then," urged Grinold. "There is not much time. When you think you have the range, loose a shaft to warn the oncoming party. They will be alerted before the bandits spring their trap."

Darting quickly through the tall grass, Cyrean moved to an advantageous point and notched an arrow. Looking at the wind's movement through the tall grass he made a mental adjustment for any effect the breeze might have upon the arrow. He pulled the string back and released it in one fluid motion. The arrow flew on its way, coming to rest in the bench only inches from the driver's feet.

"Bandits!" the driver yelled as he snapped the reins, sending the horses into a full run.

Surprised by the events unfolding before them, it took a few seconds for the bandits to realize that someone else was attacking the prey they had planned for themselves. Riding from concealment, the group quickly converged on the carriage with swords brandished. Realizing he could not outrun the outlaws, the driver pulled the wagon to the side of the road and joined the guards who had lined up facing the approaching riders.

"There are too many, your majesty!" Aurienna shouted. "I must help or we will be taken."

"You cannot endanger yourself, Aurienna. Our guards are trained soldiers. They can fight off a few ruffians."

"Perhaps, but I intend to even the numbers. Driver, give me your sword and protect the queen with your life if we should fail."

As Aurienna joined the guards to face the oncoming raiders, Cyrean and Grinold had covered the distance from their concealment to the wagon. They arrived just as guards and bandits clashed, swords and shields flashing in the afternoon sun.

"By my trow!" exclaimed Grinold in admiration. "The woman fights like a man. She has dispatched one knave and sent another running back to the trees. Quickly, Cyrean, before she wins the day herself and leaves us to look like fools."

In answer Cyrean sent a shaft that struck a rider full in the shoulder, sending him tumbling from his horse. When the ranks closed and made the bow ineffective, Cyrean pulled his sword and joined Grinold who had unhorsed another rider and was locked in a deadly struggle with swords ringing as they parried stroke for stroke. Seeing their advantage in numbers diminished by the arrival of the newcomers, the other bandits turned and fled back to the woods, leaving three of their comrades bleeding and perhaps dying upon the field.

"Cowardly dogs," cried Aurienna at the retreating riders, " run back to your holes and know it was a woman who sent you there. Lick your wounds and when they are well, perhaps you can make a living begging in the villages. Craven pigs who prey on the weak deserve no less."

"My lady, I think they will not be back. To have been bested by a woman will make them a laughingstock and no danger to anyone again," laughed Grinold as he looked at Aurienna who was still flushed from battle and shaking her sword at the retreating bandits.

"Bested by a woman? And when can not a woman best any man?" asked Aurienna, sharply eyeing the stranger before her. "Friend, my companions and I do thank you for your help, but do not presume that we could not have dispatched this scurrilous band of thieves without your aid."

"My companion meant no disrespect to you as a woman or a fighter, m'lady," spoke Cyrean. "We simply saw the men in concealment and wanted to warn you before the attack occurred, thereby putting you at a disadvantage."

"And who might our benefactors be?" asked Aurienna as she looked carefully at the two men for signs that might reveal something about them. They both obviously were trained in

The Caravan

combat and showed no fear in the battle that had just occurred. Yet they did not have the appearance of soldiers. What would they have to profit by helping simple wayfarers, endangering their lives with no guarantee of reward?

"I am Cyrean and this is my companion Grinold. We could not allow for helpless victims to come under attack and not give aid though I see that you have trained soldiers for an escort. This is indeed unusual for common gentry. Perhaps you carry a treasure that these bandits knew of in your wagon."

"There is no treasure on our wagon. These soldiers are simply riding with us until they reach their regiment, and then they will leave us. It is fortunate they were with us today."

Whatever Aurienna hoped to learn about her benefactors, she would have to discover at a later time, for she was interrupted suddenly by the driver who nervously approached her with shaking hands.

"My lady, come quickly!"

Sensing from the driver's apparent agitation that something dire had happened, she followed him back to the coach where she discovered the queen in obvious distress.

A small crimson patch on the part of the dress covering the queen's shoulder instantly alerted Aurienna that somehow she had been struck during the battle. Cutting the dress away from the wound, she discovered that an arrow had shattered and a fragment of wood had lodged in her shoulder. It was not a mortal wound, but it would need immediate attention.

"Where can we find medicinal aid for my companion?" asked Aurienna. "We carry nothing with us, and the wound she has received in the shoulder will need more care than I can give."

"I will send my companion to complete the errand we began this morning," answered Cyrean. " We were on our way to see a hermit for medicine for a wounded animal. On the same mission he can acquire herbs that will work on your companion's wound as well."

"I will return soon," said Grinold, who was already moving in the direction of the hermit's hut.

"My lady," said Cyrean looking earnestly at Aurienna. "You and your companion cannot remain here. There are other bandits, and she needs to be put into a bed to rest. I do not receive strangers into my home, but I would be remiss to leave you out here on your own. The guards are tired and have received hurts of their own in the battle. They can camp by the river until they have rested and nursed their wounds. When Grinold returns with the medicine, we will make your companion as comfortable as possible, but she needs a bed and shelter from the elements until she is well. The safest place will be in my home until that time. My friend and I will construct a litter upon which to carry the lady, for assuredly she could not walk any distance."

"I will agree for Lady Ofra's sake, but we must be on the road and traveling within three days."

"My hospitality extends to you as long as you require it, my lady. I will construct the litter while my friend is returning with the medicine."

Cyrean set quickly about gathering material he would need for the litter. Aurienna watched him as he put together the limbs and bound them with strips of cloth. He moved with practiced assurance, and she could not help but find herself fascinated by his quiet strength and resourcefulness. He was not boastful like the young men she had encountered at court, and she felt herself calmed by his presence, sensing that everything would be alright as long as he was there.

"Lady Aurienna, the litter is ready and Grinold will be here soon. He and I will bear the litter and guide you to my home. It is not the accommodations to which you are accustomed, but it will serve until you can return to better."

"Where is your home, Cyrean? Will it be very far?"

"No, my lady. It is only an hour traveling straight through the Dark Wood."

"The Dark Wood? No, Cyrean, we cannot go into such an inhospitable environment. Only demons and exiled criminals live there. It would not be safe."

"You will be safe with me and my companion, Lady Aurienna. I have lived within the Dark Wood many years. I know its dangers well and will guide you safely to my home. When your companion is well, I will bring you here again to continue your journey. My word is my bond."

Before Aurienna could protest again, Grinold returned with the medicines received from the hermit. Queen Ofra was made as comfortable as possible and placed upon the litter. After giving instructions to the guards, Aurienna joined the two men, and they took up the litter and began the return journey through the forest.

Chapter Eleven
A Fruitless Encounter

The candle flickered as a gust of wind blew under the flap of Tobias' tent, a cold wind that might have served as an omen had Tobias been a superstitious man. Such was not his nature, and he arose and pulled the sides of the shelter together as he prepared for the sleep that for too many nights now had been denied him. The burden of leadership was a harsh one. He was a commander to soldiers in whom he had very little faith. Their loyalty was his as long as he could promise them riches. They would raise their swords to fight for him as long as there was no other battle to be had. They were men of little honor and questionable courage. Yet they were the army he ruled, and if the soldiers be a reflection of the leader, then Tobias had the army he deserved.

As Tobias made his nightly preparations, he pondered the news he had received the last two days. The spies that Captain Malaban had placed in the king's castle had brought word that a caravan carrying the queen and Lord Hadreon's daughter was leaving for Alcinor under the protection of fifty of the king's best troops. Tobias had immediately sent twice that number to intercept and ambush the caravan with the admonition that the queen and Aurienna were not to be harmed. With two such important hostages in his possession, the battle might well be ended before it began.

Tobias smiled as he thought of what the king's reaction would be upon hearing of the queen's capture. Having lost two sons in the same way, this might be the act that would finally claim his life. If that were to happen, the crown would be his without a battle being fought. A part of him hoped that would not happen. He longed for battle, and a victory over the king's forces would make the acquisition of the crown all the sweeter. He snuffed the candle and lay down, pulling a blanket over

A Fruitless Encounter

himself and falling into a deep sleep, secure now in the knowledge that the crown was imminent.

It is the fate of mankind that within each victory is cloaked the specter of failure. The elation that Tobias felt when he retired the night before now was to be shattered at daybreak when Captain Malaban and his troops returned without the queen and Aurienna. Tobias listened grimly as Captain Malaban told his story.

The soldiers had planned their ambush carefully and had lain in wait for the caravan to reach the spot where the attack was to take place, the captain explained. The area was excellent for such a purpose with dense foliage and large trees for concealment. Captain Malaban had placed fifty soldiers on each side of the road. At a predetermined signal, twenty-five men on each side would attack the caravan and try to take the women. If the first wave could not accomplish the objective, the remaining fifty troops would sweep through with fresh horses and strong arms and claim the day.

The plan worked well at first. When the first wave set upon the caravan, soldiers managed to get to the wagon which they thought carried the queen and Aurienna. It wasn't until they tried to pull the women from the wagon that they realized they had been duped. The two women met the soldiers with hard steel and killed three men before they realized these were not women at all. In the confusion, the second group of soldiers were never signaled into the fray, and having accomplished their mission, the king's soldiers retreated back down the road they had come toward Eustan.

When Captain Malaban finished his story, Tobias stood up and strode outside the tent. Enraged, as he considered the deception played upon him, he swore to the skies as if there lay the answer he sought.

"The very fates do taunt me!" he thundered. "The king will

pay dearly for this trickery. No mercy will be shown to any that oppose me in battle. All will be killed, soldiers, women, and children. Not one soul will be left to mock my failure here. King Malavore has won this time, but there are many moves in a game, and I will have the final play. Prepare thyself, King Malavore, thy fate is sealed!"

While Tobias swore vengeance on all who opposed him, the king's soldiers had returned to Eustan. When the commander reported to King Malavore that all had gone well with few casualties, the old king was heartily pleased. Now Tobias had felt the sting of their determination. He would smart for a while from the bite, but the king knew it was only a temporary victory and it would only serve to anger Tobias all the more. Still, the ruse had worked well enough to get the queen and Aurienna to safety. That had been the objective, and it had been accomplished. Now let Tobias do as he would. Without the worry of the two women's safety, they could fight unhampered.

The appearance of General Draco into his chamber's interrupted the king's contemplation of the coming battle, and he motioned the general to come forward.

"General, you have arrived at a moment of triumph, however small in the greater scheme of things. My wife and Aurienna are safe and the traitor Tobias has been thwarted again."

"I heard from the returning soldiers of their success," replied General Draco. " It was indeed a stroke of good fortune that the plan went well. The queen and Aurienna are well then? Such good fortune should always be with us. If you will but tell me the whereabouts of their ladyships, I will send other soldiers to assure their safe passage to their destination."

"There will be no need for that, Commander. They are safe and close to their objective by now. The fewer people who

A Fruitless Encounter

know of their destination, the better able we are to protect them."

"But surely, your majesty, the commander of your armies should be privy to all important decisions made concerning the kingdom. How else can I carry out my duties?"

"This matter is not a concern for my generals. It concerns only me and my wishes for the safety of my family. You will have enough to worry about once the battle begins, General Draco. Now go and begin the assignments for the wall fortifications. In the first assault, we will rain such destruction upon their forces at the wall that they will think the gods themselves have taken up our cause."

"It will be done."

The king watched Draco exit the room and mused that perhaps Aurienna had been correct in her assessment of the general. He wanted to know more than was required to do his assignments. King Malvore wondered where the caravan was now and if its inhabitants were safe. Aurienna had promised to send word as soon as they reached their destination. If they had made good time, a rider should be back within three days to inform him of the troupe's safe arrival in Parvidian. Until then it was a matter of waiting and preparing for war.

The sun had begun to set when Lord Hadreon arrived and was granted entrance to the king's chambers. He too had spent a great part of the day contemplating the fortunes of war and the safety of his child. But he knew that whatever happened now was in the hands of fate. They had planned well and now it was a matter of waiting until Tobias made his next move. As he entered the king's chambers, he knew the king would be pleased with at least one message his spies had brought.

"Your majesty, I see from the imprint upon the rugs that you have walked miles today in this room. Your agitation I can understand, for I have suffered from the malady as well. It is my good fortune that I have the responsibility of the securing of this castle to keep me occupied. Perhaps it would also do you good to leave these chambers and go into the light to view our fortifications. It would encourage the soldiers and give the people hope to see you involved in our preparations."

"Your counsel I have always invited, my friend. You are right. I have deprived myself of the healing effects of nature for nigh two years. I long for light and fresh air. Since the queen and Aurienna are gone, I have no one to talk to nor read to me. It is as if the sun has been taken from the sky with their departure. These chambers are cold. Let us walk out into the courtyard and bask in the sun before it sets over yon hills."

Taking the king's arm, the two friends slowly walked out into the bright air and sat in the orchard below the king's chamber. The evening rays of the sun still lingered as if in obeisance to the king. Lord Hadreon helped the weakened monarch to a comfortable place and told him his news.

"My king, I have news that will lighten your spirits this day," began Lord Hadreon.

"I would readily hear good news. Is it of our families?"

"No, your grace. There is no word of them though I am sure of their safety. My news concerns the weapon we most dread as we prepare for this war."

"You have found the Crystal of Light? If so my greatest fear has been put to rest."

"No, I do not know of the crystal's location, but according to my spies Tobias is ignorant of its whereabouts also."

"I am a soldier, Lord Hadreon, as are you. I would not wish to use such an instrument to destroy lives. If I must fight, I will do it honorably and face my enemy at the time of death. How easy it is to kill when you do not have to see the pain and suffering inflicted by a weapon such as the Crystal of Light. There was a time when the honor in battle went to him that

A Fruitless Encounter

showed compassion to an enemy that had fought well. Soldiers need to be honorable men if theirs is a just cause. Once the objective has been achieved, pardon your enemies and send them back to their families. They too fought for a cause. In their minds, was their cause less noble? It is in the likeness of Tobias that we see the dark face of war. He fights for no cause other than his own. The spoils of war are his reward. The enemy he has fought receive no mercy from his hands. I would rather die a thousand deaths than live one life under the rule of Tobias."

"You echo my thoughts, your majesty. I would fight as an honorable soldier and die in the doing thereof as long as Tobias hath not the crystal. He cares not of the havoc which would be wrought by such a weapon as long as it achieves his ends. I would that the crystal never be found again, but I fear this is not so. Tobias had the weapon and now it is missing. If some thief took the object, then he might sell it to whoever pays him the most gold dragons. Thieves have no honor. They care not for the greater good, and, in their fashion, are much akin to Tobias himself. I fear he would acquire the weapon again from such a person."

"If my sons were here now, I would care not whether Tobias had the crystal," spoke the king sadly. "With them at my side, we would lay waste to the forces of Tobias, and the kingdom would be strong again. These old arms have lost their strength, but they would be renewed had I my sons to fire my spirit."

"Do not talk of things that cannot be, your majesty. It will only upset you and quell your spirit which I see as bright as ever. When the time comes, you will lift your battle- tested weapon and put it to its proper use again."

"I live for that day now that the queen is safe, Lord Hadreon. "She is all that I have to live for now. I pray that she is well and out of harm's way."

"As do I of her and my daughter. Come, my lord, the sun has set and the night grows cold. We will talk again tomorrow when the world is bright and heaven smiles once again on our efforts."

Chapter Twelve
A Power Revealed

Within the bowels of the forest, the Dark Wood seemed more foreboding than anything that Aurienna had heard or imagined. How could anyone want to live in such darkness and isolation? Was Cyrean an exile and, if so, what crime could one so genteel have committed? There were a lot of questions to which Aurienna could not fashion answers, and she was sure her host would be reluctant to enlighten her. The path they were traveling was not worn, but there was evidence that it had been traveled in the past. Obviously, Cyrean had safe paths to travel through the woods, and none would be discernible except to the most perceptive eyes. He led them past sand pits and other snares that would quickly have dispatched less knowledgeable travelers. After almost an hour of carrying their burden through these obstacles, the group finally reached Cyrean's hut.

The daylight had waned and the hut and its surroundings were in darkness like the rest of the forest. There was no light in the hut, and Cyrean and Grinold placed the litter temporarily outside until Cyrean could light a candle and stir the embers of the fire. They then took the litter inside the hut and gently placed the queen upon one of the cots. Wolfen stirred when he smelled his master. He had not moved and still locked in his jaws was the head of the monster. When the light illuminated the room enough for everyone to see, Aurienna was horrified by what she saw.

"Cyrean, what has this beast within his mouth? I have never seen such hideousness. Take the head from the animal's mouth and place it outside. I cannot bear to look upon it longer."

Cyrean walked over to the cot where Wolfen lay, and the great dog stirred and softly whimpered. There were strangers he did not know and he should be on guard, but he could not move without pain. Cyrean placed his hand gently on the dog's head and spoke to him.

"Ah, my faithful Wolfen," said Cyrean softly, "for us you have risked your life, and even now, still wracked with pain, you cling to that which would have killed me and my companion. A truer friend I could never have. But you must let go of the monster's head. It cannot harm us now."

Ever so slowly, the great jaws of Wolfen began to relax, and Cyrean pulled the monster's head away from the injured animal. He took the monstrosity outside and walked into the woods where the tossed it as far as he could. When he had disposed of the head, he returned to the hut and to tending the needs of its injured inhabitants.

Grinold prepared the fire and sorted the medicines while Cyrean and Aurienna made the queen as comfortable as possible. When the poultices were ready, Aurienna placed them gently on the wound of Lady Ofra and pulled a chair to the bed and sat holding the hand of her companion. After he was sure Lady Ofra was comfortable, Cyrean removed the splints from the ribs of Wolfen and dressed his wounds, applying the medicines that Grinold had received from the hermit. He worked as tenderly on Wolfen as he would have a new-born babe, realizing that without the dog's help they might not have survived the battle with the swampsweeper. Aurienna watched as Cyrean performed his tasks and marveled at the gentleness with which he tended to the needs of the wounded animal. Here was the same man who earlier that day had fought so fiercely defending two wayfarers that he did not know. This was an unusual man indeed.

"Will he live?" Aurienna asked.

"He will live but his ribs will need time to heal. These splints that I have placed upon him will restrict his movements somewhat. He will be ill-tempered for awhile, having the bindings placed upon him, but it is the only way he will heal properly."

"The animal seems to mean a great deal to you. You treat him as tenderly as you did my companion in dressing her wounds."

"More than once and even today Wolfen has saved my life. He is more than just an animal. A man could not have a more loyal companion. His loss would hurt me as deeply as any child I might have."

Aurienna turned back to the bed as she felt the queen stir. The wound was causing obvious pain, and the queen reached across with her hand and felt the dressing on the shoulder. As her senses gradually began to return, she opened her eyes and saw Aurienna above her, a look of concern blanketing her face. Looking around the hut, she realized they were safe but not anywhere near where the attack had occurred. She tried to lift herself from the bed, but a gentle, yet persuasive, touch from Aurienna was all she needed to realize it would be foolhardy to risk such a movement.

"Where are we, Aurienna? Have I been asleep long? The darkness tells me that it has been hours since the attack upon our wagon. Have you been hurt?"

"No, your ladyship. I received no hurt, but two pilgrims who happened by during the attack aided us and brought us to their hut. You are safe, but you will need care for a few days. Rest and I will prepare some soup for you."

"Do our rescuers know who we are?" whispered the queen.

"I think not, your majesty. I have said nothing to make them think we are anything other than two unlucky travelers. It would be best if I address you as Lady Ofra while we are here. It is unlikely that they will recognize the name. We do not know as yet what type of men our hosts are. If they know that you are royalty, we might have been rescued from one danger to fall into another. We will not reveal any more than is necessary until we know we are in safe hands."

Grinold brought a bowl of warm soup to the bed and handed it to Aurienna. He gently touched the hand of Lady Ofra to reassure her that she was among friends. As his hand rested on hers, a look of amazement came to his face, and he stared fully into the eyes of the woman lying on the cot. Aurienna had started to feed the queen and was bringing the spoon to her mouth when she noticed Grinold staring at her companion.

"Sir, is there a reason you gaze upon my companion so directly? Has she some wound on her person of which I am unaware? If not, you are a rude host indeed to be so familiar."

"I am sorry, my lady. I was unaware that I was staring. I simply was looking to see if she were comfortable. I did not intend to act unseemly."

Grinold moved back to the fireplace and sat against the hearth. He had felt something when he touched their guest's hand. He could not explain what the feeling was, but it was unlike any other with whom he had come into contact. There was a presence in the room that he had never felt in the huts in his village or in the taverns. This was different. It was something with which he was not familiar, and it troubled him that he could not place it into a category within his realm of experience. Though they dressed in simple garb, these were not simple peasants. The bearing and dignity of the wounded woman was evident even in her pain, and the beauty and the fierceness of character displayed by her younger companion was not to be found in peasant villages.

Cyrean had finished tending Wolfen. He returned to the bedside of Lady Ofra and looked at her with concern upon his face. He had not seen or heard the interchange between the women and Grinold, but he paused for a moment as he saw

Grinold sitting quietly by the fire. His companion seemed to be in deep concentration on some matter. Cyrean reasoned it was simply that the day's events had given him much upon which to reflect. He, too, would have to give this day much thought when the occasion was right.

Aurienna looked up at his approach and smiled wanly.

"We each have suffered today," she said. "Our best friends and companions have received a hurt. It is a helpless feeling and we wonder if there is not something more we could have done."

"Time is a great healer," replied Cyrean. "They will be well again and we will be here to support them and care for them in their time of need."

"You and your animal are obviously very close," observed Aurienna. "How came he to be in possession of the head of such an animal as I witnessed earlier?"

"Grinold and I owe our lives to Wolfen. We fought today in another part of the forest a swampsweeper, and Wolfen was the instrument of our victory. He knows no fear when my safety is at risk. He locked onto the jaws of the monster, and we had to cut away its head to bring home the injured animal. He will not loose anything his jaws have locked upon without my command."

"I have never seen such a beast as the swampsweeper," marveled Aurienna. "Are there other animals in the forest as fearsome?"

"There are many dangers in the Dark Wood, my lady. Bogbears and sand pits are everywhere, and even the warthogs and howlers can be dangerous in numbers."

"Your companion speaks little," replied Aurienna. "I feel I may have judged him harshly and spoke too rashly earlier. He seems to have a good heart though his visage is hard and his manners are rough. Have you known him long?"

"No, he, like you and Lady Ofra, was in need of assistance and I helped him out of a danger in which he found himself, being unfamiliar with the woods."

"Then you have three people indebted to you for your bravery and courage. How can we repay such beneficence?"

"It is the duty of all mankind to help when others are in need. I only did what any man would do under like circumstances."

"And what of our benefactor? You have told me little of yourself. How came you to these woods. Only criminals and outcasts have ever called the Dark Wood home. Your actions of late convince me you are neither of these."

"I now not how I came here. My earliest memories are of these woods. My mother and father lived here because it was home to them. Why they felt compelled to live a life of isolation here, they never revealed to me. When they died, I buried them in a sunny meadow far from these woods. I did not want them to have the darkness in death that they had lived in life."

"But what of you? There are no ties to hold you here now. You could take your place among your fellow men. There are many things you have never seen living here. There are adventures to be had, beautiful mountains and rivers to see, and companionship that not even Wolfen can provide."

"I cannot leave now but I have a journey planned upon which I will embark ere long. First, I must see that you and Lady Ofra are well and safely on your way."

"If that journey take you toward Eustan, I have lived there and can give you recommendation so that you will be welcome wherever you go."

"That is indeed my destination, my lady. I have need to see the king. Though a commoner may never gain audience with his majesty, I must make the effort."

A Power Revealed

"Perhaps the task will not be as difficult as you think," answered Aurienna. "The king is always available to his subjects and listens to their problems."

"Those are comforting words and will help to unloose my tongue if I am lucky enough to speak to his majesty."

"Take this with you," said Aurienna, removing a small crested ring from her finger. "Any guard will recognize its significance and grant you passage to the king."

"Then you do stand in favor with the king. I could sense that you were more than just a commoner. Your skills with a weapon and your fierceness in battle are not found in the common mob. How do you know the king?"

"I cannot answer those questions now. I ask only one favor. When you have an audience with the king, give him the ring and tell him the owner and her companion are safe. That is all he will need to know. With that news to cheer him, you will be granted anything you wish."

"I will question you no more. I would be a rude host to play inquisitor to my guests. If there comes a time when you wish to reveal more, I will be the well into which you may pour your secrets. Now we must rest. The night is cold and a warm fire and sleep awaits us. I will move Wolfen to his accustomed place by the hearth, and you will take my bed. I will sleep by the fire with Wolfen and Grinold. The hut is sound and secure against all night creatures. Grinold and I will be here to ensure that you and your companion will continue your trip safely once you are recovered."

Aurienna turned to check on her companion and found her resting peacefully. The poultices had done their work well. She lay down upon the cot which Grinold had prepared with fresh bedding. Both men were soon asleep by the fire with Wolfen between them. Aurienna had little time to reflect upon the conversation with Cyrean as exhaustion soon closed her eyes and pulled her down into the deepest of slumbers.

The morning broke, finding the inhabitants of the hut still abed. Cyrean was the first to stir as he poked the ashes of the fire and blew upon the coals, bringing them to a red glow. He piled more wood onto the coals and shook Grinold. Years of hunting and being the hunted had made a light sleeper of the tracker and he was instantly awake.

Wolfen stirred and whined softly. He raised his head and looked at the two men but dropped it again as the pain from the movement coursed through his body. He would be well again, but the ribs would cause him pain for many days. Lady Ofra had gained color in her face and seemed to be resting more comfortably now that she had gotten a night's sleep. The two men walked quietly out the door and toward the forest, happy to stretch their legs after a night's discomfort on the floor.

"You have been quiet of late, my friend," said Cyrean. "Has something been troubling you?"

"I do not know the cause of my malady," answered Grinold. "I sense that our guests are more than they proclaim to be. You have already guessed that I have a special ability to know things about people that they are hesitant to reveal. I received a feeling when I touched Lady Ofra's hand that I had never experienced before. It is nothing that would be a danger to either of us, but it is indeed curious."

"Yes, I have discovered secrets of my own in talking to Lady Aurienna. She has been acquainted with the king on some level. She will not reveal any more to me, but there are things afoot when two women of such obvious stature travel the countryside dressed in peasant garb."

"They will be here for two more days," replied Grinold. "Much can be revealed in that time."

"In the meanwhile, let us make our guests comfortable,

Grinold, my friend. We will gather wood from beneath the dead tree at the edge of the clearing. The limbs will burn well and from the darkness of its wood will come the light by which we will warm ourselves tonight."

Cyrean sat about gathering the dead limbs and piling them into a stack for retrieval later. Grinold walked beneath the huge tree and began his own pile, savoring the feeling of exercising muscles that he had not used in almost two days. Cyrean stopped to examine a small plant that might be medicinal in nature and felt a sudden gust of wind sweep through the grass and upward. The sudden movement of air shook the trees around them, causing them to bend and sway until it seemed they would be uprooted from their very foundations. Just as suddenly as it had come, the wind died to a gentle breeze. Both men stood for a moment observing the phenomenon and then resumed their work. Somewhere high in the trees above them a rotten limb swung back and forth like a pendulum connected only by a small appendage. The movement soon finished the work the wind had begun, and the limb plunged on its course of destiny. Grinold was placing a last stick on the pile he had accumulated, unaware of the danger above him. As the wooden missile plummeted toward the ground, Grinold suddenly sensed the danger. Looking up, he saw the limb and realized he had no time to evade the blow. He had time only to raise his arms in an attempt to divert the limb from his head. Suddenly, just as if another large draft had caught the limb, it veered away and landed several feet from where Grinold stood with a look of wonder now frozen on his face.

Grinold dropped his arms to his side and looked in amazement at Cyrean, who stood trembling as if he had just completed a task which had taken all the strength from his body.

"I know not what occurred here, but I know somehow you

played a hand in my rescue again," he said weakly to Cyrean. "How did you divert yon limb from my pate. No wind blew to perform the deed. How can such a thing be?"

"It is something I have done before," replied Cyrean, "but never with such a large mass. The danger of the moment made me capable of controlling a much larger object than I had ever attempted ere this."

"Then this is not the first time for such a feat. How long have you known that you possess the ability to move objects at will?"

"The first time was as a small child, only four years old. A small snake lay coiled in the dirt near where I was playing. I had disturbed it with my movements and it lay ready to strike. Even at such a tender age, I recognized the danger presented by the creature. Without thinking, I willed the serpent into the air and with my mind I threw it into the high grass a safe distance from me."

"Have you used this ability often enough to make it a useful tool?" asked Grinold.

"No. In a way it frightens me," answered Cyrean. Why do I possess such a power? How came I by such a gift and what would be its usefulness?"

"It once saved your life and now mine," observed Grinold.

"Yes, I did not think about that. It seems like such abilities often come from the forces of darkness, but if that be so I have used it twice for good. My fear of the gift, if that is what it is, has kept me from realizing its potential."

"I would guess that it would only become stronger with use," said Grinold. "My senses have grown sharper with use until they are now a part of who I am and make things known to me without my effort. But, unlike you, I welcomed the power that was given to me and used it for my own means rather than to help others. In one moment you have done more good with your talent than I have done in a lifetime with mine."

"Do not belittle yourself. It is often through trial and error that we find what is real and true and what is false. You have made those discoveries, and now the choice is simply how you are going to use your powers. I do not know what my abilities are because I have never truly used them. In time the purpose will perhaps be revealed to me. Today has allowed me insight into myself and the potential therein."

"Come, Cyrean, I am still shaken by my recent adventure. Let us walk back to the hut with our wood. Such exercise will get my blood flowing again that had almost stopped in its coursing. We will talk later of these things. There is still much to discover."

Aurienna had prepared food for the queen and herself. When she saw the two men come into the hut, she arose and ladled a portion of the contents of the pot into bowls for them.

"Grinold, a cold pallor lies upon your skin. You may have been too long in these woods. Cyrean has spoken of a journey. Maybe it is a journey you should also consider. Lady Ofra and I will soon be once again traveling on our own pilgrimage. Without us to be of concern, you will have the world before you. Eustan is to the north and fair wind and weather and a friend such as Cyrean make for good traveling companions."

"My life has been one endless odyssey, Lady Aurienna. I need to be more like the mighty Auk who soars through the skies but always returns to his nest in the cliffs. I have no place I can call home, and I see many more weary days stretching before me before I will find my own nest."

"Such is the way for many, Grinold, but I would prefer the life you lead to staying in one place and never seeing the adventures the world has to offer. We can rest when we are old and our bones will not allow us the freedom of the road."

"I have seen enough of the road for awhile, my young companion," said Lady Ofra as she made an effort to lift herself to a sitting position. "If vagabonds and bandits are what the road has to offer, I will stay home and spend my days by a warm fire."

"My lady, you should not exert yourself. The wound has not healed sufficiently to allow movement as of yet," admonished Aurienna, moving to place a large fur behind Lady Ofra's back for support.

"If your companion feels well enough, Lady Aurienna, Grinold and I will make a sitting place in front of the hut so that she may enjoy the sunshine. It comes only for a brief time each day, and it is now at its height."

"The warm sun would be welcome, and I would share its light with friends if all of you will join me," said Lady Ofra in way of agreement.

Lifting the queen from the bed, Grinold carried her to a place in the sunlight.

"What an odd place to live," observed the queen. "Have both of you always lived here?" she asked of Cyrean and Grinold.

"It has always been my home," replied Cyrean. "Grinold has been my welcome guest these last two days."

"Did your parents live here also?"

"Yes, my lady. They lived here until their death five years ago."

"The passing of our parents is a sad thing. When Aurienna and I are established in our new home, you must come and visit us, Cyrean, and bring your companion. The change will have a wondrous effect upon you both."

"Lady Ofra, we have heard of the plans that Tobias has to overthrow the kingdom. I know not what Grinold plans for that time, but I will fight for the king. I will be traveling to Eustan soon. I have news for the king that might have an effect on the outcome of that conflict. I have heard that the king is a good and worthy ruler. Nothing good have I heard about the upstart Tobias. I will throw my lot with the king. The only way I know to judge a man is by his deeds. When the time comes for war, I will leave the Dark Wood and fight not only for its preservation but for the provinces all around. The fate of us all will depend upon a victory in that conflict."

"Well said, young Cyrean. The king would welcome the aid of your strong right arm," replied Lady Ofra. "I begin to feel the cool of the night air since the sun has set. Take me in to the warm fire. We will continue our discussion there and forge an alliance in support of the king."

Grinold lifted Lady Ofra from the stool on which she sat and carried her into the hut. After placing her gently on the cot, he went to replenish the fire which now had died to a small flicker. Soon a blaze was casting its heat into the room and Aurienna placed a blanket across Lady Ofra who soon was asleep. She looked at the two men who now were sitting by the fire, Cyrean stroking the broad head of Wolfen who lay and enjoyed the attention of his master. Cyrean looked into the fire. He had made plans that day and revealed them to new friends. He had not known what he would do if war began. Now he was sure that he would fight for Lady Aurienna. Her loyalty would be his. He had never known such a woman, and something within him wanted to protect her from the darkness of the forest and the darkness of the war which now seemed unavoidable. He had the means to assure victory for the king. As he lay his head upon the makeshift bed, he finally knew what his mission was, and in two days he would be on his way to fulfill it.

Chapter Thirteen
A Like Trust

"Is it not as I told you, Darius? Outworlders have come to our forest. More and more they come until soon the Dark Wood will be the same as any Outworlder village."

Bartold and Darius sat high in a tree looking into the clearing where stood Cyrean's hut. They had witnessed the afternoon's gathering of the guests outside the hut, and now they worried as they debated the possible consequences of other beings in their forest.

"I have warned you before of befriending outsiders such as Cyrean," said Darius. "Now you have permitted others to enter. Here we were safe from the taunting and ridicule of the Outworlders as long as they feared the forest. Now that they have Cyrean to guide them, our woods will soon be full of intruders and there will be no place left for us to go."

"Cyrean's family has lived here for many years," replied Bartold. "They have never caused us harm and were as eager to preserve the sanctity of the forest as we are. These visitors to Cyrean's hut will soon be gone and everything will be as it was. You will see that I am right, Darius."

"That may be so, but I must bring this matter before the council. If they agree to wait on a course of action, I will accept that decision until we witness other interlopers in the forest. If they decide to act now, you will be expected to follow the wishes of the council even if it means Cyrean will be dismissed from the forest."

"As always. the decision of the council is final," replied Bartold. "I have no great love for any Outworlder. Cyrean is different only in that he wants to keep the forest a secret as much as we do."

"Perhaps, but now he has violated that trust. He has nothing that is of benefit to us. His loss from the forest will not be missed."

"I am not so sure, Darius. I was witness to strange activities in the woods nights ago. At that time, a group of men had come into the edge of the forest and attacked one of their own. Cyrean observed, as I did from another vantage, the death of the man. He went to where the man had deposited an object during his flight, and when Cyrean returned home that evening he carried something with him in a leather pouch. He was very secretive in his actions and spent much time observing his surroundings as if to assure himself that no one was watching. There is much afoot of which I would know. When Cyrean and his companion take the women back to their wagon, I will enter the hut and find what secret Cyrean would keep from us."

"Is not Cyrean's great mastiff always at the hut?"

"Yes, but he has been injured and cannot move. He will not prove a threat to me."

"Then may good fortune aid you in your search. I must get back and report my findings to the council. When the opportunity presents itself, search the hut for the object and bring it to us at once."

Darius turned and made his way back through the forest, and Bartold settled into the shadows of the tree to maintain his surveillance of the hut.

The next day, activity in the hut began early. Cyrean had lain awake much of the night debating within himself how it would be best to get the crystal to the king. He felt that it would be advisable to get other opinions as to how he should proceed. He trusted the other inhabitants of the hut and was convinced they could help him in his course of action. He would tell them today, and together they could make a decision that would be prudent for all involved. When he arose, he checked Wolfen, who had rested peacefully during the night.

He seemed stronger and his breathing was more regular now. The queen, too, had rested well and was still asleep when Cyrean arose. Grinold stirred when he sensed movement and was soon on his feet and tending to the fire. If things went well, the guests would all be well enough to travel the next day, and Cyrean could begin his journey to the castle. Cyrean hoped Grinold would accompany him. He had grown to trust the man even though Grinold's curiosity about the crystal at first had concerned him a great deal.

The two men stepped outside to talk, allowing the women to rest. They would need their energy when they began their trip the next day. Grinold looked at his companion curiously as he seemed occupied with thoughts that were worlds away.

"Your body performs its accustomed rituals, but your mind has charted its own course this morning, Cyrean. There is a troubled look in your eyes that can only mean you have spent a restless night worrying about someone or some thing," observed Grinold. "Are you concerned for the safety of our guests? I have seen you more than once look at the Lady Aurienna with a fondness that tells me she has smitten you with her charm. Am I right in my observation?"

"She is unlike any woman I have ever known, Grinold. Though it is true my experience with women has been limited, I can see she is an eagle among sparrows. I will be much saddened with her departure, but I have nothing to offer her to keep her here. I am but a poor peasant, and she would not deign to consider me a proper suitor for her affections."

"You carry your own worth too lightly, Cyrean. Some women consider the measure of a man to be more than wealth and position. I have seen her casting looks at you when you were not aware. Be as bold as you were the day we fought the swampsweeper. Put your heart in her care and she will not rebuff you if I am any judge of her character."

"That may be for another time, Grinold. I must first accomplish the mission I have set for myself and see the king on an urgent matter. Today, I will reveal things that I know to all of you and ask for help in the completion of that which has lately troubled me."

"I will do as you ask of me, Cyrean. Use me as you wish."

"Let us wake the women and have our morning repast. Then I will reveal a curious thing that may require all our wits to fathom."

Upon reentering the hut, Cyrean's disposition brightened when he observed Lady Ofra up and moving around the room. The poultices had worked their magic well. She smiled when they entered the hut and invited them to sit at the table. Aurienna gave each one a large portion of the morning meal that she had been preparing over the fire.

"You will have to excuse my poor offering," she said as she placed bowls on the table. "I have not the skills in this area that most women have. My father taught me the sword and the lance and how to ride a horse. Those things are important in a man's world, but I fear they have not prepared me for the role that most women aspire to, that of a wife and mother."

"A wife must be all things," observed Cyrean. "When a man is hungry, she is the preparer of meals. When he is sick, she must be his nursemaid. In those times when life throws misfortune at her family, she must be the comfort and staff upon which the members lean. When danger threatens, she must fight like the she-bear to defend those she loves. A man without such a woman is but half a man. Lady Aurienna, your presence would brighten any abode regardless of how humble it may be."

Aurienna's cheeks colored as she listened to Cyrean's praise, offered in genuine admiration to a woman whom he saw as the culmination of everything that is fine and noble in mankind regardless of gender.

"I had not seen this side of my companion, heretofore," remarked Grinold. "Lady Aurienna, you have made much of an impression on our host. He is not one to offer praise lightly."

At Grinold's remarks, it was Cyrean's turn to redden, and he dropped his head as he stirred the contents of the bowl in front of him. His feelings for Aurienna ran deep, but these things could be spoken of at a later time. He felt an urgent need to unburden himself of the secret he had kept for days now, and he rose and went to the shelf over his bed.

Pushing aside the bowls that covered the shelf, he extracted a leather pouch hidden behind them and reseated himself at the table.

"What I am about to reveal to you must remain our secret for a time," he said, placing the leather bag on the table. "Until the time this bag and its contents be in the hands of the king, no word of its location can spoken. On this I must have your solemn pledge."

"What you tell us will remain with us," Aurienna assured him. "What can be of that nature that pales your features when you speak of it?"

"Within this bag lies the Crystal of Light," said Cyrean, picking up the pouch and holding it at arm's length as if that short distance from the object would protect him from its effects.

"I knew you must have it!" exclaimed Grinold. "My senses are never wrong. I had come in search of the object on the command of Tobias, with the intention of taking it back to him."

"You have an alliance with Tobias? How can you proclaim to be my friend and the protector to these women when Tobias represents all that is evil?" asked Cyrean as he drew

A Like Trust

back the crystal and placed it into his jerkin.

"That was before I knew the truly dark nature of the man," explained Grinold. "Since that time, I have had opportunity to assess my relationship to Tobias and have found it sorely lacking. Cyrean, you have helped me to realize that Tobias can never have the crystal. Have not my actions in recent days assured you that I can be trusted?"

"Grinold, I have not the gift that you do to judge the worth of people," said Aurienna, " but I have the instincts of my father, who is a good judge of men, and it tells me you are an honorable man."

"I, too, have seen only kindness from this man," added Lady Ofra. "If it be truth that a man's worth is in his actions, then Grinold merits our trust."

"It seems that I am outnumbered though I would as well cast my lot for you," agreed Cyrean. "I will take you for a friend until you prove unworthy of my faith in you."

"Then we will remain friends, for I have renounced my loyalty to Tobias. No longer can I endure his cruel nature."

"I have heard of the Crystal of Light," said Aurienna, "but I know little of its power. It must be great indeed to attract so many men to it. How can it help the king?"

"The crystal feeds on light or any other form of energy," explained Cyrean. "It can take the smallest amount of light and multiply it manifold. Direct the rays toward an enemy, and his ranks would be decimated in a matter of minutes. Simply holding the crystal in the hands just for a few seconds can drain all the energy from the body. Placed in the hands of one who would know how to harness its potential, it could be the most devastating weapon the world has ever seen."

"And Tobias would know how to use the crystal for such a purpose," said Grinold. "The crystal can never be passed to him. The world as we know it would never be the same again."

"I must be part of the plan to get the crystal to the king," said Aurienna. "It is an adventure that would show my father that I am worthy to fight by his side. Let me go with you to Eustan. I have the means to get an audience with the king."

"But what of Lady Ofra?" questioned Cyrean. "Does she not need your assistance now more that ever with the wound to hinder her movements?"

Aurienna's eyes clouded as she saw the impossibility of leaving the queen alone. Though the wound was almost well, she would still need care and companionship on the rest of the trip to Parvidian. She could not leave her in the care of soldiers who knew nothing but how to fight. She would have to continue the trip until Lady Ofra reached safety.

"You are right, of course. I must go with Lady Ofra, but as soon as she is delivered safely to Parvidian, I will return to Eustan with the soldiers. With hard riding, I will get to Eustan not long after you arrive. Wait for me before you see the king."

"We will wait two days," said Cyrean. "If Grinold will accompany me on the trip, the crystal will be doubly safe. After the two days, we must try to get our own audience with the king. It would not be prudent to keep the crystal in our possession any longer."

"I can ask no more than this favor," said Aurienna. "My return will be swift."

"I must see the crystal," urged Grinold. "If I am to be its guardian, should I not be able to hold it and feel its power?"

Cyrean hesitated as he pulled the leather pouch from his pocket. He remembered the incident that night he first held the crystal in his hand and how it had almost totally sapped his strength in just the few seconds before he could return it to the pouch. But Grinold deserved to know what he was protecting.

"Very well," agreed Cyrean, "but I will be here to aid you if the power of the crystal should affect you adversely. Lady Aurienna and Lady Ofra, you should not look directly at the crystal as it could harm your eyes. Even the small light of the candles can be amplified to cause harm if one is not prepared."

"I am ready," said Grinold. "Place the crystal into my hand."

Cyrean untied the string from the pouch and slowly rolled the crystal into Grinold's hand. Instantly, as the crystal quickly assimilated the faint light in the hut, the room became filled with a brightness unmatched by anything other than the sun. It filled the room and became a presence that could almost be felt it its intensity. Lady Ofra and Aurienna turned away and tightly shut their eyes to avoid the brilliance. Grinold had held the crystal in his hands for only seconds when he felt the energy draining from his body. He sank down upon the floor and his hand opened, allowing the crystal to roll from his grasp.

"Quickly," urged Cyrean, "we must get the crystal out of the light and into the pouch. Extend your hand, Grinold. We must return the crystal to the bag before we all perish from the light that even now grows stronger."

"It escaped my hands, Cyrean. Search for it upon the floor. It cannot have rolled far."

Extending his hands and keeping his eyes tightly shut, Cyrean groped on the floor for the crystal. Crawling to where Grinold lay, weakened from his experience having been in contact with the crystal, Cyrean managed to grasp the ball of glass which had now begun to pulsate as it fed upon the light in the room. Moving swiftly, Cyrean returned the crystal to the pouch and cinched the string, shutting out all light from the object within.

For several minutes, all the inhabitants of the hut waited

for their senses to readjust before attempting to stand. Even Wolfen seemed to be affected as he blinked repeatedly trying to wash the glare from his eyes.

"It was unlike anything I have ever experienced!" Grinold exclaimed. "Had it not been placed back into the pouch in timely fashion, I fear we would all have fallen victim to its power."

"Whoever works with the crystal to harness its power will have to observe it through a darkened lens," observed Grinold. "It will not be an easy task to control such a weapon."

"I do not wish to make the attempt," Cyrean assured him. "When it is delivered to the king, it will become the responsibility of his generals to control its power."

Placing the bag in its original place on the shelf, Cyrean concealed its hiding place with the bowls and turned to Arienna and the queen.

"My ladies, you have been a witness to the power of the crystal. Now you see why I must get it to the king. Tomorrow, Grinold and I will escort you back to the river where your soldiers await your return. Then we must journey to Eustan and complete our mission. Remember, Lady Aurienna, we will wait only two days for your return and then we must get the crystal to the king."

"Do not wait," said Aurienna. "It is too much responsibility to hold onto the crystal if it can be gotten immediately to the king. Use the ring I gave you, Cyrean. It will get you to the king as easily as if I were present."

"Tomorrow, we will take you to the river," said Cyrean. "Then we will return for the crystal and to make arrangements for Wolfen. We can leave him with the old hermit for a few days during our absence. When we return, he will be well again."

"May God lend wings to your feet and grant you a safe

journey," said Aurienna. "All that we have is now in your hands. I will see you and Grinold again when my mission is complete."

The rest of the day was spent in preparation for the morrow. As Aurienna and Lady Ofra gathered their belongings for the next day's journey, they thought of all the responsibility that now lay in the hands of two young men whom they had only met three short days ago. Cyrean and Grinold spoke little, each burdened with the realization that within their possession lay the instrument that could turn the tide of war into the king's favor. It would be a daunting task, but each man knew he would give his life if necessary to see it to completion.

Chapter Fourteen
The Council of Twelve

Morning found the small band up and ready to begin their day. Lady Ofra was able to walk short distances without rest, but Grinold carried the litter in case the need arose to transport her as they had done on the trip into the forest. Checking on Wolfen one last time, Cyrean spoke to him in a comforting voice. Whether he understood or whether it was the close relationship between animal and master, who can say? However it was, Wolfen knew that Cyrean was leaving for a short space of time and he whined softly. Cyrean took the few pieces of clothing the women had with them and put them into a small bag that he flung across his shoulder. He closed the door but he did not bar it, knowing that only the dwarf clan would be able to work the latch to gain entrance. To bar it this time would only arouse suspicion. No one ever came into the woods, and he never worried about his possessions. He had left water and food for Wolfen on the hearth where he could reach it even in his restricted condition.

The companions set out on the trip with mixed emotions, knowing that they would soon be separating and perhaps never meet again. They talked very little and the trip to the edge of the forest seemed to go too quickly for Cyrean and Aurienna. When they reached the river, the soldiers were ready to go, having received word by Grinold the previous day that Lady Ofra was well enough to travel, and they would be resuming the duty of taking the women to Parvidian. The parting was with great sorrow on both sides, and Cyrean felt a dark gloom settle on his heart as Aurienna waved a last goodbye from the coach window.

The two men began the return trip quickly. They would have to prepare Wolfen for the trip to the hermit's hut. The litter that Grinold carried would have to be used for Wolfen since the large dog would not be able to walk any part of the distance. The round trip had taken over two hours, and the men were eager to be on their way to Eustan. As they entered the cleared area and viewed the hut, Grinold sensed instantly that something was wrong.

As they approached, the men could see that the door was open, and Wolfen lay with his body half outside the hut. He was in great pain and whimpered when Cyrean reached him and raised his head. Inside his mouth was a piece of a garment with a small stud attached. Grinold instantly recognized the decorative piece. It was identical to the one that he had seen on entering the forest for the first time. Cyrean knew it to be the type that Bartold regularly wore on all his clothing. He gently coaxed the piece of clothing from Wolfen's mouth and held it up to the light. There was blood on the remnant, and Cyrean knew the owner of the garment had received a wound. He was sure he knew who that person was. He and Grinold entered the hut and saw chaos all around. The beds had been overturned. Clothing was strewn on the cots, and the few meager belongings in the hut were scattered everywhere. Cyrean stared helplessly at the debris lying scattered about the small house. The leather pouch was gone. He did not need to search the hut. He knew it had been found by the intruder. Mentally chiding himself for leaving it in such an unprotected place, he turned back to Wolfen and examined the loyal animal. It had taken what strength he had left in his body to try and protect his master's property. He had not been able to stop the thief, but he had made him pay for his spoils. It now became imperative for them to get Wolfen to the hermit for the care he would need. Then they would need to return and go deep into the forest to the home of the dwarfs. Cyrean knew what to look for in his quest. One of them would have a large piece missing from one of his legs. Cyrean was sure he knew on which dwarf to look.

They placed Wolfen on the litter and made yet another trip to the edge of woods. As they crossed the river to the road, they heard riders approaching. Quietly placing the litter on the ground, the companions waited for the group of riders to pass, thinking it might be the same band they had encountered earlier. Cyrean was in no mood to face another quarrel, and he hoped they would simply move on toward whatever destination lured them. Grinold suddenly tensed and peered sharply at the leader as they passed the spot of concealment. He looked as if prepared to spring until Cyrean, noticing his agitation, placed a hand on his shoulder to calm him. When the horsemen had passed, the two men stood and watched the riders disappear into the distance before again lifting Wolfen and moving on toward the home of the hermit.

"Why did you almost give us away, Grinold? You looked as if it were a band of ghost riders searching for lost souls."

"I almost wish that it had been spirits. That was Tobias in the front. I should have risen and driven a sword through his heart. Even if I had been killed in the doing, I would have rid the world of one more tyrant, and the kingdom would have been safe for a time."

"No," said Cyrean. "The time is not now. You would have been overwhelmed by superior numbers, and I also would have been killed in your defense. That would not have helped the king or his cause. We must regain the crystal, for I know where it is. Only then can we be assured that the king will have the power he needs to defeat Tobias. Let us carry our precious burden to safety, and then we will visit the dwarf village. There our hunt for the crystal will end."

Grinold nodded in agreement and soon Wolfen was in good hands. With a promise that they would be back within a fortnight, the two men left the hermit and returned to the

The Council of Twelve

forest. Cyrean had been to the dwarf village just once before but he remembered the path. They would have to be even more careful when they came to the village because all manner of traps surrounded the perimeter of the grounds. It would take all of Cyrean's intelligence and Grinold's keen senses to get into the village safely.

Within the village, the elders were meeting in council to discuss the new fortune that had fallen into their hands. Bartold had returned from his mission with a great treasure. Some of the men had heard from the injured Bartold when he had limped into camp about his great defeat of the brute Wolfen. In fierce combat he had dispatched the large dog with only small damage to his leg. That was his badge of courage which he readily showed to any that wanted to hear his tale. He had killed the crystal's protector and brought to the dwarf people a great weapon that would make them the most feared of all who walked the realm. Now the Outworlders would know of true power. No longer would the dwarf clan be subjected to loathing and hatred. Bartold swelled with pride as he was followed through the street by those who wanted to know how he obtained such a treasure.

When the crystal was placed in its pouch on the table, twelve dwarfs sat down to discuss its future use. This was the Council of Twelve. All the workings of the dwarf clan were determined by these select few. To be a member of the Council of Twelve was the highest station a dwarf could receive. The honor was conferred usually only on the elders of the village or those who had distinguished themselves in some way in service to the people. Bartold hoped one day to sit at the head of the council as the Most High of the Highest. He was sure that his contribution today would soon bring him the position he desired.

This was a special meeting to discuss the crystal. When

Bartold was ushered into the room, the buzz of talking ceased, and each council member turned to look at their new hero. Murmurs of approval went around the table when Bartold's adventures were related to the ones at the council table. Bartold stood proudly as he was applauded for his bravery in the fight with the great hound, a beast nearly twice the size of Bartold with jaws of steel which he had narrowly escaped. His leg wound had received great care, and he had even been carried to the meeting in a high chair to receive his honors.

"We meet here on this auspicious occasion to honor Bartold, our champion," intoned the Highest of the Most High. "With little thought of the danger into which he boldly thrust himself, he has defeated a brute of great strength, the protector of the crystal, the most hideous of creatures in hand to claw combat. He stabbed the creature many times, eventually killing the animal and in the process has brought great hurt to himself. Let us all celebrate his victory and honor the one who has brought us the crystal. With its power, the dwarf clan will have to fear no man or beast. We will be all-powerful, and the Outworlders will pay obeisance to us when we pass. Three cheers for our champion."

"All hail to Bartold, All hail to Bartold, all hail to Bartold." The cheer went round the room and Bartold stood and beamed as the accolades rained down upon him.

No sooner had the cheers ceased than the door to the council room burst open.

"What! Is it the way of the dwarf clan to honor a thief and rogue as their savior now?" shouted Cyrean, as he and Grinold strode into the room.

The council gasped in surprise and stood as one as they suddenly realized strangers had come into their camp undetected.

"It is the two Outworlders, Cyrean and his companion

The Council of Twelve

Grinold," choked Bartold in fear. "They have followed me here and intend to kill me for the slaying of the beast Wolfen. Rally my brothers to the aid of brave Bartold who has this night done what no other dwarf has accomplished in battle. We must stand as one against the two Outworlders."

"Stop your prattling, you foolish dwarf," responded Cyrean as he looked around the room for signs of weapons. "You know why I have come. You have stolen something from me and I want it returned."

"We have nothing of yours, Cyrean. How came you here through our traps and defenses?" asked the Highest of the Most High.

"Defenses? The sightless bogbear with only his sense of smell and hearing to aid him could defeat your defenses with a mere stick in its paw. My companion and I came through your village undetected because the dwarf clan have grown lazy over the years and think that no one could ever penetrate their traps. Silly, silly dwarfs! You stand and celebrate a coward. Give me what is mine and let us return to our hut where the smell of fear is not so strong."

"Ah, Ah, Ah. Hear him, my brothers!" laughed Bartold in a shrill voice. "The great Cyrean and his companion would take on the whole of the dwarf nation. Who is the foolish one here to come into our midst and make demands?"

"Give me the crystal, Bartold. I see it upon the table. You do not know the danger you possess. I will forgive this intrusion on my home and the dishonor it has brought you. If the object is not returned, no dwarf or Outworlder will be safe. You have not harmed me or any that I love yet. Therefore, I can be charitable if the crystal is returned."

"What of the beast Wolfen!" exclaimed the Highest of the Most High. Did Bartold not dispatch him in combat?"

"Wolfen will be well soon enough. His injuries were not

received of Bartold but from a swampsweeper we bested in battle. The only injuries received when Bartold encountered Wolfen in the hut were those given to a cowardly thief when he tried to slip by the injured animal after stealing the crystal. May thy leg plague thee for many fortnights, "Brave" Bartold, for thy craven ways."

"Perhaps Bartold is not the hero we would have liked," spoke another member of the council. "Still, he did bring the crystal to us and now it is our possession, not yours."

"Is theft not accounted as a crime in the realm of the dwarfs?" asked Grinold. "I have been a thief and have often been punished for my deeds. Are you not held to account for like actions?"

"Did Cyrean not also steal the crystal?" asked Bartold. "With my own eyes, I saw him go to the place of concealment in the rocks near the highway. He took the crystal that the stranger hid in the rocks. If the crystal belonged to the stranger, was this not theft?"

"Can it be said that the crystal belongs to anyone?" asked the Highest of the Most High as he looked around the room. " I would think it belongs to the one who possesses it at any given time. The crystal is as old as the earth. No one can claim to own such a treasure. Therefore, it is ours, for we now have it in our possession."

"It is the nature of the foolish to bandy words," said Cyrean. " It is even more foolish to try to reason with them that do so. Yet, I must try, for too much depends on what we do here today."

"What reasoning could you give that would convince us to turn the crystal over to the Outworlders?" asked Bartold. "They have shown us nothing but contempt for centuries. We have been slaves and objects of ridicule for their pleasure. Now you say we should turn over the very instrument that will place us as equal to them that persecute us."

"It is not for the Outworlders alone that I make this request. The dwarf people will suffer as well if the crystal should fall into a tyrant's hands. I do not ask for the crystal for myself. My intent was not to keep it but to deliver the object to King Malvore to help him in his battle against Tobias. You say that you want your forest to remain unchanged. If you keep the crystal, the world as you know it will change. The Crystal of Light was never meant to be used for self-serving purposes. Used for the good of man, it could be our salvation, but place it in evil hands and it could destroy good and evil alike."

"Yes," replied Bartold. "There will be change but we will use the crystal to cause it, and the dwarf people will rule and the Outworlder's will be our slaves."

"Members of the council, hear me!" exclaimed Cyrean. "The very words of Bartold condemn you to the evil of which I have spoken. The crystal cannot be used for personal gain whether it be for wealth, power, or control of another people. You cannot erase centuries of persecution with a weapon. If it could be done, prejudice would not exist because it has been tried many times before without success. Weapons of war have wiped out whole civilizations, and still hatred among people of different races continues. We must learn from past mistakes. Bartold would have you believe that you can gain the respect of others through the use of power. I tell you just the opposite is achieved. If you conquer the Outworlders with the crystal and enslave them, how is that different than what you contend they have done to you?"

"My friend speaks true," agreed Grinold. "I have felt the power of the crystal. I have seen what men will do to achieve it. I have traveled much in the world outside these woods, and I know how intolerant one race is of another, but the power to enslave is not the answer. Mankind must learn to live together.

All races must unite for the common good, or tyrants such as Tobias will conquer the world. Then indeed will we be one race, for we will all be slaves under his control. I know people can change because I have felt such a transformation within myself. For many years I had thought only of myself and used the talents God gave me for my personal gain. Though I had the ability to make fools of others and play them for material wealth, I was not happy. I have recently discovered what a man truly needs to be content. It is not gold, which only has the value that we place upon it. For what is gold but a shiny metal? Will it feed you when you are hungry or comfort you when you are cold and alone? And what if you conquer the whole world but have no true friends with whom to share your conquest? How hollow would be the victory!"

"The words of the Outworlders have merit," observed Darius who held the rank of eleven in the council. "I do not want to conquer but only to live a good life with the benefits that should be afforded all men. If the crystal is a weapon and not a force for good, I do not want to keep it. Perhaps it would be best to place it in the deepest and darkest pit in the forest to be sucked down into the middle of the earth. Such a fearsome thing should not exist if evil is its only purpose."

"Sometimes," said Cyrean, "the qualities of a weapon, as also would be true in the quality of a man, is in their use. I have heard that King Malvore is a just king. His reign is under attack by one who can neither be called just nor fit to be king. I believe the crystal in the right hands could shift the outcome of the battle to the king. Give me the crystal and Grinold and I will risk our lives to see that it gets into the right hands."

"Your arguments have been strong and reasonable in their content," said the Highest of the Most High. "The Council of Twelve will meet and discuss their merits. We have no wish to be unreasonable. Stay the night with us. You will be given food

The Council of Twelve

and shelter. Tomorrow, we will meet with you and your companion again. At that time you will be allowed to leave our village with or without the crystal."

"Bartold asks that the Council allow him to meet as well and discuss the future of the crystal. After all, it was I who took the crystal from the Outworlders. I should have the right to say how it should be used."

"You have been dishonest with your own people," said Darius. "You have lied to bolster your standing among us. While we applaud the initiative you have shown in acquiring the Crystal of Light, neither your desires nor your ambitions come before the good of the people. Go from our sight and think on what we have said here."

Bartold slunk from the room and went to his home. It is difficult to say whether words can change a heart. As Cyrean and Grinold watched him walk away, they knew the ambitious dwarf would resurface at another time. Neither man wanted to make enemies of the dwarfs. In the upcoming battles, all the clans in the provinces would be needed to battle Tobias. The dwarf clan would need to fight to protect the forest which would not be inviolate against the forces of war.

It proved to be a restless night for the two men, and both were awake when the rooks' cawing signaled the arrival of morning. The village began to stir and an hour later Cyrean and Grinold found themselves once again in the council chambers. The stern looks of the members convinced Cyrean that their arguments had not accomplished their purpose. Grinold too observed the countenances of the men around the table, but he looked more keenly into the eyes of the Highest of the Most High. As he stared intently at the dwarf, Grinold's face began to relax and a smile curved the corner of his lip. He knew what the answer would be, and he placed his hand on Cyrean's arm to reassure him.

The significance of the touch did not go unnoticed, and Cyrean relaxed ever so slightly as he tried to convince himself that Grinold had never been wrong before. The Council of Twelve were all seated and the Highest of the High had begun to speak.

"We members of the council have debated long," he began. "We know little of the power of the weapon we possess other than what we have been told by others. None of the council have ever witnessed its power. We wish to be prudent in our decision. A demonstration of its abilities might convince us to lend it to the king's service. Would Cyrean and Grinold have objection to this?"

"The light from the crystal is very powerful," warned Cyrean. "It is within your right to know of its strength, but hold us not liable for its actions."

"We will take responsibility for any damages the crystal causes," Darius assured the two men.

"Then we have no objections."

The Highest of the Most High took the pouch and placed it on the table. He carefully untied the string and prepared to roll the crystal onto the table.

"Wait." said Darius. "Let us place several candles closer so that we can get a better look at its markings."

"That would not be prudent," warned Cyrean, "as the crystal takes light and magnifies it many times. I have seen what it can do with just one candle."

"We would know its full effects to judge it more accurately," responded the Highest of the Most High. "Bring forth more candles."

A dozen large candles were place around the bag that contained the crystal. The Highest of the Most High took the bag and rolled the crystal onto the table. Instantly, the tent was filled with brilliant colors. An explosion of light shot from the

The Council of Twelve

glass ball and ignited the roof of the meeting chambers, starting a fire which quickly spread through the hut. At the instant the crystal had been taken from the bag, Cyrean and Grinold had shielded their eyes with their hands. As the fire spread, they were the only ones capable of finding the door to the hut. Cries of panic came from the blinded dwarfs as they futilely searched for the door.

"The fire will consume them if we do not help!" cried Grinold. "Help me, Cyrean, to lead them out."

"Each man reach out and take the hand of another. Join hands. We will lead you through the door before the fires destroys our only exit. Quickly!" shouted Grinold.

"Start them forward, Grinold." urged Cyrean. "I will retrieve the crystal before everything is destroyed."

Shielding his eyes as best he could against the light of the crystal, Cyrean placed his hand over it and instantly felt the intense energy begin to take his strength. He fell to the floor, still clutching the crystal in his hand and began to crawl toward the door. Having gotten the others to safety, Grinold realized that Cyrean was still inside the inferno. He fought his way through the flames and located the struggling Cyrean whom he pulled to safety just as the beams of the ceiling collapsed around them. He took the crystal and covered it with a cloak, and the brightness around them diminished except for the flames that now consumed the council chamber.

All the council members had managed to escape the fire with minor burns and bruises from the falling debris. They lay gasping, trying to clear the smoke from their lungs. Others in the village had now arrived and were helping their companions to safety and fighting the fire that by now had almost consumed the hut.

Cyrean took the crystal and wrapped it tightly inside the cloak before placing it inside his jerkin.

"You have seen the power of the crystal," Cyrean said to the villagers. "My companion and I will take it where it can be used to build rather than destroy. Tend your injured. We go to Eustan where the king will receive us and the weapon we bring. Pray that never again will you see its power in the Dark Wood."

Realizing how vital was time in the equation of war, Cyrean and Grinold immediately left the village and began their trek to Eustan. With good luck in finding coach or horses, they could be at the palace in two days. With the memory of recent events to spur them, they moved rapidly toward the road and Eustan.

Chapter Fifteen
Beauty in an Unusual Place

The group of riders came slowly down the road, scanning the hills and the terrain around them carefully. A rider dismounted at the command of the leader and looked at the ground for signs that would indicate what they sought had come this way. The leader, who obviously was used to giving orders and having them obeyed, barked commands at the other riders who fanned out in different directions doing searches of their own. After fifteen minutes of fruitless effort, they rejoined and continued their ride.

A peasant wagon met the riders and was stopped. For several minutes the leader asked questions of the old man who drove the wagon. After a time the wagon continued on its journey and the leader spoke to the group of men.

"Our search has yielded nothing. I must return to camp and be sure all is in readiness for the march. The tracker is dead or has defected our ranks and gone into hiding. I cannot believe a man so skilled in hunting would fall victim to anything in the forest. With his instincts, he may have sensed my intentions for him and now has joined the army of the king or gone out on his own. Whatever the cause for his desertion, I have no more time to give to him. More important to me is the finding of the queen and her companion. Have none of the travelers we stopped today seen a wagon bearing two women and traveling with soldiers?"

"None, my lord," answered one of the riders.

"I know they would have come this way. They were not in the party that my soldiers raided in the north. This must be the direction they took. The two provinces of Arminius and Parvidian lie in this direction to the South. I must return to camp, but the rest of you are to split into two groups and search these provinces. I want the queen and her companion found and brought to me. Kill any that try to shelter them from us. With the two women as hostages, we will have the advantage that the crystal would have given us."

Tobias spurred his horse toward the camp and the remaining riders split into two groups and rode off in different directions to the south.

To the north of this band of riders, Cyrean and Grinold were making their way to Eustan. The two men had walked several miles before a peddler stopped and allowed them to climb on the back of his wagon. He was going to a small village several miles to the east of Eustan, but he could get them closer to their destination. After several hours on the road, the driver saw smoke from a campfire. The day being almost gone, he directed his wagon toward the camp where hopefully they would find food and hospitality for the night.

Grinold looked quickly over the group as the wagon pulled into the campsite. He had to be certain that it was not men from the camp of Tobias. He knew by now that he would be a hunted man and certainly there would be a price on his head. A close inspection of the dress of the clan told him they were mere gypsies and presented little or no danger to them.

The leader of the gypsies welcomed them and bade them to help themselves to food and drink, which the three men did gladly. The day's travel had been a weary time. The wagon had moved slowly, and Cyrean and Grinold had fretted often about the snail's pace at which they traveled. Horses were needed but good horses were not to be had without some good fortune providing them. As they looked around the camp, they saw nothing that would make their travel to Eustan faster.

A young woman brought the men a sweet liquor to drink after they had eaten. She was very comely, with features that were very different from those of her traveling companions. She had skin the color of cream, and her dark brown eyes were large like the young fawns that Grinold often saw when hunting in the fall. Her hair was the darkest of reds and fell upon her shoulders in waves. She smiled enigmatically as she handed Grinold his drink, and he knew the secrets behind those dark eyes would be worth exploring.

Grinold's observations had not gone unnoticed by his host who sat down on a large rock next to the tracker and cautioned him in a quiet voice.

"Stranger, I see that you have taken a fancy to my daughter. I must warn you that she has been spoken for, and the man who has claimed her is a soldier and fierce and strong. It would not be wise to try and take something so beautiful from such a man."

"Pardon my manners if I do seem rude, my host, but she has not the dark skin of the gypsy folk," observed Grinold. "And when I looked into her eyes, I saw more than a gypsy heritage. Is she truly your daughter?"

"She has been my daughter for over eighteen summers. When she was an infant, her village was raided. We happened upon the disaster soon after, and I heard her crying and found her in a basket near a small stream. The parents had hidden her there from the raiders. Her parents and most of the other villagers who had not fled to safety were killed. Since that tragedy, we have been her family, and we have loved her as our own."

"Does she love the soldier?" asked Grinold.

"What is love?" the host replied. "Marriage for a woman is a necessity. If she marries this man, she will be cared for by him. He will provide a home and shelter and perhaps love in time. And in time she will come to love him also. We have not the niceties of royalty or the high born. When opportunity comes to better ourselves, we must take the nearest way. My daughter has a strong will, and she says she will not marry a man who is not of her choosing. But he comes for her tomorrow, and I will force her to go with him. It is the only way to escape the vagabond life we lead."

Grinold watched her as she moved about the camp preparing their beds for the night. She would never marry someone she did not love This was obvious in the way she carried herself and in the fierce look of her eyes. He often sensed her looking his way when she thought he would not see. The connection between them was strong, and he knew he must talk with her again. When she took the eating utensil from him, he placed his hand upon her arm and spoke of his feelings.

"My lady, I am Grinold, hunter and tracker, and hopefully a good right arm for the king someday. I have asked of your father if I might court your favor. He spoke of a soldier who has claimed you for his own. Say that you do love him and I will not trouble you further. Say but nay and I will fight for the right to court you as would any man who saw your beauty and spirit."

"Grinold, my name is Madelyn. I have been with the gypsy clan for eighteen years now. In that time I have seen many men come and go from the camp. None have stirred my feelings as did your arrival today. It is said that the heart will know when the right suitor appears. I feel that it is so. I do not love the soldier who will take me from this camp tomorrow . My father wants to make the match because he has been promised twenty gold dragons for my hand. He does not understand what it is to be loved and to love someone who values you for what you are. I would leave tonight if I had the means to escape this impending betrothal."

" Madelyn, come with us when we leave tomorrow. I know that it is sudden and reckless to follow someone whom you have just met, but I sense a bond with you that I have never felt with another. I can offer you little now, but my fortune is yet to be made, and it will be made in the king's service. Will you come with me?"

"What of my father? I cannot leave without his blessings."

"I will speak to him and make arrangements. Has he any horses that can carry us to Eustan? The peddler with whom we travel cannot take us to our destination, and you will need a horse for the trip."

"He has two fine geldings that he favors highly. I do not think he would let us take them. If I leave, he will lose twenty gold dragons. He will not take the loss of the gold and of the horses. It is not the gypsy way."

"I will tell him that I take great news to the king and any that help me now will be richly rewarded later. He will have his twenty dragons and more when we reach Eustan. He may travel with us if he wishes until he receives his reward."

"You may try if you wish. I believe he will do what is best for me," she said hopefully.

That night before they retired, Grinold approached Cyrean with his plan and spoke to him of his love for Madelyn.

"Indeed, my friend, you move quickly," said Cyrean, smiling at his companion. "I have been witness to the signals between you both. At another time I would advise you not to rush headlong into love, but these are unusual times and who can determine the ways of the heart? Tomorrow when we leave, Madelyn is welcome to ride with us. The promise of the twenty dragons I will help you fulfill. If our host will give us the horses, double that amount will be his."

When dawn arose the following day, Grinold approached Madelyn's father with his proposal. Cyrean sat by the campfire eating his morning repast and listened as the two men bargained.

"'Twenty dragons, you say, and another twenty for the

horses? That is a princely sum. How do I know that you will fulfill your bargain? Once you have gone with my daughter and my two fine horses, how do I know you will ever return?" asked the host.

"You may go with us to Eustan. There you will be given all that I have promised," said Grinold.

Cyrean approached the two men and stood beside Grinold as the host deliberated the offer.

"Look at this ring," he said. "It bears upon it the crest of the king. We will stand in high favor once he sees we have it in our possession. He will grant us whatever we wish, and you will be paid your forty gold dragons. With such wealth, you will never have to travel the roads again. Would not such a possibility be worth taking a chance?"

"I will go with you. I will bring my wagon which can travel twice the pace the peddler's wagon makes. My daughter and her suitor can ride the two horses. Together we can make good time to Eustan and there I will receive the gold dragons."

"It is done," said Cyrean. "Let us leave now. We need to make haste before the day has run its course. By nightfall we should be close to the palace. Only when I see its gleaming towers will I feel safe."

The men quickly saddled the horses, and Madelyn and her father pulled the wagon out onto the road. Within the hour, the wagon and riders were on their way to Eustan.

Within the walled city, King Malvore waited for Lord Hadreon in the council chambers. He had not received news from the caravan carrying the queen and Aurienna. It was now the fourth day since their departure, and he was looking for word from the returning soldiers that they had been safely delivered.

As Lord Hadreon entered the chamber, he could see the worried look on the face of the king, and he understood the nature of his concern. He, too, hoped for some word soon on his daughter. He knew the plan they had formulated was a good one, but it is the nature of a father to worry about his child's safety.

"My liege, concern sits upon your face like a cloud, obscuring the hopeful visage that we must present to the people. We have done all we can do in preparing for Tobias and his forces. Now let him come. We have supplies enough to last any siege they may attempt. Entrance inside the city walls is impossible without assistance from within, and we have none that are not loyal to our cause. We will be getting a message soon about our families, and I know that will be good news. The most difficult task is to wait, and in that we must be strong, for there is little else we can do. A good soldier often has to be patient if victory is to be his."

"I know that all you say is true," acknowledged the king. "But it does not make it easier to bear. Stay with me, my friend, for a while. I will summon the servants for food and drink, and we will talk of old times when wars were honorable and families remained together."

"I am, as always, your servant, my king. I will join you and we will speak of many things that will take our minds away from present problems."

Had the king known of the dangers the queen and Aurienna had already faced, little sleep would he have had that night. Fate had placed their fortunes into the hands of two young men who were even now on their way to the castle to bring him news that would lighten his heart and bolster his chances of victory against Tobias.

"The wagon moves quickly, Grinold, my friend. With these fine horses, we will be within sight of the city by nightfall," said Cyrean. "Are you and Madelyn faring well?"

"The sands of time may course more slowly now," said

Grinold. "With Madelyn by my side, I notice not the passage of time nor the hard roads upon which we travel."

Cyrean envied his friend and he wondered where Aurienna was now. She would have reached Parvidian by this time. Did she think of him also? He looked at the beautiful countryside as they traveled to Eustan, and he wondered how long that beauty would last if the power of the crystal were unleashed. He had been tempted many times during the trip to take the crystal from his pocket and hide it deeply in the earth where it could never be found again. Even used for good, it might devastate the countryside and destroy all the beauty around along with the enemy. It was a difficult choice to make, and it would remain so until the moment he placed the crystal into the king's hands.

As Cyrean pondered his choices, a cloud of dust had formed no more than a mile behind them. He wondered about its significance, for the riders seemed to be coming on at a rapid pace. Due to the rapidity with which the cloud moved, it was probably not a wagon. The area where the raiding bands operated had been passed much earlier and no riders had been spotted. Therefore, It would be unlikely that the approaching riders would be bandits. Grinold, too, had noticed the cloud and yelled to Cyrean to stop the wagon.

"Take your wagon and daughter to the clump of trees on the left," Grinold said to Madelyn's father. "Cyrean and I will meet these riders and see what their purpose may be. If it be not harm to us, they may ride on and we will continue upon our journey. If it be any other reason for their haste, they will find ready steel to meet them."

The wagon had barely reached concealment when three riders came into view. They slowed their pace at the appearance of Cyrean and Grinold in the road before them.

"Ho, strangers, why do you bar our way upon the road?"

said the leader as he drew nearer the two men facing them.

"Why are you in such haste to trample any who travel this highway?" asked Grinold.

"We are not accustomed to telling strangers our business," said another of the riders as the two groups of men faced each other.

"We want no trouble," replied Cyrean. "If no harm is meant to us, we will step aside and you may continue your journey."

"The gypsies at the camp a half day's ride behind us told of two men who came into their camp last night and partook of their hospitality. This morning the two men left with a young woman and her father. It is that woman we seek. From the descriptions we were given of the men, it would seem they now stand before us, daring to bar our way. Do you have the woman?"

"If we did, she would not be turned over to one such as you," retorted Grinold. "The lady did not wish to go with you, and judging from your manners, hers was a wise choice."

"Perhaps cold steel will loosen your tongue to her location," said the leader. "She is my property and I will see her returned or have your head upon a pike."

"The difficulty will be in the taking of that head," said Grinold, as he drew his sword from its sheath. "If you be foolish enough to try and take what is not yours, we will treat you as we would any common bandits upon the road."

"Then feel my blade, boastful one," said the lead soldier, spurring his horse forward.

Grinold met him stroke for stroke as their blades flashed in deadly rhythms that gave and received with no quarter asked. Cyrean had taken the brunt of the charge of the other two soldiers and maneuvered his horse quickly to gain the advantage before they could flank him, making him vulnerable to both their swords. As one of the soldiers charged in, Cyrean leaned to the side of his mount and swung his sword, striking the passing rider full in the shoulder and unhorsing him. Turning to face the other, he saw that Grinold had fallen from his horse and was now at a disadvantage as his opponent prepared to charge toward him.

Turning his mount, Cyrean spurred him to where Grinold stood and came between Grinold and his opponent, meeting the charge of the soldier and allowing Grinold time to remount his horse. For several minutes the skirmish continued until the second soldier received a wound and fled toward the woods. Now facing two skilled fighters, the leader saw little chance.

"I see myself at a disadvantage," he said. "Two against the one would not seem to be fair odds."

"Yes, the odds were much better when you had three against our two," returned Grinold sarcastically. "I do not need my companion to dispatch a coward. Cyrean will stand aside and I alone will fight for the woman. If a man hath not courage to fight for the one he loves, then he is not deserving of her."

"There are other women and there will be another time," said the soldier. " Take her and welcome. We will meet again and when we are done, she will be in need of a new husband. Until then, take care that you have not obtained that which you would gladly be rid of later."

"Away, base coward, and take your friends if you can find them. Such scurrilous dogs should not be on the same highway as honest men."

"Well done, Grinold. You fight like the she wolf protecting her young. The king will make good use of your sword."

"And yours, Cyrean. Now we must hurry. The day grows late and we are not in sight of Eustan. There from the woods appears the wagon and Madelyn. We will ride until dark and make camp in a secluded place. We must avoid other encounters, or we may never reach our destination. I received a small hurt upon my arm during the fight and it will need tending. We still have some of the poultices we used earlier on the queen. They will prove useful again."

"Then let us ride until dark if the wound does not pain you too much," replied Cyrean. "When the sun sets tonight, we will be near our destination."

When the wagon joined them, Madelyn saw the wound on Grinold's arm. Taking a small strip from her garment she wrapped the wound. Having stemmed the flow of blood, Grinold was content, and the small band continued their journey to Eustan.

Chapter Sixteen
To Meet a King

The din in the hallway outside his chamber instantly brought the king out of his bed. Calling for his servant to bring his robes, he stepped down onto the floor and wondered what would bring someone to the palace at such an early hour. He had spent a restless night, sleeping very little as worry for the queen had filled his head. A knock on the door came just as the servant brought his clothes.

A guard entered and informed the king that a small party of three men and a woman requested an audience with him and had presented a ring with the king's crest. The king marveled at this news, for only three people had been given rings with such a crest. He fought the panic that threatened to grip him and steeled himself as the visitors were admitted to the room. None of the visitors had he ever seen before, and the fear that something had happened to his wife for a moment robbed the king of his power of speech.

"Your majesty, my name is Cyrean," said the apparent leader of the group. "You must pardon our intrusion at such an early hour, but the matter which we must discuss cannot wait."

"You have a ring with my crest," said King Malvore. "How came you by such an object? Few people have access to a ring like the one you possess."

Grinold looked at the king's face as Cyrean nervously searched for the best way to tell him how he had come to have the ring in his possession. Grinold could see the agitation in the gaunt face of the old soldier in front of him. Here was a man who had the demands of ruling a kingdom etched deeply into his face. Yet behind the worry that his countenance evinced, Grinold saw other things as well. There was a kindness in the eyes of the man before them. He did not have the haughty demeanor that is so often found in the character of one who is used to giving orders and having them instantly obeyed. Still in every aspect of his being, it could be seen that this was the king. Years of having to manage the affairs of a kingdom had given to King Malvore a presence that filled the room. He stood straight and firm though the strength was obviously gone from the body of this great ruler who had fought in many battles with little quarter given or taken. Grinold saw other things also, but he did not have time to sort through them for a meaning. There was much about the king that told him here was a man worthy of his allegiance.

"The ring was given to me, your majesty, before we began this trip," continued Cyrean. "I have something to give you, and the ring was to assure I would be granted an audience."

"Given by whom? Speak, Man," said the king impatiently.

"A young woman named Aurienna told me it would help me in my quest to find you," said Cyrean.

"You have spoken to Lord Hadreon's daughter?"

"I have spoken to a young woman named Aurienna, your highness. Whose daughter she is I cannot say. I sensed there was something in her bearing that belied her clothing."

"Was there another woman with her?"

"Yes, your majesty, and they told me to communicate to you that they were well, for they knew that you would worry. Know you well the two ladies, your majesty?" asked Cyrean.

"Aurienna is the daughter to my chief counsel, and her companion is my wife and the queen," replied King Malvore.

Grinold and Cyrean looked at each other in astonishment. They had tended to the wounds of the queen and had given both women shelter without any idea of who they were. Neither woman had given any indication that they had ever been used to anything more than what they had received at Cyrean's poor hut.

"I still have not had my question answered of how you came to have the ring," said King Malvore.

"Before we begin our story, your majesty," answered Cyrean, "let me say again that both women were safe and on their way to their destination when we left them. My companion and I had given them shelter for three nights."

"My friend speaks truly, your highness," averred Grinold. "We had not the knowledge at the time of their rank, but they were treated as well as we had means."

"Why did they need your hospitality for such a length of time? They should have been housed in Parvidian two nights ago."

"It is a long story, your majesty. If you wish to sit, I will tell the story and Grinold will fill in when my memory eludes me."

"I will willingly hear the story," said King Malvore.

"First, my king, if I may be so bold as to ask a boon for a friend. This is Madelyn and her father. He has been promised twenty gold dragons for her hand in marriage to Grinold. In like manner I promised him an equal number for the two horses we needed to complete our trip. We have not such treasure upon our persons, but if you will pay the debt, it will be returned manifold by the gift I have for you."

"You gave hospitality to the queen. Anything that I can do will be of small significance for such beneficence. Guard, inform Lord Hadreon that I have received word of his daughter and then go to the treasurer and tell him of my need. Bring the dragons back immediately."

"Yes, your highness."

"I thank you, your majesty. Now I will begin my story. I am Cyrean Pendrall of the Dark Wood. I have lived there all my life with my mother and father who passed away some years ago."

"You lived in the Dark Wood with your parents?" asked

the king. "Why would a family with the obvious nobility that is evident in their son want to live in such a God-forsaken place? Pendrall, you say? I once knew a man with such a name. He was once my wisest and most devoted counselor. He was exiled to the Dark Wood for transgressions in the mystic arts. Surely, this would not be the same man?"

As the king finished speaking, Lord Hadreon rushed hurriedly into the chamber. He looked at the visitors and then at the king. He studied the faces of the two young men before him and when he had assured himself that he did not know them, he turned to the king.

"My liege, I have heard that news has come of my daughter. Is she safe?"

"Yes, Lord Hadreon. These two men have recently come with news that both Aurienna and the queen have reached their destination. Sit, my friend and counselor. Young Cyrean will tell us the story of how he came to know the two women."

"Your majesty," continued Cyrean, "I do not believe the man that you knew could be my father. He would never have done anything that would have been a disservice to the king. He knew nothing of the mystic arts."

"Perhaps you are right, Cyrean. We will explore this coincidence further at a future time. For now, I must hear the rest of your story. Lord Hadreon will sit and listen with me for he has as much interest as I in the matter."

"My father lived for many years in the Dark Wood. After the deaths of my parents, I continued to live there, for it was all I knew. I know little of the world outside my forest. Then a few nights ago the man you see with me fell into one of the many pits in the woods, and I rescued him and took him back to my hut to care for his wounds. He had barely recovered when we were attacked by a swampsweeper which wounded my hound Wolfen. We were on our way to a hermit that I know for medicine when we came upon a wagon under attack by highwaymen. We did not know the inhabitants of the wagon, but we could not let them be overcome by robbers, so we encountered the band and helped to fight them off. Lady Aurienna had almost dispatched the entire party before Grinold and I could take our part in the fray."

"Ever her father's daughter would you not agree, Lord Hadreon?" asked the king.

"It is so, my liege. She has too much of her father and often takes on a fight when the odds are against her. But you say she is well, Cyrean? She has no hurts?"

"None, my lord," answered Cyrean. "Grinold and I had little more to do than finish the few that remained when she was done. The cowards took flight when they saw her skill with the sword."

"And what of the queen? She is also well?" asked the king.

"She received a small wound to her shoulder from an arrow that splintered, but we tended the wound and she is fast recovering," said Cyrean.

"They dare to injure the queen! I will have them all executed for such an affront!" exclaimed the king.

"They, as we, did not know it was the queen, your majesty," said Grinold. "Luckily, we escaped with our lives, and Cyrean and Aurienna are to be credited for their part. The queen bore up well under her injury. She did not complain and weathered the pain as well as any man."

"When this war is over, my first order will be to rid the highways of cutthroats such as you have described. Still she is safe. That is all that I need to know," said King Malvore. "Continue your story, Cyrean."

"We took Lady Aurienna and the queen to my hut in the Dark Wood. There they were given shelter and food and the queen's wound was attended. We knew not their identities, but it would not have mattered. We would treat the lowliest traveler with the same courtesy. After three days, the queen was sufficiently recovered to allow us to take her back to the road, and she and Aurienna resumed their trip. Before departing, Lady Aurienna gave me this ring with the royal crest to make it easier for me to gain an audience with the king."

"It is a story that rings well upon my ear for it hath a happy ending," said King Malvore. "I would hope that the story that we will tell of the impending battle will have such an ending. But your tale cannot be done, Cyrean. You said you came on an urgent mission with an important gift. Does it also have a story?"

"Yes, your majesty, though some of the telling will have to be done by Grinold. He has some knowledge of events that are not known to me."

"Let me see the gift," requested the king.

"It would be best to hear the story first, my liege. To know the story is not enough, for in the gift itself abide stories that would chill us to the marrow if it had voice to tell them. I have in my possession the Crystal of Light."

"The Crystal of Light!" exclaimed Lord Hadreon and the king in unison.

"How did you come by the object?" asked the king.

"The first part of the story I will tell, my liege," said Grinold. "I was the chief tracker for Tobias for many years. During that time he came into possession of the crystal. One night a servant stole the crystal and fled from the castle to bring it to you. With me showing the way, Tobias and a small group of soldiers set out to track him down. We reached a place in the road where it seemed the crystal had been hidden, but it was not there. Later, when we found the servant, he was trapped in a sand pit in the forest. He told us where he had hidden the crystal. Tobias left the servant to die in the pit, and we returned to the place the servant had revealed, but we could not find it. With the servant's death, we had no way to know the location of the crystal. Tobias sent me on a quest to find it. I returned to the place where the servant said he had hidden the crystal, but I had no more luck than on that ill-fated night when we first searched."

"That is because I had taken it," said Cyrean, picking up the thread of the story. "I brought it to my hut in the Dark Wood until that time when it would be safe to take it to you, your majesty. It was during this time that I found Grinold, who had been searching for the crystal on his own, trapped in a pit."

"What plans had you for the crystal, Grinold?" asked Lord Hadreon.

"I did not know at the time, but I came to the realization soon after my rescue by Cyrean that it could not be given to Tobias. When I saw the earnestness of my host in his desire to help his king, I felt I could do no less. The loyalty he showed to your cause I had never seen before. I wanted to be a part of that effort," said Grinold with finality.

"We welcome you and Cyrean to our ranks," said the king. "Does this story have a happy ending, Cyrean?"

"That we will not know for some time, your majesty. I know of the power of the crystal, for I have seen it displayed. Assign only your most knowledgeable men to guard it and to probe it for its secrets. It must be used wisely or it could cause as much harm as good."

"With the crystal, I have the weapon that will shift the balance of power in our favor," said the king. "Now am I young again. With the burden of certain defeat lifted from my shoulders and the queen safely hidden, I feel as free as the cliff birds. Come, my welcome visitors, and we will dine on the best of meats and fruits and drink only the sweetest of wines. This good news has gladdened my old heart and brought back a lightness of spirit that I have not felt in years."

"Cyrean and I will be with you anon, your majesty," said Lord Hadreon. "I would speak further of certain matters with him before the repast will set well upon my stomach."

"Very well, Lord Hadreon, but be not long, for I want us all to share the happiness that I am now feeling."

The king and his guests left the room, and Lord Hadreon took Cyrean by the arm and led him to the council chamber. Upon their arrival, he closed the door and spoke in a hushed voice to Cyrean.

"In your story to the king," began Lord Hadreon, " you spoke of a man named Pendrall who you said was your father. Is this true?"

"Yes," said Cyrean. "The king also recognized the name, but the man you knew and my father cannot be the same man. The king said he was exiled to the Dark Wood, but my father told me many times that he had taken to the solitude of the forest because he no longer wanted to be a part of the corruption he witnessed daily from mankind."

"What were your mother's and father's first names?" asked Lord Hadreon.

"My father was Arthur Pendrall and my mother's name was Marion," replied Cyrean.

If Lord Hadreon recognized the names, it did not show in his countenance as Cyrean searched his face for some sign that the two names meant something to him.

"Obviously, you are right," he said to Cyrean. "The two men are not the same. I hope I have not upset you with my questions. The king and his guests await our attendance. Let us go and help to make merry the gathering."

"Food and drink are welcome," said Cyrean. "We have traveled many miles to get here. Now that my burden has been taken on by others, I can eat and drink. Peaceful be the heart of he who knows he has done what is right in the eyes of God and his king."

When the two men reached the dining hall, the large table was covered with food of all kinds. They sat and feasted, and for a time all the doubts and uncertainties that had plagued the last few days vanished. Madelyn and Grinold sat and talked of their pasts and the future that lay before them. Lost in each other's eyes, they heard little of the conversations around them. Madelyn's father had received the gold he had come for and shortly took his leave of his host. Before he left, he kissed Madelyn on the forehead and gave her his blessing. Madelyn knew she would probably never see him again, and she cried softly. His grief in his loss was quickly replaced with the sudden knowledge that he now was as wealthy as he would ever be, and he hurried forth to spend the forty gold dragons as quickly as possible. The king was in good spirits and he and Lord Hadreon shared with Cyrean many exploits of their youth, causing Cyrean to long for battle so he could have stories to pass on to his son. As he thought of a son to whom he could leave a legacy, he thought of Lady Aurienna. He had not spoken to her father of his feelings for her. With so much still to be done, he did not think it was the right time to declare his love for her openly to her father. He also felt himself growing more and more concerned about the king's comments earlier in the evening. He had spoken of a man he had exiled who might be Cyrean's father.

They had both agreed that it would be unlikely that it was the same man. Yet, the interest that Lord Hadreon had shown in the matter had now cast doubts into Cyrean's mind. Was it all a strange coincidence, or was there more to the story than had been disclosed to him? Cyrean know that he would have to know the answers to these questions before long.

Cyrean looked at the king who was now engaged in another story of war. Cyrean had placed the crystal into the king's hands just before they had come into the great dining hall with the admonition that it was never to be taken from its pouch in the presence of light. The king was aware of the danger posed by the crystal and had assured Cyrean that only those with knowledge of the crystal's powers would be entrusted with its care. Now that he was free of responsibility of the weapon, Cyrean should have felt the lightness of heart that his comrades exhibited, but some small doubt still remained in his subconscious. What was it that still preyed on his mind? He knew that it must be connected in some way to the conversation he had had with Lord Hadreon earlier. He also knew he would never be totally at ease until he knew for sure that his father and the man exiled by the king were not the same man. He had just managed to clear his head of these thoughts and become absorbed again in the king's stories when a commotion in the hallway stopped the conversation. All eyes turned toward the door to see what merited the abrupt appearance of the guards in the doorway of the dining hall. The answer was quickly forthcoming.

The figure standing in the doorway was dressed in attire that might be worn by a man in hunting or even into battle. But the figure upon which the attire rested was not that of a man, and the sudden realization of who it was sent Cyrean's emotions soaring. It was Aurienna.

Chapter Seventeen
To Capture a Queen

Lady Ofra looked about her and sighed. What a long way she had come from Eustan, not only in distance but in station. The small house was comfortable enough, and the family who lived there were very happy to supply her every need within their means. Their host had once been a servant in the king's household, and when an accident left him without his eyesight, he had come to Parvidian with a small pension from the king that allowed him to live comfortably. The king trusted the man and his wife and knew that Lady Ofra would be safe under their care.

She unpacked the few necessary items that she needed and placed them on the table in the corner of the room. The bedroom was small and would have been even smaller with Aurienna there. As soon as Lady Ofra had been delivered to her new lodgings, Aurienna took a horse from one of the guards who had escorted them and rode quickly back in the direction of Eustan. No amount of royal persuasion could keep her there with the queen even though her orders were specifically to attend to the queen at all times. Having knowledge of the crystal's powers, which by now would be in the hands of the king, Aurienna was sure of their ultimate victory. She had to be there to be a part of that victory. She hesitated at the thought of leaving the queen when it was her charge to tend her majesty. But who would find her here in one of the smallest provinces in the entire kingdom? She would be safe because Tobias had too many other things to occupy his time. She left the queen with the promise that she would send a rider every week to check on her safety. Now Aurienna was gone, and Lady Ofra sighed again at the capricious nature of fate.

Having spent the better part of the morning within the

confines of the house, Lady Ofra felt a need to get outside and look over the small village and surrounding countryside. She knew there would be little chance that she would be recognized in the peasant garb that she wore. The family with whom she stayed had been sworn to secrecy, and the king knew they could be trusted. That is why they had been chosen for this responsibility. The people of the village were like those of any small village everywhere. Most of them knew of happenings at the court only through what they heard from peddlers or travelers who made their way from one province to another selling wares or adventuring. Most of the villagers had never been outside Parvidian. Few had ever been to Eustan, and none had ever seen the queen and king though stories of their generosity and love for their people had spread over all the provinces. Several young men from this small community had gone to enlist in the service of the king, and the inhabitants of the village took great pride in their loyalty to the crown. They had witnessed on more than one occasion the savagery of Tobias' cutthroats who had come into their small town and taken whatever they desired, knowing that resistance, if any, would be small. Now with many of their young men gone, there would be no resistance at all. The hope was now that all of the forces of Tobias would be involved in the war which they saw as imminent, and they would be left in peace for that space of time. There was nothing in Parvidian now that the tyrant would want, and they could go on with their lives. With good fortune, Tobias would be defeated by the king's forces, and his men would leave and do their looting elsewhere.

A young man who would be Lady Ofra's escort brought two horses to the front of the hut. He helped Lady Ofra into the saddle. and they rode to the outskirts of the village to enjoy the countryside. The young man spoke little and if he had known who the lady was that he escorted that day, he would have spoken even less. Lady Ofra was satisfied to enjoy the sun and the beauty of the fields and to be left to her thoughts. When the sun indicated it was noon, Lady Ofra told her escort to guide her back to the village. She was tired by now and the small amount of food she had eaten that morning was gone. They had gotten within sight of the village when the smell of smoke and the shouting of men told the riders that things were not well. Instructing Lady Ofra to stay in the concealment of the trees, her escort rode toward the village to see what was causing the disturbance.

Soon, he returned with an ashen look upon his face. He came to the place of concealment and dismounted, pacing back and forth as Lady Ofra waited for some news about what he had seen.

"What news have you brought, young man? Why are you so pale?" she asked.

"My lady, the village is ablaze. Soldiers are everywhere. My own home has been destroyed, and I do not know if my family is alive or dead. From the shouts, I determined that they searched for someone they believed to be in the village. When they did not get the information they wanted, they set fire to many of the houses. Many are dead and others beaten. I must go to check on my family. Do not come with me, for the danger is great. When I have found my family and the raiders have left, I will return for you."

Without waiting for an answer, he remounted and rode again toward the village. The smoke had begun to curl high into the air, and the shouting had died so that now the cries of the wounded could be heard and shrieks of lamentation for the dead came to the queen's ears.

"I have caused this," she said softly to herself as she tied her mount to a small sapling and took up the pacing that had been started by her escort earlier. "My presence here has brought death and destruction to these people. When my escort finds his family dead and realizes who I am, he will want my death as retribution, and I could not blame him. The forces of Tobias are everywhere. I would have been safer at the castle with the walls to fortify and the king to assure me of victory. Here I only bring grief to those who do not even know who I am or for what they are being persecuted. If I had known the suffering that I would bring to these simple people, I never would have left Eustan. Now it is too late to give myself up, for what would it gain? It would not restore the village nor bring back those who have lost their lives. I must wait here until the young man returns. God grant that no harm has come to those who sheltered me."

After what seemed like many hours, the escort returned. He was obviously shaken and sat down at the base of a large tree. Tears welled in his eyes, and he wept unashamedly.

"Then it is as I feared. Your family is dead?" she asked.

"My father is dead," he replied. "He went to the aid of an old woman who was being beaten and received an arrow in his back for his pains. My mother is alive, but our home is gone."

"And what of my hosts?" she asked. "Were they spared the sword and torch?"

"No, my lady. They are both dead and their home is also burned. It was said by someone in the village that a ring with the king's crest was found in their home. When this discovery was made, a general shout went among the troops and they searched each house, setting the torch to them as they went. Few homes were spared and many lives have been lost. Who they search for I do not know, but no one is worth the loss of life that I have witnessed today. Even if the king were here, I feel he would give up himself rather than witness the death of so many of his subjects."

"Yes, the king would have surrendered himself rather than see so many people killed, and so would I had I known what was happening."

"Then you are…are…the…the…"he stammered.

"Yes, I am the queen and the one the soldiers were hunting in the village."

"Your majesty, I meant no disrespect in my remarks about the king or you."

"No, young man. You are right. A king who cares about his people would not allow such things to happen, and had my husband been here he would have given himself to the soldiers to spare the village. I must do the same thing before others are killed."

"No, your majesty. You cannot give yourself up. If you do now, the death of my father, the deaths of your hosts, and those of countless people in the village will all have been in vain. Everything is gone. What else can they do to harm us now? I will see you to safety even if it means my life."

"No, your family has sacrificed enough. Your mother has lost a husband. I cannot let her lose a son also. I will travel on my own back to Eustan. They will not be looking for a lone rider. They will have the main roads covered, but I can dress as a man and use the byways to avoid detection."

"No, my lady, I cannot let you ride alone. The king would never forgive me, and I would not forgive myself if something happened to you."

"But you must stay here for your mother. She will need you now more than ever."

"I will see that she is well cared for before I leave. What are our lives when compared to the lives of our king and queen? She would want to see men like Tobias wiped from the face of the earth. We know whose men destroyed our village today, and she nor the village will be safe until Tobias is dead."

"What is your name, my young escort? I would know who fights so bravely in our cause."

"My name is William Castilian, your highness. My father spent many years in the service of the king. He was blinded in an accident, and the king provided for him when he could no longer work. Our loyalty to the king is for the generosity that he has shown to us. We can do no less."

"I thank you for your generous offer, William. I will see that you are repaid handsomely for your courtesy to me."

"Come, your majesty. Let us return to the village and get a change of habit for you. When we leave the village, we will appear as two youths riding out to seek our fortunes."

The queen was visibly moved by the destruction she witnessed as they rode back into the village. Most of the homes were destroyed, and bodies of several villagers lay in a row where they had been placed for burial later. She was now witnessing firsthand the pain and anguish that war can bring. William spoke quietly to his mother, and Lady Ofra heard a stifled gasp as he revealed the identity of their visitor. She quickly left and returned shortly with riding clothes that had belonged to her husband. Dressed in these garments, Lady Ofra at a distance would be taken for a man commonly traveling on the highway.

Within the hour Lady Ofra was ready to travel. William had made arrangements to have his mother looked after while he was gone. The departure was a sad one for him, knowing he was needed there but recognizing the greater necessity of getting the queen back to Eustan and safety.

Farther north, Tobias was again meeting with his informant for any last minute information that might hasten the end of King Malvore's reign. Riding from the woods, the cloaked figure greeted Tobias and then motioned him to follow him to a secluded campsite deep in the forest. There, he drew from his cloak a parchment and spread it out for Tobias to see.

"This is the map I promised you at our last meeting," spoke the man within the cloak. "It will give you the positions of the weapons and where the largest contingents of men have been placed. It also has the location of the pulleys that control the gate. Once the battle is underway, men that have been positioned inside the castle walls must overpower the guards at the gate. Once this is done, it will take only a short time to open the doors and allow your soldiers to enter."

"You have done well. If you can give me the location of the queen, my plans will take wing and soar above the highest cliffs. Have you news of her?"

"No, I am not privy to such information. I only know what my spies bring me. The wagon in which they traveled was attacked on the highway leading south. Word came from one of the bandits who survived the conflict that two men had intervened and turned the tide of battle. One of the women on the wagon fought like a demon possessed. This could only have been Lady Aurienna who has been trained by her father in the art of war. After the battle, the soldiers and wagon remained near the river where the battle occurred, but nothing was seen of the two women or the two men. It was thought that they disappeared into the Dark Wood. Why they entered there, no one can say and nothing has been seen of them since."

"I have had patrols covering the road from Eustan to Parvidian. I will receive news soon if they have been spotted return to the castle and go about your duties. The king must suspect nothing. I will return to camp and ready the soldiers. We will prepare to move within the next two days. If we are to capture the queen, it will have to be done by then."

"Everything will be in readiness within the castle walls. I

will await your orders."

With these parting words, the tall cloaked figure mounted his horse and disappeared into the darkness. Tobias returned to his men who waited in the small valley below. A rider had come from Parvidian with news.

"My lord, we have found evidence that the queen has been in Parvidian. A ring was found which bore the royal crest. The queen was not found, though most of the village was burned to the ground. Patrols are seeking her over all the roads in and out of the village. It appears to be just a matter of time before she is taken."

"Ride," commanded Tobias, "and tighten the noose. She must not escape. There may be a female companion with her. Take them both alive. Kill any others that are with them.
When they are captured, bring them to camp. When our army marches to Eustan, they will be at its head for the king to see. Then we will see how highly he values her worth. The kingdom or his queen. That will be the choice he has to make."

"At your command, my lord," said the messenger and spurred his horse southward.

"How strange are the affairs of the human heart," mused Tobias. "How I pity those who let emotions dictate their actions. A soldier must be focused on one goal to the exclusion of all else. His one ambition is victory and damn the cost. King Malvore can never hope to defeat a man such as I whose sole purpose is to rule. No man is so loyal nor so loved that I would not lay him on the altar of war and execute him summarily to obtain my objective. I have no wife nor child, but had I those attachments, they, too, would be sacrificed to achieve my ambition. Yea, though the river ran red with the blood of those loyal to me, still would I send them into the breech. Were King Malvore to parade my family in front of his army, I would send the shaft myself that would dispatch them rather than let them be a stumbling block to my objective. This single-mindedness of purpose is what will distinguish my victory and my rule."

"My lord, the night grows late," said one of the soldiers who waited impatiently for orders. "We should return quickly to camp and await news of the queen's imminent capture."

"Patience is the one virtue that I have tried to practice," replied Tobias. "Ride back to camp and wait for me. I will take two men and go to Parvidian. The only way to make sure the queen is taken is to be there myself. I will return in time to march the army toward Eustan. Have all in readiness upon my return."

"It shall be done."

Tobias watched the contingent of men disappear into the distance, and then he spurred his mount in the direction of Parvidian. The black of the night as he rode could have been matched only by the darkness in his heart . Within the soul of most of God's creatures abides a spark of good. It is there when he commits a wrong, for it is the part of him that feels pain. It is there when he does an act of kindness, for it is the lightness that fills his heart. Such a spark has kindled mankind to some of the greatest feats the world has ever known. Rare is the man who does not possess this gift, for it was given by God in hope that its light would always overcome the darkness in men's hearts.

That light had been slowly dying in Tobias for many years now until it had been all but extinguished. Tobias was a man with a sole purpose but without the soul which would allow him to enjoy his victory. Since the dawn of time, good and evil have been at war. This was just another battle in that long-standing conflict. In the person of Tobias the forces of darkness were personified. Within his grasp was the Kingdom and within his sight was dominion over all the world. Tobias smiled as he thought of the upcoming conflict and spurred his horse even faster into the darkness of the night.

Chapter Eighteen
A House Divided

For a moment the entire assemblage was struck speechless as Aurienna walked to the head of the table and bowed to the king. She stood stoically and waited for the king to speak, but it was her father who addressed her in a joyful voice.

"Aurienna, you are alive. I had thought so many times since the news of the attack that perhaps you had sustained some mortal injury, and I would never see you again."

He moved around the table and embraced his daughter tightly. He took her arm and led her to the table and placed her on his right hand. The king, initially shocked into silence by Aurienna's appearance, had now regained his senses and spoke sharply to her.

"My child, this is indeed a surprise. I gave orders that you were to take the queen to Parvidian and remain there to serve and protect her. Now I see you are here prepared as if for war. Where is the queen?"

"She is in Parvidian, your majesty," replied Aurienna.

"Then why are you here? Did I not command you to stay with her? Have you grown so bold that you now defy my commands?"

"My full intent, your majesty, was to escort the queen to Parvidian and there remain until the war was over. On the way to Parvidian, the wagon was attacked, and I fought off the raiders with the help of the men seated at your table. The queen received a hurt and was taken to Cyrean's home for treatment. It was there that I learned about the crystal being in his possession. When I discovered that he possessed this mighty weapon, I knew the advantage was ours. It was then that I decided to deliver the queen to Parvidian and return to aid our cause."

"You decided! You decided! And who gave you power to

override the king's direct orders?" roared King Malvore.

"My liege, hear her out before the anger of the moment places a wall between you that even love cannot overleap," pleaded Lord Hadreon. "Yes, she is rash, but all she has done and will continue to do will be in support of our cause."

"I thought only for the best, your majesty," continued Aurienna. "Once Parvidian was reached and the queen securely lodged, I saw no reason to stay and hastened here to fight with my new comrades in arms against Tobias. Did we not talk of this, Cyrean? You spoke highly of my skill with the sword. Would our cause not be served better with me here to help fight for the kingdom?"

"Indeed, you have skill that would rival any man," agreed Cyrean, uncomfortable at having to choose sides. "But, my lady, if your orders were to stay and protect the queen, then that was the mission you should have performed."

"Then I have disappointed you also," she replied sadly. "And you, my father, have I done that which will make you look down upon me with disgrace? I thought only to serve my king. Since I was a small girl, you have taught me the art of war, preparing me for that time when I could use those skills to defend the kingdom. My abilities would all be wasted in Parvidian. Here I can do that for which I was trained."

"My daughter," replied Lord Hadreon. "A soldier does that which he is commanded to do. In violating your trust to protect the queen, you have disobeyed the orders of the king and left the queen vulnerable. We had spoken before you left that it was imperative she not be captured. There are no soldiers in Parvidian to protect her. With the intelligence and skill you possess, you were the best choice to send with her. In time you could have returned to unite the kingdom should it fall in the upcoming battle. These were the plans of the king and of me, your father. You have disobeyed us both in your actions and shamed me in front of the king. My love for you must be secondary to the trust you have been given. If it is the will of the king that you return to Parvidian, then you must depart immediately."

"Then none will stand for me," Arienna said softly. "I will return tonight. But, your majesty, judge me harshly for my youth and impetuous nature and not for any disrespect to you or the queen. It was my love for both of you that has brought me here. Be not angry with my father, for none of my actions can be placed at his door."

Having said all that she could in her defense, Aurienna sat down dejectedly at the table and waited for the king's answer. The king arose and walked to the fireplace, gazing into the fire. For several moments he stood and debated within himself before he turned back to the table. Before he could speak, a disturbance in the hall outside the chamber distracted his thoughts, and within seconds a courier was admitted into the hall. He bowed to the king and stood, obviously distraught, awaiting permission to speak.

"What is the cause of your discomfort?" asked the king as he noticed the agitated state of the man before him. "What news causes your limbs to tremble and whitens thy cheeks? No, do not speak. Wait in thy discourse, for I fear that which thou might say. Is it of the queen?"

"Aye, your majesty."

"Then truly are you a harbinger of doom. Like the darkest of forest kites who feed upon the carrion in the road, your business deals with death. Tell me that the queen is alive and I will embrace thee as I would a son. Tell me she is dead and then run your sword through my heart, for I would be as empty as the air wherein those words are lodged."

"I cannot answer that which I do not know, your majesty. I have come from Parvidian at the request of a young man who was in service of the queen at the time."

"Then what news can you reveal to me?"

"Sire, Parvidian has been laid to waste and the whereabouts of the queen are unknown."

"Oh, most foul of days. The queen is missing? Should I be happy in the knowledge that her body has not been found and hope for her return, or should I fear even more that her absence means she has been taken by Tobias? If so, would that not be a fate worse than death?"

"Your majesty, think not that the queen is dead," said Lord Hadreon, placing his hand upon the king's shoulders and leading him back to his chair at the table. "Her body has not been found, and she has the will of her husband. She has gone into hiding and will return to us soon. This is what we must believe."

Aurienna's face had visibly whitened as she listened to the news brought by the courier. Her actions had brought about the pain she was now witnessing in the king and feeling within her own heart. Had she been there, she could have protected the queen. This is what her father meant about duty and trust. She had violated the trust she had been given, and the queen's death might be the consequences of her actions.

"Your majesty, it is I who am at fault for the misfortune that has befallen the queen," said Aurienna. "Let me return to Parvidian and find her."

"And let Grinold and me go as well," spoke Cyrean. "We have brought you the crystal and in so doing have pledged our swords and our lives to you and the queen. Now we can provide for you a second service. We are knowledgeable of the area the queen will have to travel, and we know how to find our way undetected through the forces of Tobias. The queen has been to my home in the Dark Wood. It is possible that she might return there to evade the soldiers looking for her. If that is her thinking, then we must hurry, for the woods hold many perils that the queen could encounter unescorted."

"This calamity has been visited upon us by your rash actions," said King Malvore angrily to Aurienna. "You will find her and bring her back safely. If she is dead, do not return, for you will be dead to me also. Take these two as your guides and companions. Cyrean, I have many soldiers that I can send if they are needed."

"No, your majesty. They would only draw attention to our mission. It is better that we three go alone. If the queen has been taken by Tobias, one man has a better chance of getting her back than an army which he would expect to come against him."

"I have been under the command of Tobias, your majesty," said Grinold. "I know how he thinks. I believe I could still enter the camp with a story to explain my absence and he would not be suspicious. If he has the queen, this might be our only recourse."

"Do as you deem wisest," replied the king. "If the queen is dead, I will have no reason to live."

"Speak not of such things, my liege," implored Lord Hadreon. "It will only cause more pain and increase the rancor you feel toward me and my daughter."

"We hope our children will be our staffs in that time when old age will overtake us," said the king sadly. "Instead, they are disobedient to our will and bring us grief. My sons are gone. Who knows but if they had lived they, too, would have violated my trust as Aurienna has done."

"No, your majesty. Aurienna has erred in judgment, but she will always be a devoted servant to her king. Say not those things which will fill your heart with hate. My daughter will find the queen just as your sons would do were they here."

"I have lived too long, Lord Hadreon. I should have died in

one of the many battles we fought. It is not good for a father to outlive his children. If my wife be dead also, little remains for me."

Rather than witness the sorrow of the king in this moment of crisis, Aurienna had taken her leave and with her two companions rode out from Eustan to find the queen. Little was said as they hastened toward the Dark Wood, hoping there they would find the queen safe and unharmed. It was unlikely the queen would have been killed knowing the value Tobias placed upon her. Hopefully, she had managed to escape the burning of the village and was now hiding awaiting rescue.

Fate has a capricious nature and with each decision a person makes, he is met with success or failure. Whether the right choice has been made will only be known after the steps are taken upon that course. Would another choice have been wiser? Perhaps. But the luxury of foresight is not given to most men. Had Aurienna stayed with the queen, she might be safe now and back with the king. Or if she had remained and fought with the men who raided the village, she might have been killed along with the queen. If the queen had not gone riding that fateful day the village was burned, she would have been captured, perhaps sparing the lives of many villagers. The ride that Aurienna and her companions now made was another choice. Whether it was the right one would only be determined in time.

The object of Aurienna and her companions' search was even now riding slowly and cautiously toward Eustan. Lady Ofra and William had made good time, considering the meandering path they had to travel to avoid other riders. They did not know if groups of riders were bandits, Tobias's men, or simple wayfarers, but they could not risk encountering anyone with the stakes so high.

"William, we are close to the place where I entered the

Dark Wood," she said as they approached the area where she had been attacked and wounded. " I do not know if it would be safer to continue traveling or to try and find the hut where I stayed previously in the forest."

"Your majesty, I fear the unknown much more than I do any man," William replied, looking at the darkness of the forest before him. "If you command, I will enter, for my life belongs to the queen, but it is not a choice that I would make if I were alone."

"It is strange that we do think of the supernatural and magic as evil things. But I feel they can be used for good also. Many years ago, in the king's council was a man with skill in the mystic arts. This man had the knowledge of foresight. How far he could look into the future was uncertain. But he felt he was limited to those things that would occur within the lifetimes of those with whom he came into touch. He was my husband's most trusted advisor and teacher to Lord Hadreon who would eventually take his place."

"What happened to this man," asked William.

"He was banished to the Dark Wood by the king."

"Banished? But what of the favor in which he was held by the king?"

"The banishment was for an unpardonable offense in my husband's eyes. He had given to this man the care of his two sons. He was to teach and instruct them and prepare them in the skills they would need to protect themselves and the kingdom when they became men. They were just babes at the time and little instruction could be given. However, with so many plots against the king's life, he feared that the King's two sons would be at risk also. It was years later before the truth of what occurred that day was known. The ability to see events in the future prompted this man of magic to bestow certain gifts upon the two sons."

A House Divided

"Were these gifts not good?" asked William.

"We now believe they were, but the king did not know that at the time. A young commander named Draco was in the king's army. This man, who is now a general, felt that this advisor was plotting against the king and was using magic to harm the infant sons. He had the ear of the king and brought distrust between him and his advisor, for the king loved his sons dearly. One day the king happened upon the magician while he was chanting over the two small boys and assumed it was a curse he was putting on the infants. He had the magician taken away and placed on trial. With no one to support his claims that he was protecting the children from harm, he was branded as evil and sent into exile with his wife. This was over twenty years ago, and the king still is not sure if the sentence was just. For my part, I do not trust Draco, the man whose accusations banned the magician forever. I feel there is more to the man than meets the eye. Others feel as I do toward Draco, and I have often advised my husband that the man bears watching. He is too ambitious."

"But what of the magician?" asked William.

"As far as we know, he spent the rest of his life in the Dark Wood and never used his skills in magic again. He and his wife both died here. I met their son a few days ago. He is the young man who tended my wounds. I will always be grateful to him for his care, and his kindness to me makes the treatment of his father all the more bitter."

"You are not responsible for a decision that was made by the king, your majesty. You are not accountable for the banishment."

"I have the king's ear at all times. Something I might have said to him could have prevented the injustice to his advisor."

"What of the two sons? Did they suffer from the supposed curse place upon them?"

"We will never know, for within days of the banishment, our two sons were abducted and have not been heard from since. They were never found and the king has never been the same. I tried to be strong for him, but I could not take away the guilt he felt. He blamed himself for the abduction. I am afraid if I do not return soon, he may think me dead also. With the circumstances so similar, his guilt would be redoubled. Such an event would end his life, for he would not want to live with all his family gone. It is imperative that I return to Eustan before the war begins."

As they spoke, a sound of hooves along the road in front of them prompted William to take the reins of the queen's horse and lead it off the path. In the distance he could hear the sounds of a man's voice giving orders. On each side of the road, a small camp had been established so that watchers could see anyone traveling the road day or night. It would be almost impossible to pass through the narrow distance between the river and the cliffs without being heard or seen.

"Your majesty, we cannot get through until these camps are deserted," cautioned William. "It would be best for us to go to the hut of the man you mentioned. Can you find your way in the dark?"

"I was carried in while I was in a delirium, but I walked out and I think I can remember the path."

"I would make a camp outside the forest," said William. "But we have no food and I cannot make a fire. It would alert soldiers or bandits to our whereabouts."

"We will go into the forest if only a short way," replied the queen. "If I cannot remember the path, we will return here and wait until the soldiers leave. Some hunger and discomfort will have to be endured by us both. We have not the niceties of the court here."

The two companions tied their horses to a tree and slowly

made their way into the fringes of the Dark Wood. The small bit of light that remained as the day waned would soon be lost as they moved deeper into the forest. After a time, Lady Ofra stopped and looked about her as if unsure of what step to take next.

"William, this does not look like the path that I traveled before. Adjust your steps to the right and look for signs that someone has passed this way. In the darkness, it is difficult to determine where it is safest to place our feet. I have heard Cyrean talk of bogs that will swallow unwary travelers. Be careful that you do not fall into such dangers for I have not the strength to pull you out."

William walked, carefully peering into the darkness, hoping his eyes would adjust as the light faded even more with the approach of night. He stepped toward a dead limb that had fallen from the tree above him. If he used the limb to probe ahead of him, he would be able to avoid any of the bogs that may lay in their path. Suddenly, the ground disappeared from beneath his feet, and he felt himself pulled upward by some invisible force. When his body stopped swaying, he realized he was suspended in the air his head toward the ground. He sensed a tightness around his legs, and he knew he had stepped into some sort of rope trap probably intended for some animal of the forest.

"William, what has happened? What was the noise I heard?" asked the queen, now fearing to move in any direction.

"I have stepped into some sort of trap, your majesty. Do not move. There may be others all around us."

"You must have help, William. I will return to the edge of the forest and go to the men camped there. We will have to hope that they are supporters of the king. I will return soon with torches and men to cut you down."

Just as Lady Ofra turned to retrace her steps out of the

woods, a slithering sound came to her ears, and a torch was suddenly lit only feet from her. Into the light of this torch appeared a face unlike any that she had ever seen before. The light before her eyes seemed to suddenly dim as the blood left her head and she fell unconscious to the ground.

Chapter Nineteen
To Plan a Rescue

When Lady Ofra regained consciousness, light had begun to filter into the forest. She opened her eyes and found herself in a crude cage so small that she could not stand erect. She looked for William but she could not see him anywhere. She discerned many small huts as her eyes began to adjust to the dim light. It was still early morning, and the inhabitants of this village were not yet astir. She felt her head for cuts but none were evident. The only pain was a dull ache in her head which was probably received when she fell to the ground. She wondered how she got to this place, and then she remembered the face in the torchlight and shuddered. Where was William? He had been captured in a snare, but he was not put into the cage with her. It was unlikely that her captors knew who she was, and she sensed that it would be best not to reveal her identity. She had little time to debate the question further, for she heard the sound of voices approaching. She saw in dim outline William with his hands bound, escorted by four of the smallest men she had ever seen. As they got nearer, she recognized the face she had seen in the light of the torch and realized why she had fainted. The grotesqueness of their features was compounded by their actions as they beat at William's legs and back while prodding him toward the cage.

"Stop that," commanded Lady Ofra. "He has done nothing to you. Who are you that you think you have the right to beat an innocent man?"

"My name is Bartold, and I have the right to do as I wish. You cannot come into our forest and think to order us to do your bidding. You are trespassers and, as such, subject to whatever punishment we deem appropriate."

Bartold approached the cage and looked closely into Lady Ofra's face. Repulsed by the grossness of the features of the dwarf, Lady Ofra instinctively drew back.

"Does my face make you afraid?" he asked. "Do you not think that your face might be as repulsive to me? I recognize this woman, Darius. She is the one we saw at the hut. She was the guest of Cyrean."

"Cyrean? Do you know him?" asked Lady Ofra. "We are his friends and his guests. As such, we should not be bound and beaten by his neighbors."

"We are his neighbors in name only," responded Bartold. "We tolerated his presence once because he seemed to hate the Outworlders as much as we do. Now he is bringing them into the forest. We owe him no allegiance, and his guests are the same as intruders to us."

"You know not whom you have in your cage," said William. "If you did, you would tremble in terror at the knowledge and fall on your knees asking forgiveness for your boldness."

"She is but a woman and were she the Devil, I would have no fear of her, for I am Bartold the Brave, the scourge of the Outworlders."

"Tell them nothing, William," said Lady Ofra. "There will be time for that later. Cyrean will be here soon, and then he will regret his bold actions against innocent wayfarers."

"But they need to know, your majesty, whom they are mistreating."

"Your majesty? Darius, we have royalty among us," said Bartold gleefully. "The woman in the cage is the queen."

"The queen?" repeated Darius doubtfully. "Are you sure, Bartold?"

"Note the bearing, the haughtiness," said Bartold. "She cannot hide those things behind peasant dress. Her companion defers to her and addresses her as 'Your Majesty.'" This is the queen."

"Bartold, we must get her back to the king," urged Darius.

"If we harm her in any way, the king will bring his soldiers and destroy us all."

"Do not be such a coward, Darius. Do you not realize the king's days are numbered? This very day is Tobias readying his army to march on Eustan. When the battle is done, there will be a new king. I have a plan that will make us wealthy and powerful in the new regime."

"Bartold, you have always coveted those things that are out of our reach. We will never stand side by side with the Outworlders. They will use us and then cast us off."

"This is different," assured Bartold. "We have something that Tobias needs almost as much as the crystal. He would reward us handsomely if we were to bring the queen to him."

"We should bring this to the council," replied Darius. "Such an action would have far-reaching effects and should involve all the dwarf clan."

"Don't be stupid, Darius. This plan will elevate us in the council and make us the most powerful dwarfs of all. We simply tell the others that we are taking the Outworlders to the edge of the forest and turning them over to the soldiers. The others do not have to know that we have the queen and that we will ransom her to Tobias."

"The better part of me tells me this is dangerous and foolhardy, Bartold."

"Then listen to that which is the worst part and help me to take them to the camp of the soldiers. We will be hailed as the greatest of all the dwarfs when we present her to Tobias."

"Listen to me, Darius," said the queen. "Convince your companions to take me to the king, and all of you will be richly rewarded. Bartold does everything for his own gain. You can help all your clan by taking me to Eustan. Your people will stand in favor again. This I promise you."

"We are through listening to the lies of the Outworlders,"

said Bartold. "Uncage her, Darius, and we will quickly begin our journey before any of the village can say us nay."

Darius hurriedly opened the cage and helped the queen to her feet. Bartold pushed the hapless William before him and instructed the other dwarfs to say nothing until they returned.

There was light enough in the forest to make a fast journey to the camp of the soldiers, and Bartold knew the forest well. Soon they had arrived at the edge of the Dark Wood. In the distance Bartold could see the camps of the soldiers and smelled food cooking over the fires. He pushed his captives forward, and they made their way to the first encampment.

The captain and leader of the soldiers saw the approach of the small party and a smile formed on his face.

"By my faith," he said. "Here is a strange sight indeed. Two of the smallest creatures I have ever seen have captured a woman and a boy. How did you come to apprehend two such dangerous rebels, dwarfish ones?"

"You may laugh until you know who our captives are. Then the smile will leave your face," said Bartold haughtily.

"The little man speaks with the bluster of a giant," said the captain. "Such defiance befits a much larger body."

"I am Bartold and this is Darius. We are soldiers and warriors. We have captured that which the great Tobias covets. He will reward us handsomely when we tell him what we have."

"And what do you have that would be of interest to a man like Tobias?"

"This woman is the queen. He has been hunting for her and we have captured her. It will be our reward when she is brought before him."

"The queen, eh?" the captain mused as he looked at the woman in front of him. "I do not believe this is the queen. Look at the way she is dressed."

To Plan a Rescue

"Just like an Outworlder fool to judge something by the way it looks," said Bartold derisively. "Do you think she would wear her royal robes if she were trying to avoid capture? She would not want to look like the queen."

"Before we take her to Tobias, let me confer with the men," said the captain.

Soon a small group of men were discussing the situation. They would look occasionally at Bartold and Darius and then at the queen and her companion. Bartold could only catch part of the conversation as the captain spoke to the others.

"I do not believe it is the queen," the captain said to the others around him. "She has not the royal look to her."

"None of us have ever seen the queen," said another. "If we take this woman to Tobias and she is not the queen, he may put us to death for our ignorance."

"If she were the queen," spoke another of the men, "we could take her from these small creatures easily and tell Tobias that we captured her and get the reward for ourselves."

"Then it would be well if we were sure," replied the captain. "Since we are not sure, let the dwarfs come along. If the woman is not the queen, the dwarfs will get the blame. If she is the queen, we will say that we captured them together and the dwarfs were trying to help her escape."

This appeared to be the safest course of action and all the men agreed. The captain came back to the two dwarfs who had waited impatiently as the men discussed the situation.

"We have decided to take you and your captives to Tobias," he said. "I hope for your sakes that this is the queen. Tobias is not a man with whom to trifle."

"It is the queen and we will see what Tobias thinks about two dwarfs achieving what all his soldiers could not," said Bartold sarcastically.

The queen, William, and the two dwarfs were all placed into

a wagon, and the soldiers mounted their horses and began the trip back to their camp where Tobias waited, hoping for some good news before beginning their march on the morrow.

Eager eyes watched the movement of the riders as they pulled out of their camp. Three pairs of eyes saw the queen being placed into the wagon and three hearts yearned as one to ride into the group of soldiers and remove her from captivity. Yet, they could not, for to commit such a hasty action might endanger the queen. The soldiers numbered twenty or more and the three companions knew that even their superior skills could not overcome so many. They would have to wait until the right time to make their move. They knew the riders would make camp once more and try to reach the army of Tobias before he marched his troops the following day.

"My soul burns to ride into the middle of these cutthroats and remove the queen from harm," said Aurienna angrily. "Look how they handle her as if she were a shoulder of meat they would cook over their campfires. They will pay for their impertinence."

"We feel as you do, Lady Aureinna," said Grinold. "But they are too many. This is a time when cool heads must prevail. They will have to camp tonight. When they do, we will have a plan to rescue her majesty and her companion. I care not what happens to the dwarfs. Do you think they had a hand in her capture, Cyrean?"

"I am sure of it," he replied. "I know Bartold and his desire for wealth and position. He will do anything to achieve his ends. He is much like Tobias in that way except he has not the cruelty. Bartold feels as is the world owes himself and the dwarf clan for all the misery they have suffered over time. He will play the fool and fawn and scrape to Tobias, but he will always be searching for ways to enrich himself as he does so. But we cannot concern ourselves with anything that Bartold

To Plan a Rescue

may do. It is the queen we must consider. Grinold, you spoke of a plan. Have you any way to get into the camp without being detected?"

"We will not have to sneak into the camp," replied the tracker. "We will walk in as if we belong there."

"I do not understand," said Lady Aurienna. "That would be foolhardy to give ourselves away and never lift a sword."

"We will go into the camp together. Some of the soldiers know me and will be hesitant to do anything, for they know of my closeness to Tobias in the past. I will simply tell them that I am returning from my quest to find the crystal. It was not a success, so I was returning for the march to Eustan. Cyrean will be a rebel whom the king has cast out for treason. He has come to join the army of Tobias."

"But what of me?" asked Aurienna. "The queen will see me and before she knows what we plan she may give us away."

"I have thought of that, and I have hit upon a way to make us even more welcome in their midst."

"We must not do anything that will endanger the queen," cautioned Aurienna.

"We may not have to strike a blow," said Grinold smiling. "When we enter the camp, we will have you as a prisoner. We will tell the captain that we caught you trying to sneak into the camp in an attempt rescue the queen. The queen does not know us well enough yet to know for sure what side we may favor. She will have to bear her disappointment for a time. When Aurienna and the queen are reunited, Aurienna will look for an opportune time to tell the queen what we have planned so that she may be ready when the moment presents itself. With Lord Hadreon's daughter and the queen to deliver to Tobias, we will be welcomed into the camp."

"But the dwarfs will try and turn the soldiers against us also," said Cyrean. "How will we evade their accusations? They know that I had the crystal and took it to the king. This would be the downfall of your plan."

"I have given great thought to the dwarfs, and I have something that may teach them a lesson and help us in the rescue at the same time. This is where you will play an important part in my plan, Cyrean. Even Lady Aurienna will not know what you are going to do. It will be as much a surprise to her as it will to the soldiers."

"I will do what I can to help. Come, let us ride ahead of Lady Aurienna. She is absorbed deeply in thought of what lies ahead this night."

Aurienna was indeed seeing the events of the night as she hoped they would be. She must rescue the queen. It had been she who had abandoned the queen and disobeyed the orders of the king. It must be she who now rescues her. This was the only way she could ever be in the good graces of the king again. Her two companions were good soldiers and loyal to the king. They would be strong allies in any battle they might face, and she did not fear anything with them at her side. She looked at Cyrean now in deep conversation with Grinold and wondered if he knew of her feelings for him. The events of the last few days had left little time for them to talk. She hoped that after the events of the night were over, she would have that chance. With God's help, the queen would be safe, and she could turn her mind to other things. Her mind snapped abruptly back to the present. Grinold and Cyrean had stopped. Looking back, Cyrean waved her forward, and she moved up to join her companions.

Chapter Twenty
The Confrontation

A bright moon directly over their heads illuminated the way as the three travelers kept pace with their quarry. It would not be long before they made camp at the place of the Three Oaks. This was a common resting place for travelers since it had adequate shelter, and a nearby stream provided an excellent water source. Grinold had gone over his plan to rescue the queen with Cyrean and Aurienna. Each knew what part to play, and now all that was left was the successful execution of what they had devised. They traveled in silence, each lost in his own thoughts and eager to do what must be done.

They had ridden for some time, and the companions began to worry that the soldiers might travel all night and make the entire trip without camping. However, a short time later their fears proved unfounded as horses and travelers alike grew weary and stopped at the Three Oaks. The queen was lifted off the wagon and was placed with her hands tied at the base of a large oak. William soon joined her after he had gathered wood for the fires and was tied the same as the queen. The dwarfs sat alone by their fire and sullenly accepted the stew that was offered to them by the captain. After everyone had eaten and the horses had been bedded, most of the soldiers gathered around the fires to gamble or to tell stories of their deeds and conquests. The queen and William were allowed to come to the fires for warmth and were even allowed to have their bonds removed for a short time. It was regarded as unlikely that they would try to escape in the darkness without horses or without knowing the countryside well enough to travel at night. A lute played by one of the soldiers lifted its melody into the air and soothed the aches and pains of travel. The captain and several soldiers sat at a campfire with the queen and William, each hopeful that something one of the captives said would verify that this was indeed the queen.

Soldiers by nature are a superstitious lot. They trust their lives to fate and with each new battle they survive they thank some pagan god for deliverance. They face death almost on a daily basis and confirm their courage in the face of the enemy. There is nothing of flesh and blood that can instill fear into their hearts. Yet, every one can relate a story of encounters with demons and sorcerers that made their blood run cold and their limbs shake. It is this fear of the unknown that makes cowards of the bravest men.

"It is true what I am telling you," one of the soldiers remarked in concluding his tale to nervous laughter. "For sorcery, the man was beheaded and the grisly member was thrown into the fire where it refused to burn. It was taken to the Dark Wood and cast into a sand pit where it sank, never to be seen again. I saw his grave the day after he had been beheaded. It was empty. To this day they say he searches the Dark Wood for his head. I would never go into the place, for the body of the sorcerer might not be fussy about the new head he places upon his shoulders."

"Such an ugly head as yours he would never deign to place upon himself," said another soldier to the speaker as the others laughed, glad to be in front of a blazing fire and far from the Dark Wood.

"I have lived in the Dark Wood," said Bartold, listening to the conversation and now approaching the group. "It is all superstition, these stories you tell. No one can walk abroad without a head. I knew a sorcerer who lived in the Dark Wood. Never did I see anything that would make me think he could use the dark arts. He threatened me once with a curse, but I laughed and asked what could he do that would be worse than the misshapened creature he saw in front of him. If any

The Confrontation

beings should have control of the dark arts, it would be the dwarf clan. For centuries they have toiled in the earth's bowels, making mystical weapons. They know the secrets of the greatest sorcerers who have ever existed. Who is to say that I, the Great Bartold, am not the greatest wizard who ever lived?"

"You, a wizard?" scoffed the captain. "If you have the power of a wizard, why do you not change your appearance, small one?"

"Who is to say that your appearance is handsome and mine is ugly?" Bartold replied to the captain. "Beauty can be interpreted in different ways. True, as a sorcerer I could change my features, but that would not change the ugliness of the human heart which sees what it wants to see."

"Perhaps he is not a sorcerer," said the captain. "It seems he is a philosopher who speaks of tolerance toward others. I would say that in your dealings with others you do not practice the wisdom you speak. Your actions in giving us the queen for ransom tells me you are more mercenary than monk, more selfish than selfless, and more boastful than beneficent."

The debate between the captain and Bartold might have gotten more heated had not a commotion suddenly begun in the camp. Three riders had entered, and instantly, all the soldiers had gotten weapons and were on alert. The captain moved to where the riders were now surrounded and looked at the three. They seemed harmless enough and perhaps were only seeking a night's rest there by the stream. But by nature a cautious man, the captain knew these could be spies or an advance scout party for the king. He would take no chances.

"Strangers, you have wandered into a serpent's den it would seem," the captain said. "State your business here."

"We are but weary travelers," said Cyrean, "seeking shelter and food for the night."

"We have both," answered the captain, "if indeed you be

but poor wayfarers. Alight from your horses and join us at the fire."

"We accept your hospitality, Captain," said Grinold. "It seems that you are a large party to be in the middle of nowhere. Do you travel to do battle at some later date?"

"We do not tell our business to strangers, but if you need food and warmth, both are available."

"I did not mean to be inhospitable with my questions," Grinold explained. "We rarely encounter this many soldiers who have not a battle impending."

"Then come to the fire and perhaps we will talk of these things and many others," said the captain. "I see by the rope that binds the hands of the female that you have a prisoner. She does not look like a bandit or rogue. What is her offense?"

"Neither do we tell our business to strangers, Captain," rejoined Grinold. " But some food and drink may loosen our tongues and then we will tell our story."

The three companions dismounted and followed the captain back to the fire. When they walked into the light of the campfire, Lady Ofra saw it was Aurienna and stifled a gasp. She did not know what had happened in the interim since she had last seen Aurienna. Cyrean and Grinold had seemed to be their friends and had helped her when she was wounded. She sensed somehow there was more here than met the eye, and she remained silent, hoping that soon she would be able to talk to Aurienna and discover the unusual circumstances behind her captivity.

"Find a place by the fire," said the captain. "We will place the woman with the female captive when we retie her to the oak tree. We will untie her hands and give her food. A guard will be placed with them while they eat, and in the meantime you can enjoy the comfort of our fire."

After all the men had resettled around the fire, Cyrean and

The Confrontation

Grinold were given food, and the captain asked them again to tell their story. Cyrean surveyed the soldiers and the positions of the queen and Aurienna as Grinold began to speak.

"I am Grinold, the tracker. This man, my companion, is Cyrean. Under the command of the Warlord Tobias, I have been seeking a precious object for many days now. I did not find it, but the captive we have may serve as well."

"Grinold? Come closer into the light," ordered the captain. "Yes, you are the man that I have often seen in the company of Tobias. Who is the man with you and how did you come by your prisoner?"

"I could not find the crystal," replied Grinold. "But in my search I stumbled into a pit in the Dark Wood and would have died but was rescued by this man. He heard my story of the search for the crystal and became enthusiastic for adventure like I had experienced. He has had little communication of the outside world, but with Tobias he would get the adventure he craves. He wants to be a soldier, so I have brought him with me."

"He has the air of command about him," the captain replied. "He is welcome to join us as we journey back to camp. Now, how did you come by the girl?"

"We saw her following your caravan at a distance and became intrigued with her suspicious behavior. We followed her at a distance and when we saw her spying on your camp, we captured her. She told us that her name is Aurienna and she is the daughter of Lord Hadreon, the king's chief advisor. What do you have traveling with you in which she would have such an interest?"

"Daughter to the king's chief advisor. Yes, that would explain much," mused the captain. "She was trying to rescue the woman whom we have captive. The dwarfs who brought her to us swear that she is the queen."

Bartold and Darius had been listening with great interest at the conversation between the two visitors and the captain, waiting for the right time to speak. Bartold had recognized Cyrean and Grinold immediately. He believed the woman to be the one that had been with the queen at Cyrean's hut. If this were the woman, then Cyrean and Grinold were obviously planning a rescue of the queen. Knowing that the dwarfs might give away his plan, Cyrean must have something that he was holding back. Bartold decided to wait a while longer before revealing what he knew about their visitors.

"Yes, it is as I have told you," said Bartold, now coming forward with Darius to join the circle of people. "This is the queen that we have in our midst and now the chief advisor's daughter. Tobias will have much to be thankful for."

"It is Bartold, my neighbor from the Dark Wood," said Cyrean as the dwarf completed his remarks to the group. "How came you to be in the company of these soldiers, my small friend? Have you been plotting again, and, if so, who will be the benefactor of your secret intelligence?"

"Yes, I have many secrets," replied Bartold. "Before the night is over, most of them will be revealed, and Cyrean will know how it is to be treated poorly."

"Bring the captives to the fire," ordered the captain. "Apparently, there is much I do not know. Before the night is out, all will be revealed concerning the connections among our guests. We will let the dwarfs speak, and Cyrean and Grinold will be allowed to answer. Then will we determine the truth of the events taking place this night."

A soldier brought the queen and Aurienna to the fire where they were seated close to Cyrean and Grinold. In the time she had been with the queen, Aurienna had managed to tell her most of the plan than Grinold had devised. The queen knew that there had to be more than what Aurienna had told her. If

The Confrontation

not, there would be very little chance to escape.

"Now that we are all here, we await your story, Bartold. How do you know our visitors?" asked the captain.

"I have been in the Dark Wood many years," Bartold began. "During that time a man and woman came to the woods. He was the sorcerer I talked about earlier. Soon a son arrived and there the family lived for many years. The son is the man called Cyrean. After his parents died, he remained in the forest, and from that time, ours has been an uneasy but manageable relationship until recently. He has of late had visitors to his hut. The two women you have in captivity were those visitors. I have seen this with my own eyes. Be wary of these two men, Captain. They are devious and not to be trusted."

"Is this so Cyrean? You have been accused. How do you respond?" asked the captain.

"Believe nothing that this dwarfish creature tells you," answered Cyrean. "Since I have known him, he has done nothing but evil for his own gain. He would take the queen and Lady Aurienna to Tobias because he thinks it will make him rich beyond imagination. His duty is not to king or to Tobias but only to himself."

"This in itself is not unusual among men such as we are," said the captain. "We see nothing in your accusations that would not be true of all of us."

"He speaks of riches and power," rejoined Bartold. "But this man has possessed that power which would have made the world tremble. He has had the Crystal of Light in his hands."

"Can this be true?" marveled the captain. "Have you the crystal in your possession?"

"He has it no longer, Captain, for he took it to the king," interjected Bartold. "Does this not make him a traitor? Likewise a traitor should his companion be branded, for he sides with Cyrean against Tobias, a great leader who has given him everything."

During the accusations hurled against him by the dwarf, Cyrean had remained silent and the queen and Aurienna had huddled closer together. Grinold had brought his hand close to his sword, awaiting what could be a fight for their lives. He knew he could not be captured, for to give up now would only mean execution later at the hands of Tobias. The time was now if Cyrean was going to make his move. He looked at his companion who had listened to the captain and Bartold and had now begun to speak in his defense.

"Listen to the ravings of this cowardly dwarf, Captain, but be aware of the evil within this creature who tries to convince you with lying words. He stole from my father many secrets of wizardry and can use these to his advantage whenever he wills it. Often he is overcome by his own spells and cannot control them. Then there is great danger, for anyone close to him can be affected by a charm even if it was intended for another."

"What lies are these?" blustered Bartold. "I have no charms or wizard's tricks. It is a ruse to try and to save himself and his companions."

"It is true that he spoke of himself as a wizard earlier," said one of the soldiers standing near the captain. "I was afraid, for his features are much like those who dabble in the mystic arts."

"Aye," said another. "He spoke as one who knew magic and could change shape. This bears further examination. I do not trust his looks."

"Again the Outworlders band together. Had I magical powers, I would use them now to banish all of you into darkness forever. Remember who had the crystal. He came into possession of this object because he had the wizardry to obtain it."

"Do not anger him," Captain," answered Cyrean. "His

The Confrontation

powers will manifest themselves even stronger when he becomes angry. Even he cannot control them at that moment. See how his eyes redden and his features become even more distorted. I fear it has already begun."

As Cyrean spoke, a collective gasp arose from the group of soldiers who had stood listening to the arguments. The stories that had been told earlier in the night were still fresh in their minds, and it might have been this that chilled their blood as they witnessed what was now happening to Bartold.

He had been sitting in a squatting position on the ground. Now, he suddenly began to rise without the use of his legs until he hovered several inches above the ground. When Bartold realized what was happening, he screamed in panic, throwing his legs and arms outward in wild gesticulations. The soldiers shrank back in fear, not sure what to make of the scene before them. As Bartold continued to rise into the air, his shouts intensified and he turned three times rapidly until his eyes rolled back into his head, culminating in a scream that would have chilled the bravest among them.

"He has lost control of his powers!" yelled Grinold as he looked at Cyrean whose brow was now beaded with sweat as if involved in some feat that required all his strength. "Do not... Do not let him touch you. If he touches any man during this time, it will mean a curse has fallen on him that will plague him forever. Run! Run! Hie to the woods and safety."

As Grinold finished speaking, the helpless form of the dwarf circled the fire, fanning the flames and sending sparks among the circle. The sudden movement toward them send the soldiers fleeing in different directions, never looking back for fear the form of the dwarf was upon them. The captain, who had stood transfixed during much of what had transpired, now regained his power of movement and he, too, joined his comrades in seeking safety far from the floating form above him.

When the body of Bartold finally fell to the ground, scattering ashes and sparks everywhere, the camp was empty. Cyrean collapsed to the ground, his strength momentarily sapped by the mighty effort he had performed. Grinold reached down to help him to his feet where he stood shakily for several moments before he could move under his own power.

"Hurry, my ladies," Grinold said to the two women. "We must leave while the soldiers are still in flight. Some will come to their senses soon and return to see if their eyes deceived them. We must be gone before that time."

"But what happened here, Grinold? asked Aurienna. "Does this dwarf possess the wizardry that we have witnessed?"

"No, he has no such power. But I can explain all that later with Cyrean's help. We must not remain here. First, we must find safety and then we can talk of the night's events."

Cyrean had regained enough composure to gather the horses. Grinold hurriedly untied William who stood unsteadily for a moment and then immediately went to check on the queen. He helped her to her feet and moved hurriedly to the horses as Grinold and Aurienna did the same. Quickly they mounted and were soon miles from the camp.

Riding as fast as would be comfortable for the queen, the small band never stopped. Within three hours of the rescue, they had come within sight of Eustan and slowed to rest the horses. Grinold knew the soldiers would not come this close to the city, and they would be safe until each had recovered sufficiently to continue their journey.

Cyrean and Grinold had set about gathered wood as soon as they had camped, and a cheery fire now blazed, dispelling some of the bone-chilling events that had occurred just hours earlier. William had made the queen and himself comfortable

The Confrontation

by the fire, and they both sat talking of the night's events.

"Tell me how such things could be possible," marveled the queen as she sat trembling, the fire making little impact upon the coldness she felt all through her body. "I saw the dwarf suspended in air and it was not my imagination, for the fleeing soldiers saw it as well. Had not Aurienna restrained me, I was tempted to seek the safety of the woods with the others. Aurienna, were you not afraid at such sights? Even the bravest of the soldiers fled when they saw this strangeness. How could you bear it?"

"I had been warned by Cyrean to expect something my eyes would not believe," answered Aurienna. "I did not have full knowledge of what it would be, but I was as prepared as I could be."

"I have seen similar things before," said Grinold, "but I know not how they occur. I will let Cyrean explain, for it is he who wields the power."

"What power does he mean, Cyrean?" asked Aurienna looking at him expectantly.

"Since I was just a small child, I have had the ability to move objects," explained Cyrean. "I do not know how I came to have such powers, but over time I have used these abilities enough to strengthen them until what you witnessed tonight is possible. I have been afraid to call upon them unless it was for such an occasion as this, for I feared they might have a dark purpose, but more than once they have saved those who are dear to me."

"Your father was the wizard that the king banished many years ago to the forest. Could he have bestowed such powers upon you?" asked the queen.

"It is possible that this is so. I do not know for sure," replied Cyrean. "He might have known that the dangers of the Dark Wood would be ever present, and this gift would protect me. He would have had the gift of foresight if this is true, for it has served such a purpose more than once."

"Though the dwarfs tried to give us to Tobias, I feel sympathy for them," said the queen. "They seem to act selfishly, but I believe they are misunderstood, and this is the reason they behave as they do. What will happen to them, Cyrean?"

"I'm sure they will be allowed to return to their homes. The captain will have no need of them. He believes they would make poor soldiers, and Bartold will need tending with the burns he received from the fire and the hurt to his pride. Darius will see that he gets home. The adventure he has gone through will stifle his ambition for a time and perhaps make a better person of him. It is hard to say what events will change a person for the good, but this might have been such a one for Bartold. But he is worth no more anguish from us. How is your wound, my queen. Has it healed?"

"Your poultice has worked its wonders, and I am as new," she replied. "The hours upon my horse have not done it harm. Your efforts on my behalf have not been in vain both in the tending of my shoulder or in the rescue you have performed tonight. The king will be most grateful for the service you and Grinold have performed."

"We could not have done any of them without the help of Aurienna. The king must be told of how bravely she has played her part."

"He will know," assured the queen, "for I will relate with great pride how she has done those things that few soldiers could have accomplished."

"It will be good to be within his graces again," said Aurienna. "The mark of a good soldier is that he learns from his mistakes. It was rash of me to abandon you and think only of glorifying myself through battle. But youth is served by such a mistake in that it will not be made again."

"For that we will both be grateful. Now, my companions, if we all have rested, let us ride to the castle. I miss my husband and would alleviate his fears in my regard. He will be most joyed by our appearance. With us home safely and the crystal in his possession, he will be as a young soldier again, looking forward to the battle."

"Within the hour you will see his face, your majesty," assured Cyrean. "Until that moment, let us give thanks for the good fortune we have experienced."

Helping the queen onto her horse, Cyrean thought back on the night's events, and he was indeed thankful for the victory they had won. The queen was safe and Aurienna was again by his side. He did not know what other dangers awaited him when they reached Eustan, but he knew he would meet them without fear with Aurienna by his side.

Chapter Twenty-One
A Force of Thousands

The tall figure stood upon the hill overlooking the large encampment. Thousands of tents dotted the countryside, and thousands of soldiers now milled around outside those tents in preparation for the march which was only an hour away. Today was the day that the army of Tobias would begin its move to Eustan. The soldiers were eager and up early to check their weapons and to tear down the tents which had been their home for many weeks now. A sense of urgency was in the air as the anticipation of action spread like a fire throughout the camp. Tobias looked at the activity and smiled, but he had little time to enjoy the spectacle before him. A small group of about twenty riders had topped the small knoll in front of Tobias' tent and were rapidly approaching. Tobias could tell from the stern looks upon the faces of the men that what they brought was not good news.

"Captain, I do not see any captives in your possession. Then you have not been able to find the two women?"

The captain shifted uneasily in the saddle and averted the gaze of Tobias as he spoke.

"Yes, my lord, the women were captured, but we lost them while bringing them back to camp."

"Lost them!" shouted Tobias. "How can twenty men lose two women? I send some of my best troops to bring in two women, and they return to me empty handed. How can two females escape my elite troops, Captain?"

"We were victims of sorcery, Lord Tobias. As all men here can attest, witchcraft was used to help the women escape."

"Who has knowledge of witchcraft? You were deceived. How did this happen and who is responsible?"

"It was Grinold," said the captain. "And with him he had a

man named Cyrean that I had never seen before. They came into the camp under the pretense of joining our ranks. While they enjoyed our hospitality, they plotted to take our captives, which they did with the aid of a spell placed on one of the dwarfs."

"Dwarfs? You addlepated simpleton, how did dwarfs come into the camp?"

"They were the ones who captured the queen, my lord, and brought her to us. We sent them back when the prisoners escaped. They could serve no other purpose for us."

"They captured the queen and you let her escape. My purposes would be served better if you had traveled elsewhere and the dwarfs had come to serve me. You cannot capture her nor hold onto her after she is captured. I am plagued by idiots and simpletons. Now that the king has back the queen and Lord Hadreon's daughter, his efforts to thwart me will redouble. Has he the crystal also?"

"According to the dwarfs who identified the two men, the one called Cyrean had delivered the crystal to the king."

"Then are my worst fears realized," muttered Tobias as he glumly stared at the darkening sky. "Grinold has deserted our cause. I am surrounded by men who cannot carry out the simplest mission. Even the heavens show a dark portent as we prepare to march. But I am in too far to pursue a former course. The gods frown upon the man who shows fear at the first obstacle that is thrown onto his path. We will march our soldiers and hope that the spies that we have within the castle will aid our cause and find a way for our army to push within the gates."

"Then we still march within the hour?" asked the captain.

"Assemble my commanders," said Tobias as a way of dismissing the captain and answering his question at once. "There is no turning back. All that I have strived for is now at arm's length, waiting for the taking. How often is the path of ambition strewn with the clutter of high design, thwarted and dashed to earth because the traveler let the specter of doubt bar his way. I am buoyed by that which stands as a barrier between my desires and their acquisition, for that resistance only makes me stronger. It emboldens me and speeds the blood through my veins until my heart is filled to bursting. This is the time that I have lived for, a time that will write my name into history as the greatest conqueror of all. See how the clouds now part as the pride of my ambition wills the sun to come forth and smile on my undertaking. Before this day is over, King Malvore will know my might and my resolve."

The clouds indeed had parted and the sun now shone forth as if a testament to assure Tobias that the time was right for his ascension to the throne. He mounted his horse and rode to the top of a small hill where he could be seen by all the soldiers encamped around the plain in front of him.

"Soldiers in the army of Tobias!" he shouted. "You are gathered on the morning of a great march. By sundown we will be within sight of Eustan. When the feeble king sees our might, he will shake and tremble in fear. Ours will be a noble victory, for we will all share in its triumph. Those that survive will be given wealth and land and the love of your new king. You will not need to travel from conflict to conflict, selling your sword to the warlord who has the most gold. You will own the land which I will bequeath to you. In return all I ask is that you will support me in my rule. Mine is a noble ambition. All that I do will be in concern and compassion for the people that I will govern. I care not for wealth, nor am I an ambitious man. There will never be hunger nor poverty in the kingdom that I rule. There will be no men who slave all year only to give up that which they have gained in taxes to a tyrant king. We set out on a glorious mission to make the kingdom whole again by

A Force of Thousands

deposing a weak and selfish monarch. Under my rule all men will be free to benefit from his efforts. Who will join me in my quest?"

From thousands of throats came the shout that resounded through the hills.

"All hail, Tobias. "All hail the next king."

The sound of horns set into motion a thunderous din as soldiers mounted their horses, and huge catapults on wheels began to move from the camp. The army had begun its march. Even Tobias observed in awe the juggernaut as it moved toward Eustan and marveled that so many men with so many varied backgrounds could be united in a common cause. Tobias smiled as he thought of whom that cause would most benefit. The brain of a soldier was a very simple organ. Give him a weapon, tell him of gold, and point him in the right direction. Tobias knew the only man who would benefit from the carnage that was to come would be Tobias himself, but no one else needed to know. A man will fight for a lie as quickly as he will the truth. When this day was done, many men would be dead on both sides. The number was incidental to Tobias as long as he achieved his objective.

Tobias motioned his aide to his side and spoke briefly to him. He sped away on his horse and soon the captain was riding to meet Tobias.

"Have you contacted my spy at Eustan?" he asked the captain.

"He will meet you at the appointed spot when you are in sight of the castle," the captain replied. "He says that he has news that will be welcome to your ears, Lord Tobias."

"Good news is most welcome. Join your men and keep up their spirits. This day will see an army gathered that has seldom been seen in the history of war."

The captain turned his horse and moved to join the ranks

of soldiers that were marching to Eustan. Tobias and a small contingent of soldiers rode off to the right flank of the army and soon were away from the congestion of the mass of the procession.

The day lengthened and gradually the enthusiasm that had been so evident at the beginning of the day had settled into the tedium of any march. Men cursed tired horses as they plodded in the dust and wake of hundreds of others before them. Carts with broken wheels sat on the side of the road, waiting for repair. Huge machines of war had to be maneuvered past obstacle after obstacle until the handlers of these massive weapons grew tired and short tempered. When at last the hills surrounding Eustan could be seen, it was a weary contingent that welcomed the sight.

When camp had been made and the soldiers had settled in for the night, Tobias set forth to meet his contact from the king's palace. After a thirty minute ride, he came upon a small grove of trees and, using the signal they had established previously, he whistled three short bursts and a figure soon emerged from the trees.

Leaving the small force that had accompanied him, Tobias rode to meet the hooded figure. They stepped down from their horses and soon were in earnest conversation.

"Is everything in readiness?" asked Tobias of the cloaked figure.

"My men are positioned as we planned," he replied. "All that remains to be done is to find some way to get the crystal. Even if it cannot be put into your possession, having it away from use by the king's forces would be just as advantageous. I have means to get to the crystal. It is well protected but with my position in the king's chain of command, I can gain access quickly."

"Are the men positioned close to the pulleys on the gate so

that they may be opened at the critical juncture in the battle?"

"They are so placed and have their orders."

"Then what else remains for us to do?" asked Tobias.

"I have discovered that in the mountain wall behind the castle are a series of caves that apparently had been used by cave dwellers long before the building of the castle. I have been told that there is a passageway into and out of these caves from the back of the mountain. If this passageway can be discovered, then soldiers can gain entrance to the castle by this means."

"This is good news," said Tobias. "But if such caves exist, the king will know of them also and of the passageway. He will try in the moment of our victory to get his family out through these caves. We must be prepared for that that possibility."

"I have many men now scouting the area from the north side," said the cloaked figure. "The sea is at the base of the mountain and prevents any access to the cliffs other than by boat. The people of Eustan can go into the caves, but there is no escape on the other side, for the sea breaks upon the rocks there and no ships can come into the area. The only escape would be to hurl themselves into the sea and that is certain death. If we are fortunate enough to find the entrance to the caves, a few of our men could gain access to the castle by this route. In the event escape should be tried through this means, a small force such as we would have lodged there could prevent such an effort."

"Have some men stay with the search and keep me informed," said Tobias. "Such knowledge could be a turning point in the battle."

The hooded figure nodded assent and mounted his horse. He had soon disappeared into the grove of trees, and Tobias rode back to rejoin his men.

As in all historic events, many lives and many conflicts play a part in the outcome. The large drama of war has room for many intangibles, some of which will be instrumental in the struggle. In the Dark Wood, one of those intangibles was now becoming an actuality.

Bartold and Darius had returned to the dwarf village in shame. Bartold had dreamed of becoming a hero of his people, and now he had to bear the shame of those people knowing he had failed. Not only had he failed, but his scars were always going to be constant reminders of the time when he almost had more power and wealth than he had ever known. As he dressed the burns on his arms and legs, he reflected upon the events of the past few days. He did not know the ways of fortune, but there was one thing he did know. Each time he had attempted to gain advantage for himself, he had suffered misfortune. Was this the curse of the dwarf clan or a curse on him alone? What determined that one man prospers while another fails? Could a man with the failings of character so evident in Tobias actually conquer the world they knew? If such a man could be rewarded with the crown, why could not Bartold achieve a similar, if somewhat lesser, status using the same methods? He had tried and failed. Somewhere in the depths of his conscience, Bartold knew the answers to the questions he had been asking himself. If mankind succeeds by using force to conquer others, he has gained nothing. A servile connection to a governing force will never achieve a lasting bond. Tobias would never have the loyalty that King Malvore had achieved through years of dedication to his people. And in the end, if Tobias had power but not the love of his people, then his rule was a farce and doomed to rot from within until nothing was left but the fragile shell upon which the kingdom had been founded. In their own small world, Bartold had seen similar workings in the dwarf clan. Only when they had strived together toward a common cause had they been successful. If there was a chance that Tobias could succeed, then it was time to make a choice among themselves. Bartold had decided on what course he wanted to pursue. Now it was a matter of convincing the council when they convened to listen to what he had to say.

That night the Council of Twelve met to discuss what had been plaguing Bartold with doubts since his return to the village. Each member of the council realized that the war would affect them in some way. Whether the king retained his crown or Tobias stripped it from him, it would cause a change in the Dark Wood and in their lives. They could not remain neutral and hope that the world would not change. They knew that was not possible and not to make a decision here would simply mean it would be made for them later. When the Council had been seated, Bartold stepped forward to speak.

"To the Council of Twelve I address these remarks. I do not expect to have a strong voice here in this chamber. My actions of late have proven to be selfish and contrary to the welfare of the dwarf clan. But hear me for what I have learned if not for what I have accomplished. I have been witness to man's inhumanity to man, not only in the outside world but also in this wood we call home. I have also witnessed the good that resides within us all. In all of us, whether dwarf or Outworlder, resides a mixture of good and evil. But we have the power to choose which will rule our lives. We are capable of ambition and greed just as surely as those that we would condemn for exhibiting those frailties. It is not the size of the man that is important but the size of the heart that matters. I have seen in the Outworlders' nobility and courage. In times of crisis, one has risked his life for another. Yes, men like Tobias exist and I have done those things that would make me worthy of his company. But we are men also in spirit and soul, if not in size, and we can change those things that are base in our natures. I stand here before you to exhort this council to take a stand for the king and the kingdom. Let us not languish here and let others decide our fate. Regardless of the decision of this council to what I have proposed, I will go to Eustan and serve as the king sees need to use me. Make the decision to join me, and we will go together this night to the king."

The Highest of the Most High arose from his chair to address the council and, looking at Bartold, he began his remarks.

"We have seen the baser qualities of the dwarf who stands before us, my brothers. He has made a powerful plea. It is now for us to determine how much truth is contained in his words. He has proven false to us before. How do we know this is not a ruse to achieve that which he has sought and been denied? I ask that all of you consider carefully what you are being asked to do, for it will determine whether our small clan will continue to exist once the war is over."

"I have been with Bartold," answered Darius. "I have seen the transformation of which he has spoken. I believe his words and vote to go to Eustan."

"If we are to take sides, I wish to be with the old king," said another. "He has never done anything to harm us or our way of life. I cannot say what Tobias would do, and it is that unknown that frightens me. I vote to go to Eustan."

When the voices of all the council had been heard, Bartold had gotten that which he had wished for his people. The decision was made and Bartold was made the leader of a small contingent of dwarfs who would go the king and pledge their allegiance. When the village was assembled and volunteers were requested, threescore and two small men stood in the village courtyard awaiting orders. Bartold in an unselfish act had finally achieved that which he had sought so long. He had a following at which he was the head and a purpose which would benefit not just him alone but all those in his village. The pride he felt in his heart could not be bought with money or gained through manipulation. It was achieved through a selfless act that would change Bartold for all time.

Chapter Twenty-Two
Prelude to War

The King paced the conference room, waiting for news from Lord Hadreon. Advance scouts had brought news that the army of Tobias was on the move. The kingdom's defenses were as well prepared as they could be due to the diligence of Lord Hadreon. No word had come to them concerning the queen. If she were a captive of Tobias, the three companions sent out to find her would need all the skill they possessed to free her. The king could only pray that they were not taken also in their mission.

"Ah, young heads and a passion for adventure are not a good combination," mused the king. "I fear that they will be rash in their zeal to rescue the queen and in turn will endanger themselves. I cannot remember being so bold and reckless as a young man. Now, even our women leave the safety of their homes and rush into battle to prove themselves. Once there was a day when even war was honorable and fought by honorable men for what they believed. Today, wars are fought to conquer and enslave, and honor lies buried under the heels of tyrants like Tobias. I long for those days when a man judged himself by his courage against a foe in combat face to face. Now, weapons of great force such as the Crystal of Light have taken away the sword and replaced it with a fire that consumes all in its path. Such a weapon belongs in the bowels of Hell where it was forged. No good can come from a weapon that can wreak such destruction. I will not call upon it even in defense of my own family. It shall remain hidden and when this war is over, it will be cast into the deepest and darkest part of the sea, hopefully to remain forever buried under its shifting sands."

"My liege, I see that you have heard the news that has come from the camp of Tobias," said Lord Hadreon, upon entering the conference room and finding the king in deep contemplation. "You have paced many times through these chambers. Your worry will not start the conflict any quicker nor bring home the queen any sooner."

"It is in the nature of a leader to worry. The crown sits heavy upon my brow, Lord Hadreon. Have you any good news of our young people in their search?"

"Nothing at present, my lord. Though it has not been discovered by our spies that they nor the queen are in the clutches of Tobias."

"Then that is good news and until worse shall make itself known, I will take joy in its hearing," said the king.

"Our most renown scholars are examining the Crystal of Light," Lord Hadreon assured the king. "By the time Tobias' forces arrive on the morrow, we will have unlocked its secrets. With such a weapon, we cannot lose."

"I will not use the crystal, Lord Hadreon. It has been a weapon that has demonstrated time and time again that it knows not whether the wielder is good or evil. Through all wars in which it has appeared, there was no clear victor, for it distinguishes not one from another. I order it hidden away until that time when we can destroy it forever."

"But, my liege, in so doing we are throwing away certain victory. The crystal, if used wisely, will turn the tide in our favor with little loss of life."

"We do not know enough about the weapon to control it," replied the king. "If there were more time available to us to unlock its potential, I might be more favorable to its use in our cause, but we cannot risk our own people in unleashing its power without a thorough understanding of its capabilities."

"I have ever heeded the commands of my king, and I will not disobey them now before the most important battle of our lives. I will go to the advisors who possess the crystal and tell them to hide it until the battle be won."

"I thank you for your loyalty and your understanding, Lord Hadreon. Send General Draco to me when this news is given to our troops."

"I will send for him immediately, your majesty," replied Lord Hadreon turning to take his leave.

The questions which had plagued the king before the entrance of Lord Hadreon earlier now manifested themselves manifold as King Malvore sat at the table waiting for General Draco.

"Am I doing the right thing for my people?" he questioned himself aloud. "With such might at our disposal, perhaps it is wise to harness the knowledge we have and use it at any risk. Perhaps it would be best to use it as a deterrent. Tobias knows that we have it. If we only display it for him to see, that could be enough to have him restrain his forces for another day. But no, the soldier in me says that the time is now if ever we are to meet, for we are as prepared as we can be for the onslaught of his forces."

Tired from the strain of so many internal conflicts, the king placed his head into his hands and bent forward until only a hunched form could be discerned in the growing darkness of the room. He remained this way for several minutes until the sound of footsteps brought him back to the present, and he straightened as he saw the form of General Draco enter the room.

"You sent for me, my king?" asked General Draco, standing squarely at attention as he addressed King Malvore.

"Yes, General Draco. Are your troops in readiness for the battle tomorrow? Tobias will be at our gates when the sun arises. Is all as it should be for that time?"

"We will not fail in our duties to the kingdom, your majesty. With the crystal at our disposal, we have a weapon

Prelude to War

that will turn Tobias on his heel and decimate his army."

"The crystal will not be used, General. Our battle will be fought as of old, with swords and lances at close quarters. We will see how the cowardly forces of Tobias will fight when they come face to face with their opponent. It will be a glorious battle, General, and many will be the stories that we will tell of the conflict in years to come."

"But, my liege, with the crystal the conflict will be short and many lives will be saved. I will carry it into battle myself. Place me in charge of its keeping and I will bring you a great victory."

"I have spoken and my word once uttered is law. You, General Draco, will fight the battle of your life without the crystal. Rally the troops as only a great leader can. The crystal will remain hidden until the battle is done."

"Where has it been hidden? I will need to know so that I can have troops ready to protect it, your majesty."

"I have given orders that it be tossed into the sea if it becomes apparent that defeat is our curse. No one will ever make use of it again for means of conquest. It was not meant for mortal man, and I will not allow it to fall into Tobias' hands a second time."

"Time and time again you have not entrusted me with the means to protect the kingdom, your majesty. How am I, the general of your armies, to fulfill that trust if you tie my hands by not allowing me to have the weapons I need?"

"Trust is earned over time, General. Many have been the occasions when you have taken it upon yourself to use men of questionable loyalty to the kingdom to carry out missions that were not of my direct command. You have stopped just short of treason to the crown on many occasions, General. If it were not for your family, I would have replaced you long ago. Your father was one of my best fighting men years ago. He gave his life defending the kingdom, and I promised him as he lay dying that you would be placed at the head of my armies. I fulfilled that promise, but bear this in mind, General Draco, what I have given I can just as easily take away."

"Then I will prove myself worthy as I have done in the past. All that I have done was in concern for the kingdom. If you think so little of my skills, your majesty, this battle will be my last. I have long been aware that you listen closely to the advice of those who would have me replaced. The scars that I have upon my face are there because I was appointed by you to defend the realm. That I have done and this is my reward. A dog in the streets begging for food holds a greater place in your esteem than I do. So let it be said now that I will fulfill my duties until this battle is won, and then I will quit my station here to pledge my loyalty elsewhere."

"If once the battle is done and you have fought an honorable fight, I will be the first to greet you and ask for forgiveness, General. The measure of the man is in his deeds. Do those things that are necessary of a great leader, and you will stand on my right hand when the honors of battle are given forth."

"I go to prepare, your majesty. We will talk again when the battle is won."

King Malvore watched as the general strode from the room and wondered if he had placed the fate of the kingdom in the hands of a man that could not be trusted. The general had used questionable methods many times before in defense of Eustan. Yet, in the end the kingdom remained strong. If the ends do justify the means, then General Draco had done what was expected of him. Still, King Malvore worried that he had allowed too much latitude in those methods used by the general and that he and the kingdom would be judged by the general's actions. Nothing could be done now, for the battle

Prelude to War

was upon them, but future indiscretions on the general's part would be met with harsh discipline.

King Malvore walked from the council chamber and out onto a balcony overlooking the courtyard. In the distance he could see the light of many campfires, and he knew that soon a great army would be massed at the gates of Eustan.

As the king turned to reenter his chambers, a loud commotion arose in the courtyard and then a general laughter lifted from the ranks of people who were standing at the opened gate. King Malvore strained to see what had caused the gates to be opened, but he could not make out the figures of the visitors. He made his way down to the courtyard where General Draco and Lord Hadreon had already taken command of the situation. Upon seeing the king on the steps of the castle, a hush fell upon the mass of people and they all bowed in reverence to the king.

"Lord Hadreon, what is the meaning of this commotion? Why are the gates opened when an army waits to attack us at any give moment?"

"Your majesty, it seems that we have the great honor to be witness to a significant event," replied Lord Hadreon. "The dwarf clan has come to help us in our battle at dawn and stand here now with a mighty force of threescore and three. Will these new recruits come forward for the king's inspection?"

A shuffling began within the crowd and people parted. Through the throng and through sounds of laughter marched a group of small men to stand before the king.

"Who are you?" asked the king. "How do you plan to serve our cause?"

"I am Bartold the Brave," said the leader of the group, "and these are men of the dwarf clan. We come to serve the king in whatever means he chooses. We have always been a people apart, but with war threatening to destroy our homes, we meet now to defend that which is ours."

"A noble cause indeed and your small army is welcome to fight with the forces of the king on the morrow," said King Malvore.

"No!" said General Draco, stepping forward to address the king. "As commander of our army, I will not allow my troops to fight with this band of misfits. They are not soldiers. Two of them would not make one good soldier for our ranks. They have never done anything for the kingdom before. Why would they desire to do so now? They have been sent by Tobias to cause mischief to our efforts. When the time is right, they will turn on us and allow Tobias to gain an advantage."

"We do not fight for a blustering general," rejoined Bartold. "We fight for the king and the kingdom. We do not take orders from anyone other than the king. If it is his will that we stay and fight, that is what we will do."

"The toad dares to insult me! I will run him through with my sword!" thundered General Draco, removing his weapon from its scabbard.

"No, General Draco, sheath your sword," commanded the king. "These men have come to help us and we will graciously accept them into our ranks. We will find places for all of them on the walls. The sting from a small scorpion is just as deadly as that of the adult. Welcome, men of the Dark Wood and know your efforts here will not go unrewarded."

Knowing that he had no choice but to obey a royal command, General Draco took his leave of the king and returned to his post. All the dwarfs but Bartold were taken to points on the castle walls where they would be most useful. Bartold was taken to the council room where he could be questioned about what they had seen as they journeyed to Eustan.

"We had to be very careful, for the soldiers of Tobias cover all the roads," said Bartold as he answered one of the questions concerning the enemy's troop deployment. "Being small, we could move through the high grass and scrub brush undetected. They have large machines that can rain rock and fire upon the castle. It is an army such as I have never seen. Tobias is confident that victory is inevitable."

"Did you see others upon the road?" asked Lord Hadreon. "We have waited long for news of a small band that we hoped would be here by now."

"Then the queen has not arrived?" asked Bartold puzzled.

"Do you know of the queen?" asked Lord Hadreon, suddenly alert.

"Yes, I was in the camp when she made her escape with Cyrean and Grinold. She and Lady Aurienna fled to the woods where I assumed they joined up with their rescuers and had made their way back here. It is strange that they have not arrived."

"Then they did escape," said Lord Hadreon. "Your majesty, our prayers have been answered. They have encountered difficulty getting through the troops that are stationed along the roads. I will send out a small garrison to search for them. A few men can still move through the byways undetected."

"Yes," agreed King Malvore. "Something within my heart tells me they are alive and well. We must get them within the safety of the castle walls. If they are in hiding and spot our search party, they will reveal themselves and be back here before dawn. It will make the rising of the sun a welcome event rather than the darkness that accompanies an impending battle."

"Your heart has ever been right when it has touched on me," said a soft voice from just outside the door of the council chamber. The king arose from the table with a speed that belied his fragile condition. He looked at the guard who now was opening wide the doors of the council room. Framed there in the glow from the hallway lamps stood the queen.

Chapter Twenty-Three
The Return of the Queen

It took just a moment for the king to regain his senses. Then he rushed to meet the queen, and they held each other for several moments. The queen cried softly as she embraced her husband again for the first time in many days. Behind her, standing in the doorway, was Aurienna, who smiled and brushed a tear from her eye. Aurienna and her companions entered the chamber and Lord Hadreon hastened to welcome his only child.

"My daughter," he said softly, "we never lost hope that you would return safely with the queen, and now our prayers have been answered. I will never send you away again. The fate that awaits us we will meet together."

Lord Hadreon welcomed Cyrean and Grinold and ordered food and drink for them. When everyone was seated at the table, the king spoke in a hearty voice.

"Our families have returned to us and for this we are thankful. These old eyes have seen many things but never anything more beautiful and inspiring than the small band of family and friends that has just returned to us. My wife is safe. My counselor's daughter is well and back in our good graces for her fearless devotion to the crown. The young men who have fought with her are most welcome, and we will come to know them more fully before the night is over."

"I echo the king's heartfelt words," said Lord Hadreon. "When our small ally told us that you had escaped from Tobias' men and had not returned, we feared some other misfortune had claimed you."

When Lord Hadreon acknowledged the contribution of Bartold, all eyes turned to the dwarf whose head was barely above the level of the table.

"Yes," said Grinold, "the little man has had more

adventures and escaped harm more times than someone with twice his bulk."

"Why are you here?" asked Cyrean of Bartold. "You have always been quick to condemn those who live outside the Dark Wood. Yet now you sit at the table with the king and queen. How have you grown so bold that you now sit with those that you once hated?"

"Like the wind, a man's mind can change directions," replied the dwarf. "Man was given a brain so that he could decide right from wrong. It may have taken some time, but my mind has been fired to support the king."

"More than your mind has been fired," joked Cyrean good naturedly. "It is good to see that you are recovering from your injuries."

"I know not what happened to me," said Bartold, "but I know that somehow you played a part in the events at the camp. But be that even so, I will not harbor ill will toward you. I am a changed man who has come to fight for the king. We are comrades now, Cyrean. Those days are gone when we could be foolish, and I would mock you and throw stones upon your hut. The time is not right for levity. You have returned in time to stand with me and my brothers on the parapet, and we will hurl stones together at the tyrant who would destroy our way of life."

"Yes, all of you have returned in time," said the king. "Your lateness cast a shadow across my heart for a moment, but it has been dispelled with your safe appearance here."

"We would have arrived sooner," said Aurienna, "but we saw the dwarfs making their way to Eustan, and we waited to see which force they would join. Their reluctance to reveal themselves to the soldiers camped in the woods told us which they had chosen. We simply followed them in when the gates were opened."

"Now we are one again with no harm to any," said the king. "I would hear more of your escape from Tobias' men."

"If all of Tobias' army are like the ones we encountered, our victory will be swift," promised Aurienna. "They are superstitious buffoons, your majesty."

"Do not underestimate the power of your enemy, my child," the king warned. "That is the first lesson that a soldier learns. Tobias is no fool and he will be a formidable enemy regardless of the simpletons he commands. How did you escape the camp with so many men to prevent movement?"

"I am not sure of the means myself, your majesty. Somehow, unknown to me, some wizardry was used. Cyrean and Grinold have not explained all to me. Perhaps with your persuasion, they will confess the matter."

"Cyrean, when we met earlier, we had no time to speak of familiar matters. And once this day begins we know not what may transpire. Tell me of your family."

"You know them well, my husband," said the queen gently.

"How do I know them? What is your father's name, lad?"

"It is Arthur Pendrall, your majesty. He once served here in this very castle."

"Pendrall? Of course!" exclaimed the king, his eyes widening in surprise. "He was my closest counselor at that time. I did not know he had a son."

"I was born in the Dark Wood, your majesty. I know very little of the event that separated my father from your affections. What I have learned of that time, I have learned mostly through others who were there. My father would not speak of it and even at the edge of Death's door never revealed more to me. I sense it was a dark time in his life and that he felt he had been betrayed by someone. Were you that man, your majesty?"

"I have thought many times of that occasion and whether I

made the right decision in banishing my closest ally to the Dark Wood. I was stirred to action by General Draco who said that he had witnessed the wizard placing a spell on my sons. When I witnessed the action myself, I became enraged and allowed my emotions to overcome reason. No one spoke for him at his trial, and he refused to speak in his own defense. It seemed as if he felt the revelation of his purpose would cause some great calamity to occur."

Cyrean stirred uneasily in his chair as he witnessed the flood of emotions that swept across the king's face.

"I know little of those events so many years ago, your majesty. But of this I am sure. My father would not have hurt your sons. In the twenty years that I knew him I witnessed only kindness in his actions. He loved me and my mother, and all that he did was for us. I never saw him use the mystic arts. If he possessed that ability, I was not aware. The only way that I know that he was different is through the gift I have. I feel that somehow it came from him, and I was unsure of its purpose until the events of the last few days. Now I know it was given to me for some higher purpose. Perhaps in the next few days that purpose will be revealed."

The king had listened with interest to Cyrean's testimony in regard to his father. He turned to Grinold and spoke to him.

"Have you witnessed this gift, Grinold? Was this the ability that was used to free you and the others?

"Yes, your majesty. It has saved my life more than once in the time I have known Cyrean. Now it has saved the queen and Aurienna."

"I have much to sorrow for, Cyrean," said the king sadly. "I cast out your father and now his son returns to save my family. In our lives we do those things that we think are right, but even the king has not the gift of hindsight. I know now that your father was doing those things that would protect my sons

The Return of the Queen

and the kingdom, but I refused to see. A king should have better insight into those people in whom he puts his trust. Can you forgive a foolish old man who acted too quickly and too harshly in judgment?"

"My father never spoke harshly of you, your majesty. I am his son and I carry his blood within my veins. I will not judge you and say that you acted unseemly, for I know little of the motives that compelled your actions. Only you can look into your heart and know the answers. When you can do that and forgive yourself, you will not need mine."

Lady Ofra placed her hand on her husband's arm and caressed it as she would a child's as the king fought back the tears that came into his eyes. Suddenly, as if she had forgotten the most momentous occasion of her life, the queen turned to the others.

"Where is William?" she asked as if his absence meant the circle was not complete as the king had said.

"He was taken to one of the chambers to bathe and sleep," said Aurienna. "I do not believe he has rested since he undertook the protection of your majesty's person. Do you wish that I awaken him?"

"No, let him sleep," said the queen. "You will like the young man, my husband. He reminds me so much of you at his age. If he so desires, I would like for him to stay with us. His mother can be brought to Eustan and they can make their home here, unafraid that a raid will ever harm any of their family again."

"Then that order will be given when the battle here is done," said the king.

As the talk had begun to center around family and friends and those near at heart, Grinold had become more and more restless. He had taken a hurried leave of Madelyn to go with his comrades to find the queen. He knew that she would be worried and anxious to hear of his safety. She had agreed to stay under the king's protection in the castle and had often brought the king's meals when he did not feel well enough to rise and walk about.

"Your majesty, I also have a story to tell," said Grinold. "But if you will grant me leave to find Madelyn, my story will be easier for me. She has feared for my safety, and I would let her know that I have returned."

"Oh, yes, Madelyn. She is a beautiful young woman who has adapted well to life here in the palace. It is as if she was born into a higher station but fate played her falsely.
Send a guard to bring her to the chamber. She shall enjoy your return with us. In the meantime stay and tell us your story."

Grinold had hoped to see Madelyn alone. The things he had to say were for her ears only. Soon the morning would break, and the uncertainty of his fate in that battle made it all the more important to speak to her of his feelings. But he was a guest of the king and, as such, he knew he should remain at the king's request.

"Your majesty, my story is one of degradation, of sloth, and of wasted potential. You see before you a man who has spent his life in gaming and debauchery. My parents were killed in one of the many raids on my village when I was just a small boy. With no one to guide me, I took to the streets. Before long I had learned the ways that humanity can take advantage of frailties in others. I gambled and rarely lost. Like my companion, Cyrean, I had a gift. Where I received it I may never know. Unlike my companion, I used it for evil purposes and selfish gain. I could read a man's eyes, yea, even his soul as I sat across the table from him. My spoils I wasted and even to this day I have nothing but the clothes that I wear. I was taken in by Tobias when I was in the depths of despair and, through his use of me, my soul took on a darkness that even I could

not fathom. I have escaped that darkness now and, though it mean my death, I will not go back to that time in my life.
Bartold has said a change was wrought in him, and I can say now that a like change has brought me here to serve in this conflict. If I die here, it will be an honorable death among good friends."

Madelyn had entered the chamber just as Grinold was finishing his story and with a stifled cry went to the table and sat by his side.

"Now is the circle complete," said the king in satisfaction. "Cyrean and Grinold, you will take positions of command into which I would have placed my sons were they here today. Bartold, you will command your troops, but you will be under the charge of General Draco. You do not have to respect his character, but his ability to lead has never been questioned. If the day is to be won, he will have to inspire his troops to fight as they have never done before. Aurienna, you will obey your father's wishes regarding the part you will play. I cannot say that you will fight if that is not his wish. There will be a time when you will be needed. If it is not today, then it will be at another time when the fates have decreed so. Now I must rest. It will be dawn soon and we know not what the day holds for us."

The king and queen arose and took their leave of the guests. Little rest would there be for any of the castle that night. The others soon followed and the chamber was deserted except for Grinold and Madelyn who sat with hands clasped. Little was spoken but no words had to be said to convey what was in their hearts. Aurienna and Cyrean had gone out to the wall to look over the preparations. Their talk was about battle and heroic deeds, but they too spoke of what life would be like for them after the battle was over.

"I know my father will let me fight by your side," said

Aurienna. "He has taught me the skills of a soldier, and I can fight as well as any man. At times like this, we cannot think of me as a woman or the daughter of the chief advisor. All able hands are needed, and my hands and heart are eager for what lies ahead. Do you fear that war will separate us forever, Cyrean? I know it sounds womanish of me to fear losing you, but to have found someone that I could spend my life with only to lose him so quickly would darken the rest of my existence."

"I fear that war may take some of those we love, Aurienna. I will not let it take you. Promise me that should I receive a wound that you will not put your life in peril to try and save mine."

"I cannot make such a promise, Cyrean. It would not be in my nature to do so. Let us not talk of war. Instead tell me what our lives will be like in the days to come."

"I do not know what I will do when the battle is done, but I will not return to the Dark Wood. Wherever I go, I want you with me, Aurienna. There are many things to see that my limited boundaries have denied me up to the present time. Aurienna, will you go where I go and be part of the new discoveries I hope to make?"

"Where you go, I will go. Where you sleep, I will sleep. Your enemies will also be mine, and none there will be who can come between us. To you, Cyrean, I pledge my heart and my life."

"Then let us enjoy the next hours until the first blow in the battle is struck. Look, there is Grinold and with him his lady Madelyn. They will rejoice with us in our union."

"It seems that sleep eludes you as well, my friends," said Grinold as he and Madelyn made their way to the wall. "The anticipation of such an event as we will see today denies us the rest our bodies need. But the excitement I feel is not in anticipation of the battle but the pledge I have made to Madelyn. When this battle is done, we are to be wed. I have never known such happiness until today. With the light heart that beats within my breast, I could fly over these walls and conquer the army of Tobias as easily as I draw breath."

"Now my happiness is redoubled," replied Cyrean, "for Aurienna and I have also plighted our love. We will stand together when that time comes when two shall be as one."

"It is agreed," responded Grinold. "You are the one true friend that I have had in my life. It is only fitting that our wedding day should be the same."

The light conversation among the four friends was interrupted abruptly by a shout from above as a terrified scream came from a soldier on the wall. Suddenly, a body was hurled from the wall and plummeted into a twisted mass of arms and legs only feet from where Cyrean and his companions stood.

"Let this be a lesson to anyone else who falls asleep on his post!" thundered the voice of General Draco. "Every man who is not at his post and alert will be subject to the same punishment. There will be time for sleep when the battle is done. Be not prepared, and your sleep will be a permanent one."

"Is there not a better way to discipline, General?" asked Aurienna as she looked scornfully at the imposing figure high above them. "How can a dead man help us to fight a war?"

"Ah, it is the young daughter of the Chief Counsel. Yes, the one who would be a soldier. You have often presumed to tell me how to conduct my affairs. I have not the time nor the disposition to listen to the banal whines of one who has never fought a battle but presumes to tell me how to do so. Be watchful, young Aurienna, that when the battle is hottest you guard your back carefully. There may be some who do not like your impertinence."

"And you should watch, General Draco, that you do not overstep those boundaries that even one of your rank has to observe. It is obvious that human life means little to you. A soldier to you is simply a weapon, to use until it has served its purpose and then cast away. The king abides you, for he feels an obligation to your father. I have no such obligation, and I will do everything in my power to have you removed when the this battle is done."

"I would treat you as I would a fly that buzzes about my ear and annoys me until I crush it with my hand. The threats of a mere stripling girl do not concern me. Come to me again when your weapon can provide the sting that your words cannot."

The general turned and moved back into the shadows of the wall high above them. Cyrean reached for Aurienna's arm as she moved to ascend the steps to where the general was now repositioning two of the soldiers.

"No, Aurienna. This is not the time to let our emotions outweigh the greater good. You cannot lift a weapon against the commander of our army. It would not be wise for the others to see dissension in our ranks. Time has a way of revealing human nature. The general will make a mistake that will show the king his true allegiance. When he makes that mistake, we will be there to help remove him from our lives forever."

"You are right, Cyrean. This is not the moment, but I see a time when the general and I will talk again. That conversation will prove who is the better soldier."

As the four companions turned to leave, a shout was given by the lookout. A rider from Tobias' army had come to the gate demanding to talk to the king. The gate was opened to admit the rider and he was taken to King Malvore. Cyrean and Aurienna hurried to the council room to hear the news.

"I come from the camp of Commander Tobias, your majesty," said the messenger. "He has a proposition that could prevent this war."

"The only concessions I will make will be when I see his army turned away from Eustan," answered the king. "Give me the message and then be on thy way."

"Commander Tobias asks only that you turn over the Crystal of Light to him. If you will do this, he will take his army from Eustan. He says to inform you that Eustan will be safe. The world is a large place and there are other, less resistant, kingdoms he can rule. He asks only that you reply before sunrise. After that time, nothing can save your kingdom and he will take the crystal by force."

"Then take him my answer now and let the sun rise on his defeat, for I will never turn the crystal over to such a tyrant. Does he think that I feel less responsible to the people who live outside my rule? As long as I draw breath, he will not have such a weapon at his command for use in enslaving people in any part of the world. Let the base coward bring his army to the castle, for he needs to know how a free people will fight to keep what is rightfully theirs."

"I hear and will deliver the answer," said the messenger.

As the gates were opened to allow the messenger passage, Cyrean and Aurienna went and stood by the king who looked out at the horizon. Streaks of light were just appearing in the sky. The night was over and the day of reckoning was about to begin.

Chapter Twenty-Four
The Conflict Begins

The sun that rose slowly over the hills was obscured by clouds of dust as the war wagons and catapults moved into position in front of the castle. All along the walls of the fortress, archers stood in readiness waiting for the command that would rain arrows down upon the soldiers below. Fire arrows were prepared to shoot into the large catapults that were now being readied to do destruction to the walls and fortifications inside the castle. General Draco walked along the walls positioning his men where they were needed. Each man knew this day could be his last, and the beating of each heart increased in intensity until the sound seemed as if it reverberated through the war drums themselves. From out of the clouds of dust, a small band of soldiers rode to the castle gates with Tobias at their head.

"I have a final offer for the king!" he shouted. "I will ask again that the crystal be given to me. If I have it before I ride back to my troops, all within these walls will be spared. If I have it not, then the stone walls of this fortress will collapse like sand dunes in front of my army. Tell the king my words."

The king had gone to the wall to witness the advance of the enemy ranks. He stood looking at the swelling of the mob before the castle gates and uttered his own ultimatum.

"I hear your words, traitor and coward, as I would the wind as it passes by my ear. You will have the crystal when it is taken from my bloody body. Know that before this day is over, the forces of Tobias will lie in a field of blood before these walls. The kites of the air will feast upon the carrion, and I will personally mount your head upon my lance for all to see."

Tobias took his sword from its scabbard and thrust it into the air.

"Then with those final words you have sealed your fate. Let

the deaths of those that fall this day be on your head. I give to you the opportunity to save thousands of lives and you rebuff me. Prepare for the apocalypse, for it now has come."

Tobias turned and rode back into the ranks of men now no more than a mile from the castle walls. Within minutes the huge catapults had moved into position and all awaited the fateful orders that were to come.

High upon the walls, Lord Hadreon and General Draco paced back and forth over the fortifications. Set at intervals were cauldrons of boiling oil. Rocks were piled along the wall to rain down on any of the soldiers who might attempt to scale the walls themselves. The night had been spent reinforcing the gate. It would take a mighty force to destroy the heavy timbers that now added extra strength to the portal.

Cyrean and Aurienna ascended the steps to the parapet and joined Lord Hadreon as he paced the length of the wall, making sure all was in readiness. Upon seeing his daughter, Lord Hadreon paused in his preparations and led her aside.

"Again I ask is there nothing I can say that will convince you to join the other women in safety within the castle's chambers, my daughter? I have prepared you for battle, but I did not prepare myself for the time you would actually take part. I would not consider it unseemly if you left these walls for safety within. Can a father's concern not persuade you to go be with the queen until the conflict is done?"

"You know that this is where I want to be, Father. I am not afraid. Since I was a mere girl, I have looked to this time for which I have prepared so long. If I fall, it will be as a warrior in battle and not like a coward, waiting for my execution. The bearer of the sword that takes my head will have to risk his live in the doing, and that will not be an easy task."

"Then I leave you to do what you must. Never have I been more proud nor more fearful. May God guide your weapons true and place into your arm the strength of a thousand men."

"Your father worries for your safety as I do," said Cyrean, rejoining Aurienna. "It is the nature of a father and of a suitor to be concerned for the woman they love. You put yourself in harm's way, but I know I cannot change your mind. Heaven guide us in our actions today."

"I would expect no less concern from the one I love, but it is what I must do, Cyrean. Let us talk not of it. See the preparations that have been made. It will take a mighty effort to penetrate these walls. When enough men have died, they will see how fruitless is the battle and withdraw."

Their walk along the parapet had brought them to where Bartold and his small group had finished piling stones at intervals along the wall. The approach of the couple caused him to pause as he laughed in anticipation of what was to come.

"Ah, Ah, Ah, Ah, Cyrean, my friend. All the practice I have had casting stones at you and your hut will now serve me well. Many will be the broken pate that lie in front of the castle when the sun dawns tomorrow. My men and I will rain stone down like the thunderbolts of the gods upon the heathen that attempt to scale these walls. When stone is exhausted, then boiling oil will be our weapon. The few that survive both will taste the sword of General Bartold."

"General? I would not have thought that such a rank could have been obtained so quickly," said Cyrean. "Is the king aware of your ascension in rank?"

"He gave me command of the dwarf army. Such a position requires that I be elevated to proper stature. The king has not had time to confer the status officially, so I have taken it upon myself to do so until that time when it will be made official."

"Then I will need to take orders from you," said Cyrean, bowing to the dwarf, "until that time that I can make myself a

The Conflict Begins

general also. I would not have thought it would be so easy to do."

With a gesture of disgust, Bartold turned back to his duties as both Cyrean and Aurienna, laughing quietly, continued on their way.

Shouts from the walls suddenly arose as observers began to see a stirring in the vast army before them. The movement of the men began slowly and then became a surge as line after line of bodies pushed forward like waves rushing to shore. The mass of humanity continued to move forward until the rock foundation of the castle walls ended its impetus. Huge ladders were moved forward and placed at the lowest part of the stony fortification. In a seemingly never-ending line, bodies began to move up the ladders only to be met with stones that rained down upon them in a continuous barrage. Bartold moved among his men, exhorting them to greater efforts as all around them men ran yelling, rushing to fill voids where bodies now lay, arrows jutting from their lifeless bodies. Solid balls of flame flew over the wall, hurled from the catapults below and igniting fires all over the compound. Men and women alike rushed back and forth working to extinguish them.

"The gate!" yelled Grinold. "We must move them back from the gate. Bartold, bring your men and come with me. Bring the oil to pour among them. If we do not move them back, the entrance could be weakened."

Instantly, all the soldiers in the area of the gate moved to roll the huge vats of oil to the point designated by Grinold. With a great effort, the vats were overturned, raining hot oil over the combatants below. Instantly, the mass of bodies in front of the gate dispersed, screaming as the hot oil stuck to them like a second skin. Time and again bodies massed at the gate until repelled by the torrent of oil that rained down upon them. After a time the troops pulled back, leaving bodies of dead or dying comrades in their wake.

"What a horrible way to die," observed Aurienna sadly. "There is much suffering in such a death, for the end comes slowly."

Cyrean also seemed moved by the scene of the human tragedy below them.

"They are little more than human fodder. Wave after wave they are ordered forward by Tobias until a virtual wall of bodies provides added protection to our fortifications. Yet still they come and will come until the madman achieves his objective."

"I look about for General Draco, but I see him not," said Grinold. "Why is he not upon the walls where he is needed most?"

"Perhaps he went to see the king," answered Cyrean. "He wants very much to use the weapon of light. He has asked the king to give it to him more than once. I fear he grows impatient and will use it if he can locate its hiding place. I still am not sure as to which army he would destroy. Better it remain hidden as long as we can hold with the forces we already have at our disposal."

"Look," said Aurienna. "The soldiers are withdrawing. They will regroup and rest. I do not think they will attack again until tomorrow. We, too, must eat and rest in preparation for that time."

The army below them was slowly retreating to their camps. High atop a nearby hill, Tobias sat on his horse and gazed at the castle. Discouraged by the lack of progress he witnessed, he turned his horse and spurred the animal to the place where even now a tall figure awaited him.

"General, the battle goes not well for us. When we formed our alliance, it was with the assurance you could help me gain

The Conflict Begins

advantage to those things that could win this conflict for us. Why have the gates not been opened? You said there were men stationed at points where the gates would be breached at the opportune time."

"Things do not always go as we have planned," said the tall figure removing his hood and revealing the face of General Draco. "The time for secrecy is past. When next I enter the castle, someone will tell me the location of the crystal. Only its power can get your troops inside. The gates have been reinforced with heavy timbers. Until these are removed, the gates cannot be opened even from within."

"What of the route that you take to come to me? Can we not send men through the same passage to gain access to the inside of the walls?"

"The number of men needed to gain an advantage this way is not possible," answered General Draco. "There are several caves that open upon to the back of the mountain but only one small passageway that allows access to the outside of the walls. That is the route I have taken to come here. But to move large bodies of men through such a small place would make for immediate discovery. Continue the battle as we have begun. Within the next two days I will have found the crystal even if I have to kill the queen to get the information. Once it is in my possession, destroying the gates will be a simple matter. Then will your army enter and take the spoils within."

"I am an impatient man, General Draco. Find the crystal and you will be richly rewarded. Fail, and you will be to be like any other soldier that thwarts my ambition. Choose wisely your next move. Eustan will be mine even if I have to lay a siege to the city that will last for the next hundred years."

"Then if you see me again, you will know that I have succeeded. If I do not come to this place at the appointed time, then I have been discovered and killed. But know this,

Tobias. It is only in death that I will give up the effort to locate the crystal."

Without waiting for a reply, Draco turned his horse and spurred it into the night. The journey through the passageway into the walled city was not long once initial entrance had been gained. It was too narrow for a horse and rider and on those nights when Draco knew he had to use this method instead of the gate, he left a horse stationed nearby. As he moved through the narrow passageway, many were the places where he had to maneuver his large frame carefully around jagged rocks that protruded from the walls. When he had first searched through the caves on the orders of the king, he found most to have been lived in at some time by a primitive people. Pieces of shaped stone, most broken, had obviously been used for weapons. There were rough drawings on some of the walls and animal bones had been unearthed in some of the bigger rooms. But no one knew of this passageway other than Draco. When he first stumbled upon it, it was only a small entrance covered with shrubs. After he had worked his way into the narrow opening, he realized that it had been used at some time as an exit from the walls. With the sea to the back, this would have been the only escape in case of attack.

When he had made his way back inside the walls, Draco discovered most of the soldiers had left the parapet for the night, leaving only a few sentries to sound the alarm should it be needed. The bodies of the dead soldiers had been removed from the top of the walls and laid in a remote area inside the compound. A covering had been placed over the corpses until such time as a burial could be afforded.

Within seconds he had blended into the general commotion of the activities as if he had never left. He knew the need for secrecy would soon be over. If his plans went well, within a short space of time he would have the crystal of

The Conflict Begins

Light and victory would be a formality. He hoped the king survived the battle. He would take great joy in sending the king to his death. If he were lucky, maybe even Aurienna would fall before his sword. With these thoughts to spur him, he entered the palace, and sought audience with the king.

Chapter Twenty-Five
The Past Revisited

The king and queen sat in the throne room and talked of the day's events. Casualties had been few, and the king was in a lighthearted mood. The walls had stood firm against the enemy's assault, and the royal troops had fought well and distinguished themselves as King Malvore knew they would. The king felt that the walls would continue to hold unless Tobias had weapons that he had not used in the first day's battle. If the second day proved fruitless for Tobias, he might well lay siege to the castle and wait until supplies ran out and the king had to surrender. The king had foreseen such an eventuality, and the stores were well stocked to last as long as was necessary. General Draco had the troops well prepared, and regardless of how he felt toward Draco, the king knew any force trained by the general would be ready for battle. When King Malvore was brought the request that General Draco sought a conference without the presence of his advisor or the queen, the king sensed that this was not an ordinary meeting.

"General Draco stands without," said the guard after bowing in the king's presence.

"Then do not keep him waiting. Send him in," replied the king. "My queen, I must ask you to leave me for now. The general and I must talk alone. It is of war and not worthy of your ears. We will meet shortly in the dining hall with our young warriors. Until then, rest and be peaceful in the knowledge that Tobias will never find a way to penetrate our forces."

"I leave you to your talks. It is ever the lot of woman to be kept in secret in regard to war. Come to me after you have met. I look forward to the company of the young people who have come to us in our time of need. It is their energy and courage that enlivens me and enables me to look forward with

The Past Revisited

hope that this cursed war shall soon be over."

Soon after the queen's departure, General Draco was shown into the chamber. The king looked at the commander of his army and motioned him to come forward and speak. The look of impatience on General Draco's face could not be suppressed as he addressed the king.

"Good evening, your majesty. The battle has gone well. We have slain many of the enemy today with loss of few of our own men. Still, we must be ever vigilant and aware of the might that Tobias has in reserve. We have seen only a small part of the power at Tobias' command. I fear tomorrow will reveal to us a darker day. Tobias must wonder why we have not used the Crystal of Light. If we do not use it tomorrow, he will grow bolder still. Each day the crystal is not used will encourage his belief that we do not have the weapon or are fearful to use it. We must show him that we are willing to do what is necessary to win the war. Allow me, King Malvore, to take the crystal atop the battlements tomorrow and demonstrate its power. When Tobias sees what the weapon can do, he will give up his mad quest for power, and the kingdom again will be safe."

"General Draco, many times I have questioned my reasons for not utilizing such a powerful force. If there is a chance that this war can be won without the wanton loss of countless lives through such a weapon, then I feel we must keep it hidden. If I knew that we could wipe out every man under the command of Tobias tomorrow, I would hesitate still, for it is not the honorable means to defeat an enemy. Those who follow Tobias are men with families, and desires, and aspirations no less than our men who defend the kingdom. As long as we have the crystal, the advantage is ours. Soon the men under Tobias' command will grow weary and long for home and family. Then will they desert their leader to return to those who await them or they will seek easier conquests elsewhere."

"You understand not the resolve of the enemy, your majesty. He will come again and again with a vengeance until he topples the walls around us. He is an impatient man who will use all means at his disposal for victory. Even now he could have spies within the gates who will work to steal the crystal and put it into his possession. At least reveal to me its location so that I can put men of trust around it."

"That I will not do, General Draco. The fewer who know of the crystal's location, the safer it will be. Go, Commander, and tend to the needs of your army. I am not foolish enough to think that one battle wins a war. Tomorrow will bring new surprises and more deaths within these walls. We must be ready when that time comes."

The general turned to leave and then turned back to the king and spoke sharply.

"This weakness within you to preserve the lives of our enemy will be our downfall. Heed me, King Malvore. Defeat will fall upon your shoulders when it comes, not upon mine. It will be remembered that I urged you time after time to bring to bear all our resources and you refused. Look about you and be wary in whom you place your trust, for the enemy is all around. Those in whom you place the most esteem can sometimes be the most deceitful."

The king studied carefully the stony face of the man before him and wondered what secrets he knew but would never reveal.

"If you know of such men, then tell me their names so they can be purged from the kingdom before they harm our cause."

"You would not believe me because you see in me one who only seeks to benefit himself. I will go about my duties, but look to those close to you who have secrets of their own. They seek to bring down the kingdom from within and are more dangerous than a dozen such as Tobias."

With these parting words, General Draco left the castle and returned to his duties. The king pondered the warning and wondered how much trust he could put into the words of a man who obviously had ambitions equal to Tobias. His warning only served to heighten the king's resolve to watch those who would profit most from his fall.

Curious eyes had watched with interest General Draco's exit from the king's throne room. Lord Hadreon knew that the general was once again pleading his cause to the king to use the Crystal of Light. What other mischief he had whispered into the king's ear he could only surmise. Lord Hadreon had known for years the ambitious nature of General Draco. He had watched him rise in rank until, upon his father's death, he had been given command of the king's army. His own ascension to Chief Advisor to the King had come about in almost the same way. As a young man, he had been an apprentice to the king's chief advisor, Arthur Pendrall. He had a receptive mind but not the skills of the wizard who had tried to teach him the arts that only a select few would ever come to know. He had learned much about human nature by observing his mentor and the easy skill with which he could manipulate charms and spells with seemingly little effort. Yes, Lord Hadreon had been an eager student, but his skills had never matched his enthusiasm. The one vital quality he had obtained from his master was that of loyalty to the crown. Everything was secondary to the survival of the kingdom. When Arthur Pendrall was imprisoned, awaiting trial for crimes against the king, he saw that his service to the king was coming to an end. Before he was sentenced to exile, he summoned his young student to his chambers and spoke to him secretly.

Lord Hadreon still remembered that conversation with

Pendrall. It was as strong in his mind now as it had been when he first heard the words many years ago. He had been asked to do that which Pendrall could not, now that he was being exiled. He had listened to a dark prophecy, and the gravity of the message imparted to him caused him to tremble. The charge entrusted to him was more than he felt himself capable of handling. Yet the burden had to be placed upon him, for Pendrall had no one else he could trust. It was a task that would have been daunting for someone twice his age and experience. When his master was exiled to the Dark Wood, Hadreon put into motion those plans that had been devised in the conversations with Pendrall. Within a year of his being appointed Chief Advisor, the mission had been accomplished and no one was ever the wiser. He had carried those events with him for many years now. They had changed him from a scared boy into a man who would be chief counselor to the king through the triumphs and the failures in the campaigns ahead. During that time, he would have many opportunities to look at his actions and wonder if in his own way he had not been guilty of treason.

Lord Hadreon looked at the events of the last few days and knew time was running out for the king. He needed to know the truth about Pendrall and what had motivated his actions. Too long had he let the king believe in the accusations hurled at his former advisor and closest friend. Lord Hadreon had been sworn to secrecy, and that necessity had silenced the one voice that could have saved Pendrall from many years of isolation. From observations he had made in recent days, Lord Hadreon now knew certain things that he had only guessed at earlier. If his information was correct, everything the wizard had told him was now coming to pass. Tonight he would make known to the king those things that would hopefully ensure that the kingdom would remain unchanged and safe from

The Past Revisited

tyrants like Tobias.

With the departure of General Draco, King Malvore was left alone with his thoughts. It was evident from their conversation that General Draco wanted possession of the crystal. How he would use it and to what lengths the would go to obtain it were not certain. It would only be a matter of time before the commander ferreted out the information he sought. The crystal would never be safe as long as it was in the hands of the many scholars who were trying to unlock its secrets. Tonight at the dinner he would return the crystal to the one man he could trust to take great caution with it. In Cyrean's care he knew it would be safe. Not even General Draco would suspect that it would be in the possession of Cyrean, a commoner who had just recently found favor within the king's circle of friends and advisors. With the decision made, the king sent for the scholars who were instructed to bring the crystal to the king's personal chambers. Within the hour the crystal was in his possession. Now all that remained was the planning for the battle which he knew would resume at dawn. The words of General Draco had caused him to waver somewhat in his resolve not to use the crystal. Knowing it would soon be in the possession of Cyrean, he felt a calm come over his spirit and he moved to join his subjects and friends in the dining hall.

Chapter Twenty-Six
The Past Revealed

Everyone arose from the table as the king entered the great dining hall. The king's face bore a relaxed expression that had been too long absent as the threat of war for years had rarely allowed him the occasion to smile or laugh. He took his accustomed place at the head of the table and signaled the servants to bring the food. Soon the sounds of laughter and the warmth of friendship permeated the room. Gone were the rigors of war, at least for the moment. All knew that within the next few hours they again would fight for their lives and the kingdom, but for the time being, no one spoke of the conflict.

"Eat, my friends," said King Malvore heartily. "We are gathered as friends to celebrate the time we have together. We know not what fate has in store for each of us, but we have the present to laugh and share each other's company. Bring in the musicians. I would hear a lively song that would brighten our spirits."

At this command, three musicians entered the hall and began playing for the king and his guests. The music mixed with the talk and laughter would have been disconcerting for Tobias if he could have heard. It was not the sounds of people who thought of defeat on the morrow but the sounds of people who were free and who had resolved within themselves to remain that way.

"Have the musicians sing of love," requested Aurienna. "I have thought of war too long. I would hear of the love between two people who know not of war."

When the request was made, the musicians sang, accompanied by their lyres.

> On windswept heights where cold mists curl
> And windy peaks bespeak a nether world,

The Past Revealed

There walks a maid full fair of form
Across a land by time unworn.

This lady looks not left nor right;
She moves as if bereft of sight.
It's unknown where she wends her way,
Her world devoid of night or day.

Another time, another place,
Perhaps a painting her beauty graced;
How came she here so all alone?
She wept and sighed and softly moaned.

There darkly on a cold hillside
She found a knight his mount astride;
"Sir, what manner of place is this?
What be this land of fog and mist?

The dark knight looked into her soul,
Into those thoughts past her control;
"The world you see is yours alone
Until for another you atone."

"Not for misdeeds are you placed here,
No sin within a soul so pure;
Your love instead you wrongly gave;
So died a heart you now must save."

"Thus be aware when once again
You walk the world of mortal men,
There beats a heart within your care
That voids this world and its despair."

Then she awoke; the knight was gone;
She looked above and saw the sun.

> She looked around and saw all clear;
> No fog nor mist now lingered there.
>
> The knight's last words lay on her heart;
> What message to her did he impart?
> We fail to learn so oft it seems;
> "A dream," she whispered, "just a dream."

As the song concluded, the lyre's last sad renderings brought a tear to Aurienna's eyes.

"How dark was this ballad," she said sadly. "Pray that the songs henceforth be merry. I do not like to hear of lovers with broken hearts."

"Yes," agreed Cyrean. "It seems that the dark lady in the song made an unwise choice, and her heart knows she has erred even though her mind would deny it."

"That has not happened to my heart, Cyrean," Aurienna said reassuringly. "My thoughts and my heart have belonged only to you since that time we first met."

"As have mine belonged to you," he answered. "Perhaps the knight was Grinold. He has a way of looking into the souls of others."

"It was indeed a sad song," answered Grinold to his friend. "But tonight I see no sadness in anyone around this table. When I look into the eyes of my Madelyn, I see nothing but happiness. May it always be thus for us, Cyrean. We have found those who are the most courageous and most beautiful of women. They will share our dreams and sustain our households for many years to come. Kingdoms are built when two people love each other and vow to spend their lives together. We are indeed fortunate."

When the guests had finished eating, the king had more wine brought to the table. When all the guests were occupied

The Past Revealed

in their own conversations, he motioned for Cyrean to follow him to a small adjoining room just off the dining hall. Cyrean did as he was asked and left the room and followed the king to an area where they would not be observed. When they reached their destination, the king turned to Cyrean and, after glancing about to make sure no one was near, he spoke to his companion.

"Cyrean, I have a great fear that the crystal may fall into the wrong hands unless I move now to see that it does not happen. I do not want to use it in our cause, for I feel it is too destructive to be unleashed even as a last resort. You are the one who brought it to me and the one to whom it should be returned."

"I do not understand, my lord," answered Cyrean, puzzled as to the king's intent.

"I must put the crystal into your care, Cyrean. That is the only way that I will know it is safe. No one would suspect that one of our soldiers would have the weapon on his person. You have shown a great willingness to help the crown by bringing the crystal to me. Who could I trust more with its keeping? Will you secret the crystal upon your person until I know it is safe from the grasp of Tobias?"

With his request, the king carefully removed the crystal from beneath his robe and handed it to Cyrean who quickly concealed the bag containing the crystal in his own pocket.

"I am at the command of the king. If it is the wish of the king for me to take possession of the crystal, then I must obey. I will prove worthy of its guardianship though assailed by the mightiest army upon the earth."

"I would expect no less from one I have come to trust as much as one of my own sons," said King Malvore. "Come, let us return to the dining hall and enjoy the company of our friends. It will not be long until daylight will come and bring forth the forces of Tobias once again. We must steel ourselves for that time. Let us talk to our friends and partake of wine until the warmth of both sends us to our beds for a good night's rest. It will be needed when the morrow comes."

When the two men returned to the dining room, the table had been cleared except for the large goblets of wine which the servants quickly refilled as each was emptied.

"This toast I propose to the king and queen," said Lord Hadreon, lifting his container high into the air. "May the battle be short, may your rule be long, and may our victory tomorrow reveal to all tyrants the willingness of the crown to protect its territories and their people."

"To the king and queen," said the others in unison and drank heartily to their health. When the toast was ended, Lord Hadreon placed his cup on the table and turned to the king. He nervously clasped his hands together and sought for the words he would need for the revelation he was about to make.

"When last we met in this manner, your grace," said Lord Hadreon, "we spoke of matters pertaining to the lives of our guests. I would like to enlarge upon that subject tonight. I have some things to reveal that will shock and awe those present. These are things that I have kept to myself for all these years but now feel compelled to reveal before fate intervenes and stills my tongue forever."

"We welcome the words of a man of such imminence in our hearts," replied the king. "Speak freely of those things that are troubling you, Lord Hadreon. You are among friends who will support you though you have the darkest of sins hidden within your soul. We will hear what troubles a man of such honorable qualities."

"I have not always been honorable, your grace. I have done that which has haunted me for all the many years that I have been in your service. It is only now that I have discovered those things that I feel will bring me forgiveness in your heart."

"The paleness upon your cheeks tells me that this revelation is of some import," said Queen Ofra, laying her hand upon his arm. "We would hear your story. Tell us of that which brings the whiteness to your face and a palsy to your limbs."

Turning to the king, Lord Hadreon began to speak in a hesitant voice.

"Your majesty, as you know, many years ago I was apprenticed to your closest advisor. Arthur Pendrall was the greatest of wizards, and I was fortunate enough to be placed into his care and learn from his teachings. He was a man greatly skilled in the magic arts. He had the ability to look into the future and ascertain events before they happened. It was this ability that at once was his greatest gift and his greatest failing. Through this gift he had discovered that the king's sons would be kidnapped and slain, eventually resulting in the downfall of the kingdom. He did not know if the fate of the sons and the kingdom could be changed, but he knew he had to make the effort. I was but a young apprentice at that time, but he had no one else he could trust. Thus he brought me into the intrigue that was to follow and thereby made me an accomplice for good or bad."

"Was not the plan that my father devised one that would save the kingdom?" interrupted Cyrean.

"Everything your father did was for the king and the kingdom," reassured Lord Hadreon. "What your father asked me to do was after long hours of deliberation. He felt he had no other way to save those he loved than the plan he revealed to me."

The king was listening intently to the words of his Chief Advisor. The color now seemed to have left his face also as he listened to the man he trusted more than anyone in the world.

"Your majesty," Lord Hadreon continued, "when you felt your trust had been violated by Pendrall, you had him placed into prison and eventually exiled. You did not know that he had conferred onto your small sons certain gifts that he felt would protect them as they grew into men. Conspirators were already at work to make sure they never reached that age. Though not directly involved in a plot himself, General Draco did not like Pendrall's relationship with you. He hoped to be rid of Pendrall by poisoning your mind against him, thereby improving his own station in your eyes."

"I should have taken my sword to him," said Aurienna. "I have never trusted him. Cyrean, he has hurt your family and mine. Bitter will be his end for his misdeeds."

"When I finish my story, Aurienna," said her father, "perhaps you will look at me with the same distaste that I see in your eyes for Draco. The general was simply fulfilling his part of the prophecy. I knew the events that were to transpire and became a willing accomplice. Pendrall knew there would be numerous attempts on the lives of the sons, and they would eventually be successful if they remained in the castle. Pendrall advised me to tell you that the safety of your sons could only be achieved by getting them to safety in secret seclusion. This I did and you agreed to the plan. Pendrall knew that others would hear of the ruse and be prepared to stop the caravan. I made sure to have my own band of soldiers to attack the caravan first and remove the sons to a secret place I had designated. When the sons were placed into my hands, I then carried out the rest of the plan that Pendrall had begun."

The look upon the face of the king had lost the pallor that it had taken on earlier in the story and now had been replaced by shock and amazement.

"You kidnapped my sons. Regardless of the motive, that is

The Past Revealed

the worst of treasons," he hissed at Lord Hadreon, standing and preparing to call upon the guards at the door.

"Please, your majesty, hear me out," implored Lord Hadreon.

The king looked at his chief advisor for a moment and then sat down in his chair.

"You have a short time more to convince me of your motive for such a treasonous act before I have you thrown into prison," King Malvore warned.

"I had been told by Pendrall to take the sons to different families where they would be safe until that time the kingdom had been rid of all those who were scheming to overthrow it. Of course, one of those men was Tobias, who is distantly related to the king and would have a legitimate right to the crown if the sons were dead. The sons were taken to different families to assure that they could not be found together, making the job of killing them that much more difficult. When I had placed the sons in homes where I knew they would be safe, it was then only a matter of waiting. I knew this would be hard on you and the queen, but I thought it was all for the best. Pendrall had never been wrong, and I felt the fate of the kingdom rested on my following his directives. Who knew of the resolve of Tobias and that it would be so many years before the sons could be safely returned?"

The King's face suddenly came alive with hope.

"Tell me my sons are still alive, and your punishment will be a quick death rather than being exiled to the Dark Wood forever."

"Your sons are alive, your majesty."

The queen gasped and placed her hand over her heart. The king grew pale and clutched the arms of his chair as he sat back, his eyes widening in amazement.

"Where are they?" he finally managed to stammer as he

rose from his chair. "We will win this war tomorrow if it means I will have my sons returned."

"The youngest son was given to a man and woman in an outlying province. The man is a distant relative of mine. They had just had their young daughter taken in a raid upon their village. The fate of most children taken this way was death or being sold to gypsies. I approached them with this young boy, and they willingly took him into their home. It was only a few years later that a similar fate struck them again. Only this time they lost their lives, and after the raid the young boy was never located. After listening to the stories of those sitting around this table, I believe I now know where that child can be found."

"Where is he?" said the king. "If I have but one son still alive, I am blessed. Tell me where he is."

"Having some knowledge of the gift that was conferred upon him and hearing his own story about his childhood, I believe that young boy to be now a man sitting at this table. He is Grinold the tracker. Somehow, fate has brought him home and back into the arms of his parents."

A collective gasp came from the members seated around the table and a stunned Grinold sat and stared as all faces turned his way.

"I, the son of a king? Can it be possible?" Grinold finally managed to gasp as he and the others tried to assimilate the revelation placed before them. "How is that possible?"

"My old heart wants to believe that what you say is true, Lord Hadreon," said the king at last. "But before I rejoice in his return, how can we prove this is my son?"

"I have only the things that I know to be true," Lord Hadreon replied. "The family to whom I gave the son was killed. The boy disappeared but a body was never found, so he could have survived. Grinold does remember his family and how they died. From all he has said, that is the same family I knew. He has a gift that no other man possesses and has demonstrated it effectively on many occasions. It is the same gift that was received by one of the sons from Pendrall. This is your youngest son, my lord. There can be no doubt. Look into his eyes and look at his bearing. Royal blood runs in his veins. Your son has returned to you."

Gone was any hesitancy on the part of the king as he rose from the table and embraced Grinold. Tears flowed from the eyes of both men as the bond of father and son was again united, this time forever. The queen took the hand of her son and caressed it tenderly. Grinold sat down at the table, his legs seemingly unable to bear the weight any longer.

"I am the king's son," he repeated as if in saying the words he could finally convince himself of their truth.

"Yes, you are my son," said the king. "How could I have not known instantly? All these years in my mind I have imagined how you would look. Gaze, my wife, upon the son who has returned to us."

"My heart is full to bursting at the sight," Lady Ofra replied. "Though you were removed as a babe from my breast, my heart knows my son. We will never lose you again, Grinold, though a thousand like Tobias come against us."

"I salute you on this day of your good fortune, Grinold," said Cyrean, approaching the newly found heir to the throne and bowing.

"Do not bow to me, Cyrean. I have no claim to royalty other than that of birth. We have been comrades now for many days. Twice, you have saved my life. I owe you a debt that I can never repay. It is I who should bow to you. Fate has brought me home, but without your guidance and faith in me, I would not be here. Take my hand as a friend that will forever be in your debt."

The two young men embraced, each realizing that their fates were tied each to the other, and the friendship they had formed would remain forever.

Aurienna came forward to stand by Cyrean and give her blessing to the newly found prince. In this revelation would the king rejoice and his efforts to preserve his kingdom now would be redoubled. Such a revelation would reach Tobias she was sure. It could change his plans for conquest. At the least it would give him cause for concern now that another leader had emerged.

Madelyn had listened to the news of Grinold's being the king's son with mixed emotions. In the short time she had known him, she had grown to love him with all her heart. She knew that he loved her, but would that now change? She was a commoner and, as such, might be denied the love of a member of the royal family. She arose from the table and went unnoticed into the hallway outside the dining room. She knew she would have to leave Eustan. To be in the presence of Grinold and know she could never have his love would be more than she could bear. She walked softly to her room and lay down across the bed and cried. The night would be long, but regardless of what the morning's battle might bring, she knew the relationship that existed between her and Grinold now had changed. When the opportunity presented itself, she would have to leave and find her own way in the world. It would be difficult, but she had lived through hard times before, and this would not be any different except for the void that would forever remain in her heart.

Chapter Twenty-Seven
The Caves

Tobias walked restlessly up and down the small hill that led to his tent. Things had not gone well in the first battle. He had lost many men, but he had expected this and was not concerned with the lives of a few mercenary soldiers. The resistance had been much fiercer than he had anticipated, and now he had begun to realize a frontal assault against such an impenetrable fortress was not the answer. With the crystal, the battle could have been won in a day. He did not understand why King Malvore had not used the weapon himself. As the battle had gone in his favor, perhaps he was waiting for a more desperate time to utilize its power. Yet, there could be another possibility. Perhaps he did not have the weapon at all, and the news that it had been given to the king were only false reports. Whether he had the weapon or not, it was almost a certainty that the gates would not be opened by force. He would have to find a way inside the walls to have any hope of victory.

General Draco had not returned since their last meeting. He had promised to find the crystal if it existed, but thus far Tobias had heard no news. Tobias had little patience left, and if Draco did not find the weapon quickly, he would have to use a different strategy. With Draco's guidance, he could send soldiers into the caves in small numbers. Eventually, the number would be enough to prevent anyone escaping from inside the gates through those passages. General Draco had found numerous caves that honeycombed the mountain behind the castle walls. Some of the caves linked to others and some did not. Most of them had a rear exit, but it was to the sea and that would be an impossible means to escape. The back wall was a sheer drop into the sea. The only escape that way was suicidal. Tobias knew these caves were known to the king. Should defeat be inevitable, King Malvore would try to get his family to safety through this means. It would be General Draco's responsibility to see that such an escape did not occur.

Tobias had just gone into his tent to try and sleep for the few remaining hours before dawn when a runner approached carrying a missive in his hand. Tobias received the message and took it to the light to read. After a minute perusing the note, he frowned and burned it in the flame. Could it be true? The king's son suddenly has revealed himself and is within the very castle walls. Surely the fates were conspiring against Tobias if the news were true. With one of his sons returned to him, the old king would now be more determined than ever to hold on against all odds. A noise outside the tent indicated that someone had approached his tent and had been stopped by the guards. The flap opened and General Draco stood in the entrance.

"General Draco, I had begun to wonder at your absence," said Tobias. "Have you found the crystal?"

"The crystal is no longer with the king's advisors. He has removed it and its whereabouts is now unknown. But even more disarming is the news that one of the king's sons has revealed himself. With his son at his side, he will be more formidable than ever. It is time to move before the son's reappearance can strengthen their resolve."

"I have just received the news about the king's son," said Tobias. "I agree that we must move quickly. I want to see the caves and the entrance that you have discovered into them."

"Then we must go now while it is still dark. Bring some men and torches, and I will show you the entrance. We will station the men within the caves, and by the end of the battle tomorrow we should have most of the caves fortified against escape through them. Once the men are stationed within the caves, I will order the entrance sealed and no one will be able

The Caves

to use it again."

Tobias sent for a body of two dozen soldiers to accompany them. When the men arrived, Tobias and General Draco moved quickly to their horses and in a short time had reached the well concealed entrance to the caves. The men dismounted and tied their horses in a secluded area near the cave entrance. General Draco led the way to the cave mouth and pushed aside the shrubs that hid the entrance. It was a narrow opening but wide enough for a man to enter on his hands and knees for the first few feet. Then the passageway opened wider until a man could stand and walk between the narrow walls. Eventually, the passageway led them to the first large cave. As Tobias examined the walls and floor, it was evident that they had been used for habitation at one time. He held his torch close to one of the walls, and General Draco immediately pulled him away.

Feeling a hand upon his person, Tobias reacted instinctively and pulled his sword from its scabbard.

"A man who puts his hand upon me takes his life at little value, Draco. What is the meaning of this assault?"

General Draco released Tobias' arm and held his own torch up so that the light reflected off the dark substance that streaked the cave walls.

"It is not a personal affront. Look about you, Tobias. All the walls are laced with a dark mineral that runs all through them. This mineral will sparkle with fire when a flame comes into contact. With so much of the walls composed of this substance, the cave itself could explode if the fire of our torches touch it. I have often thought that if the mineral's power could be harnessed, it could be as powerful as the crystal."

Tobias took his sword and dug into the wall, extracting some of the material from the wall. He placed it upon the ground and lit the powder with the flame of this torch. It immediately burst into flame, throwing sparks around the cave.

"It does have an explosive quality, General. But the odor of the mineral when burned is offensive to the nostrils. It smells much like eggs that have rotted in the sun. When we have made our conquest here, we will explore the qualities of this substance further. Let us continue through the other caves. We will station most of the men at the central area of the caves and leave the others to guard the exit. How are the caves accessed within the walls, General?"

"There is a stairway carved into the stone that allows ascension to the first cave. It is narrow and allows only one person at a time to walk the step until the first level is reached. Once that level is reached, the walkway extends across the face of the wall to all the other caves."

Tobias mused upon this information for a moment.

"Then the entranceways are too narrow for a large group of men to enter at one time and thus can be easily defended by a small force. With the caves blocked, anyone wanting to exit the fortress will have to do so through the front gates. Those gates tomorrow will receive a bombardment like never before. I will have my archers send hundreds of flaming arrows into the wood. If we cannot knock it down, we will burn it down. I do not intend to spend years in siege to win this war. I have waited too long already."

"I have been gone too long from my post," replied General Draco. "I must return before the king is informed that I am missing. He trusts me not and I am almost past the point of trying to hide my deception. Tomorrow's battle will reveal many things. If the fates should conspire to throw the fate of the king into my hands at a crucial moment, then he will die by my sword, Tobias, denying you the one victory that would

The Caves

satisfy you the most. My hate for the king is no less than yours. My father served the king loyally for many years. But I have never had the respect given to me that was accorded my father. The king thinks that I am cruel and have not the compassionate nature to lead or rule a people. Before tomorrow is done, he will see my cruelty at its height."

"How the king dies is not important to me, General. I would prefer it be at my hands, but if you are given the opportunity to send him to his god, then I will be content with sending his family to join him. If the son has returned, that will just make my victory so much the sweeter. Go back to your post. We do not want anyone to know our plans until it is too late to avert them. I will post my men and return to my camp to prepare for the dawn's activities."

Before Tobias exited the cave, he again took his sword and extracted some of the mineral from the cave walls. After placing the substance into a small sack that one of the soldier's carried, he returned to the mouth of the cave. Four men he left at its entrance and then mounted his horse and returned to the camp. Once inside his tent, he took the bag and extracted a small amount with his fingers. He sprinkled it over the flame of the light in his tent and watched entranced as the tiny particles of the substance made small popping sounds and send sparks into the air. He closed the sack and sat pondering the material before him. He went outside the tent and again began his pacing up and down the hill. Suddenly, he stopped and signaled to a guard who immediately appeared in front of him.

"Go quickly to our armory and bring to me the one who mends our weapons. I have a task for him."

"At once, Commander."

The man hurried off on his errand and Tobias returned to his tent. He took a small bit of the black substance and tightly wrapped it in a piece of parchment. He tossed it into the flame of the small fire just outside his tent entrance and marveled when the small package exploded, scattering fire and ashes all about. Smiling, he reentered his tent and waited for the weapons maker.

Chapter Twenty-Eight
The Circle Completed

As Madelyn made her way to her room, the news of the Prince's return spread like wildfire through the castle until the lowliest servant knew that the king's son had returned. Within the great dining hall, many tears were shed and many were the toasts that went round the table as the old king basked in the revelation that had been placed before him. Lord Hadreon had remained on the outskirts of the celebration, bracing himself for the rest of the news he had to deliver to the king. After the welcoming and the elevation of Grinold to his rightful position as heir to the king, the party settled themselves at the table to discuss all the events that had led to this great reunion. The king toasted once again his newly found son and then turned to Lord Hadreon.

"Lord Hadreon, this news has revived my spirits and given new life to this tired old body. You have said my sons are alive. The one I see before me but what of the other? If he be alive, when can you produce him before my eyes? When I can see he is alive and well, then will I again call you friend."

"Yes, my liege, both of your sons are alive. Sit and listen to the rest of my story. Then if you can forgive me, my oath to Pendrall will have been fulfilled and I can die on the morrow with a glad heart, for I will have done my duty."

"We will listen, Lord Hadreon. By my command, no one is to speak until you have told me the location of my firstborn son."

"Your majesty, when I took Grinold to his new home, my work was only half done. Your oldest son would have to be hidden even more carefully away. I had no other relations that I could trust to perform such a service to the crown, so I had to look elsewhere for aid. I had done all that Pendrall had asked except for the placement of the oldest son in safety.

Pendrall had been released from prison and sent into exile in the Dark Wood three months earlier. Having no other recourse, I again sought out your former advisor. I went to the Dark Wood with the child. Some god must have watched over me and the child, for against all odds I survived the traps of the forest and found the hut of Pendrall and his wife. Never such a dark environment have my eyes witnessed. Pendrall the Wizard, who had once had the ear of the king, was now living among the most savage place and most savage beings on earth. He had built the hut with his own hands from the trees he had cut. All around stood the Dark Wood, but, somehow, around the hut many beautiful plants and flowers grew in abundance. There was a warmth in and around the hut that radiated around the clearing that surrounded the small dwelling. Somehow, Pendrall had created his own Eden within the bowels of the Dark Wood. It had to be some wizardry that my eyes beheld. It was as if Pendrall had used his last magic to make a home for him and his wife that they could enjoy for the rest of their lives. It was a small recompense for the loss of the privileges they had known in Eustan, but it was all he could do."

"Then my old friend was happy?" asked the king.

"He had adjusted to his new life and found things to keep himself busy. He was a woodcarver and had made their furniture and many other beautiful pieces from the wood of the trees of the Dark Wood. It is amazing how so much beauty can come from something so dark and sinister in nature. When they saw me approaching through the dark wood, they found it difficult to believe their eyes and welcomed me into their home. When Penrall saw the child, he grew highly agitated and paced the small hut back and forth many times. He sensed why I had come and gazed upon the child to be certain that no harm had come to it."

The Circle Completed

"Was no other child present in the hut at the time?" asked Grinold, his curiosity causing him to forget the king's warning not to speak.

"There was no other child, but ask me not to get ahead of my story. All will be revealed in due time. The baby was fed and placed on a small cot to sleep as I told Pendrall the story of the kidnappings and my attempts thereafter to put the two sons where they would be safe. He listened with a concerned expression as I told him of the difficulty of finding a suitable hiding place for the oldest son. I told him I had come to him for advice, but even as I was speaking a plan had begun to form in my mind."

The king had been listening fearfully, barely breathing until he looked as if he had turned to stone in the chair where he sat. His mouth hung open as the import of what Lord Hadreon was saying suddenly began to make an impression within his mind. Lady Ofra touched his arm to reassure herself he was still alive and that the revelations now being made had not had an ill effect upon his health. When he stirred at her touch, she turned to Lord Hadreon.

"Lord Hadreon," she said almost inaudibly, "What are you saying?"

"I believe the innate instincts of the wizard warned him of my intentions, or perhaps he knew all along and my coming to his house was all just a part of the great plan that he had formulated those many months ago. Whatever the reason, when I walked over to the child and picked him up, I had already decided what needed to be done. I placed him in the arms of Pendrall's wife, who instantly understood, and tears immediately welled in her eyes. I turned to look at Pendrall, and I did not have to convey my message. He knew what I was asking them to do."

"Oh, my!" Aurienna gasped when she realized what her

father was saying. "If there was no other child in the hut at the time, then the child given to them by you, my father, must be…"

"Wait, Daughter. I must finish my story. Pendrall was not totally convinced that the Dark Wood was the place to rear a small child. With all the dangers present, there would have to be constant vigilance, or a growing child with normal curiosity would fall prey to the dangers in the forest. I reminded him of the efforts to which he had gone to give each child a means to protect himself. Further, regardless of the dangers in the forest, he would have two loving parents and the safety that the Wood provided because of the very dangers it possessed. In his heart Pendrall knew it was the best choice, and I am sure he could not but wonder at the irony of what was occurring. The king's son was being given over for protection to the very man who had been exiled by the king for fear that he would harm him. I think that Pendrall had to smile a little inwardly at the situation. Grinold I was not sure about because of the circumstances surrounding his disappearance after the raids, but of this I have no doubt. That small child that Pendrall and his wife took to be theirs that day in the Dark Wood was the king's son. That child was named Cyrean by the couple, and he grew into a man of which any king would be proud. Your majesty, you now have both your sons again at home. Cast me out for what I have done if you must. But I have now fulfilled the promises I made to Pendrall. It was for the love of you and your sons that I did these things that I have revealed. I could do no less for those people who were as close as my own family."

At first all the guests around the table sat in stunned silence and looked about to confirm if others had heard the same story they had heard. Surely the odds of two brothers separated as infants coming together now at such a time and such a place would have to be extraordinary. Grinold was the first to stand and move to his brother's side.

"Then he whom I have called brother because of the friendship we share is indeed my brother by birth," Grinold said joyously. "Can it be that such happiness can come to a man who is as undeserving as I? My life had no meaning until I met Cyrean and Aurienna and my fair Madelyn. Now I have discovered I am the son of a king and the brother to the heir to the crown. How can this wondrous thing happen in such a short time?"

Aurienna stood and embraced Cyrean as the others stood and surrounded the pair.

"It is beyond belief," said Aurienna. "If I were not beholding these events with my own eyes, I would think that this was a dream."

"It is not a dream, young Aurienna," said the king now embracing his son tightly. "All the years of pain have been washed from my body. My heart soars with the eagles, and I have malice toward no man. If Tobias were standing in front of me now, I think I would give him the kingdom. That is how much the return of my sons lifts my spirits. Come, Cyrean, tell us your story. My sons, sit on my right and left hand while Cyrean tells us of his life in the Dark Wood."

"I cannot speak, my father. A tide of confusion washes over my being as I strive to contain the surging emotions within me. I have another father? My father is the king, not the woodcarver that taught me and watched over me, keeping me from harm all those years? How can this be? I have only known one father, and now I find that I have two. I must sit and think. Forgive me, my friends, if I seem unmanly by this flood of tears, but I have to reconcile within myself the meaning of that which has been revealed."

"And who among us would not feel the same?" said Queen Ofra, moving to comfort her son as he placed his head in his hands and wept. "I will find tears to weep at another time. My family is complete again. Seeing my husband this happy was a dream that I thought would never be fulfilled. All of us have much for which to be thankful. Send the news through the kingdom and to the soldiers who would invade our home that the heirs to the throne have returned. Let them be afraid of that which they now face."

As Queen Ofra finished speaking, William came into the hall leading Madelyn who looked at the people surrounding Cyrean and wondered at the cause of such emotion.

"I found Madelyn alone and crying within her room," said William. "I feared that some tragedy had occurred and did not want to leave her alone. I have brought her back here to determine the cause of her tears."

"It is nothing," said Madelyn. "I was simply overwhelmed by the news that Grinold received. I had a desire to be alone just for a moment while I thought over its meaning to me. Grinold, I did not mean to desert you in your moment of happiness. It was a moment for you and your parents to share, not for one such as I."

"I do not understand," said Grinold as he moved to take her hand. "Come sit with me and we will talk of these fears that have taken you from me if only momentarily."

"Come, William, and join our group," said the queen. "You have been missed. For the services you have shown me, I want you to be present at such occasions. Before long you will be Sir William and a member of our court. Would this be acceptable to you?"

"It would be an honor to serve my king and queen," replied William. "I will accept with pride the honor you wish to bestow upon me."

"Then let us continue to marvel at what we have discovered tonight," said King Malvore. "Cyrean, tell us of the years you spent with Pendrall. Did you want for anything that you might have had as my son here in the kingdom?"

"I wanted for nothing," replied Cyrean. "My father gave me all that I needed to become a good man. Now that I discover that I have two fathers, I am doubly blessed. I am thankful for the knowledge of my birth family, but I can never forget the blessings I was given by my parents in the Dark Wood."

"That in itself shows to me the strong values they have instilled within you," said King Malvore. "Pendrall was my closest friend for many years. I wronged him in the measures that I took against him. He was falsely accused of treason, and I let my emotions overrule my heart. I can never have his forgiveness, but I know now that I was wrong. I can never repay what he has done for you, Cyrean, except to become more tolerant of those around me and to listen more with my heart."

"Then you can do now that which you wish to do for Pendrall," said Cyrean. "Before you stands Lord Hadreon, your chief advisor and close friend as once was my father. Forgive him now as you would my father were he here. Lord Hadreon did only that which he was asked to do. He performed the duties well and he did them for love of you. Now you have an opportunity to repay him for the kindness he showed and the risks he took with his own life. If you want to be the father that Pendrall was to me, then fulfill this one favor. Forgive Lord Hadreon and welcome him again as friend."

"That I can do and will freely do," replied King Malvore. "Such a boon would have been granted even without your request, Cyrean. How could I deny my closest friend and a loyal follower of my former counselor? Those lost years away from my sons have faded into nothingness, and a new life has begun for me. I would not live out my last years with my sons being bitter toward a man who only meant to save my family. In those efforts, he was successful. The possibility exists that had he not done those things commanded by Pendrall that my sons would not be here today. I will not look back and be bitter but forward to better times now that my sons are safe. In a short time we will all be engaged in a battle with an enemy who would destroy what I have spent my life building. I want my sons to be at my side when that enemy is vanquished. Together, we will build a stronger kingdom than ever where men like Tobias will fear to tread. For now, Cyrean, fulfill my request to hear your story before the dawn breaks and the battle renews."

The king settled into his chair and his guests around the table looked at Cyrean, all anxiously awaiting to hear of the life of the Prince while growing up in the Dark Wood.

"My story is not as adventurous as that of Grinold. He has many stories of bold and dangerous encounters. I had few of those due to the watchful eye of my father. Truthfully, I have lived through more excitement since I have met Grinold and Aurienna than I did in all the years I spent in the Dark Wood. My earliest memories of my father and mother are warm with the tenderness and affection they gave to me. I had no brothers or sisters, so they doted on me as would be expected considering our solitary environment. My father worked with his hands and created beauty from wood. In all the time I lived with my father, I never saw him use the magic you say he knew. Perhaps that part of his nature was taken from him when he was exiled. Maybe it disappeared when he knew that he had done all he could for the kingdom. More likely than these, he saw no further need for those things that he could not create using his own hands and abilities. I believe the gift was there, but he never used it again because he felt he had all he would ever need around him."

"Did he ever talk about his life as counselor to the king?" asked King Malvore.

"He never spoke to me of those times, but many were the occasions when he would sit and meditate for hours upon the qualities of flowers and plants. He knew how to make medicines and wondrous cure-alls from the simplest of plants. That part of the magical nature in him he never lost. No, I knew not of his life in the king's service. Perhaps he was afraid that I would long for that life, and he would lose me if he revealed its lure."

"Do you wish now that you had known of your other life and family?" asked Aurienna, intently looking into his face for some indication that such a desire existed.

"My life is what it is and I cannot change it," said Cyrean quietly. "I won't say that there was not a time when I was older that I did not wonder what lay beyond the limited confines of the forest. But to look back and regret is not part of my nature. I look at what I have now, and I am thankful to those who protected me and allowed me to live for this moment when I have family and friends around me."

"Who could have known," mused Grinold, "that when fate threw us together we would one day discover ourselves to be brothers? Surely the gods do move us around like pieces on a gaming board, letting chance decide which will live and which will die, which will find love and which will be forever alone. Can we truly determine what will happen to us, or do we cast our lot and hope for the winning card? If the fates have led me to this point, it may be that it has now become my destiny to take my life into my own hands. If that is true, then I will take my place among the soldiers on the wall tomorrow and show Tobias his error in letting me live until the present time. For now, I have more pressing business. I would know what has caused the tears that stain my lady's face. Come, Madelyn, and we will talk of many things before the dawn again separates us. I have the words to bring a smile to your face."

"Would that you could do so," Madelyn replied. "I will go with you and we will talk of the future. I pray that my sadness has not created a pall on the joy of the king and queen. This is a happy time for them. It is selfish of me to think of myself at such a moment."

"Nothing can dampen the joy in their hearts now that we are all together. Come with me to the wall where we will watch the sun rise on a new day. We cannot know what each day holds for us. There is only now and we should not spend this precious time worrying about those things beyond our control. We have each other for the present, and that is all we need for happiness."

"Return soon, Grinold," said King Malvore. "We must plan for the attack at dawn. I will send for General Draco. He will find ready use for your strong arm. Cyrean, Lord Hadreon and I will walk with you and Aurienna to the planning room. We have much to decide on before dawn finds us in battle again. Join us, William. As you have ever protected the queen, that will remain your duty as the battle escalates. Guards, go and summon Bartold. He will need to know of any strategy that is being formulated. His dwarfs fought well the first day of battle. Courage can reside in the body of the small as well as the largest of men. Since the caves have a limited space for bigger men, we can put several of the dwarfs there to assure that they are available if we need them. I have never gone through the caves, but General Draco told me years ago that there is a chamber through the caves that exits near the woods not far from the castle walls. In the event that the battle goes against us tomorrow, the queen will need to be taken to safety through those caves. Have Bartold to explore them carefully and be prepared to defend them should any of Tobias' men

The Circle Completed

find the entrance."

The guards hastened to perform the duties assigned them. Cyrean and the others walked with the king to the planning room and seated themselves around the table. The map of the fortifications had already been placed on the table, and Lord Hadreon had just begun pointing out areas of the fortification that would need strengthening when General Draco walked into the room.

"Ah, General Draco, I thought that you had deserted our cause," said Lord Hadreon as Draco seated himself at the table.

The color began to rise in the face of the king's top commander, partially in anger and partially because the clandestine mission that he had just completed was too close to making a truth of the statement uttered by Lord Hadreon.

"I do those things that are needed to protect the kingdom," he said heatedly. "That requires that I be in many places. I would think, Lord Hadreon, that you would have more vital concerns that spying on me and my activities."

"It was a casual observation, General, and not intended to disparage your efforts to win this battle," said Lord Hadreon.

"Then let us complete what plans are necessary, and I will get back to my duties of protecting the kingdom. Since I am denied the luxury of the crystal to use as a weapon in our defense, I will assume there is great strategy afoot that will win the battle without it. I have heard also that the sons of the king have returned to help us in our battle. I am most grateful for their presence, and I know that you, King Malvore, have been greatly heartened by their safe return to their rightful place by your side."

"Yes, General," replied the king. "I know you will use their skills wisely when the battle begins. Put them in places where the fight will be most fierce. They are soldiers, and though I stand to lose them again, I would not have them protected simply because they are my sons. Their relationship to me instead necessitates that they fight more fiercely because they have my blood within them. Honor is not bestowed upon cowards. Put your trust in them, General, and perhaps tomorrow the forces of Tobias will suffer a critical blow that will send them running like the dogs they are."

"Do not concern yourself, your majesty. I will place them in the heat of the battle where they can stand as examples to the other men. I will be at their backs and ever watchful to lend my sword to the fray if they are overrun."

"There is one other point that you will oversee, General. You have told me of the caves and the exit that can be used if it becomes necessary to do so. I am placing half of the dwarf force in the caves as a final measure should we need to use them. They will ensure that an enemy force has not found their way into their confines to foil our retreat if it be necessary. You will show Bartold the exit chamber, and then he will place his men where he deems it necessary to defend them."

"The dwarfs are not needed in the caves, your majesty. I need them more upon the walls. The brunt of the attacking forces will be at the gate. It is not difficult to see that is where the bulk of our men should be. You will be taking thirty men from the walls that will be sorely needed. The enemy can never find the passageway into the caves. I will stake my personal honor on that belief."

"Your personal honor will do us no good when our people are slaughtered because they are denied access to the caves. Ah, here is Bartold now. Welcome, my small friend. Did you hear the charge that I have given you?"

Bartold came into the room and bowed to the king, looking sidelong at Draco in the process. Bartold had no use for the

General. Like others who had felt the wrath of Draco vocally, if not physically, he knew the cruel nature of the man and bore a dislike for him that he did not try to hide.

"Yes, your majesty. I hear and obey. I do not need General Draco to help me. I will send my men into the caves and within the hour, its secrets will be revealed to us. We will protect the wall should you have need to come into the caves. We have an advantage in such a place because I have been told they are narrow at many points. I will take thirty of my best men, and we will take torches and move into the caves immediately."

"Then it is done. General, return to the walls and place your men as I have directed. Tobias will come with a different approach tomorrow. We must be ready for any plan that he has devised."

"Once again you have failed to heed my advice, your majesty. Let us hope that this decision does not endanger us all."

"Your skill is in implementing those plans that we employ, General, not the formulation of such. Make haste. The sun will soon arise and they will be once again upon us. We must be ready."

"I do as I am commanded," said Draco darkly and exited the room.

"I still care not for the commander," said Aurienna. "He says that he will guard the backs of you and your brother, Cyrean. See that he stays not too close, or he may be the one who runs you through with his sword when you are most assailed."

"Daughter, it is good to see that the recent events we have shared have not changed your high opinions of the General," laughed Lord Hadreon. "I think Cyrean's back will be well protected if you are there in the thick of the fight. And I pity the general if he should try to harm him."

Aurienna flushed at the remarks of her father and quickly left the room followed by Cyrean who smiled at Lord Hadreon as he made his exit. He knew Aurienna's father held him in high regard, and that knowledge made his feelings for Aurienna just that much stronger. He did not know what the fates would reveal on the morrow, but he knew that whatever happened he would let no harm come to Aureinna as long as breath remained in his body.

Chapter Twenty-Nine
The Battle of the Caves

The mountain wall that stood only a short distance from the castle was a formidable structure. The rock that Tobias would have to penetrate to take the city had been removed from this very mountain and placed where it now protected the front of the palace as well as the back. The wall was almost vertical and climbing it would have been almost impossible, but people of another time had carved steps into the craggy face of the mountain that allowed the wall to be scaled to a point where a walk led along the face of the cliff and allowed admission to the caves there. For a man normal in size, this would have been a difficult climb. For the dwarfs, it was an effort that left them exhausted by the time they had reached the walk. When Bartold had made sure that all had reached the walk safely, they moved to the entrance of the first cave and entered.

Tobias' men had already entered the chambers that led to the cave from the forest entrance. As they made their way toward the central cave, they often had to struggle with the narrow passageway. At times the corridor would open until a man could stand upright and have room to move freely. At other times the passageway narrowed until they had to stoop and turn their bodies to get through the openings. When the passageway opened into one of the caves, more freedom of movement was allowed. Almost all the caves had ample headroom and space enough to move around freely. The central cave area was large enough to hold several people at one time. It was here that Bartold and his men found themselves. From this point the smaller caves on the left and right could be reached by connecting chambers. Bartold left half the men with Darius to guard the chambers to the left and the central chamber while he took the others and went to explore the chambers to the right. If he had been informed correctly, the exit to the forest lay in that direction.

Rarely did the dwarfs find any impediment to their movement. Surely, Bartold thought, it must have been a people much like himself who had occupied these caves at one time. Men like Grinold and Cyrean would have trouble maneuvering through the narrow openings as they moved from one cave to the other. Some of the caves had an opening to the sea wall and others did not. As they moved forward, Bartold noticed the sulphurous smell that seemed to permeate the chambers. The light of the torches flickered as currents of air played upon the flames. Suddenly, Bartold stopped and listened as the wind brought a sound to his ear from one of the caves they were approaching.

"Listen!" he whispered to the others who were following closely in the rear. "I hear a voice somewhere in the direction we are moving. There are other beings in these caves, and they are not dwarfs. Somehow, Tobias' men must have discovered the entrance and are moving to fortify the caves, thereby denying escape through them."

"What are we to do, Bartold?" said the nearest dwarf. "Would it not be best to return to the main body of our force and meet the enemy in the central cave where we have room to fight?"

"No," said Bartold firmly. "That would put us at a disadvantage. We would be fighting taller men with longer swords in an open, spacious area. We would be at a disadvantage there. Most of these caves allow little movement, and the passageways allow only one person at a time to move through them. The cave we have just passed through was spacious enough for three or four of our men to move around freely, but it does not allow such freedom for taller men such as we will face. In groups of three men to each cave, return to the ones we have covered and wait. The rest of the men and I

The Battle of the Caves

will go forward and meet the enemy as they come through the passageways. If we meet them there, we have the advantage. Any enemy we kill will block the passageway, and his body will have to be removed before another can move forward. Placed at strategic points along the corridor, we can hold off a small force of soldiers for a time. If we can gain access to the entrance of the cave, we can post a few men there to guard it and surprise others that may attempt a like maneuver."

Six of the dwarfs moved back in the direction that they had come to occupy the two caves they had covered. Bartold and the others moved forward until they reached the next cave and three more he placed there. Perhaps they could not stop all the men that might be in the force now making their way through the caves, but at each one there would be stiff resistance from the dwarfs and the advantage should be theirs.

The voices had gotten louder, and Bartold knew that a meeting was soon inevitable. The corridor now had opened sufficiently to allow a small amount of freedom. At various points along the wall, clefts in the structure were large enough to conceal a small body and in each that afforded such space, Bartold placed a dwarf until he alone was moving through the passageway.

The first man to spot Bartold gave an exclamation of surprise. It would not have been nearly as much of a shock to the soldier to have seen someone comparable in size meeting him, but to see a dwarfish creature with the facial features of Bartold staring fiercely at him, surely he must have thought he had fallen into the middle of the earth.

Bartold allowed the man little time to debate what he looked upon. With the element of surprise on his side, he rushed forward before the shocked soldier could bring his sword into play and ran him through to the hilt. With the shock still etched on his face, the man pitched forward, dead instantly. The next soldier had been directly behind the first and had managed to extract his sword from the scabbard. The element of surprise now gone, Bartold backed up only slightly to avoid the fallen body. The next soldier would not only have to avoid the slain man but try to maneuver in the cramped space afforded him. The only stroke he could make was directly at Bartold who inched back until the walls closed tighter and then waited. As the soldier stepped over his fallen comrade and moved to thrust his sword at Bartold, the dwarf rushed inside the opening he was given and again his sword found its mark. Now pandemonium had been created in the ranks of the men still trying to get through the narrow openings. There was no space to retreat so the only option was to move forward. They advanced again and soon Bartold found himself in one of the caves. Here he found the three dwarfs he had stationed there, and they waited for the assault they knew would come.

As the first man made his way into the cave, Bartold met him and was forced back by superior strength. Two others had made their way into the open area, and now the fighting began to escalate as wounded and dying men on both sides filled the small space. One of the dwarfs had been forced to the walk outside the cave and was knocked by a sword blow off the walk and to the rocks below. When another was quickly lost to superior strength, Bartold motioned for the remaining dwarf to retreat to the next cave, and he and Bartold backed into the passageway. Knowing that stiff resistance would be met at each new cave and unable to maneuver in the close quarters, Tobias' men halted long enough to discuss the development that now faced them.

During the time the men were planning their next move, Bartold and his companion had reached the next cave. Placing two of the dwarfs outside on the walkway, Bartold and the

The Battle of the Caves

remaining two dwarfs waited. Realizing they would have to get into the cave itself to be able to maneuver, the first man through the opening tossed his torch to the floor and swung wildly, driving the dwarfs back until two others had come to his aid. The disadvantage was quickly obvious to Bartold who whistled shrilly. From their concealment outside the cave, the two dwarfs rushed in and met a fourth soldier who was trying to squeeze through the small space to join his companions. He was met by both dwarfs who, striking together, dispatched the man instantly. His body still wedged between the two walls, the movement of men was temporarily stopped and the battle inside the cave had swung in the favor of the dwarfs. Bartold had fought fiercely, but his arms grew tired as he had to parry stroke for stroke with a larger opponent. Another dwarf had fallen and as Bartold backed away, he prepared his sword for one last defense. Seeing his advantage, the soldier rushed forward, tripping over the body of the dead dwarf and falling forward on the sword that Bartold had thrust forward. The man cried out in disbelief and died at Bartold's feet.

Two of Bartold's men had been forced to the mouth of the cave and dangerously close to the walk from which one of their companions had already fallen. Seeing their plight, Bartold swung his sword at the leg of the nearest soldier, cutting through muscle and tendon. The soldier fell back, screaming in pain until Bartold's next stroke ended his agony forever. The remaining soldier, seeing his advantage gone, retreated out onto the walkway. Bartold started to pursue the man, but it was evident that time would not allow him to do so before the body of the man blocking the passageway would be removed. Backing again through the cave walls, the dwarfs now controlled only one cave before the central area would be reached. Bartold did not know the number of men still moving forward against them. But if they were allowed to reach the main cave, any advantage they now had would be lost.

Leaving the three dwarfs he had stationed there to meet the invaders, he and the others moved into the central cave. Sending one of his soldiers down to inform General Draco that they had encountered resistance, Bartold gathered the others about him.

"Fellow soldiers," said Bartold, "I do not know the number of men still within the caves that we will encounter, but this I do know. We have been give a trust that we must not fail. If the enemy gains control of the caves, then they have gained a large advantage against the king's forces. We must fight until the last man. I doubt that Draco will send others, for he cares not if all of us die on this wall today. The task for us is to defend this area regardless of our loss. Fight like the soldiers you are. Fight until the last dwarf has given his life. We will leave a legacy on this mountain that will endure for generations, not only among the dwarf clan but for all people."

"General Bartold," spoke one of the dwarfs looking down the cliff wall, "your runner has returned and no one accompanies him."

"It is as I feared. Draco will not send others to help us. The battle is ours alone. What is General Draco's message?" he asked the returning dwarf who was still trying to catch his breath from the run and climb he had made.

"His message is that his forces are needed elsewhere, and he will not send men who are needed to defend the gate. He says to tell 'General Bartold' to use his skills in warfare to save himself."

"It is as I thought," said Bartold. "We must prepare ourselves. The small force that is defending the last cave cannot last long. When the enemy arrives, we must be ready. This area is the largest of all the caves. Here we will not have an advantage if we are outnumbered."

"Perhaps we should abandon these caves and let the enemy have them," said Darius. "This is not our war. Why should we risk our lives for a kingdom that has done nothing for us?"

"Whether we fight for them or for ourselves now matters very little," Bartold replied. "The exit is blocked. To leave by that method requires that we go through the soldiers still within the caves. If we desert the walls here, then our path is blocked to the front by Tobias' army. What other recourse do we have but to fight?"

"I will stay with Bartold," spoke another. "What is life under a tyrant's heel? I would rather die here than be a servant to Tobias."

"The choice has been made, my friends, whether we agree or not," reasoned Bartold. "All we can do is face the enemy bravely and die, if we must, with courage befitting a member of the dwarf clan."

"General Bartold," said a dwarf closest to the passageway. "I hear movement in the caves. I fear the enemy has overrun our last resistance and is now moving toward us."

Bartold moved quickly forward and placed four men at the entrance to the cave. Taking the remaining men, he placed them with their backs to the walkway should they need that area as a retreat. Removing his sword from its sheath, he looked at the blood just now beginning to dry from previous encounters. He knew it would not be long until it would be replaced with fresh blood from his enemies. He joined his comrades at the entrance and steeled himself for what was to come.

Chapter Thirty
The Assault

The first volley of arrows came just as a hint of light broke over the hills to the east. Huge clouds of dust arose as the giant catapults moved into position and began their barrage on the walls and gate. Inside the walls soldiers were already in position and rained oil and stone on the soldiers below. A huge battering ram had been placed on top of a wagon and was now being rolled into position in front of the gate. Scores of soldiers pushed the great machine forward until the log made contact with the gate, sending tremors up and down its length. But the huge doors remained firm. Again and again the wagon was pulled back and then sent forward in a new assault, but no ingress was made.

From the walls, rock, oil, and arrows continued to rain on the soldiers below until they fell back out of range to plan their next move. Tobias looked at the conflict before him and silently cursed their futile efforts to penetrate the gate's defenses. He rode his horse forward and surveyed the scene before him. The gate remained as firm as ever. Now would be the time to test his new weapon, and he called for his weapons maker to be brought forward.

"Have you completed the tasks I asked of you?" he asked the burly man who now stood before him.

"Yes, Commander Tobias. Everything was done as you asked. I placed the compound within a metal canister and it is ready for firing."

"Place the container into the catapult and send it over the walls. Then we will see the effect it has within. Perhaps the power of the crystal is not as powerful as the weapon now at our disposal."

"I will make the weapon ready," said the arms maker and moved to prepare the machine. Lord Hadreon looked out over

The Assault

the walls at the mass of soldiers awaiting orders to begin a new attack. He did not have much time to analyze the activities before him, for news of the battle being fought in the caves was now being brought to him.

"Your lordship," said the dwarf before him, gasping for breath. "We are under attack in the caves. Our appeal to General Draco has gone unheeded and we are overrun. We cannot hold the caves much longer unless we have reinforcements there."

"We cannot lose the caves," Lord Hadreon responded fiercely. "Draco knows that. He has purposely given the enemy a way into our stronghold. Find Grinold and Cyrean. Have them take what soldiers they need and secure our defense of the caves. I cannot leave here. General Draco has deserted the wall and I do not know his whereabouts. Go quickly and do as I have ordered. Secure the caves at all costs."

"As you command, Lord Hadreon."

The dwarf hastened away to find the brothers and Lord Hadreon again turned to look at the preparations taking place at the catapults stationed in front of the walls. Something was afoot, but he could not tell of its nature.

He did not have long to wait for an answer. With a mighty fling the catapult released a flaming object toward the castle. The missile cleared the walls and landed in the compound, exploding and destroying a small building that was being used to house supplies. The explosion startled Lord Hadreon as he realized that a new weapon had been brought into play. This was a weapon that could cause great devastation. He would have to inform the king. Should this new weapon be used on the gates, there would be no doubt of the outcome. This could be the weapon that would make the king rethink his command not to use the crystal. A decision would have to be make quickly if one were made at all. Even now he could see the huge catapult being pulled back into a new position, undoubtedly to focus its new assault on the gate itself. Calling a soldier to him, Lord Hadreon sent a message to the king before directing his attention again to the preparations being made for a new attack on the gate.

While Lord Hadreon's attention was focused on the defense of the gate, Cyrean and Grinold with a small force of soldiers were making their way to the cave walls where Bartold and his small band were waiting. They were only minutes away from their battle with the soldiers now making their way through the caves. Having overrun Bartold's last reserves, nothing stood between them and the central cave. Bartold knew that when they reached the central cave his small force could never hold them off. If help was to come, it must be soon. As he debated his fate, he suddenly heard movement below and a familiar voice came to him from out of the darkness.

"Bartold! Bartold! Are you there?" called Cyrean in a strained voice from below.

"Yes, I am here," Bartold replied.

"We are coming up. Do not mistake us for the enemy."

"Quickly," urged Bartold. "Soldiers are just minutes away from making their way to this point. I have only thirteen men left and myself to defend this cave."

"Then we are not needed after all," Cyrean returned, trying to relieve the tension evident in Bartold's voice.

"This is not a time for jesting," Bartold responded. "Many soldiers tonight have tasted Bartold's sword, but we cannot hold out much longer."

"Then fear not, my small friend, for Cyrean and his brother are here to lend their swords to your cause, and never has the enemy encountered such a force."

"Are you not forgetting someone, Cyrean?" said a female

The Assault

voice from the dark.

"Aurienna, is that you?" Cyrean called out.

"Ever close," she replied. "I have made a promise to be at your back and there I will be."

"Then come forward and stand with me and my brother. We must dispatch this pack of dogs quickly. I have heard strange noises and seen bright flashes of light in the area of the gate. I fear that a renewed assault has begun there. We must be prepared to defend the castle if the walls have been breached."

"Here they come!" yelled Bartold, cutting off any other thoughts Cyrean had about the security of the gates.

From the passageway soldiers suddenly flooded the central cave and Bartold and his dwarfs encountered them as they came. Fierce was the fighting and friend and foe alike fell until the floor of the cave was red with blood and bodies lay scattered about, limiting the movement of those still standing. Grinold, seeing Bartold driven back until he was only feet from falling into the sea at the cave's back, moved forward and ran his blade through the enemy soldier, sending his body crashing onto the rocks of the sea wall. Still they came through the passageway and each new wave was met with a renewed ferocity by the two brothers and Aurienna. Bartold was near exhaustion, having fought since the enemy's presence in the cave had been detected. Two wounds, one to the shoulder and one to his side, now limited his movement, and he had to depend on his comrades for the bulk of the fighting.

"Bartold, descend from the wall and have your wounds attended," commanded Cyrean. "You have fought well, but to remain with your wounds would cost your life. The soldiers have momentarily stopped coming through the passageway. The ones that are here sense defeat and are making their way back to the exit. We will stay here with your remaining comrades until we know the caves are secure."

"I need only to rest for a short time," Bartold replied. "I will stay here and tend my wounded."

"Very well," said Cyrean. "Aurienna and I will remain with you. Grinold, take the remaining soldiers and return to the wall. If the gates are under attack by some new weapon, then they may fall quickly. Should that happen, draw all your men back to the castle and defend it at all costs. The king and queen must be protected."

"I will go immediately. When I have determined the status of the gate, I will send a runner with news. Should all else fail, I will bring the king and queen to the caves. Send soldiers to sweep the caves and secure the entrance. That might be our only means of escape."

With these last words, Grinold descended the steps with his men and returned to the wall. When he arrived, he discovered a part of the gate had been destroyed by a blast from whatever weapon Tobias now had at his disposal. All soldiers who could be spared had been summoned to fortify this area, and fierce fighting had taken place with many deaths to both sides. Whatever weapon had been used to inflict damage upon the gate now was silent. There had been no explosions for some time, and it was assumed that the explosive material had been exhausted. If the soldiers could manage to mend the rift in the gate, the day might still be won.

Grinold put his soldiers into the group of men now attempting to fortify the gate and sent one man back to Cyrean with news of the situation. When the soldier arrived, he was startled to see a figure quietly ascending the wall to the caves above. He was a large man and in the darkness it could not be ascertained whether he was an enemy or friend. To the companions standing guard in the caves above, it could not be said for a certainty which he would turn out to be.

The Assault

Cyrean had tended to Bartold's wounds as best he could under the circumstances. The dwarf now sat resting with his back against the cave wall. Cyrean drew Aurienna to him and assessed the situation.

"Bartold needs more care than can be afforded in these caves," he said. "My knowledge of medicine is adequate, but I have not the poultices needed to help the wounds heal. He should return to the castle to have his wounds tended."

"Take him, Cyrean. I will stay and defend the caves. He has fought bravely and needs care. Go with him and return when he has received aid."

"I will take him to the castle. I have much respect for the small warrior. Gone are those days when he played the fool by casting stones and disrupting my daily activities. He is a soldier and has fought bravely. He has earned a time to rest and heal. I will return when I have delivered him safely to the castle. I will leave with you the most powerful force I have to guard you," said Cyrean, pulling a pouch from his pocket.

"I recognize this bag," she said. "Does it contain what I believe it does?"

"Yes, it is the crystal. Should you be assailed before I return, use it in any means you can. The safety of the king and the kingdom are paramount."

"A noble sentiment," said a voice from the front of the cave and Cyrean and Aurienna spun around to see General Draco facing them.

"General Draco, I had wondered where you were," said Cyrean, placing his hand upon his sword.

"And I had wondered about the crystal. Now I see my search has ended. Give the crystal to me, and I will see that you and Aurienna are allowed to go free when this war is ended. Tobias wants only the weapon. Perhaps he will even spare the king and queen."

"Traitor!"

Aurienna spat out the word as if she could rid her mouth of the distaste she felt for the man standing in front of her. She drew her sword and started for him when Cyrean stepped in front of her barring her way.

"This is a fight that I must finish," he said. "Even with your skill with the sword, your strength is no match for his. Stand back and guard the crystal. If I should fail, you are the only one remaining to safeguard it. If all our efforts fail, cast it into the sea where no man can ever again use its power."

Aurienna looked into his eyes and saw the determination there. She backed away, holding the crystal in her hands. General Draco observed her movements and licked his lips as he saw the bag in her hands. Knowing that he was so close to possessing what he had long dreamed about, he drew his sword. Cyrean turned to face the soldier before him, realizing that he would face the greatest battle of his life. Mindful that all the kingdom was now hanging in the balance, he braced himself and advanced to the center of the cave, prepared to give his life if he must to protect those things he loved.

Chapter Thirty-One
How Great a Sacrifice

The sound of metal upon metal resounded through the cave as both men fought with a ferocity fueled by mutual hatred. Full sunlight now illuminated the mouth of the cave, and the swords flashed as they parried a thrust or sought a weakness in the opponent's arsenal.

Aurienna stood as if frozen, praying that Cyrean had the skill and strength to match an opponent who had been tested in battle many times and still lived to tell stories of the encounters. The scarred features attested to his success in those battles, and the frowning visage bespoke a brutality that would not give nor take any quarter. She longed to be a part of the conflict before her, but she knew that Cyrean must fight the battle alone. Should he fall, no mercy would be shown to his killer. She would succeed or they would fall together against a common enemy. If death were to be their fate, then they would die knowing they had done all they could.

As the combatants moved about the cave, each trying to gain an advantage, Cyrean found himself hemmed against a wall. Trying to move laterally, he tripped over the body of a soldier and went down. But instead of pressing his advantage, General Draco suddenly lunged at Aurienna, knocking the sword from her hands. Surprised at the suddenness of the attack, Aurienna found herself in the powerful grip of her attacker. Holding her, Draco grabbed for the bag and tried to wrestled it from Aurienna's grasp. During the struggle, she managed to wrest her hand from his grip, but in so doing, flung her arm outward, losing her grip on the bag. Throwing Aurienna to the back of the cave, Draco lunged toward the bag which had struck the cave wall an opened, allowing the crystal to roll out onto the cave floor.

All this had taken but seconds to occur. Cyrean had

managed to regain his footing, but before he could act, he saw Aurienna tossed to the back of the cave. Unable to regain control of her body, the momentum carried her to the cave lip where her body fell over the edge. Grasping the ledge, she tried to hang on long enough for Cyrean to reach her. But Bartold arrived first and grasped her wrists, holding as tightly as his diminished strength would allow.

Suddenly the cave exploded in light as the sun's full rays hit the crystal. General Draco, who had been reaching for the object, received its full impact as the cave almost exploded with the energy released. Bartold, who was still clutching Aurienna's wrist, hoping to pull her to safety, now found himself propelled forward by the blast and over the ledge, and he and Aurienna disappeared from sight. As suddenly as it had begun, the light diminished and Cyrean looked to see General Draco lying dead on the cave floor, his body covering the weapon he had coveted.

Fighting to refocus his sight, Cyrean looked to where Aurienna had been clinging to the cave wall for life. He saw nothing and fought back an urge to scream as he stumbled to where she had been only moments before. Reaching the back wall, he looked down, expecting to see her body on the rocks below. What he beheld was a miracle. Holding on for her life to a small shrub that jutted out from the mountain wall was Aurienna, and still holding on to her wrist was Bartold.

Cyrean knew any hope for rescue rested on his ability to act quickly. Aurienna would not have the strength to hold both her weight and Bartold's long, using only one hand to clutch their lifeline. He looked around the cave and there was nothing to lower to them. The two figures below were about ten feet away. He could not reach them with anything at his disposal. A descent down the sheer face of the cliff was impossible. No resources seemed available, and Cyrean knew time was running out.

"Cyrean!" Aurienna called out and the sound froze the very marrow in his body. He rushed back to find her frantically trying to maintain her grip but slipping ever so slowly with each passing second.

As he realized that she was going to fall to her death, Cyrean was instantly struck with a realization. He had the power to save her. He had only to utilize the gift he possessed to pull her to safety. Exerting all the mental force in his body, he trained his mind on the form of Aurienna, and her body discernibly rose inches up the cliff. Straining even harder, he tried again, and again her body rose slightly.

"He cannot lift such a great weight, Aurienna," came the voice of Bartold. "Our weight is too great even for his power. You have no choice. Save yourself. Release my hand and Cyrean can pull you to safety."

"I will not release you, Bartold. If you are to die, it will not be because I released you to save myself."

"There is no time to debate whether it is right or wrong. Release my hand, Aurienna. I have obtained all that I have ever wished for myself. To die now will be no shame for me. You must live to carry on the battle. Think of me with fondness. Remember what I and my people have done here."

"No, I will not release you...."

Before she could finish her entreaty, Bartold jerked his hand from hers and, pushing his body away from the mountain wall, he plummeted into space and fell into the sea below.

"No! no! no!" Aurienna cried as she felt the weight lifted from her body, which now began to rise up the face of the cliff. Within seconds she felt the arms of Cyrean close around her as he pulled her inside the cave and collapsed on the ground beside her.

Stroking his face, Aurienna lifted Cyrean's head into her lap and cried as she realized the sacrifices that both men had made for her. Cyrean slowly began to revive and looked up into the eyes of the woman he gladly had risked everything to save.

"You are safe," he cried, reaching to touch her face to reassure himself that she was real. "For a moment I dreamed, and I thought that I had failed and you had fallen into the seas below."

"No, it was just a dream, Cyrean. I am here. But another we love has fallen in battle. Rather than both of us perish, Bartold gave his life for me when he removed his hand from mine and fell into the sea."

"Then Bartold is gone? I gained a friend and lost him just as quickly. In the end he sacrificed all that he had for another. Can any man do more? Who could know that such courage and sacrifice lay in such a small body? I will miss him."

"And I. I do not know if I could have been so brave. I should have had more strength to hold on to him."

"There is no fault in our actions. We did what we could, and Bartold knew we could not give more. Come, we must report what has happened here and learn the status of the battle. Even now the enemy is at the gate. Let us hope that he is not within. One viper has been dispatched, but another shows his fangs without. With his death will end this struggle. I will place the crystal back into its bag, and we will go to the king. I have a plan whereby the crystal could be used without it harming those who employ it. Its power must be controlled before it can be directed at the enemy. I now believe I know how that can be done. Let us hasten to the king and present my plans to him. He has been hesitant in the use of the crystal, but I feel he will agree to what I can do with its power."

Quickly descending the steps to the base of the wall, the two companions hastened to the castle. To their amazement, enemy soldiers had begun to penetrate through the wall and there was escalation of fighting within the walls. It would only be a matter of time before the gates collapsed, and the entire enemy force would be within. Aurienna ran to find the king while Cyrean raced to the arms room and took up a shield made of burnished metal. He place the shield upon a table, and, removing the bag containing the crystal from his pocket, he placed it close at hand upon the same table. Removing his sword from its sheath, he drove the sword with great force into the middle of the shield and made the opening wide enough to accommodate a small, thin piece of metal which he bent on the back side of the shield, thereby fastening it tightly to its host. This done, he bent the metal in the front creating a pocket into which he placed the bag and bent the metal inward until it securely held the crystal. With the shield prepared, he ran to find the king.

Aurienna had gone through castle and after an exhaustive search found the king taking the queen to the tower atop the castle. After informing him of Cyrean's plan, she raced back to the arms room where she met Cyrean.

"Where is the king?" Cyrean asked, never stopping in his hurry to obtain the high walls of the castle.

"More and more soldiers have penetrated the gate," answered Aurienna. "He has taken the queen to safety and will return soon. William and Lady Madelyn are with her. He has commanded you to do what you deem best in defense of the castle."

"Then I must hasten to the wall. Come with me, Aurienna. What I must do may take more than one person to accomplish."

Without responding, Aurienna quickly moved with Cyrean in the direction of the wall. A battle now raged just inside the gate as enemy soldiers slowly began to make their way through the breach. Taking the steps up a side wall to the walkway, Cyrean and Aurienna arrived at the area just above the gate. Only a handful of soldiers were there, most of their number having been moved to the front gate by Lord Hadreon. Cyrean motioned them away and positioned himself with the shield directly in front of him facing toward the sun.

"Take your sword, Aurienna, and pull away the bag from the crystal. Once that is done, stand with me behind the shield, for that is the only place where we will be safe."

Placing her sword up to the leather bag containing the crystal, Aurienna pulled the cover away, and instantly the sun's direct light penetrated the crystal all the way to its core. Cyrean felt the shield vibrate in his hands, and a blinding light shot from the crystal, intensified in magnitude by the burnished metal of the shield in which it was placed. Cyrean slowly lowered the shield until the rays came into contact with the catapult most directly in front of the castle. Instantly, the machine exploded and burst into fame. Again, Cyrean directed the beam toward another wagon, and it exploded in the same manner, sending debris and fire into the men manning the machine. Cries of pain and of terror arose from the men closest to the explosions, and all eyes turned to witness the power of the weapon Cyrean had wielded. Directing the weapon at a downward angle, the beam struck the ground around the front of the gate, sending men and weapons flying as it cut a swath through the area where the enemy had gathered the heaviest. Panic stricken, the soldiers bolted and fled the area, retreating to the safety of the woods. Cyrean leveled the beam until it struck the trees of the forest, sending flames into the tops of the trees, which burned with an intensity hotter than any caused by a lightning strike. Now in full flight, the men rode as quickly as they could, hoping to put a safe amount of distance between themselves and the terrible

How Great a Sacrifice

weapon in the hands of Cyrean. The landscape in front of the castle was empty now except for the bodies of soldiers dead or dying. Placing the shield where the rays would be directed into the sky, Cyrean spoke to Aurienna.

"Aurienna, remove your short cloak and place it over the crystal. It must be done quickly or the rays will destroy the cover itself."

Aurienna stood in shock and unable to move. She had just witnessed a sight that had stunned her beyond words. Cyrean spoke again and yet again before his words began to make an inroad into her consciousness.

"Aurienna! Aurienna! I need you!" shouted Cyrean. "Place your cloak over the crystal."

Now aware of what she was being asked to do, she removed her cloak and advanced slowly toward the crystal.

"Quickly throw the cloak over the crystal," directed Cyrean, "but be careful you do not get too close to the rays coming from the center of the weapon. Sure death would follow."

Aurienna slowly drew the cloak to a point where she could safely toss it and let it go. It settled upon the crystal and instantly the weapon's power was gone. Aurienna rushed to Cyrean who was just now recovering himself from the horrifying display of destruction he had wrought.

"Cyrean, we have won the day. Havoc lies all around us but the weapon struck none of our people."

Cyrean was only half hearing the words spoken to him as he sat down against the wall and tried to collect his senses sufficiently to let his mind digest what had just occurred. Suddenly he stood and looked at Aurienna.

"Where is Tobias?" he asked in alarm. "Throughout the battle I saw him not and even now when the soldiers were fleeing the field he was not among them. We must move quickly to the castle."

As Cyrean and Aurienna made their way down from the walls, the activity around the gate had ceased. The few remaining enemy soldiers had surrendered their arms. Nowhere among them was Tobias. The two companions raced into the castle and toward the council room. It was empty and Aurienna looked to Cyrean with an expression that Cyrean had rarely seen in all the time he had known her. A pallor had come into her face as if the blood itself had drained from her body.

"Where is the king and queen, Cyrean? Where is my father?"

"Come with me, Aurienna. They cannot be far away."

As the two raced to the tower, Aurienna tried to shake the fear welling up inside her. If she had allowed her father and the king to be taken, she would never forgive herself.

The sound of voices came from a corridor just above them. Racing up the steps, they were greeted with a sight that momentarily stopped their hearts. Tobias stood against a wall with his sword directly at the throat of Lord Hadreon. Facing him were Grinold and the king, both with swords in hand but unable to move for fear of causing the death of Lord Hadreon.

"It seems that now we are all here," said Tobias triumphantly. "It is evident that I have the upper hand. I must thank you, Cyrean, for leaving the passageway to the caves unguarded. I have Lord Hadreon at sword point, and two of my men are now making their way to where the queen is hidden in the tower. Their orders are to kill the queen when they discover her. Only I can stop them. Bring me the crystal and I will let Lord Hadreon live, and I will call back my men before the queen is slain. Consider my offer quickly, for little time remains."

While Tobias had been speaking, Grinold read his eyes and

looked into the soul behind them.

"How many men have you sent to slay the queen?" Grinold asked. " I saw no men enter this part of the castle. You lie, foul tyrant, to protect yourself from the death that awaits you at the end of my sword."

"I do not lie. Even now the soldiers are battering at the door of the tower room. Soon they will make forfeit the life of the queen. You must give me the crystal, or her death will be on your hands."

"He lies, Father. I can read it in his eyes. The queen is safely ensconced within the tower. He holds only Lord Hadreon as a barrier to our swords."

"Then kill him even as his sword slits my throat," said Lord Hadreon. "I am a soldier and prepared to die if it means this tyrant will never live to harm anyone again."

"No!" screamed Aurienna. "Do not endanger my father's life. I will take his place. Take me in his stead."

Before any of the men could react, Aurienna ran forward and fell at the feet of Tobias. Realizing the advantage he had, he quickly brought his sword to her neck and ordered Lord Hadreon away.

"Well, Lord Hadreon, you have been spared for the moment. How wonderful it must be to have a child willing to sacrifice herself for her father."

"Harm not my child, Tobias, or once my sword has taken your life, I will strip the hide from your body and place your head high atop the tower for the kites to feed upon."

"Your threats do not sway me, Lord Hadreon. I hold the upper hand here."

"Do not harm Lady Aurienna, Tobias," pleaded Cyrean. " I will stand in her place. As the king's son, I promise you safe passage from this castle. You may take me as assurance that I speak true. When safety is reached, then take my life if you must claim such from the families of King Malvore and his counselor."

"Foolish boy," said Tobias. "I care for only one thing. Bring me the crystal. That you have the power to do. Once that is done, then you have my promise that I will leave this castle with no harm to any member here."

"He lies, Cyrean," said Grinold, moving to clutch his brother's arm as he prepared to leave the room. "If you bring him the crystal, we will all be destroyed. I see it in his eyes. I have been in his company for many years. I know what cruelty he is capable of administering."

"Another son speaks while the king stands idly by and refuses to take action. Order the crystal brought to me, old man, or my blade will cut her throat like a ripe apple."

"Let me go, Father," said Grinold. "Cyrean should remain here. Perhaps there is a gift he possesses that might serve your cause."

A light of understanding came into the king's eyes, and he nodded assent to Grinold's request. Grinold hastened from the room, and placing the blade firmly against Aurienna's throat, Tobias waited for the weapon that had long been kept from him. Realizing that time was running out, Cyrean closed his eyes and prayed that what was to come would end without the tragedy that now seemed likely.

Chapter Thirty-Two
A Kingdom Reborn

The time needed for Grinold to cover the distance from the castle to the front wall would not have been long, but to the small group huddled in the corridor of the palace just below the tower, it seemed a lifetime. No one dared to move, knowing that the least slip could cost Aurienna her life. A thousand avenues of escape ran through Aurienna's mind, but she scarcely dared to breathe as she felt the sharp edge of the sword against her throat. Any move on her part and the sword would slice into her neck. She looked at her father and tried not to reveal her fear, but she knew that his fear was far greater than hers. What would happen once the crystal was delivered to Tobias? She did not trust him, and the likelihood was great that not only would she perish but the ones she loved as well. If only Tobias would drop his guard for a second, there might be a chance for escape. If it did not come soon, she knew she would have to sacrifice herself to save the others. Could she be as brave as Bartold? A strange fear lay deep in her heart that she could not. Again she looked at her father for some sign that a plan had been formed, but she saw only concern in his eyes.

Cyrean's eyes searched the room for some means of diverting Tobias' attention and perhaps getting the opportunity to move against him. He knew that the slightest movement could mean Aurienna's death, and that had to be avoided at all costs. If only she had not allowed herself to be taken hostage. Yet, though what she had done had been foolhardy and rash, he admired her bravery and determination. The love she had for her father would be redoubled for the man who would be her husband. Such a woman he could not lose. Soon Grinold would return with the crystal. Once Tobias had it in his possession, who could say that he would not kill Aurienna in malice? No, there had to be another way to rescue her without Tobias gaining possession of the crystal. The walls were covered with weapons of all types, but getting the use of them would take too long. Their swords were equally as useless. By the time the distance between them was covered, Tobias would have killed Aurienna.

Further deliberation was halted by the return of Grinold who carried the shield carefully in his arms, the covering still carefully wrapped around the crystal. Upon seeing Grinold return, a strained smile came to the face of Tobias.

"Ah, at last the weapon is in my presence. Tracker, place the shield on the floor and remove the rystal carefully from its metal clasp. See that you do this carefully. Any untoward move will result in death for more than one person in this room."

Grinold took his sword and bent the metal clasps that connected to the back of the shield holding the crystal to its surface. He wrapped the short cloak wherein it lay securely around the object and arose. He hesitated and looked at King Malvore for some sign that he would not have to give up the crystal. But no sign was forthcoming.

"Bring the object to me, Tracker. You of all here know the cruelty of which I am capable. Once I have the crystal, all of you can remain in safety here. But know that I will return. As long as I live, none in this kingdom will have a moment's peace. You will never know when I will return with the crystal and destroy the whole kingdom. I must commend Cyrean for showing me how the weapon can be used safely by the person who wields it."

"No, you cannot give him the crystal," Aurienna pleaded. "If my death is the price we must pay to see the kingdom remains strong, then so be it. I am willing to die for those I love."

"How noble," growled Tobias, tightening his grip even

more. "But nobility bleeds as well as any commoner. Perhaps a demonstration."

Tobias made the slightest movement with the blade and a small drop of blood formed on Aurienna's throat. Lord Hadreon instantly started to move forward and had to be restrained by Cyrean who knew it would mean instant death for Aurienna.

"Yes, Cyrean. Hold the father wolf who would protect his cub. He is dangerously close to losing her forever. The blade can cut much deeper and will if the crystal is not delivered to me immediately."

Cyrean knew that the time for talk had ended. He was also aware that Tobias had only one means of escape. As long as Aurienna remained alive, he could hold them at bay. If he killed her, then he had no protection other than his skill with a sword to protect himself. As adept as he was with weapons, he could not defeat four men whose skills almost rivaled his.

"Bring me the crystal," hissed Tobias. "Your time grows short."

"Father," said Grinold, "Your word has always been law and inviolate. We can give the crystal to Tobias with your promise that he can leave the castle safely if he will release Aurienna. Let us take what we can and hope for better opportunities tomorrow. Yes, he will have the crystal, but now he also knows our will and that regardless of his weapons, Eustan will stand firm. Give him the weapon for the release of Aurienna. We will all live to fight another day."

"No, Grinold. End it now," pleaded Aurienna. "I have no fear of dying."

"I will not lose my child, Sire," said Lord Hadreon. "Let him have the crystal and take it from this castle. It is not worth a single life whether it be my daughter or your sons."

"What of this truce, Tobias? I, as king, will give my word

that you may leave unharmed with the crystal if you will release Aurienna safely. It is the only recourse open to you. Do you accept?"

"That is a weakness that you possess that will always leave you vulnerable to men like me, King Malvore. You care too much for the ones around you. You have given your word and I accept. See, even now I remove my blade from her throat. Now bring me the crystal."

True to his word, Tobias released his hold upon Aurienna, and she stepped away and ran to the others.

"Now, Father," said Aurienna, "he has no hostage. Take your blades and end his tyranny forever."

"No, Child," said King Malvore, "the royal word has been given and it is law. Tobias will leave with the weapon. Take it to him, Grinold. Let him leave this castle forever. The next time we meet, Tobias, there will be nothing to save you, whatever lives it may cost."

Grinold handed the cloak to Tobias, who clutched it to him and looked about as if to see if there existed any treachery he could read in their eyes. He knew what he would do if the circumstances were reversed, and he expected no less from his enemy.

"King Malvore, your own morality keeps you from doing that which you know to be best. By releasing me, you are putting your kingdom at risk. All this for the life of one girl. What fools you are and how easily will I defeat you because of this flaw in your nature. You will never triumph over me until you use the methods I do. I will always be stronger because I care only for myself. I will return and when I do, I will be well versed in the use of the crystal. Remember then that your decision cost you a kingdom."

"Take the crystal and remove your presence from Eustan," said Grinold. "I have seen too much of your cruelty. Be wary of the weapon you carry, for it can destroy good and evil alike. Do not remove it from this cloak in the presence of light or your life will be forfeit. I do not care for you, but others would be endangered."

"Ever the noble hearted, Grinold. I once had hopes that you would follow me and learn my ways. You could have been second only to me as the most powerful man on earth. But you have the same moral disease as the king. It is with no reluctance that I take my final leave of you and this accursed palace."

Tobias strode past Grinold and the others, never looking back. Within minutes he was through the palace gate and riding from Eustan.

Lord Hadreon hugged Aurienna close to him as she cried tears of relief that none of them had been harmed. The king had gone into the tower where he found his wife and Madelyn safe. Grinold had been correct. There were no soldiers. When the door was opened, William met the king with sword drawn, but lowered it and bowed when he recognized King Malvore. When they joined the others, it was a time of rejoicing. For now they were safe and the city stood firm. There would be another time to worry about Tobias and the crystal. This was a time for celebrating, and each of them silently gave a prayer of thanks for their deliverance.

"Come, all of you," said the king. "We will attend our duties making plans to rebuild the walls and tending to our dead and wounded. We will post sentinels at the gate and on the morrow, rebuilding will begin. Tonight we will feast in the great dining hall and celebrate our victory. Go, each of you to your duties and I and the queen will attend ours in the palace. Meet tonight for the great feast."

Cyrean and Aurienna walked out into the grounds surrounding the palace. Destruction lay on all sides and the smell of death was all around. Knowing there would be little they could do until morning, they returned to the castle to talk of their future, which for now seemed bright with promise.

Grinold and Madelyn had taken their own walk out into the gardens behind the palace walls, and in the waning sunlight they sat and talked.

"Grinold, I thank God that he has guided you safely through this battle. I was ever fearful for your life. I wish I could be more like Aurienna and be there in the conflict with you. Alas, I am not a warrior nor even of noble blood. How can you love me when I have none of the trappings of nobility?"

"Madelyn, love does not require a certain station. I need not those things of which you speak. Though you are not a soldier like Aurienna, I know that you would gladly give your life for mine if I were in peril. And what of nobility? Who is to say that you were not born into nobility? You were taken by gypsies when you were very small. We do not know your family. To me you are Lady Madelyn, the woman that I love. If you can love me with all my failings, then I can return that love thousand fold. Tonight, I will make our intentions to marry known. Though I have known my father for only a short time, I know he will allow the marriage. Such happiness as ours knows no rank nor station. Will you stand with me tonight when I ask the king's permission to marry?"

"Yes, Grinold. I feel as you do and will gladly marry if the royal family agrees."

"Then let us return to the castle and the happiness that lies within its walls. Tonight will be a night of feasting and celebration for victory and for our lives together."

That night in the great dining hall, a feast was set unlike any other that had been seen in the king's lifetime. The talk was lively and many the toast that went round the table for the victory over Tobias and the lives that had been spared. When Grinold asked the king's permission to marry Madelyn, it was given with the blessings that only a father who has found his son can bestow. King Malvore stood and looked at the sons he thought he had lost and raised his cup.

"My youngest son has asked my permission to marry Madelyn. That permission I gladly give, and to Madelyn I say that you henceforth shall be Lady Madelyn with all the privileges of any member of the royal family. To Cyrean and Aurienna, who have already asked for my blessing, I also give assent. My sons are returned and are to wed. Now do I know true happiness. My only sadness is for those who have given their lives for the kingdom. Great is the sorrow of the Dwarf clan with the death of Bartold. His death weighs heavily on our hearts also, and I have plans that I will announce soon to honor Bartold and his brave soldiers for the sacrifices they made in our cause. But as I look around this table, the cares of the day have melted away and not even the loss of the crystal can weigh on my heart."

At these words, Grinold stood and looked at his father.

"As you have given me a boon, so can I in return give that which would please you most, Father. I have kept this secret since our encounter with Tobias in the tower. I knew that Tobias could never be allowed to have control of the crystal, and when I went to the wall to get the object, I devised a plan. I took a piece of leather from the coat of a fallen soldier and wrapped the crystal within. I placed it upon my person and put a small stone into the cloak that I gave to Tobias. Father, he has not the weapon. This gift I now give to you."

Grinold reached into his cloak and withdrew a leather pouch. He placed it on the table in front of his father and returned to his seat. The King looked in stunned silence at the object before him.

"Then Tobias does not have the crystal? He carries nothing but a rock?"

A smile crossed the king's face at the thought of Tobias carrying a rock, thinking it was the most powerful weapon upon the earth. From somewhere in his chest a laugh began and swelled until the hall echoed with the sound. The laughter spread like an epidemic, and soon all around the table had joined the king in the healing sound of joyous celebration that had been absent too long from the kingdom.

"Grinold, you have given me a gift, but it is more than that," said the king. "It is a gift to the kingdom. Tobias will never plague us again. Without the crystal he knows he can never hope to rule. This object before me must be put where it will never again plague mankind. Let Tobias believe we still have it, but on the morrow it will be taken to the darkest of places and buried forever. No longer will a weapon that can destroy thousands be placed into the hands of those who would plunder and murder. Soon, I will call the people together and set the new order for the kingdom. Until then, eat and rejoice in the knowledge that never again will we have to fight to preserve our way of life."

And with these words, the king let it be known of his intentions to reunite the kingdom and strengthen its boundaries until men such as Tobias could no longer terrorize its people.

The next day a great assembly was ordered, and all the people in the outlying provinces were invited to hear the king speak of the battle that had been waged and of his plans for rebuilding the kingdom. For three days people from all the provinces came to Eustan to see and hear the king. A great festival was held and all, commoners and nobles alike, took part in the eating, entertainment, and games provided by the king. On the last day of the festival, the king came forth to greet his subjects and tell of a future which would unite them all in a common cause. When the king arose to speak, the thousands stood silent to hear.

"People of Eustan, hear these proclamations to the brave warriors, both dead and alive, who fought for the freedom we enjoy today. Many were the times when it seemed that defeat was inevitable, but the courage of our soldiers would not let the sun dawn on a traitorous regime. We stand before you now to establish a new rule. My sons have been found. Let us rejoice as we face many more years of peace and prosperity with them as your rulers. Upon my death, my oldest son Cyrean will rule Eustan and all the provinces to the north. My youngest son Grinold will rule from Eustan to the southernmost of our provinces. Together, they will establish a kingdom unlike the world has ever seen where all are given rights that should be afforded them as loyal supporters of the realm. No one will be judged on size, color, or his beliefs. It is the dawning of a new age, and all shall share in its bounty."

The king halted in his proclamations only briefly as the crowd cheered wildly and chanted the king's name over and over. When at last the tumult had subsided, he continued.

"To the south of Eustan Lies the Dark Wood. To that wood years ago I exiled my former advisor and friend Arthur Pendrall. It was he who foresaw the dangers to the kingdom and took steps to overcome them. It is to him that I owe my continued rule. No more shall his name be accursed in my kingdom. From this day, the Dark Wood exists no more. It shall henceforth be called Pendrall Wood, and on the morrow woodcutters will be sent forth to change its face forever. The woods will be cut back until the sun can reach into the forest, and bright plants and grass can grow. Dangerous bogs will be filled in, and paths will be built where the inhabitants can walk without fear that they will die in the watery clutches of the swamps. Bartold's people will live in peace with the knowledge that they are always welcome in this kingdom and will be protected by the realm as would any of its citizens. Within the village of the dwarf people, a monument will be erected to honor his memory and the sacrifice he made for our kingdom. From this day, the things I have proclaimed let them be done. Go to your homes with the knowledge that fear and want never again will be your lot. Let it be seen by people all over the world that this kingdom will stand forever and that all are welcome here."

And the words of the king spread to all the people in all the provinces regarding the nature of the things the king had pledged to them, and there was a great rejoicing throughout the kingdom. In the years to follow, the words of the king were proved true. At his death, his sons took their proper places, and the kingdom thrived under their rule. As the years passed the gifts that they had been given disappeared. It was never known if the gifts disappeared because there was no need for them again. Perhaps Pendrall had foreseen that also. The Dark Wood was changed forever, and fear and superstition were no longer associated with its name. The small flower garden that surrounded the hut of Arthur Pendrall and his wife and son grew into a paradise. Cyrean and Aurienna often visited the site with their small son and Wolfen who no longer had to protect his master from the dangers that had once existed there. Pendrall Wood became an Eden, beckoning any who traveled within its boundaries to partake of its bounty. If one traveled far enough, he would reach the village of the dwarfs. There he would be welcomed, and there he would be taken to a monument within the village square. Upon its base, he would read these words:

A Kingdom Reborn

In memory of Barto the Brave
This monument proudly stands.
The face mirrors not the heart;
And size measures not the man.

The End

Other Books by This Author:

Letters From The Hills
'The Clodhopper Chronicles'

Roger Lee Scott

ISBN 978-1-4092-8152-8
A wonderful story that is told through letters written
by the two main characters...who eventually meet
to fall in love and wed... it is very humorous
in content thus making it a true joy to read...
Publisher: apfpublisher.com

Other Books By This Author:

ISBN 978-1-4092-4373-1
Publisher: apfpublisher.com

Publisher: Publishamerica.com

A.P. F. P. Authors & Book Titles:

Patricia Ann Farnsworth-Simpson: Windows of Light: Life's Carousel: A Bundle of Muse: The Twinkles: Flick The Karate Pig: The Wizard the Witch and Joe the Toe: A Compilation of Tales to Thrill and Chill: Stories To Thrill and Delight: Jack the Lad:
Carolyn Sconzo   My Garden is Growing:
Christina R Jussaume Amazing Pets & Animals: Spiritual Living Waters: Jseph's Star Of Eternal Promise: To God Give The Glory: Spiritual Enlightenment:
Erich J Goller   The Trojan Horse: Groovy:
Jacquelyn Sturge   Live, Love Laugh A Lot: Live, Love Laugh With me Through Poetry A to Z
J. Elwood Davis   The Blue Collar Scholar:
Jennifer Lee Wilson   Fantasy and Foibles:
Joanne Agee   Born To Be A Rebel:
Joe Hartman Pieces of Existence:
John Henson   Shadow Dancer
Joree Williams   Ariella: Living With Cancer:
Kathleen Charnes-Zvetkoff   Embroidered Limericks:
Mary Ann Duhart From Out of The Pit I Cried: Duhart Expressions Writing With Styles:
Michael L Schuh   But Its Mine: Mike and Joe: The Cross: Spiritual Thoughts on Love and Life: The Porter Family:
Ralph Stott   Legends for Lunch Time
Richard A Rousay   Choose the Right and Walk With Noah: Choose The Right and Walk With Ruth
Choose The Right Walk with Alma:
Robert Hewett Sr   Down The Road We Came:
William Garret & Rochelle Fischer   Rosewood: Poems & Promises:
*All these Authors can be seen on their own web-page with their books at   www.apfpublisher.com

www.apfpublisher.com

E-Mail: apfpublisher@gmail.com